WARRIOR WENCH

THE ASARLAÍ WARS TRILOGY
BOOK 1

MARIE ANDREAS

BOOKS BY MARIE ANDREAS

The Lost Ancients

Book One: The Glass Gargoyle
Book Two: The Obsidian Chimera
Book Three: The Emerald Dragon
Book Four: The Sapphire Manticore

The Asarlaí Wars

Book One: Warrior Wench

DEDICATION:

To all my family and friends who believed in me.
Thank you.

ACKNOWLEDGEMENTS

Writing is a solitary process, but it can't be done alone. I couldn't have gotten this far without the love and support of all of my family and friends.

I'd like to thank Jessa Slade for editing magic—she continues to keep me from falling into plot holes. For my most awesome team of beta readers who plowed through the entire book and helped tighten it up: Lisa Andreas, Patti Huber, Lynne Mayfield, Sharon Rivest, Ilana Schoonover, and Tami Vahalik. Any remaining errors are mine alone.

My cover artist, Aleta Rafton, creating yet another awesome work of art. And to The Killion Group for formatting of the entire book and print cover.

CHAPTER ONE

"Where the hell is my ship, Skrankle?" Captain
Vaslisha Tor Dain slammed the salvage dealer against the
peeling office wall and pressed hard on his neck. The
putrid orange slime he oozed in self-defense crept toward
her feet and she stepped sideways. Damn it! If he ruined
her second favorite pair of boots, she was going to do
more than choke him—providing the smell that came
along with the slime didn't suffocate her first.

Vas was a simple sort of mercenary. All she wanted in
life was her ship, her crew, and a good fight. Now this
whimpering scumbag had destroyed that. Her gut knotted
up as worry and anger fought inside her. Anger was an
old friend. Worry was a stranger and she liked it that way.
Skrankle was getting to share all of her feelings first hand
and wasn't faring well from it. The dark blue patches
covering his red fleshy cheeks couldn't bode well for his
continued survival.

Vas squeezed his neck tighter.

More orange slime dripped down the wall behind
Skrankle. His left arm twitched out and tugged futilely at
her hand. He got enough air to choke out a few words. "I
said to you, Captain, *Victorious Dead* is in slip five.
There she's been all month."

Vas increased pressure on his throat until he darkened
at least two more shades, and eventually let him collapse.
She wiped her hands on her heavy brown duster. While
not traditional starship mercenary garb, it suited her just

fine. "Slip five is empty, Skrankle. You were supposed to fix her. Not lose her."

The Ilerian gathered himself and slithered to his desk. He slurped into his chair with a heavy sigh and a nasty sucking sound. The rustle of bureaucratic skill he demonstrated in calling up his vid-screen indicated he'd recover from her stranglehold. Unfortunately.

"Records of mine say the *Victorious Dead* docked here twenty-nine days ago. Scheduled decommission ten days ago…"

Vas pulled her heavy blaster free of its hip holster the instant "decommissioned" left his thin purple lips. "You ripped my ship apart?" The polished muzzle of her weapon found a home against his temple. The urge to pull the trigger made her mouth go dry, but the need to find her beloved ship forced her finger to stay still. An odd feeling slammed into her, starting in the pit of her stomach and clawing its way up to her throat. It took almost a full minute to recognize it as fear. She forced it back down.

Skrankle whimpered, and frantically pushed a few more buttons. "No, I'm sure there's mistake—a mistake. Yes, yes. Mistake, I'm sure."

She kept the blaster to his head and leaned over to look out into the space station shipyard through the slimy window of his office. Vas tried not to think what he'd done to the window to leave that light green ichor on it.

The Lucky Strike space station was just large enough to provide enclosed berthing and repair docks for a handful of questionable salvage and repair dealers who couldn't afford to go anywhere else. The vast majority were stuck here paying off debts owed to the gambling dens on the shiny planet below. The planet Tarantus IV was a playground for the rich and infamous of the Commonwealth, and its castoffs ended up on this space station.

The view out the window didn't give her much hope. Rusted and dented airlocks kept the vacuum of space from the battered vessels within. The small dock managed to look roomier than it actually was due to the lack of ships; only two ancient Arelian scout ships and one Gallant-class cruiser languished there. The Gallant-class cruiser appeared to be a few years newer and far flashier than her own beloved ship. The outer skin was so polished that it softly glowed in the dim repair bay— definitely not the type of ship typically found on the Lucky Strike. The damn thing even looked to have some elaborate ship tats decorating the lower and upper decks.

She shook her head. Tats were possibly the most useless thing on a ship; who in space cared if your ship had filigree markings running down its sides? Probably retrofitted for a rich, inner-planet bureaucrat who wanted to show off how well he could waste Commonwealth funds. And who spent his last minutes in some back alley down on the planet below. The cruiser may have started out as a warship like the *Victorious Dead,* but it sure as hell had left that life long ago. There was no way anyone could have mistaken that for her ship.

Not even someone as stupid as Skrankle.

Vas turned slowly back to Skrankle. Tiny beads of sweat clustered down the sides of his neck. He was dead the instant she found her ship.

He erupted into a series of grunts, his five arms furiously typing queries into the battered vid console. He knew he was dead.

"You see, Vas—" He froze when her blaster pressed deeper into his temple. "Captain. Orders confused with the other Gallant-class. That ship taken in smuggling raid and scheduled to be decommissioned and parts sold." The words tumbled from his lips so rapidly it took five seconds for the meaning to reach Vas's brain.

"You're telling me that you took my ship apart because you got the wrong ship? How in the hell could you have confused a fighting ship like the *Victorious Dead* with a gilded yacht like that thing out there? " Her grip on the blaster tightened until her palm burned. The need to splatter Skrankle's brains on the wall was so bad that her back teeth started to ache.

"Yes, well—"

"Get it back."

His head bobbled back on his neck, shortening it to ridiculous proportions. "Pardon?"

"My ship. I want my ship. *All of it.*" She accented each word with another nudge of her blaster. For added impact she withdrew her dagger and lifted his chins with it. Orange ooze filled his chair.

"But, but, but...I told you. Pieces. It's in pieces."

Vas pulled the dagger free of his neck folds. Ilerians had a tendency to shut down completely when scared too much. She wanted him dead, but not until she had her ship.

"You said that. So, now find those pieces. Every. Single. Damn. Part. Put them back together." She nodded toward the shipyard and the lone Gallant-class sitting in the docking bay. "I'll take that ship for now."

"But I can't...the Council—" Skrankle stopped talking when Vas's dagger resumed its place against his throat. "Acceptable, she is yours. Keep her and we're even?"

"Give me the code so I can do a run-through. This is a loaner, Skrankle. I get my ship within two months or I'll leave your slimy carcass on the nearest desert planet." Swamp grass was the only export for the Ilerian home world. As a race, they didn't fare well in dry air.

He quivered and pushed a code pad at her.

With a nod, she grabbed the pad and jogged into the narrow corridor, then down the short stairwell leading toward the dock and the new ship. The ship tats were a full series of elaborate, ornate, and utterly ridiculous markings done in a clean gold line. Tats were unheard of on anything as large as a Gallant-class cruiser, but the designs made it look larger than its class. The Gallants weren't designed to hold more than two hundred or so crew and this looked ready to take on at least four hundred. The closer she got, the more she realized that it wasn't just the designs making it look big. The ship was huge. Half again as large as the *Victorious Dead*. The remodel had been done so subtly that the shape of a regular Gallant-class was still there, just larger. *Now why would someone increase the size of a new Gallant-class ship instead of just upgrading to a Regulator-class?*

Her engineers would need to look over the changes carefully. They were stuck with this thing for now, but they might as well take advantage of any upgrades they could.

She aimed the code pad at the ship and flipped through the scans. The bones of the ship scanned solid. Walking inside verified that it was as clean and tight as the outside appeared. The command deck brought out an unintended whistle of admiration from her. The bridge held thousands of credits' worth of extras. And that was only what she could tell at a glance. The navigation station was enough to make her nav officer chain himself to the command deck. The newest FG-8 nav console that filled the space was so new that the screens still had installation protectorate on them. A glance past that told her she was going to have a problem with her two pilots. Those two hot heads would fight to the death over the prototype of the X-5 pilot web. Those babies weren't supposed to be on the market for another seven months at least.

However, it was the weapons console that made her feel like she needed to go get a cigarette. She couldn't help but fondle the Lazerous missile controls. Who in the hell would put these things in a flouncy pleasure cruiser like this? Hell, she'd never heard of them being installed in anything lower than a Regulator-Command cruiser. Yet, here they were, both forward and aft versions, neat as could be. Finally forcing herself away, she leaned against the command chair. White leather conformed to her shape where she leaned in against it. Damn. Reluctantly, she let herself slide into it. The chair cradled and supported her body better than a grandmother holding a newborn infant. A sigh escaped her as she investigated the controls on the arm consoles. Two systems were complete unknowns. They appeared to be high-grade military, but the coding was different. She'd have Gosta investigate them before she thought about using them. She forced herself to leave the white-leather wonder. With one more pat on its arm, she headed off the bridge and toward the crew quarters.

The longest corridor led into the captain's quarters. She let out another low whistle as she palmed open the doors. It reminded her more of a luxury barge than a Gallant-class cruiser. The room was twice as wide as her old quarters with the overstuffed bed swallowing more than half of the space. The fixtures were delicately carved of Litharian green woods, something she'd only seen in museum vids. Artifacts from twenty worlds she could recognize were embedded into the marbled surface surrounding the bed. The artifacts alone were worth more than the *Victorious Dead* and included six bladed weapons from the dead planet of Hosset. Vas wondered if she could pry them free when they finally found her own ship.

Satisfied that this extravagant ship would at least get them to their next battle intact and ready to fight, she finally ventured to the one place she hadn't gone yet: the captain's ready room.

On a practical level she knew it wasn't her ready room. There would be no deep dents accenting the walls from some of her more memorable benders. No stains from thrown cups of hot solie. No memories of the ghosts of long-lost crewmates. However, logic played little in the visceral reaction she had upon staring at these pristine powder gray walls. She told herself it was just fatigue that caused her eyes to blur. However, the fact was, more than any other place in the galaxy her ready room had been *hers*. The place she could run to when the deaths of those she cared about got to her. A mercenary captain needed to be strong. Not even her closest friends could know how the deaths ate at her. But her ready room knew.

The sterile and perfect room before her rammed home how far she was from setting foot in that refuge again.

She shook her head to clear away the ghosts and let the door slide shut. She was half-way to the airlock before she thought to check the ident chip for the ship.

The official name and all of a ship's history was stored in those idents, and even she hadn't found a way to change them for long. The Commonwealth kept tight controls over ship names for security purposes. The ident should be in the code pad Skrankle gave her, but it wasn't in the first dozen documents on file. After a judicious bashing of Skrankle's code pad against the bulkhead when it tried to die on her, Vas managed to find the ship's identity.

Her swearing at the ship's name would have peeled the paint off the bulkhead if this ship hadn't been upgraded with the top of the line sealant. That explained the over-the-top upgrades.

She ran out of the ship and kicked open the door to Skrankle's office. "What the hell are you trying to pull? That's the *Warrior Wench*. I can't be seen taking my people for mercenary jobs in a brothel cruiser. Get me another ship."

The corners of his mouth twitched, but he stopped before a full smile appeared. "Sorry. Only ship. Gallant-class cruisers hard to find right now."

Vas reached for her dagger. Granted the blaster would be more efficient, but she didn't want efficient. She wanted slow and messy. With no way to change the ident, she'd be hauling her sorry ass around in an interstellar whorehouse. She and her crew would be the objects of ridicule everywhere.

"Yiiiii!" Skrankle burst into a horrific screeching noise that quickly climbed out of her range of hearing. Then he slid under his rusty metal desk. Considering how much bigger he was than the space, he couldn't be comfortable. Vas didn't care; she could slice him into smaller bits so he'd fit better.

"You can die under there or out here, but you're getting me a damn different ship. Mercs can't use something like that. *I* can't use something like that." No way in hell she would risk her hard-earned rep slinging that gilded tart around the space lanes. Female mercs had to work three times as hard to get the same jobs as males. It didn't matter what species. Even in the matriarchal races, female mercs had it worse than males. The idea of trying to terrorize her opponents while in such a horrifically ill-named vessel made her want to see how long Skrankle would last in an open airlock.

Skrankle continued to blubber as he burrowed further under the desk.

Vas pinched the bridge of her nose and closed her eyes. Today should have been simple. Get her damn ship, retrieve the crew from their extended shore leave, and get out to the Olestle system for the upcoming war they'd been contracted to fight. She never could understand why some cultures planned their fatal disagreements months in advance. Nevertheless, it did make scheduling easier for her.

"I need a ship by tomorrow at the latest." She'd given herself an extra day, but they needed to be out of this system by this time tomorrow if they were going to make it to the battle in time. Being late wasn't an option with the people who'd hired her crew. Her ground forces were some of the best around, but ground battles still took a lot of set up.

Skrankle executed a few horrific contortions and managed to turn around without coming out from under the desk. "Only one ship of that class available in sector. *That* ship. Could get you different in month, no sooner. Look for self."

Vas turned the holovid toward her. The interstellar shipyard screens were up so she didn't need to search his system. She swore as the results returned. With a kick at the blob under the desk for good measure, she ran one more query. Nothing. Even a month was optimistic, and the ship that far out should have been sent to the great ship graveyard ten years ago according to the records.

She was out of options.

"Get out from under there." She kicked Skrankle when he tried to turn around again. "I won't kill you. Let me rephrase that…I won't kill you right now. And if you sign over that wretched ship's full ownership papers, and if you find all of my ship within two months, you'll continue to live and ooze. I'll be tracking the parts too. You lose a limb for each part I find first." Not that she really wanted his seeping limbs, but fear motivated people.

More burbling from beneath the desk.

Eventually the business owner side of him, the part who saw the wisdom in staying alive long enough to rip off more customers, won over the fear and he slithered out from under the desk.

"Deal." He coughed when the word came out as a squeak. "That is deal, Captain. I will not risk limbs." In an amazing show of speed, he scurried across his office to a torn painting that partially concealed a battered wall safe. Muttering in his native tongue, he fumbled open the lock and pulled out a collection of papers and disks. Obviously, now that he decided she wouldn't kill him, he wanted her out of there as soon as possible. "Here are the ownership papers, former logs, all documents. *Warrior Wench* is yours."

Vas briefly glanced through the documents and read the disk labels. She glanced up to find his beady purple eyes peering at her anxiously.

"You go now?"

As much as she would love to stay and make his life hell, and as much as he deserved it, she knew she didn't have time for it. The new ship was bad enough, but her crew had been on their own for a month. The break should have been only two weeks, but lately things hadn't been turning out the way they were supposed to. She shuddered at the thought of what they'd been doing for the last month. "I'll go now," she said, as she leaned in and narrowed her eyes. "Two months, worm."

Vas slammed the door behind her.

CHAPTER TWO

She scanned the papers and files while she made her way back down the filthy corridor and the uneven stairs toward the dock. The ship was five years younger than the *Victorious Dead* and worth at least twenty times as much. Which made her wonder why Skrankle would have tried to scrap it. Which of course meant he hadn't planned to do that at all. Which meant he'd had a different plan for that ship; one she just interrupted. Vas believed there were always a finite number of problems in any situation. The name of the game was to find them all before they became fatal.

Why Skrankle had this ship and what he had planned on doing with it was problem number one. Number two continued the theme with why he felt safe enough to take apart and sell her ship. Unless he lied and it was intact. Why hadn't she thought of that before? Her month off had turned her brains to mush.

Swearing under her breath, she ran across the catwalk and palmed open the airlock to the *Warrior Wench*. The unbreakable idents meant that ships could be found by anyone, including a mercenary captain, provided they knew how to hack into the Council's systems anyway. Fortunately, she had one of the best hackers in fifteen galaxies on her payroll and he'd taught her a few tricks over the years.

She ran across the bridge and activated the console connected to the command chair. It took a few minutes of tricky computer maneuvering, but she got into the Council's ident tracking system. If the *Victorious Dead* had stayed intact it would show on the logs on the screen before her. The scan pulled in nothing. At least nothing intact. A few false readings that pinged back from the scan told her Skrankle had spoken the truth for once; her ship had been pieced out. Which again brought her to problem two: why had he felt safe taking apart one of the best-known merc ships in the league?

When she'd dropped the crew off a month ago on Tarantus IV for some downtime, she'd taken a shuttle to deal with some personal business in a neighboring star system for two weeks. Business that seemed both private and harmless until now. The two weeks had turned into four weeks. She had no answers as to how those weeks doubled, but nothing bad had happened. Time just got away from her.

A faint buzzing in her head told her she was missing something, but her memory argued otherwise. She'd finished her business deal, one of the few she couldn't win. To console herself, she went to Hillet and followed one of the ongoing parties. Partying wasn't her usual pastime, but the booze had been free and the company not awful. She rubbed her right temple as bits and pieces, like chopped up vids of someone else's life, came flooding back. Along with a building pressure that quickly turned to pain. She couldn't recall whom she had been with— just flashes of a big party. She pushed past the pain in her head, concerned at the missing memory. Comfort flooded her mind as an image came forward. Ah yes, that Larakian trader. How could she forget him after those three nights?

Clearly her newly acquired partying lifestyle had led to more than a few holes in her memory. Now that his identity had been cleared up, her headache vanished.

While her extra two weeks were more or less accounted for, the question of Skrankle's actions was not. Had someone not expected her to return for her ship? He wouldn't have done this on his own; he didn't have the guts. Whoever managed to convince Skrankle there was safe profit in scrapping her ship would meet his very own version of hell once she caught up to him.

None of these were things she could address right now. She needed to find her wayward crew, get them dried out, and make sure they were ready for the upcoming battle.

With a thoroughness and paranoia born of years of killing people for a living, she changed all the ship's codes, including simple lockouts in the galley and crew cabins.

The first campaign with Gosta, her resident computer hacker extraordinaire, had created her code paranoia. Within minutes of engaging the enemy, a Dirthian heavy cruiser, he'd taken complete control of the ship and sent it into life-support lock down. He'd gained entrance to their entire system through an old unchanged lock code from the captain's personal environmental controls, a.k.a. he climbed in through the toilets. While she admired the ingenuity, she chilled at how quickly he did it. She'd changed all ship's codes every cruise since then.

Satisfied that the ship was secure, she set out to reclaim her crew. They should be together in one of the small shantytowns outside the giant casino conglomerate of Liltikin. Hopefully. If any of them had disappeared in the extended down time they could just take up permanent residence there.

The shuttle she'd arrived in was docked on the other side of Skrankle's docks. She could take it planet-side, gather her crew, and get the hell out of this area of space within a few hours.

Her plan went into the crapper the minute she went to pull up the clearance codes that would let the *Warrior*

Wench leave the space station once she got her crew on board. They weren't available. She finally tracked the codes down only to find they were still secured in the space station's main office. Whatever Skrankle had been doing to this ship he clearly hadn't planned on it leaving anytime soon.

She secured the ship's airlock and went down the dock to the station corridor. Like all of the locks in this part of the station it was rusted and pocked. However, it managed to keep the air out if a breach occurred in the repair yards. Or so she hoped.

Few people walked the main corridor of the space station and many of the shops were closed. Station time worked on loading and unloading times. When ships were in, shops were open.

The intoxicating smell of fresh fried capsina fish caught her when she strode past a new pub. Her mouth watered even as she tried to keep going down the corridor. She made it policy never to eat at new places and certainly never at one too new to even have a sign. But she let the smell of her favorite food drag her into the small, dimly lit pub regardless.

She'd grown up on Kjaria, a mostly empty desert planet in the Pleanterian system. Her obsession with food from the ocean was an ongoing joke to her crew. One of her favorites was capsina fish, with its delicate light orange flesh. Her love of it was something she would hurt people for. Even people she liked. None of her crew joked about capsina fish.

Looking at her watch, she decided she had enough time to get some food to go. Her crew turned into night owls when on shore leave and it was still too early for them to have recovered from the previous night.

A waitress started to approach her, but Vas beat her to the punch, forcing the small, blonde human to follow her while she strode to the bar. There were advantages to being tall and imposing—people often did what you wanted them to do.

"Capsina fish, large order. Side of whatever produce you have that's planet grown, and a huge container of ale. To go." She thought about it for a second. "Make that a small. Just a small container of tavaan ale." Being drunk in the middle of the day wouldn't be a good idea under the current circumstances. Besides, she'd be in a happier mood if she drank, and she needed to "keep the bitch up" as Deven, her second-in-command, would say to convince her crew to accept the *Warrior Wench*.

The waitress nodded and went to get her food.

Vas studied the pub. Jagged construction poles jutted across the back indicating a future dining area. Deep green jacadin wood planks appeared real until she tapped at the planks on the bar. The tinny sound the wood made indicated it only looked like jacadin timber. Obviously the owners wanted to come across more upscale than they were. She turned while she waited so that she could see the entire room, including the kitchen door. Paranoid she may be, but it had kept her alive all these years. Few people from her home world could say that. Her family sure as hell couldn't. Her brother had taken care of that.

The waitress appeared with her food and drink packed in cheap foamlian-core containers. Vas hoped she could finish the food before they disintegrated. She toyed with staying and eating at the bar, but while she needed to give her crew time to regain consciousness, she really didn't want to give them enough time to wander off. She needed to be down planet-side just after sunset.

"Will you need anything else?" the blonde asked.

"I need my—" Vas said as the bill keypad was shoved into her hand "—bill." She shrugged and put her chip code in. The waitress entered her code into the small machine, then snapped the printed paid receipt on the table.

Vas left the empty pub and made her way down through the intermittent groups of gray-suited freighter mechanics and the usual narrow-eyed shopkeepers to the station office. In the few minutes that she'd been in the pub, a new life had come to the station. She picked up speed and started drinking her ale as she walked.

The station office was like all station offices; whether they were planet based or space based, they all used the same decorator and must have cloned their staff. The room was painted an unappetizing puke beige and felt crowded even when she was the only one in the lobby. The countertop protecting the back area was made of Ilerian granite, possibly the weakest stone in the known galaxy. The dissolving edges were receding rapidly and would soon vanish completely.

A tiny Dliari scuttled sideways out from a back room. Ancient spectacles perched on her long snout bobbed as she gave Vas an odd sideways glance.

The species changed, but all bureaucrats acted the same.

"What does you need?" The voice came through an old series two translator at the base of the Dliari's throat. Even better, a bureaucrat too lazy to learn Common.

Vas sat her food and drink cautiously on the counter. "I need the clearance codes for the *Warrior Wench*. I'll be taking her out in a few hours."

The crustacean Dliari peered closely at her and her food before finally shaking her head. "You is not brothel owner, not your ship."

Vas had expected problems, and carefully placed the required documents on the counter next to her food. The resulting groan from the Ilerian granite made her snatch her food container.

The Dliari clicked her mandibles as she made her way forward in her zigzagging walk, snatching the files with a clawed hand as if Vas was going to take them back. "Will take hours. You come back when I done."

Vas shrugged and walked back to the only chair in the lobby. "I'll just wait here, thank you." She popped open the food container and smiled as the lovely fish odor filled the room.

"You can no eat here!"

The squeal at the end was interesting; Vas didn't think that the series two translators could make that sound. She grinned and bit into the perfectly cooked fish. It was just luck she got a Dliari. Her eating fish would be a vulgar insult to a member of that sea born species.

"But I have to wait for you to find my codes." She gave a shrug. "I can't leave until I get them."

The Dliari swore something the translator couldn't handle, and vanished into the back room.

Vas was just licking the last of the fried fish off of her fingers when the Dliari returned. She pushed the files back across the counter.

"There. You go."

Vas smiled. It seemed that everyone she encountered on this station wanted her to leave. And she was more than happy to give them what they wanted.

"Thank you so much." She checked the codes. They looked correct and the time stamp was good. With another smile, Vas tucked the files into her inner pocket and left the office.

She was congratulating herself on the quickest bureaucrat interaction she'd ever had when a man lunged out of a maintenance corridor and slammed into her. The collision knocked both of them to the decking, her arms and legs tangling with his. Struggling to her feet, she considered ripping him a new one for his clumsiness, but was stopped by the look his face. His blue eyes were rimmed in white and beads of sweat ran down his face as he stared at the corridor he'd just run out of. His eyes held the panic of a man ready to jump out an airlock without a suit to get away from whatever pursued him. With a whimper, he scrambled to his feet and bolted away. Vas let her hand drift toward the butt of her blaster as she methodically—and with practiced caution—turned toward the service corridor that had ejected her clumsy assailant into her path.

Leading with the muzzle of her blaster, she took three steps into the corridor. The barren gray walls were unremarkable and the empty corridor didn't give her a clue as to what had caused that flyboy to flee.

Shaking her head at yet another delay, she holstered her blaster into the gun belt then continued toward the shuttle. Thoughts of her difficult crew filled her mind as she marched through the empty corridors toward the shuttle dock. For their sakes, they all better be in the same spot. She slapped at the shuttle's airlock control and strode onboard.

She tried to contact her second-in-command as soon as she landed the shuttle on the planet, but he didn't answer his comm. She briefly thought about contacting her other officers, but she wanted Deven to know about the ship first. Telepaths got touchy when others knew about things they felt they *should* know first.

The days and nights on Tarantus IV went faster than her internal clock; one reason she would never pick this for a vacation spot. Although it felt like early afternoon to her, night had already fallen on this part of the small planet and the Lucky Strike space station gleamed like a third moon in the desert air. Her crew should just be getting up and about now.

Loud gambling halls, with daylight-mimicking lights, were another reason for her dislike of this world. Tarantus IV had even less to offer for survival than her own unlamented home world. But thanks to an ingenious miner six hundred years ago, it had gambling—lots of gambling—the types of gambling that were illegal everywhere else.

She hated gambling. Her money was earned at the cost
of lives. The idea of wasting that money didn't set right
with her.

The cool night air smelled fresh and clean once she got
away from the landing pad. That is, until she approached
the mass of giant buildings known as Liltikin. Not really
a city in the proper sense, Liltikin was a collection of
massive casinos that cooperated for mutual benefit. Each
one was a kingdom unto itself with its own unique style
and odor. Moreover, all of those smells hit her about a
hundred yards out from the first behemoth.

Stepping inside the casino, she knew her second-in-
command wouldn't be in there. He had a level of class
that warred with his chosen lifestyle. The flashy pink
signs, horrific pink carpeting, and pink–colored air didn't
even come close to Deven's requirements. She wasted a
few seconds wondering just how or why someone would
color air. Shaking her head, she fled for the next casino.

The second den of ill-lost funds appeared promising.
The open entry was wide enough for a small shuttle to
dock, and provided a view of the elegant interior. Light
golds and sea blues dominated the color palette, with a
few dark wood accents on the ceiling and far walls.
Carefully draped fabrics from thousands of worlds flowed
from the five-story-high ceiling to be gathered against the
walls creating a space both intimate and generous at the
same time. The gambling tables were all carved out of
pure rare stones. The five-card ta-long table immediately
before her was once a single block of rare Elierian jade.
The fast-paced calir game table gleamed an ebony that
could only have come from a single lump of Wavian coal,
a substance so protected that a single ounce could buy a
fleet of ships. The entire decor invited those of delicate
sensibilities to come in and donate their money.

She definitely didn't fit in.

For the first time she realized she still had on the
clothes she'd worn yesterday. And her duster carried

more than enough proof of its name. She couldn't remember when she last braided her hair; but the telltale red wisps near her waist told her it had been a while. The sneer on the face of the casino host told her the same thing. She glared back. Robots should never be programmed with facial expressions.

She held up one hand instead of reaching for her blaster, as she wanted to. "I don't want any trouble and I'm not staying."

The skinny droid rocked back on his metallic heels.

When the droid didn't say anything, she continued, but kept her voice low. "You don't want me here; I don't want to be here. I'm trying to find my second-in-command. The sooner you help me find him, the sooner I can stop leaving dust on your floor, got it?"

A faint humming emanated from the yellow man-shaped machine, and it nodded. "Agreed. Who is it you are searching for? What does he look like?"

She did a quick surveillance around the gambling floor even though she knew Deven wouldn't be there. His gambling usually took place in private rooms. As a rule telepaths, or espers as they were commonly called, didn't like crowded spaces. Deven might be different from most espers, but he had reasons for gambling alone.

"He's about 6'2", a bit taller than me, pale gold skin, likes to show lots of it, and has tar-black hair hitting past his shoulders unless he hacked it off again. He'd probably be in your tao-go room or a private suite." She'd give the thing Deven's name, except that he never used it on casino planets.

The droid cocked its head, another annoying mannerism, and then froze. An instant later it turned in her direction. "I believe I have found your friend. He is indeed in a private suite." The droid's eyes gave pale reflections of the images he scanned. Most likely tapped into the security cameras. "You did not say he was an esper."

She frowned when an image of Deven entering a suite appeared on the droid's eye-screens and focused in on the two linked metal bracelets on Deven's right wrist. No esper above a level one could travel without them. The laws may have given them equal rights eighty years ago, but that didn't mean people felt safe around them. Which was one reason that Deven usually wore a heavy inlaid bracelet over the telepath-blocking metal bands.

"I don't think that's a concern. He's not breaking any laws; you obviously have seen the bracelets." She folded her arms and glared at the droid. Not really at the droid, more at the small army of security most likely watching her every move through the droid. "Tell me, *droid*, is there a problem here?"

"Not a problem. However, he will leave with you, yes?" The droid turned on a metal heel and quickly strode toward the depths of the casino where the private rooms were.

Vas jogged to keep up with it.

The droid's sharp rap on the door lead to muffled swearing in two different languages. Which told her two things: they'd found Deven, and he wasn't gambling for money.

Her second-in-command had many appetites.

She stepped around the droid and added her own pounding to the door. "Deven, it's me. Get your ass out here." She paused, and added, "Clothed. Get your clothed ass out here." Better to be safe. He preferred stark naked.

An increase in the swearing signaled his acknowledgment of her command. The door swung open and a curvaceous blonde stumbled out of the room, a dazed glow on her face. Obviously, Deven had been the one making the extra cash in this scenario.

Her second-in-command was next through the doorway, looking as fresh as if he'd had time for an hour-long sonic shower before he dressed. Tall and exotic looking, Deven seemed to glow himself as he came out of

the room. His standard issue flight suit looking like he'd
had it personally tailored to fit his body like a glove. He'd
always been good looking, but he seemed different now.
She shivered. Maybe absence did make the heart grow
fonder. However, it certainly wasn't going to make her
break her rule about getting involved with a member of
her crew. Or a telepath.

Deven's sharp green eyes glinted with mild
amusement at whatever he thought was going on in her
head. Then he smiled and pulled his hair into a ponytail at
his nape.

She hated him for always looking perfect. No matter
the situation, Deven stayed calm, clean, and relaxed.
Somehow she was sure he did it to piss her off. Maybe
that anger could chase off whatever other unhealthy
feelings were going on in her head.

"We've got a problem, a job, and a missing crew." She
didn't wait for him to respond before she marched toward
the casino floor.

She didn't hear his steps, but the powerful presence at
her side told her he'd caught up.

"You were supposed to be here two weeks ago."

"Yes." A two-foot-tall Jerlian in a permanently
wrinkled suit, sloshed synth-cohol on her boots as he
tried to hug her knees. Had Skrankle not already managed
to ruin said boots, she would have seen how far she could
kick a Jerlian on a low-grav planet. Instead, she took two
steps around him and moved toward the exit.

"You didn't call."

"No, I didn't. My being late has nothing to do with
you or our next job. Can we move it, please?" She didn't
want to discuss her recent travels, and certainly not in the
middle of a casino. Nothing had happened. She was just
late. There just wasn't a reason to talk about it. She
squashed the tiny voice that said she needed to talk about
it.

"Vas saying please? Now I know something is wrong." Deven pulled up short before the casino exit.

It would take a week to get off this rock if her entire crew decided to be this chatty about her private issues. "I don't ask what you're doing," she said and held up a hand. "I don't want to know. I'm not going to tell you what I was doing. We have a job and we have a ship. Do you want to earn some money on your feet for once or not?"

"Ouch, got me." The smile he flashed caused two nearby women to swoon as Vas and Deven left the casino.

"Turn it down, damn it," she hissed with a glance down at his bracelets. There were times he pulled a glamour that had to be esper powered, bracelets or no. He didn't need it; he was freakishly good looking enough on his own. "I can't have you jailed at this point.

"Do you have any idea where—" She stopped mid-sentence as Deven suddenly turned toward a dark alley. With night vision far better than hers, she let him take the lead. He hadn't gone for any of the dozen or so weapons she knew he had on him, so she relaxed, the tension fleeing down her arms.

Deven moved toward the entrance of the alley.

"That's sad. I didn't think he came back here." His voice dropped while he flicked on a glow rod.

Vas followed him in. The alley lived up to expectations: dingy, nasty, and smelling worse than a week-old dead Ilerian. She stayed at his side as Deven approached the tall man who sat in the wide beam of light from the glow rod, muttering to himself. Odd, but not as odd as his seat. He'd created a throne out of what had to be biscuits stolen from the nearby casinos and restaurants.

Only Deven would be friends with someone who used baked goods as furniture. Vas kept her hands loose and waited to see how this would play out. The pathetic being before her didn't look dangerous, but fatal mistakes often came from underestimations. Dozens of people had died at her hand for that very reason before her reputation caught up with her.

"Who approaches? Who dares to interrupt Jeof, the God of Biscuits?" His slurred voice gave evidence to the alcoholic assistance he'd had getting to his current state. The way he leaned dangerously to the left reinforced that assessment.

"I'm surprised this is the first time I've seen him, he's usually in one of the main thoroughfares." Deven lifted his right wrist to her face. "I can help him if you help me?"

"No. You can't keep taking those things off when you feel like it. Do you want to end up in jail again? Cause you'll be alone this time, bucko. I'll tell them you overpowered me and made me take them off. Within city limits. Which is illegal." Vas hated Deven's charitable streak. It was going to be the death of him one of these days. Or her.

"Point one, you didn't get me out of jail on Pallite, I got you out," Deven said. "Point two, you never quibble about laws when it's for your benefit. Point three, this guy used to be royalty. Maybe if you help him now he'll repay you with unimagined riches."

She glanced at the loony behind Deven. Former royalty or not, he wasn't the man he used to be. His hair seemed to be shaved down the middle and the remaining chunks stuck up like braided rat-tails. His clothing consisted of a collection of fabrics and posters stolen from various casinos. She wasn't sure how it stayed on him and didn't care just as long as it did. "I'm not going to address the other two issues. But if he's royalty I'll eat one of those biscuits."

Deven laughed. "Which will be a fine sight I'm sure."

She sighed and reached for his wrist. "I'll code it off. But do it quickly. I have no idea how tight their sensors are, and I *will* turn you in if they get triggered."

He nodded, but didn't say anything as she coded the bracelet off with a few keystrokes on the thin command bar. The metal itself started out as an inert gas, but settled into a metal outer skin once coded properly. The gas inside the metal shorted out all esper skills.

Honestly, she had no idea what esper level Deven was. However, the highest of them, the tens, were all insane, so she knew he couldn't be one of them. His goal was to drive her crazy, not go for a trip himself. The bracelets were coded to one person with the ability to deactivate them for specific purposes. The code consisted of not only the right keying in, but also the touch of her skin. And her skin had to be warm. She made a point of regularly reminding Deven that he'd best work on keeping her alive unless he wanted to be trapped in those things forever.

He rubbed his wrist after she removed the bracelets and tucked them into her pocket. He seemed the same to her, but she knew any sensors would pick up his telepathic abilities in minutes. That was the major reason why she made it a policy to never take jobs on gambling planets. Too many damn sensors.

Deven slowly approached the self-proclaimed God of Biscuits. His voice dropped to a tone one would use with a scared infant and he seemed to shrink in height. The tall, skeletal man before him peered at him with squinted eyes as he approached.

"Hello, Jeof. How are you tonight? Do you remember me? We talked a few months ago."

Jeof frowned and pulled at one of the disintegrating baked goods. "It's God of Biscuits; Jeof, God of Biscuits." A pouty undertone filled his voice now, but the influence of clearvac alcohol lingered. No doubt he'd stepped out on his drinking bender a few days ago.

"It's okay, Jeof, God of Biscuits. I'm a follower."

Vas felt the tendrils of Deven's mental influence flow over Jeof. A faint low-level tickle floated in the back of her mind as if she'd forgotten something and it was just out of reach. Deven's influence hit its target as true as any blaster. Within a few seconds, Jeof's face took on a look of mild confusion as Deven's mind encouraged him to rest.

"But I need to speak to my people today. They told me to come here, give away the biscuits…there was someone I had to give a biscuit to…." Jeof's voice trailed off as he plucked another molding biscuit from his throne. Vas's stomach turned when she thought he was going to put the nasty thing in his mouth. Instead he turned his watery eyes toward her and shoved it into her hand. It happened so quickly she held it for a second before dropping it to the ground. With a shudder, she wiped her hands on her duster and took a judicious step backwards.

"It's all right, Jeof. You just need to rest for a few minutes." Deven laid his hands on either side of the drunk man's head. Jeof closed his eyes with a sigh. "When you wake up you'll go find a hotel room. You have money near your heart. It's enough to get you off this planet. Go to Chaslisten and speak to the healers. You want to be a farmer."

Deven's left hand quickly darted into the man's jumbled clothing, and then back to the side of his head. Vas knew he'd most likely just given Jeof all of the money he'd earned this last month. Jeof would probably be a happy farmer on the ag planet Chaslisten before the month ended.

A shudder crept across her shoulders and a cold pit grew in her guts. She knew Deven had power but she'd never seen it wielded so subtly. Her hand slipped into her pocket and she fingered his esper bracelets. Things would be better when she got these back on him. While she trusted Deven with her life, she didn't feel the same about trusting him with her mind. She would never trust an esper in her head again.

Deven released Jeof and rejoined her. "We should go. It'd be best if he doesn't see us when he wakes up."

She held out the bracelets with a raised eyebrow. Deven usually put them back on immediately.

"All right, but let's get out of sight." He all but pushed her out of the alley and around the corner.

"What's wrong?" She hadn't picked up on anything in the alley beyond the obvious smells of refuse and abandonment. However, something rattled Deven. That alone was a rare enough occurrence to have her fingers linger near the butt of her blaster and the hilt of her dagger.

Deven held out his arm, wincing slightly when the metal clamped around his wrist and sealed in on itself. "I'm not sure. Something didn't feel right about Jeof, something deep in his psyche. Whatever it is I didn't want to disturb it. There were webs of mind treatments dropped over each other dating back at least a year. I think it would be better if he didn't see us again."

Vas shrugged. She had no problem with avoiding the loon. The well-being of one clearvac junkie was of no concern of hers. Not to mention that no matter how much she rubbed she couldn't get the prickly feeling of the moldy biscuit free of her hand. "Agreed. Let's go make sure the rest of our crew is intact. You haven't seen any of them recently have you?"

Deven replaced the leather band over his esper bracelets. "No, but to be honest, I didn't try."

Vas laughed as they made their way to the small part of town that welcomed the more salty spacers. The invisible grunt labor found in any community lived in shantytowns set a few miles out from the casino conglomerates. To pull in extra money, many of these small towns created zones for the crews of visiting starships to stay at. The casino workers got much needed extra funds, and the crews of ships had places to stay they could afford, and the casinos avoided having riff raff sleeping on their floors.

He turned to her as they walked. "I think all of them are still in Expreia. They were talking about getting a group bunkhouse so they could all stay together cheaper. I sent out a comm-alert that you had sent out spy-cams to keep an eye on them after the first week you were late."

"When have I ever spied on my crew? I don't want to know what they do most of the time." Vas took a moment to enjoy the cool night air as she watched him.

Deven smiled, his dimpled charm reminding her how he always came out of gambling houses ahead of the game. "No, but they don't need to know that. Gosta said they were getting restless."

"God's balls, you should have said that first off." Vas picked up speed—there wasn't time for a nice evening stroll anymore. Restless was never good with her crew.

The muted lights of Expreia were coming into view when pain stabbed into her stomach. Vas grunted and doubled over as fire flooded her insides. It disappeared as quickly as it came.

"What is it?" Deven took her arm, but she shook him off.

A deep breath washed away the last vestiges of the attack. "I've no idea what happened, but I'm—" Her words ended in a scream when her insides burst into flame. She collapsed to the sand and grabbed her stomach. She felt like she'd been gutted by a beam weapon. Her fingers felt nothing, but the pain kept expanding. The tissues inside her body were being torn apart at the smallest level. Her screams filled the night.

Deven grabbed her head in one hand and her hand in the other. "You have to get the bracelets off of me. Now."

She tried to focus on the gold and black figure before her, but the ripping inside her took too much energy. She couldn't think. For only the second time in her life, terror froze her mind.

"I." Pain swallowed her world again. Blood slammed in her ears. "I can't." She tried to lock her jaw, but pain forced out another scream.

Cool hands rubbed her own. Deven held her head cradled in his lap and rubbed both of her arms. "You're dying. You only have minutes left. It has to be now." The sharpness in his command made her reach for the bracelets without thinking.

She fumbled with the metal bands, but her fingers couldn't close on them. Fear, pain, and darkness swallowed her in a massive rush of wind and sand. He was right—she was dying. She knew the way dying felt; she'd been here before. But she had never wandered this far down the path. Wrong about one thing though, she didn't have minutes left.

She had far less.

CHAPTER THREE

Deven swore and ripped the painful metal off his wrist. He wasn't supposed to be able to take them off himself, and would be dropped in a deep pit somewhere if it were discovered that he could do so. But he didn't have a choice. Vas was dying.

Vas's head lay in his lap, her breath rasping along the bottom of her lungs. He grasped both sides of her head and reached deep in his mind for his telepathic power. Gathering his strength, he mentally dove into her body. Poison flared around him, as red and violent as a discharge from a blaster, shredding her from the inside. New swear words were invented when he finally realized what the poison was. He hadn't seen that class of poison since Vas's great grandparents' lifetime, and he had hoped to keep it that way.

He could count the number of breaths Vas had left. He psychically grabbed hold of the poison and tried to drag it out of her. Instead of freeing her, the red of the poison flared brighter, tightening its hold on her heart. He dug deeper inside himself, pulling in reserves far beyond his normal ability. A new pounding echoed in his head—that of his own heart fighting to keep beating. He couldn't keep working at this level much longer.

He fought the darkness swallowing his mind, and pushed at the deadly poison one more time. He almost wept when it released her heart. Vas lost consciousness and an instant later the darkness claimed Deven as well.

"So we found you two collapsed over each other in the desert. Next time you and the captain decide to go on a bender, you might want to stay where folks can find you. Just luck we picked up a signal from the captain's comm." The voice was nearby and loud. Too loud.

Vas groaned as the voices slammed into her skull like tiny little Arelian throwing darts. Why did every pore of her being feel like it had been blown apart and put back together by a blind man? More specifically, a one-armed blind man having a bad day?

"Gosta? Report." She didn't need to open her eyes to know it had been her Navigation Command officer speaking.

"Two hours ago, Fron and Hrrru picked up your comm signal and went to investigate. They found both of you out cold but with no marks. We carried the two of you here into Terel's lab in the compound, set up cots, and tried to figure out what you'd done this time. Deven woke up a few minutes ago." Gosta paused and his voice dropped. "He is very heavy to carry, Captain."

Vas chuckled at Gosta's observation and winced when a ripple of pain shot through her body. "Ow. Don't make me laugh. Any of you." She cracked open an eye and peered up at Gosta's gangly body. The small upper body of his Syngerin ancestors appeared precariously balanced on his almost human lower half. It left him appearing constantly leaning forward. Syngerins reminded Vas of very large walking stick insects, however, she was very careful never to let her opinion come out. Besides, she'd always been fond of bugs; they were the only kind of pets available on her home world.

Shifting her glance to the man in the bed across the large room, Vas let a few swear words sputter silently. If she felt this bad, Deven should at least look winded. Instead he looked like he'd been lounging in a spa. God damn that man.

"I only remember pain." A chill took hold of her at the flash of memory that hit, but it didn't fill in any of the gaps.

Deven didn't answer, but nodded toward the low-ranking officers lingering in the doorway. Whatever he had to say, he didn't want it to go out to the rest of their crew.

Vas motioned for Gosta to lean closer. "Clear the doorway and post a guard in the hall. You and Terel can stay." Vas glanced past Gosta toward Terel. By the tiny lines that creased the medical officer's forehead and the narrowing of her molten silver eyes, Terel would probably knock down anyone who tried to make her leave her patients' sides. Having a best friend who was so protective was a good thing, but having ones' doctor be that protective could be a bit much at times.

Gosta nodded and motioned toward Xsit who leaned in the doorway. The tiny birdlike woman bobbed her head at Gosta's words, then turned toward the other junior officers. In an instant the hallway was cleared and the door secured.

"You were poisoned." Deven swung out of his bed, waving Terel's muttered protests aside as he did so. "I tried to draw the poison out too fast and my system collapsed." He tried flashing one of his charming grins. "You know us pretty boys are fragile."

Vas knew the futility of fighting with Deven about staying in bed; he stayed in bed when he had a good reason. Being injured didn't happen to be one of those reasons.

Terel finally shrugged. Her eyes flashed briefly to lighter silver, the only outward sign of her annoyance.

Vas wasn't going to step into any battles of will between those two. Besides, she had her own issues to fight.

"What in the hell happened?" Vas said.

"You died." Deven's jaw tightened in a rare show of emotion. It vanished an instant later. "Okay, you were about a second away from dying. We were ten minutes out of town when you complained about a pain in your stomach." He sat back on the edge of his bed.

A phantom pain hit her low in the abdomen. "I remember." Her voice stayed low. "I thought I'd been hit by a beam weapon."

"I wish." Deven shook his head. "That would have been easier to fix. You've been poisoned. Someone slipped you some Larkerian drell recently. You should have been dead twenty seconds after it went active. It's a designer poison and it can be set to activate anytime within thirty days of insertion."

Terel blanched at his words and slid back into her chair. Although the name meant nothing to Vas, it clearly did to her medical officer.

"What is it and how did they give it to me?" Vas racked her brain to think of where someone could have poisoned her. Had Skrankle done it? Who knew what lurked in that slime he oozed. Except she didn't think Skrankle could pre-plan his next meal let alone a murder.

Which left at least fifty or more of her favorite enemies as prime suspects.

"The drells are a class of designer poisons from the Westergail Wars." Everyone turned to stare at Gosta. Along with being a crack navigation officer, he laid claim to being a master hacker and computer wizard. However, none of his interests usually included historical facts.

He continued without noticing their looks. "They were one of the last inventions of the Asarlaís." Gosta frowned; his pronounced jaw mandibles clicking loudly as he finally noticed that the others were all focused on him. "I read, people. Something the rest of you might do once in a while."

"But the Westergail Wars ended eight hundred years ago," Vas said. She wasn't happy that after twenty years as a mercenary she almost left this world thanks to a poison. It being from the homicidal and self-destructing former master race of the Asarlaís just increased her annoyance level. That the universe managed to out-survive the Asarlaís was a miracle still taught to schoolchildren.

Gosta shook his head. "Clearly some of their creations continued. However, I've not read of the Larkerian drell before."

Deven leaned back partially on the pile of pillows on his bed. Vas couldn't tell if fatigue had caught up to him or he adjusted himself for her benefit. "The Larkerian is a rare one. I haven't seen it in a very long time."

She knew he meant to say something else. His mystery man persona was designed to increase her urge to space him. Some days resistance was harder than others.

"So someone slipped me an ancient and obscure poison sometime in the last thirty days. We have no idea who, why, or where." Vas wanted to go and find something or someone to beat up, but she didn't know if she could move. Deven may have taken her off death's path, but she'd come far too close not to feel the effects. She told herself the lump of ice in her gut was just a side effect of the poison.

"How long will it take to go away? We do have a battle to fight, you know." Vas picked at her med officer. She knew she was an awful patient, but it did seem to make doctors work harder to get her out of their sick rooms.

Terel scurried over to the holo vid, humming as she did so. She hummed when agitated, happy, or sad. Vas couldn't think of an emotion that went through Terel that she didn't hum about. Maybe it was a species thing. The question would be which species. Terel was an Exotic, her heritage made up of so many unique species that no single one could be claimed. Tall and elegantly thin, almost human looking, but with long dark orange feather-like hair that never would be found on a human. Even with the odd hair, she still looked like so many others she didn't stand out in a crowd. She had an eerie ability for balance however—physically, mentally, and maintaining the internal balance of her patients. Came in handy on a ship full of hot heads.

"You won't find much, unless you start studying archives." Deven ran his hand through his hair, then sighed as if weighing something. "I know a fair amount about poisons. No, I won't talk about it, nor will I develop any for you. But I haven't seen a Larkerian drell in over two hundred years." His dark green eyes narrowed as he watched all of them.

Vas didn't think Deven was a pure human, not many espers were, and none that were past a level three. However, *over* two hundred years?

"How old are you anyway? Your records say you're thirty." She wasn't surprised that his records were wrong. She'd be more surprised if any of her crew had accurate files. But she didn't like not knowing they were that far off.

"I lied." Deven shrugged and flashed an honest grin. Far more unnerving than his glamour grin in Vas's thinking. "You don't need to know how old. Take it on faith I'm older than you. And I haven't seen nor heard of the Larkerian drell in over two hundred years." His grin vanished and the lines in his face deepened. "And that I almost couldn't save you."

Gosta rose from the computer screen he'd been hunching in front of. "Captain, I'm going to need to use the *Victorious Dead's* computer system to find information. This is a rental and is useless for a deep search. Where is the ship docked?"

"That's a good question." Vas watched all three faces as her words hit.

"You lost our ship?" Deven went pale and a line that hadn't been there before appeared between his brows. This was why she had hoped to tell him before the others—she knew he wasn't going to take it well. The other two sat back down and stayed silent but both watched her with eyes found only on kicked puppies.

"First of all, it's *my* ship, not our ship. Secondly, what I would have told you had you not been playing with the deity of baked goods all evening was that Skrankle took the ship apart." She held up her hands as all three tried to speak at once. "Skrankle says he mistook it and parted out the wrong ship. Considering that no one could mistake the *Victorious Dead* for our current loaner, I seriously doubt it. Also considering that said loaner is in top shape, and has lots of brand-new state-of-the-art goodies and treats, I can't imagine anyone wanting to part her out."

Vas studied the ceiling; no easy way to say it. "Our current ship is conspicuous." She frowned but no easier terms came to mind. "And very ill-named."

"Well?" Gosta prodded when she waited too long to tell them.

"We've got the *Warrior Wench*."

She closed her eyes, and slid into her pillows as all three shouted at once. None of them said anything that she hadn't already said to herself. The majority of her negotiating for pay on jobs came out of her reputation and that of her crew. What her clients would think of the fierce merc Captain Vaslisha Tor Dain tooling around in the metal version of a fluffy pink whorehouse was enough to make her sick. She vowed that for every job they didn't get hired for, Skrankle would also lose another body part. Lucky for her, Ilerians had lots of body parts.

She finally waved them to be silent. "It sucks. Trust me, I know. But there isn't anything we can do now. We need to be on Lantaria by this time next week for the Honth battle. We also need to have a ship to find the *Victorious Dead*. I did a quick scan of Skrankle's orders on his holvid. He didn't do a full breakdown; the ship won't be in small pieces, so our job won't be as hard." She didn't know if she convinced them or herself.

"But we can't do anything until I can stand. Doc? Any clue as to how long I'm laid up?"

The gleam in Terel's eyes told Vas she wanted to continue asking questions about the ship. Long-time spacers often cared about their ship more than their families. Muttering under her breath, Terel turned toward her computer.

"Now that we know what you were attacked with, Gosta and I should be able to find something to combat it even on these computers. Hopefully there won't be much more to do, I think Deven pulled most of it out of your system." Her tone implied that she wanted to take him apart to find out how he'd done what he did as well. However, as with the issue of their missing ship, Vas knew Terel would just quietly wait until the proper time, then corner the guilty parties when it was least expected.

As Gosta joined Terel and they conferred in low tones, Vas pointed in Deven's direction. "What I need *you* to do is go round up the rest of our happy crew, tell them to pack up all their stuff, and get them ready to bug out. Then contact the fighters at Home and have them meet us in transport ships in route. We can't swing by and gather them this time. We'll need about six hundred fighters from Home, low-tech ground pounders only. We're with a few other companies on this one." Her crew sometimes complained about her rule for taking all personal belongings off the ship for any extended shore leave. She seriously doubted they'd complain after having the entire ship go missing. At least they all still had their stuff.

While the officers and primary crew of forty-five or so stayed on the *Victorious Dead*, the grunts all lived off ship on a large, yet very empty, world Vas had won with her first major battle. It didn't have much land mass, a few small continents scattered across gigantic oceans, but it was all hers. Keeping the fighting force intact and on call made her fighters happy. Many of them had families and this way they could be with them in a secure location. Vas herself even had a house there. Moreover, she made a point to visit it at least once a year.

Vas rubbed her hands across her face as fatigue pressed at her again. She let her eyes slide shut and kept them that way.

She felt Deven's presence next to her as he sat on her bed. She'd never noticed his smell before today. Light and green, as if a forest imp from Gflasia sat next to her. A very big forest imp—she fought to keep from sliding into him as the side of the bed went down under his full weight.

"You sure that will be enough?" He said.

Vas slid over further, but didn't open her eyes. "We're taking point, but in terms of bodies our participation will be minor. We have other fights coming up in a few months, and I don't want to commit too many to this one."

She'd expected Deven to get off the bed, but he stayed still.

"You scared the hell out of me." His voice dropped so low that she popped her eyes open to make sure he had spoken. "You died out there."

The intensity in his eyes rattled her, but she forced a smile. "Good thing I had you to save me then. Now can you please get the rest of our merry bunch together?" She let her eyes slide back shut. Maybe he'd leave her alone if he thought she needed sleep. She kept her life as drama free as possible. Right now those green eyes were screaming drama. They were saying other things as well, deeper things. But she really wasn't dealing with that right now. Something had changed in Deven or in her during the time they'd been apart, and she didn't think it was a good something.

Deven's weight lifted off the bed after a few minutes, but Vas waited until the door closed before opening her eyes.

Terel glanced at the recently shut door, then to Vas and slowly arched her left brow. Vas held up her hand at the other woman. "Whatever you're thinking of saying, don't say it. I need to get us all on track and get my damn ship back." She waved a finger when Terel took a breath to argue. "No, nothing."

"I have no idea what is lurking in your psyche, and I'm sure I don't want to know. I just wanted to tell you Gosta and I have synthesized the treatment that should eventually chase the remaining poison out. The fact that no one has survived a poisoning from a drell longer than a minute after activation actually gave us a number of options." From the look on her thin face, she hadn't intended to say that at all. She'd clearly picked up on whatever Vas was trying to ignore between Deven and herself.

Vas frowned, but refused to be embarrassed at the implication. She'd never reacted to Deven in a sexual manner. Never mind his looks and charm, he was a telepath and a crewmember. Which violated the only two requirements she held fast to for lovers—not an esper and not a member of her crew.

However, that changed when she first saw him in the casino tonight. Nothing extreme, just an awareness of him that hadn't been there before.

It scared the hell out of her.

However, even Terel's status as her best friend didn't entitle her to that information. Shaking the contraband thoughts out of her head, she turned back to the issue at hand. "Give it to me and let's move on."

Terel's eyes danced as she came forward with one hand held behind her back. "It's not one treatment. We'll have to give you injections for the next few days to get your system cleaned out and back to normal." She pulled her arm forward as if presenting a great medical discovery. "With this." The weapon she held up had to be longer than an infantry fighter's sword.

"What do you mean—injections? What the hell is that thing?" Vas tried crawling to the end of her bed, but gave up when she figured Terel could reach her before she could move far enough. "Where is the hypo spray? Why more than one? Nothing needs more than one."

Terel's grin went feral enough for Vas to rack her brain for anything antagonistic she'd done to the doc lately. She winced when a few items came to mind.

"This is called a needle. It's what our ancestors used to inject things into a body. I need something more invasive than a hypospray. It must be multiple times because it won't stay in your system without constant boosters." Terel held up the needle to Gosta. "Isn't it great? I read about these in bio-med school. Never thought I'd get to use one. Luckily, I bought a few from a local midwife as souvenirs."

Vas flung herself off the bed and hit the floor on all fours. "You've never used one of those things? What if you do it wrong?" She scrambled to her feet and grabbed her pillow to brandish at the advancing doctor. However, her grip was so weak it tumbled out of her hands.

"I do know what I'm doing." Terel stopped in front of her and folded her arms. "Do I tell you how to run your ship? What about the Company? No? How about you let me do my job and I'll keep letting you do yours." She grabbed Vas's arm and swabbed a section of skin. "I won't say this won't hurt; it will. But nothing compared to what you're used to on a battlefield."

Gosta picked that moment to drop a book. Terel stabbed Vas with the wicked needle at the same second.

Terel nodded toward Gosta who bowed, his double-jointed knees lending a unique flair to the old-fashioned move. Both of them headed toward the door. "You'll feel the effects soon. However, you need to sleep. You should be ready to board our new ship in the morning. Being as you lost our old one."

"I didn't lose it, damn it," Vas said around a huge yawn. "Waitaminute, what is in that stuff?" Her eyes were dropping faster than a drunk after a week on clearvac.

Terel gave an evil grin as she paused before closing the door. "I knew that even as tired as you were you wouldn't sleep. The sedatives in the syringe along with your treatment will assure me otherwise." She flashed a genuine smile this time. "Good night, Vas."

Vas fought to wake up as a giant with a bad hangover picked up one end of reality and shook. However, the pounding came from inside her head, not outside it. Lifting her head was a painful experience.

Falling back into the mattress, Vas muttered about revenge-driven doctors. Eventually the pounding dropped to a dull thud. It still hurt, but her head wasn't shattering and the black dots in front of her eyes were gone.

At least Terel's treatment gave Vas the strength to go after Terel and give her a piece of her mind about the resulting headache. On second thought, if the headache was going to hit this hard each treatment, she needed to stay on the doc's good side.

"Better?" Gosta's dry voice entered an instant before he lumbered into the room. Probably a safe approach if he had an inkling of how she felt right now.

"Not much. Doc needs to give me something for my head." She sat up and slowly got out of bed. "At least I can move now. Any luck tracking how I got this drell crap?"

Gosta's long legs clicked softly as he strode closer. "Not yet. Terel and I will have to use the computers on the ship." He cocked a ragged black eyebrow at her. "The new ship does have a computer system, yes?"

She turned her back to him and put on a clean shirt, clearly one Terel had found, as she hadn't brought anything down to the planet with her. "Of course it does." She glared over her shoulder at Gosta. "In fact, I hate to say it, but the system looks better than ours. When you check it out, see what things we want to take with us when we get the *Victorious Dead* back."

She had just finished lacing up her boots when Deven came in.

"We're mostly accounted for. A few took some convincing to move fast enough, but we're here. Xsit sent someone to go find Mac and Jakiin, but they can't be far. No one in town will rent them a vehicle after the last time they were here." He folded his arms and scowled at the room. "This is the only room that's not ready to go." The tone in his voice made it clear that whoever he had been during his extended vacation here, he had mentally returned to being her second-in-command.

"I couldn't disturb her, you know." Terel pushed him through the doorway and wandered over to her workstation. "No worries, I can get my lab packed up in minutes." Terel set up her lab everywhere. Vacations were just a time for her to play with it more. She turned to Vas. "Where is the shuttle anyway?"

"At the main landing pad, just past the casinos. I didn't want to bring it closer until we were ready to head out." Vas said. A sound idea that she now regretted. Time would be lost getting the shuttle to the pad outside the shantytown and they'd already lost time with her poisonings. Both of them. She counted Terel's 'cure' a second attack.

Terel bustled around picking things up and fitting them into tiny boxes. "Well then, Second, I'll have this lab picked up before you return." She gave Deven a curt nod and went back about her business.

Deven looked ready to say more, but instead shook his head and stomped out.

Vas laughed. "You two are back to getting along famously, I see."

Terel had most of her equipment taken apart and boxed already. "I will repeat this again, it is not my fault that he got buried. I can't be responsible if people have physiological abilities that they choose not to share with their doctor. Even though I'm the one who has to save their lives. Even if my say so can keep them breathing or leave them in a pile of dust. No, some people don't feel that I need to know that they go into a shallow breathing coma to repair major injuries." She threw a small box with particular force, but it still landed perfectly in the pile near the door. She pointed another box toward Vas. "He's damn lucky that his species card insists on a ground burial. Being buried alive is far better than what could have happened. He would have been dusted long before he could recover."

Vas took the box from the doctor's thin hands and carefully laid it on the pile. Even with Terel's amazing aim and leveraging skills she didn't want to take a chance with a box of vials in her current agitated state. "Hey, I'm on your side. He didn't tell me either." She shrugged. "He doesn't hold you responsible. Not really." Vas knew that at this point the battle between her second-in-command and her doctor was more for show than anything else.

"Not that I care. He can huff and puff all he wants. But it will be nice when he accepts his mistake," Terel said as she made a final pass to make sure all of her belongings were removed.

Vas started to respond when a huge explosion rocked the room and knocked her to the floor. Scrambling to her feet, she grabbed the snub blaster on the table next to her.

This time she knew the explosion didn't come from inside her head.

CHAPTER FOUR

Vas ran outside with her blaster primed. She had no idea who would be stupid enough to attack a shantytown, but she was willing to show them the error of their ways. Not that it wouldn't possibly improve the place. Her crew had chosen to stay in one of the shabbiest towns she'd ever seen. She really couldn't understand them sometimes. They made good money, but usually chose to stay low-end when planet-side. Even if the larger gambling town wouldn't have welcomed common mercs, there were far better places than this one.

The only evidence of a disturbance was a sickly plume of green smoke at the far edge of the village. She couldn't see what caused it as it came from behind the only part of town with multi-storied buildings.

"Gosta, come with me. Terel, secure the landing area in case Deven comes in." Vas returned to the doc's lab and grabbed the rest of her weapons.

Her crew rushed out of their quarters, buckling on their weapons while they ran. It appeared that most of them had kept their wits through their extended vacation.

"Gosta, you, and the flight squad follow me. The rest of you split up. Half stay here, half go with Terel." It might be nothing. However, considering all the nothings that had turned out to be somethings lately, she didn't want to take a chance.

Aside from surprised muttering from the locals, Vas didn't hear anything coming from the smoky area. That held promise. In her experience, bad things were often noisy.

She slowed to a walk as she rounded the corner. While she didn't know what to expect, she knew it wasn't the scene in front of her. Her two missing pilots stood there covered in green soot, poking at a smoldering pile of rubble with a stick.

"Mac? Jakiin? What the hell have you done now?" Vas held up her hand before either could talk. "Wait." She turned toward the people behind her. "Gosta, take everyone else back and make sure everything is ready for Deven."

Not waiting for a response, she jogged forward to the interesting tableau before her. She didn't like interesting. It often changed from interesting to painful to deadly without so much as a by your leave.

Jakiin and Mac continued rummaging about the mess in front of them, but faster. They also tried to rub off the green soot from their faces. Mac even had dusty smoke drifting up from his strawberry blonde head.

Taking a deep breath, Vas switched into full merc captain mode. Whatever her officers had done, they most likely shouldn't have been doing it. If they weren't two of the best pilots in seven galaxies she would have spaced them long ago.

"What the hell did you do?" As she strode forward, Vas cursed herself for changing into Terel's shirt. The thing was pink, for crying out loud. She normally didn't care about clothing, but there were some times it mattered. Such as getting her pilots out of whatever trouble they'd dove into. Trouble didn't follow these two; it stalked them like a jilted lover.

Mac wiggled his sunburned nose. "Our product had an accident." Mac's voice came out quick and high pitched, never a good sign with him. One of the few pure humans on her ship, he appeared out of place with his pale skin and light strawberry blond hair. The kid didn't have the coloring or temperament for lying. However, he seemed to be the last to realize that.

"What product?" Vas sighed. Mac and Jakiin were always trying to get rich. Pathetically, as officers on her ship for the last ten years, they could have been rich, if they would stop spending money on get-rich-quick schemes.

Jakiin shuffled his feet and Vas shifted her glare to him. The thin Foorlian usually let his partner in crime deal with everything. If Mac's coloring didn't suit a life of swindling, Jakiin came from an entire race of failed liars. Pale, hairless, and frail looking, his double lidded eyes had a constant look of surprise. Or abject terror.

She got closer to the wreckage. "A still?" She rubbed her eyes and wondered how hard it would be to replace Mac and Jakiin. "You built a still. On a gambling planet." With each sentence she took another step toward her pilots. She thought Jakiin turned whiter, but with his coloring she couldn't tell.

All of the gambling planets tightly controlled their alcohol. They didn't want to take a chance that someone started serving watered-down stuff. The casinos counted on their patrons to be drunk; drunks let go of money, money made the casino owners happy. The patrons were happy because they had free, and very potent, booze. Even if they quickly had no money.

"Which one of you wants to explain this? And which one of you wants to spend a week in the brig?"

Mac and Jakiin practically split their guts trying to tell their tale the fastest.

She needed more time to deal with them, time she couldn't spend planet-side.

"Never mind. Both of you can tell Deven when we're on the ship." She waved at the smoldering mess behind them. "But first take that thing apart and destroy it. You

have ten minutes or we leave without you." She started to
walk away, leaving the two pilots furiously ripping metal
pieces apart. "No shortcuts. I will be conducting a fly-
over before we head back to the ship."

She made her way to the shuttle landing pad and the
rest of her people; carefully ignoring the odd and curious
stares the locals threw her way. More than likely a new
R&R planet should be picked out for future down time.
Her people had been a little too interesting lately.

It had taken far longer than expected, but Vas finally
got her command crew, Mac and Jakiin included, on the
shuttle and headed toward the space station. It was a bit
tight in the shuttle, but all she needed was body space for
her crew. They didn't have to be comfortable.

Deven approached the command chair. "When are you
going to tell them?"

Vas took her eyes off the star field before them and
smiled. "When we get there. Telling them now will only
annoy me. We can't change it, and I think even Mac and
Jakiin will notice."

Vas entered the rest of the codes. Mac swore as she
took over his controls completely to do so. Normally
entering the codes would be his job, but since he'd be
entering the ones for the wrong ship, she took over.

A squeak in the chair next to her told her that Deven
had taken his seat although he hadn't the entire ride to the
station.

"What?" Ignoring him wouldn't work, perhaps
terseness would. She prided herself on her ability to stay
focused; it kept her and her crew alive many times when
they should have been slaughtered. However, Deven was
still messing with her focus. Once they got to their new
ship, she was going to have to set up an appointment with
her ship's mind doc, Nariel. Find a way to block
whatever she was starting to feel about Deven.

"Vas, we need to talk."

That was not what she needed right now. Her previous drug-induced sleep didn't leave her rested and it was taking everything just to stay functioning at this point. She felt as exhausted as she had during the fifty-day siege they'd led on the planet Salis two years ago. Without the perk of getting paid.

"Ya know what, no, we shouldn't." She ran her hand through her long, snarled, red hair and grimaced. "I'm sure whatever it is, it's important. However, things have been going far worse than usual lately. I know we need to talk about whatever it is we need to talk about. There's always something that needs talking about. Something deep, meaningful, and that will no doubt provide me with insight into my poor self." She folded her arms and glared at him. He retaliated with a smirk that could have knocked out a dozen suns. "What?"

With a grace envied by professional dancers, Deven levered himself out of his chair. "I wanted to tell you we're docking."

A bump as a docking bracket slid against the side of the shuttle jolted Vas back to the screen.

Muttering a few swear words, she completed the docking. By the time she unbuckled herself from the harness and sent the last codes to the control tower, Deven had herded the crew out to the space station dock.

For a large group, her crew could move with surprising silence when the situation demanded it. They failed to demonstrate that today. Honestly, by the amount of noise they made you'd think they'd never been on a station before.

Mac jogged up to her, his pack slung over his shoulder. Soot still hung around his eyes and hairline. It was probably the cleanest he'd been in weeks, although his strawberry blond hair had a new green tinge.

"Captain, why did you take over? I didn't drink that moonshine," he said with a frown. "We couldn't get the damn thing to work before it blew up."

Vas ran her fingers through her hair again, still hitting the same knots. She either needed to cut it, remember to keep it in a tighter braid, or find a crew that didn't exasperate her.

"It had nothing to do with that. But, I do...." Vas let her words trail off in shock as she realized Mac dared to look away as she spoke. Snap pilot or not, he was a dead man. With a growl she turned around to see what could be so important he'd risk his life by ignoring her.

The damn *Warrior Wench* hung there gleaming for the whole crew to see. There were no other ships in dock.

"That's the *Warrior Wench*. What in the eight hells of Glaxion V are we doing here?" Bathshea said out loud. The engineer had never been shy about her opinions, or anything else for that matter.

"Um, is that supposed to be named after you, Captain?" Jakiin would be joining his partner in crime in death. Soon. That someone would make that joke had been a given. She didn't think it would be one of her own people.

The instant the words were out of Jakiin's mouth, the entire crew froze.

"You didn't say that." Vas kept her voice low but watched as the crew, including Mac, stepped away from Jakiin.

"I made a joke?" Jakiin stepped backwards, his hands held up to ward her off.

Stupid git, as if hands would stop a blaster. Or a sword for that matter.

Luckily for her, Deven stepped behind Jakiin. At least now she wouldn't have to waste energy chasing him. A mercenary's worth consisted of her reputation. If her own people were making that connection between Vas and the ship's idiotic name, things did not bode well.

"Say you made a stupid mistake, Jakiin." Deven spoke softly.

"I know what he said."

Deven's green eyes met hers. "I'm sure he meant nothing by it. Right, Jakiin? Beg the nice captain for your life *now*."

Jakiin seemed ready to jump off the gangway and take his chances at learning to fly before he hit the bottom. "I...I...I...."

Vas stalked away from him. Killing petrified idiots didn't sit right with her. Even if he deserved it. Old age had made her soft. Funny, she hadn't felt old a month ago. The previous Vas would have sliced Jakiin and tossed him over the railing before the last word cleared his lips. Or at the very least punched him. However, as much as she hated to admit it, he wouldn't be the only person thinking it. Nor would he be the only one saying it. At least none of the rest of her command crew would be stupid enough to make that mistake again. They could spread it to the grunts when they hooked up.

"You live. For now." She turned mid-step as an idea came to mind. "But Deven gets to watch out for you. The entire campaign. You'll answer to him, and he'll have new tasks for you each day." Her grin grew while she watched both men's faces cloud over; neither of them liked babysitters.

She marched over to her ship. "Yes, boys and girls, we have a new ship. No, I won't discuss it. As you just saw, I'd recommend you don't discuss it either."

CHAPTER FIVE

The crew loaded the ship in record time, with only a few fistfights along the way. The problem arose because there were more crew quarters on the *Warrior Wench* than had been on the *Victorious Dead*. More variety meant more fighting over the selection. She now had forty-five of the best mercenary-trained five-year-olds in the Commonwealth.

Unfortunately, as much as she might like to space most of them right now, she needed all of them. The Commonwealth consisted of an eclectic collection of planets ranging from state-of-the-art technology to one level above hunter/gatherers. A few even mixed it up, creating odd conglomerations of technology. The Commonwealth kept its worlds culturally intact when it added them, and allowed autonomy for each world. Strictly enforced autonomy. They frowned on any group who brought the wrong level of tech to a planet. Since mercenary crews had to be hired through Commonwealth channels, the most successful crews were ones gifted in multiple styles of killing. Vas knew that her people were experts in their fields, each one with a unique skill set. Nevertheless, they were going to drive her mad with arguing.

"You'll deal with this?" Vas nodded to Gosta as the squabbling continued. The last twenty-four hours had left her drained and irritable. It would be safer for her people if she didn't deal with them right now. She might accidentally space a crewmember she'd need in the next fight.

Trying to get her quarters in order might bring her peace. At least it would get her away from the bickering.

Vas was just starting to feel better, and her collection of antique blasters and martial arts edged weapons had found a perfect home on her walls, when her door started rattling.

After almost dropping a rare Nlarian two-handed ritual death sword, she yelled for the door to open.

Deven leaned in the open doorway.

"What do you want?" Talking to him right now was one-step above dealing with her fussy crew.

Without waiting for her to invite him in, he walked in and sat down on her bed. "We need to talk."

"What is it? You've been saying we need to talk since I found you. Which, by the way, was not a lot of fun. Most captains don't have to grab their second-in-command out of a brothel. At least not the charging end of the brothel."

"How do you know I charged them?"

She swung her desk chair around and sat down facing him. "Don't give me that. I swear, between you, Mac, and Jakiin I'm spending more time babysitting than I am earning money. Do you think it's easy supporting an entire planet? In case you haven't noticed we've lost about half of our smuggling space on this damn trollop of a ship. Even if we can mask the idents, which seem pretty damn secure, we won't have room to carry enough cargo to pay for living expenses." She bounced to her feet and stalked the room. "Which is another thing. Damn it, they took *my* ship! And now I have to deal with this thing." She pounded an offending bulkhead. "Do you realize

what those other companies are going to say when we get
to Lantaria?" She didn't know where all of that came
from but it felt good to say it out loud. With a sigh she
resumed her seat. "So what did you want to talk about?"

"A few things." He looped one long arm around his
knee and rocked back. "That being one of them." He held
up his other hand. "No, I didn't scan you. You're
projecting so loud any esper within eighty miles felt you
on Tarantus IV." His eyes darkened. "It's more than
being mocked for the name of this ship. Although you're
trying not to show it, that poisoning scared you. But you
have to get your emotions under control before we set
camp for this battle. There will be espers there."

Vas stewed as he spoke. She never lost control. He
couldn't feel anything. "I know they are sanctioning
espers. *I'm* the one who made the contract for this fight.
What is your point?"

"If I can feel your unease, other espers can too."

"If there happens to be any others out there as strong
as you. Which I seriously doubt." Trusting telepaths
didn't come easily for her. Her home planet practically
worshipped them, and that had almost ended very badly
for her as a child. But she trusted Deven as much as any.
He might be telling her the truth about projecting. She'd
felt out of sorts since she hit the space station yesterday.

And that was before she knew how exciting her life
had become.

"That's the problem. A level-one esper would read
you from a mile away on the planet. Hell, you probably
ruined every espers' game in that casino planet-side." He
leaned forward. "It's more than the ship, or the attempt
on your life. You've had people trying to kill you as long
as I've known you. Whatever is causing the problem, we
need to shut it down before we get to Lantaria."

She stared out the porthole. The answers certainly
weren't in the docking bay before her. If they were
anywhere they lurked in her own head. Deven might be

able to help her, but she had lifelong rules about telepaths. They were an asset on her crew, great as friends, but she would never let one in her head, her bed, or her heart.

"For the record, most people only try to kill me in battle. Never with centuries-old poisons from the Westergail Wars. I think I have a right to be unnerved about that. As for whatever I'm projecting?" She shrugged; she couldn't deal with this now. "I have no idea. I am pissed about my ship. However, I also want to know who ordered it to be taken apart. There's no way even an idiot like Skrankle could have confused the two ships, and this one isn't anywhere close to a decommissioning. He honestly didn't think I'd be returning."

Deven nodded. "What happened to you on your trip? Skrankle is a moron, but he's also a coward. It's not good that he felt safe enough dismembering our ship."

"My ship," she said, but only half-heartedly. Semantics aside, the *Victorious Dead* belonged to the entire crew and meant a lot to them. "Nothing I can think of." She couldn't think of much that happened during her trip that could be deemed threatening. Nothing beyond bad pick-up lines in a few bars anyway, and a few nights with that trader. A recon to go see about a planet for sale. It ended up being longer than she'd intended, nothing to be concerned about.

Except that something in her didn't want to talk about it to anyone. She shook off the undefined feeling of unease that rose whenever she thought about talking about her trip.

"Look, since we're not going to find out what's causing this great psychic leak anytime soon, and since you think it's going to be a problem, can't you find a way to block it? Do some of your mumbo jumbo?" She wiggled her fingers at him.

Now it was Deven's turn to look away. When he turned back to her the lines around his eyes and mouth had deepened. "We have a few days before Lantaria. We should try and get to the bottom of this. Any patch I do may or may not hold since I'm not sure what I'm patching."

She took an involuntary step away from him; a feeling of utter terror at him prying into her head flooded her. Which was stupid on many levels. One, she never gave in to fear. And two, she trusted Deven with her life.

Granted, she'd never allowed telepaths in her head, but this feeling went beyond that. Her stomach threatened to climb up her throat at the thought. "No. I've got too much work to do before battle. We have to be spot on, and the month off won't have helped." She waved her hand at him. "Block it."

He sighed, but went ahead and placed a simple telepathic block that should keep anything in her head from leaking. He'd had to put one on once before for a mission, and he'd explained it very thoroughly at that point. He didn't explain it this time, but the feeling was the same—sort of as if he'd just put a swimming cap on her head.

There was nothing more to be said, so they went to see how the crew was faring. They were almost back on the bridge when they were slammed to the floor and bounced along the corridor a few feet.

Vas rolled to her feet and ran the rest of the way, expecting to see part of her new ship blasted apart before they even got out of dock. Deven was right behind her.

"What was that?"

"Are we under attack?" Both Deven and Vas spoke at the same time, and looked to do so again when Gosta raised his hand.

"The explosion was on the station." He flipped the screen toward them and showed what had blown up— Skrankle's office. Actually his office, the building it was in, and two unlucky nearby scout ships. A gaping hole opened the bay to space before the station's seals locked in. The sirens that filled the station indicated help would be there soon.

Vas ran her fingers through her hair, finally ripping out the remains of the braid. Who in the hell would want Skrankle killed? Okay, lots of people would want Skrankle dead. And dismembered. And strewn to the far corners of the universe. Nevertheless, she didn't think most would go so far as to blow him up. Joy at an irritating life blown to bits collided with annoyance at being beaten to the punch. In addition, the fact he might have actually come through on getting back parts of her missing ship.

"Damn it, we'd better see if there's anything left, I'm positive he knew more about what happened to the *Victorious Dead.*" She turned toward the corridor leading to the hatchway.

Deven blocked her. "You probably shouldn't go." His frown was as solid as his arm.

"I have a right to see what happened." She glared at him.

"Can I talk to you first?" He propelled her toward her ready room. It probably looked like she walked with him by choice. She couldn't pull away without looking like they were fighting. Which would only lead to more drama and gossip. Her crew might be some of the best at what they did, but they gossiped more than a gaggle of grandmothers.

With a sigh, she followed him into her ready room and shut the door. "Why don't you want me out there?"

"Who do you think is going to be the number one suspect in Skrankle's demise?"

"Me? Because I had a disagreement with Skrankle? I only kill people I'm paid to kill, no freelance. Besides, I've been with all of you." Vas paced around the small room. She hadn't taken the time to personalize it yet, so the room still felt cold and sterile.

He nodded. "Yes, and if you hadn't been poisoned where would we be by this point?"

"Probably half way to Lantaria if Mac had his way...." She swung around. "You think someone wanted it to look like I did it? Someone stupid enough to not check if we'd left dock yet?"

He raised his hand, the esper bracelets clinking lightly. "Or someone desperate enough. This ship was probably being fitted to be sold to someone, they might not have been happy about him giving it away. And, you said yourself that you roughed him up pretty bad. He had more than enough time to tell the entire station about your attack on him." He shrugged, the movement tightening the fabric across his chest. "Maybe someone decided to take advantage of a merc captain with a noted temper."

Vas rolled her eyes to the ceiling; she swore Deven had the nagging skill of a matron. "The minute the masses stop believing I'm a tough-ass bitch is the minute we stop getting jobs."

"So you're going to say that you're not a tough-ass bitch?"

"Not at all. If anyone knows how much of a tough-ass bitch I am, it would be you. But, that image has to be built upon. I built upon it for Skrankle's benefit. In this case, an obvious waste of perfectly good bitchiness." She frowned. "I had to dump my second favorite boots because that slime ball oozed on them." She paused and shook her head. "What the hell were we talking about?"

"How you were going to stay on the ship, and that you'd get Flarik to talk to the station security that you're sure are coming this way." Deven folded his arms and leaned against the door.

"I didn't say that." Although she agreed with his logic, she had a policy of never giving in without a fight. Especially when it involved Deven.

"No, but it's a good idea."

The grin had moved into insufferable by this point. Vas toyed with banning grins on her ship. No matter how nice he looked wearing them, she never trusted any of Deven's grins.

"I suppose so," she said finally. "What gender is Flarik this month? Isn't it in hibernation yet?" Wavians had the ability to switch genders on a regular basis, the male version being more difficult to deal with most of the time. They also had a habit of sleeping through space flights. As a lawyer, Flarik was rarely needed until they reached their destination, so the sleeping habits worked well.

"Female, and yes, she started her sleep cycle as soon as we got on board. But you're going to need her."

She rubbed the side of her face in thought. Getting Flarik involved might be a good idea for more than station security deferment. "Wonderful idea. I'll call her immediately." She fussed with papers on her desk, then glanced up, feigning surprise at his appearance in her ready room. "Isn't there something you should be doing?"

The sly grin flashed again, someday she would really have to number them, and he slid out the door.

Vas's annoyance level rose when she had to search to find the code for Flarik's room. She knew all the rooms on her old ship by heart. A twinge reminded her that those rooms were missing now. She swore again at the recent explosion. Killing Skrankle should have been her job.

After a few minutes she found the number and tapped it into the ship's comm system. "Flarik? I know you're going down for sleep, but I need you." Vas tried to sound as understanding as possible but she'd had a shitty twenty-four hours and wasn't in the mood. However, pissing off a sleepy Wavian often led to a radically shorter life, even for a mercenary captain.

A low voice chimed in after a few seconds. "What is it, Captain? I need to hibernate."

"You'll have time to go under before we take off. But I need you to come to my ready room."

A sigh on the other end told Vas that Flarik fought off her sleep. "I will be there."

Terse, but not bad for a Wavian who had been awake for a month.

Deven's idea of bringing in the lawyer was a sound one, even if he did it to keep Vas out of the space station cops' way. She also needed someone who enjoyed mystery, deceit, and drama to look into other things for her. A lawyer, particularly a Wavian lawyer, would be the perfect choice.

Flarik had only taken a few minutes to get to her ready room, yet as always, she arrived impeccably dressed and groomed. No matter which gender she chose, or those disturbing times of being neither, Flarik always appeared immaculate. Vas fingered her wild red hair and sighed in envy.

She waited until Flarik took her seat with a slight ruffle of her perfect white feathers. The feathers were very short, but perfect, whatever color they were at that moment. Along with switching genders, Wavians could change their coloring at a whim.

"What did you need to see me for, Captain?" Flarik folded her delicate, clawed hands neatly in her lap. She looked prim and proper until she went into action with those claws. Vas would have hired her regardless of her legal skills based on the claws alone.

"Sorry for dragging you out. But there's been an explosion." Vas called up the images from outside the ship on her screen. She quickly played the explosion and resulting fireball. "That was Skrankle, the bastard who's responsible for us being on this ship."

Flarik nodded as Vas spoke. "You mean the fine individual who gave us this ship as recompense for the accidental dismemberment of our own? He did give you the papers, yes?"

Vas laughed softly. "I forced him to give them to me, but yes, he gave me the papers. This is ours."

"Excellent," Flarik said. "I will explain this to the officers when they arrive. I'm sure they will not wish to detain us." She flashed a grin, but unlike Deven's it didn't comfort. Even after all these years Vas still wasn't used to those teeth. Three rows of razor sharp, albeit very tiny, teeth. She didn't want to think about the rumors that went around about those teeth before the Wavians joined the Commonwealth.

"It's a good thing that we were still in port when this happened. It might have appeared as if you were leaving the scene of a crime." Flarik rose and turned toward the door. "Good day, Captain."

"Actually, us still being here is something else I wanted to discuss. How long will you be sleeping this time?"

Flarik clicked her teeth in thought, literally reading her body. "I'd say through the arrival at our next battle. It is in six days, yes?" At Vas's nod she continued. "Yes, I would say I should wake right when we get there." She cocked her head. Her golden eyes focused sharply, giving the unhealthy impression of staring down prey. "Why?"

"There have been too many unhealthy things happening lately. I need someone to see what the pattern is. I'd like to have Gosta start looking into it. He can hand off anything he finds once you wake." A surge of embarrassment snuck in, but she pushed it aside. Vas had always dealt with her personal problems on her own, asking others was a new and uncomfortable situation. Delegating was needed for her line of work—she didn't like it in her personal business.

Flarik gave a tight nod. "That will be acceptable."

Vas waited a few minutes after Flarik left then went back on the bridge.

"Gosta, can you come here?" Vas motioned for him to come over to a small console near the command chair. "We need to find our ship, our real ship. I pulled up the idents before I left Skrankle's, but I couldn't get a clear fix. I need you to find at least the star systems where the *Victorious Dead's* parts went." She frowned. "Skrankle might be gone, but the damage he did continues. Can you locate the parts?"

"I think so," Gosta said as he fiddled with the computer. When he didn't find anything immediately, Vas went to her own console and fussed with pulling up system records for Lantaria.

"Captain? You may wish to see this." Gosta beamed, a few minutes later. "A few bits of ship you might want to see again." He tapped a few green spots on the crowded screen. "It looks like Skrankle parted the ship out quickly once you didn't show. Or he did it right after you dropped it off. Regardless, those parts took a fast trip to the outer rim. But most of them aren't incorporated into any ships yet."

She studied the screen; once he pointed them out she saw where the parts were. "So, fourteen? He split her up into fourteen parts?" Not too bad. The main part to find would be the core. That held the brain of the *Victorious Dead*. "You said they weren't all incorporated. Which parts? Are they in a nearby ship?" The idea of raiding a ship stupid enough to take illegally removed parts sounded lovely. Especially after the way things had been going lately.

Gosta practically rubbed his hands with glee. "That, my dear Captain, is the best part of all." He pulled the screen toward him and fiddled with adjustments. "See here? This is the *Warrior Wench*, as we sit in dock waiting to leave." He tapped the center. "And this is the core of the *Victorious Dead*."

Vas poked at the screen. That idiot Skrankle had put a warship's core in a pleasure cruiser? "Are you certain? Is it damaged?"

"Yes, I'm certain. And it's not damaged. Skrankle put a block on it so the *Warrior Wench* would work without tapping into the *Victorious Dead's* memory portion of the core, but she's there. He didn't clean her. He simply overlaid the block."

She allowed herself her first real smile that day. The most important part of her beloved ship was with her; she only needed to dig it out. The rest of it would have to be gathered, on principle if nothing else.

Finally she shook herself. No reason getting too happy. Things were still far from normal. "Can you check to see if the *Warrior Wench's* core had been damaged?"

The grin faded from his face. "Already thought of that, Captain. No damage. The *Warrior Wench* is only a few years old, her core still factory perfect and I hate to say it, more advanced than the *Victorious Dead*."

She swore. "So why did Skrankle gut my ship to add its core into this one? We're missing something."

"We may never know now that Skrankle's gone."

Flarik broke up the introspection as she came on deck. "The officers completely understand our loss, and hope that we continue to enjoy this ship as the last gift of our gallant supporter, Skrankle."

Vas continued to be amazed at Flarik's ability to keep a straight face in any circumstance.

"If you no longer need me, I will resume my sleep preparations." More statement than request, but Flarik did wait until Vas had acknowledged her with a nod before turning and marching down the hall.

"Why do I always feel like I've been chastised when she does that?" Deven spoke from behind her.

"Because you are being chastised," Vas said. "We all are. I'm grateful she's on our side. Now, Gosta—"

"Now, Captain," Terel cut her off as she came into the bridge. "I've been calling you for the last ten minutes. We have to get another shot into you. And I want to do more tests on that poison."

Vas started to argue but Terel wouldn't let her. "If you'd prefer we can stop the treatments and see if what's left of that stuff in your system can find a way to kill you." The look on Terel's face said there were two options: her way or her way.

"So be it." Vas raised her hands. "I'll go let you shoot me with that archaic torture device. Let's get this over with."

 *

Deven waited until Vas and Terel were gone before turning toward the rest of the room. "Mac, prepare to move out. Gosta, you have the bridge." He turned toward his own small ready room. There were too many things that he needed to sort out.

One of the most disturbing items concerned his recent reaction to Vas. The last two days he felt an odd tingle in his telepathic senses whenever she stood close. Like he would when near a lover. However, while he and Vas were close, they'd never gone past a solid friendship. Not that he would say no—his captain was a stunning woman. However, she made it clear from the first time they'd met that she would never be involved with a telepath. So why was he thinking about it now?

Something had happened during her extended trip. He'd venture to say a lot of somethings happened. Vas had never been an hour over-due let alone two weeks. The fact that she wouldn't, or couldn't, talk about what she had been doing disturbed him. The fact that he couldn't tell which was the case made things even worse.

He fingered the cuffs on his wrist in thought. If he took them off he would know instantly what had happened to her. However, alarms would go off in Vas's comm, and he couldn't risk anyone, even her, knowing that he could remove the cuffs himself.

He'd come close to exposing his ability in the desert, but Vas obviously thought she'd stayed conscious long enough to free him. In truth she had been all but dead when she fell to the desert floor. He'd barely been able to rip off the cuffs in time.

Drells were rarely used even before the Asarlaís were destroyed. The making of them was so arcane, so deadly, that half who tried died slow horrible deaths as the creations destroyed the creators.

So how did one end up on an obscure gambling planet in the body of his captain? A woman who, while well respected in her field, wasn't anything more than a merc captain. Far more gifted than any he'd ever seen, and after four hundred and fifty years of life he'd seen more than his share, but still not a person who should have people trying to slaughter her with such a weapon when a blaster would do the job.

Had someone tried to poison him and got her? Or decided to poison her to find out how strong of a telepath he really was?

Deven swore under his breath as he packed a small bag. Either could be true. And he knew who to get answers from. He'd be cutting it close to get where he needed to go and be back before the battle began, but he didn't have a choice. If someone had targeted Vas, he needed to find out why. And if someone had done it to find out the level of his esper abilities, he needed to leave the Commonwealth immediately.

Too many people both inside and outside of the Commonwealth council would love to get their hands on an esper of his level.

He pulled up the star charts, looking for a small planet that he knew would be hidden from him. It took longer than he wanted, but he found it. Now he needed to find a way to jump ship, get his answers, and then return before the battle. And he was going to have to try and talk to someone who would rather kill him. Slowly. Repeatedly. Someone the Commonwealth would also love to get their hands on.

Not all of the Asarlaís were dead.

CHAPTER SIX

"Where's Deven? I need to talk to him." Vas scowled at the console while she called the bridge. She hated when Deven turned off his comm. Even though she had said to get the med work done quickly, Terel had managed to confine her for two hours to run "one more test". Now Deven had wandered off.

"Out. He's gone out." Mac spit out the words and cut the comm.

Vas concentrated on the documents she needed Deven's opinion on, for now ignoring the abrupt cut off from Mac.

A few minutes later she buzzed the bridge again. "Out? Out where? We've only left dock, which, by the way we seem to be doing at an advanced speed." She called up their specs. "Take it easy, Mac. Flarik managed to get the nice cops to leave us alone, but she'll come out and chew off a few heads if we have to wake her again to deal with a speed warning."

The silence told her that he weighed the danger. Nevertheless, even he wouldn't want to be on Flarik's bad side. "Aye Captain, two clicks below posted speed until we're out of the station." Then he cut the comm. Again.

Vas called back. "Mac, where did you say Deven went? I wanted him in my ready room five minutes ago."

"He's out. Didn't tell me where he went. Took that shuttle we came up on and said he'd meet us at Lantaria." The words came out so fast it didn't sound like Mac speaking.

It took a few seconds for his gibberish to sink in.

"Wait—he left?" Without so much as a, *hey I've got errands to do*? She strode out onto the bridge. "Xsit, flag down that damn shuttle. I want to talk to him now."

Xsit cringed, and the light yellow feathers on the back of her head ruffled up. "I'm sorry, Captain. He cut communications and left the station." Her voice went softer. "It looks like he is blocking us."

Vas stomped around the deck. She'd kill him. Then toss the body in the nearest black hole. She glanced up and noticed how carefully her command crew watched her. She'd stomp in private. The issues between Deven and herself were growing stranger, but the rest of the crew didn't need to know about them.

"I knew that. He mentioned something. I didn't think he'd go so soon." She tried to ease her pace as she went to her ready room. "Gosta, you have the bridge. Keep Mac under control."

If her crew chose not to believe her, there was nothing she could do. But for now she could leave menacing messages for that bastard and plan how many ways she might kill him.

*

Deven carefully ignored the flashing message light on the shuttle's console. He knew Vas would be pissed, but he also knew he couldn't explain what he needed to do. Hell, he hadn't wanted her, or anyone else on that ship, to know he was old enough to recognize a two-hundred–year-old poison. He sure as hell didn't want to explain anything beyond that. Marliress would take a lot of explaining.

Marliress Gtill Sorlian kept a lower profile than even Deven did. The Asarlaí had been a race of beings with enormous powers, technology that even Deven's people hadn't reached yet. They had ruled this entire quadrant, Deven's home galaxy as well, for thousands of years. Two thousand years ago they were brought down by the weight of their own cultural demands. They lingered on for centuries but only as a shadow of their former power, finally dying out during the Westergail Wars.

Marli was the only Asarlaí left as far as Deven knew.

Deven watched as the comm light continued to flash. With a sigh he covered the light and continued entering his destination into the shuttle's navigation system. He couldn't let Vas distract him. Marli might decide to follow through on her threats and kill him; he needed to be alert if he was going to survive. Even if she didn't, she could make things extremely uncomfortable for him.

He took out the vial of Vas's blood he'd smuggled out of Terel's lab. He hoped the answers he found were worth the risk he was taking.

⤡

A few hours later, an alarm squealed over the ship's system and pulled Deven out of his thoughts.

"Whoever you are, if you don't clear my airspace now, I'm blowing a hole in your aft." Deven leaned forward with a grin. At least he knew he'd found Marli.

"Marli? It's me." He hoped that he would be able to bring up the heavier shields before she guessed who it was. Marli was a wanderer, one who made herself immortal long before the Westergail Wars for the sole purpose of having enough time to see all the wonders of creation. She also had a temper and a memory to match her eons of life.

"Damn it." The response coincided with a drop in energy coming from the small artificial moon below him.

Deven swore; he hadn't realized she'd already taken aim until she dropped her charge.

"Deven? What are you doing out here? Didn't I say I would slaughter you if you ever came back?" The rich dry voice brought back memories. Usually things were great between him and Marliress. She knew his secret, he knew hers, and they protected each other. However, twenty years ago she'd been in a mating cycle when he'd come for a visit.

Not that he had issues with assisting females with sexual needs, but the Asarlaís' natural mating form wasn't conducive to sex with other species and often ended up with the non-Asarlaí partner dying or losing a limb. Marli wouldn't have wanted him to die, but she thought a good friend should be willing to lose a limb. He could get a new one, right?

He left immediately and they hadn't spoken since.

"I knew you didn't mean it." He checked the readings coming from the moon. "Besides, you powered down. You could have blasted me once you knew who was up here."

Marli's laugh echoed in the small shuttle. "You always were a cheeky bastard. I forgive you. Get your ass down here and share some wine before I change my mind."

Deven shook his head. If all of the Asarlaí had been like Marli, it was amazing the rest of the universe survived.

"Aye, ma'am. I think I have an interesting mystery for you to go with your wine."

Her laugh deepened and she uploaded the landing coordinates. "You know I do love a good mystery."

After landing, Deven locked up the shuttle. The terra-formed moon seemed to be abandoned, but if Marli was here, others could be as well. Besides, depending on Marli's mood he might want it locked against her.

The tall woman waited for him outside of what looked like a pile of rocks, her long white hair reaching the ground. At just under seven foot tall that was a lot of hair. Marli honored him by letting him see her in her natural form, or as natural as she could be seen by non-Asarlaí eyes. The Asarlaí appeared differently to their own people, or so she claimed.

"So, did you change your mind?" Marli folded her arms and tilted her head; her ruby red eyes peered at him closely. The serious look she gave him stopped Deven dead in his tracks. Had he miscalculated and she was in state again?

Marli held her pose for a minute, and then let a huge laugh loose. "I'm kidding, boyo. I'm good for a few more years yet. And I found a species outside of the Commonwealth who isn't as fragile as you to take care of my needs anyway." She turned and walked toward the pile of what Deven had thought were rocks but were in fact three fighter ships, or rather the remains of three fighters. Marli smiled as she saw him study the ships before turning into a hidden doorway to the right. "Get inside. Dinner is getting cold."

As they ate, Deven enjoyed the comforts of Marli's secret home. Far larger than a single person needed; artifacts from thousands of worlds covered the walls and floors. He relaxed and for a moment allowed himself to forget why he came.

However, Marli wouldn't.

"As much as I know you enjoy my company, why are you here?" Her grin revealed tiny fangs, also usually hidden by glamour.

He pulled out the vial. "I have a friend who was poisoned by a drell, a Larkerian drell to be exact. I'd like your help on finding out why, how, and whom."

A series of emotions flashed across her sharp features. That surprised him; Marli rarely showed any emotion. The emotion that stayed unnerved him though: pity. "I'm sorry, Deven. Did your friend die quickly? Poison is such a coward's way to kill."

"She's not dead. Not yet any way. And when she does go it won't be because of the poison. I neutralized it and we're working it out of her."

Marli knocked over a plate as she jumped to her feet. "You saved someone from a drell?" She began pacing, muttering more to herself, or voices only she could hear, than to him. "Of course it has been quite a while since my involvement with any of the drells. I suppose cures could have been found. And he is powerful. But still...." She stopped in front of him, peering down as if he were an errant child. "What did you do? Exactly what steps did you take?"

Deven rose to his feet to close in the distance between them. "I purged as much of it out of her blood as I could. We found a counter poison and she's getting injections to chase the rest out."

Without asking for permission Marli placed one hand on either side of his head. Her long fingers covered his skull completely. She stared into his eyes, her clear red ones searching with a frightening intensity.

"Ah yes, you have grown stronger. But why? How were you able to...?" Marli released his head and stepped back. "Have you had recent gene therapy?"

The release of his head and her question slammed Deven backwards. More than that, a brief buzzing almost brought him to his knees. "What? No. What did you just do?"

With a frown she went to a small chair next to a desk that faced a blank wall. A few terse commands opened a large vid screen. She turned to him before calling anything up on the screen. "No gene therapy, yet you have changed." She placed her hand on the screen and series of codes filled the blank space. Calling up a keypad, she entered more numbers.

"This is my recent scan of you. Don't worry what the numbers mean, nothing but an old out-of-date Asarlaí way of tracking species." Marli punched a few more numbers and a second series joined the first. They hung there one suspended over the other for a few seconds, then overlaid each other. "The second set of numbers I put in was you twenty years ago. Your abilities have grown."

Deven crashed back to his seat at the casualness of this ability. He was used to being far more advanced than the people of the Commonwealth, but he felt like a child next to Marli, especially now. She'd never been so open with showing him her technology before.

"Bio implants? Do you have them in your hands?"

Her laugh carried an odd bitterness, but she still smiled. "Not unless you call my entire body a bio implant. It's part of who I am, part of who the Asarlaí were. In my youth I wouldn't have had to touch you. Alas, it's not that easy anymore." She punched a few more buttons, shaking her head when the results weren't helpful. "Unfortunately, I can't tell what's changed in you; something has though. If you didn't do it deliberately, then it must have been another person trying to change you. Do you know who is doing this? Who knows what you are?"

Deven tried to process all of the information. He began to understand how Vas felt when he threw too much detail at her. "No one knows who I am, not even my shipmates. As for enemies," he said, "I'm a mercenary now, sometimes a smuggler, and on occasion a pirate. I have a feeling I have more than a few enemies. But that's not why I'm here."

Marli studied the screen a few moments longer, glancing back between it and him with a growing frown on her face. "I don't like it. But very well, tell me about your friend, how did she get poisoned?"

"I don't know how she got poisoned. My understanding is that the drell poisons could be activated any time within thirty days of contact?" At Marli's nod,

Deven continued. "Then we have no idea. Vas had been gone for the last month."

"Vas? Your lover?" A mischievous light filled Marli's sharp eyes.

"Vas, my captain." Deven scowled at Marli, but couldn't hold it. "There is more to life than sex, you know. She almost died yesterday. I want to find out if you know of anyone who's bringing back the old ways."

Marli's frown deepened.

"Damn it, you know something." He didn't grab her. To do so would mean a slow, painful death. But he wanted to. This new Marli was far more open than the old one, which was more disturbing than the drell itself. He was pretty sure knowing Marli's secrets could be deadly.

"Let me see the blood. At least I assume that's what's in the bottle?" She held out one long-fingered hand. Once he placed it in her hand she stared at the bottle for a few minutes, her frown growing deeper. Finally she glanced up and handed the vial back. "Your friend still has the drell in her system. Whatever your people are doing to remove it is too slow. I'll give you another drug that will purge it completely." She tapped her fingers on the small desk. "They poisoned her sometime in the last two weeks. I can't get any closer than that since you were able to get so much of it out of her system. One other thing, does she know she's also got a tracker in her blood?"

Deven pocketed the vial. "How can you track blood?"

"It's an old trick, not as old as the drell, and not one the Asarlaí created, at least not officially. However, I have a bad feeling more of my extended family are alive out there. Or someone who wants them to be." Her eyes lost focus for an instant then snapped back. "A blood tracker is an insidious artificial insect that is transmitted into a person through a thin needle. It spreads throughout the bloodstream quickly and once established it is impossible to remove. Within a month it would be fully integrated into her body and unmovable. Someone recently decided they wanted to follow your captain. Very recently."

Deven ran his fingers through his hair. He came looking for answers and found nothing but more questions. "How could they have given it to her?" He tried to think of Vas's habits on a space station. "Could they have put it in her food?"

She shrugged, sending a ripple down her silver hair. "Possible, but unlikely. The needle could be hidden in food, but the person doing it wouldn't know they'd gotten her. Judging by the lack of spreading, I'd say it was given to her in the last thirty-six hours, no more." She stood up, walked over to a small kitchen, and came back with two glasses. "I'd like to know what this mercenary captain of yours is up to that she has one person using blood trackers on her and a different person or persons trying to kill her with a drell."

Deven gratefully took the short glass, grimacing as the fiery liquid made its way down his throat. "I'd like to know that too. Which comes back to who do you know who might be messing around with drell-class poisons?"

Marli drained her glass in a single gulp, making Deven cringe more than his own sip had. "This is only hearsay, rumor drifting around the space lanes as it were. But folks are saying there's a cult focusing on the Asarlaí, on the darkest side of my people. They believe there are still enough immortals left around to lead them into a blessed land. Which is a hell of a thing because if there was such a land, my people would have already destroyed it."

He noticed a slight shake in her right hand. "You're drunk."

She cackled as she went back to her kitchen and came back with a huge half-empty bottle. Amber liquid sloshed around the exotic golden glass. "And here I thought you were nothing but a pretty face. Righto, my boy, I am completely drunk. Or as drunk as an immortal with a viciously fast metabolism can get." She sighed and peered at the bottle. "Which isn't much, sad to say. Back to the cult. They have been around for the last ten years or so. Sneaky little bastards. They mostly stick with stealing anything rumored to be from the Asarlaí. However, there are darker rumors too. If someone has brought back the drell poisons, I'd say it's them."

She reached out as a hidden slot in the wall spit out a slim disk. "Here's all the information I have. If you're with a merc company, you might have better luck finding them." She started to hand him the case, but didn't let go. "One thing though." She waited for his nod before continuing. Her grin was the darkest he'd even seen. "When you find them you have to tell me where they are. I want to show them what a real Asarlaí is like before I destroy them."

CHAPTER SEVEN

"Captain, Deven is flagging us on line one." Xsit's voice carried the frown Vas knew she had as well. "And he's got three wrecks in tow."

Vas thought of new things to call him. After six days she had begun to wonder if Deven planned to come back at all. "Patch him through."

The console *fizzled* once.

Xsit gave a chirp of apology. "I'm sorry, Captain. His line went dead. He did request the docking bay to be opened and docking for the shuttle plus the other three."

"He better have bought that damn shuttle."

Xsit heard her. "What did you say, Captain?"

"Never mind let the bastard dock. I'll meet him down there." If Deven had run off without buying the shuttle she would send him back in pieces. Last thing she needed was unsanctioned stolen property.

Her anger at him returned on the walk down to the docking bay. It had almost died down to a simmer in the last few days.

Deven maneuvered the shuttle and the three towed ships with the ease of moving a chair from one side of a room to another. Vas admired his skill even if she still wanted to space him.

The three extra ships looked vaguely familiar, but were little more than piles of rusted metal bones. She wondered what sob story Deven had believed to take the wrecks.

When the bay pressurized, Deven let himself out of the shuttle and came into the docking waiting room.

"Where the hell have you been? Why didn't you tell me where you went? Did you know we're now two hours behind rendezvous time?" Not that two hours really mattered with a battle like this, but it was the principle. She paused on her tirade long enough to slap her hand against the window looking into the docking bay. "And what in the scathrian abyss are those three things doing coming into my ship? They look like scrap metal."

Deven hung back. "I had errands to run. Not all of those errands involve you or this company." He cut her off as she started to argue. "Are you willing to talk about where you were before? I didn't think so. When you are, then we can talk. And a big part of my being late involved those three beauties that you insulted."

Vas swore under her breath. She liked ships as much as the next space rat, but the members of her crew went completely bovine shit about the weirdest things.

"What are those pieces of rusted crap?" She stepped forward and drummed her finger into Deven's chest.

"That crap, as you so tactfully put it, is three Furies," he said with the pride of a new papa.

Vas ran her hands over her face. "You brought three broken Furies on my ship?"

"Our ship." He frowned. "Why aren't you happy? Furies. Three of them. Ours."

"Great, three ships no one properly knows how to use and that look like they're broken to bare bones? They're ancient. No one has known how to fly those things right for the last hundred...oh."

Deven beamed as she caught on. "The last hundred years? Correct. The people who designed them are long gone."

She sighed. He definitely didn't lack in the balls department. Furies were a fatal disaster waiting to fire. "Except for someone who's been around long enough to know how to cure a two-hundred-year-old poison? I might forgive you for going AWOL." Furies were mythological in power and unpredictability.

"I can't be AWOL. We're not military." Deven held up under Vas's stare for about two minutes. "Next time I'll be more detailed about my comings and goings. When I can." He folded his arms and stared at her. "Let a guy have some secrets."

Vas didn't bother to argue. Deven could be as pig headed as her. She sure as hell wouldn't want him busting her about her past; she'd grant him the same courtesy for now. "Just don't take off without letting me know in advance." She walked away. "I could have been worried about you."

"Were you?" Deven yelled after her.

"I said 'could have'." She paused at the door. "Secure your toys and get cleaned up. We're behind schedule. And you damn well better have a bill of sale for that shuttle."

Vas went up to the bridge, leaving her wandering second-in-command to deal with his mess. It would be a cold day in hell before she let him know she had in fact been worried about him. Thoughtless bastard.

"Are the rest of the troop carriers with us yet?" Vas asked Xsit once she got to the bridge.

"Aye, Captain. The whole group is here. ETA six hours. We were supposed to be there in three hours." Xsit bobbed her head quickly. As a Xithinal, she shared a long-lost bird-like ancestor with the Wavians. However the two lines were as diverse as a massive bird of prey verses a small bird kept in a cage. Xsit's bobbing was her inherited way of asking a predator not to eat her. She wasn't aware she did it, and Vas had learned to ignore it.

"I know. Deven's errand ran longer than expected."
Vas turned to Mac and Jakiin, "Without losing the rest of
the ships, can you shave any time?"

Jakiin shook his head, but Mac nodded. "No problem,
Captain."

 *

Four hours and one harrowing trip later, Vas glared up
into the cloudy sky on the planet of Lantaria as she set up
her command console. Deven's little stunt cost them
some ground; they were still at least an hour behind
schedule. Not to mention that the two smaller troop
carriers had to run like hell to keep up with Mac. After
this, she and Deven would be having a long, ugly talk.
She said she'd leave him alone, but she hated being
behind schedule.

All of her ships would land near each other, but their
late arrival put them a few miles from the other merc
companies and the side they would be fighting for. There
were supposed to be four other companies fighting
alongside them for this side. It looked like all were full
complements and in place.

Not only were they far away from the rest, the ragged
ground made it difficult for the two smaller troop ships to
find a clear landing. The rest of the troops had
disembarked from the larger two transports and were
jogging toward her command center. But interestingly, no
one from the paying side had shown up yet. Usually folks
wanted to meet her and her officers. You didn't build the
reputation she had without gathering a few awe-inspired
fans.

The clouds grew heavier and she considered ordering
bad weather gear. With a few choice swear words, she
glanced up to determine how nasty the weather would
get.

She froze.

Those weren't clouds.

Silent ships filled the sky above the battlefield, lurking in massive cloudbanks that may have been created by the ships themselves. The ships were still too high to fire in the atmosphere, but wouldn't be for long. A dozen things flashed through her mind: this was a ground battle—no ships; she'd never seen any ships that size hanging as low and silent as these were trying to do; nor had she ever seen anything with those markings. Heavy and gray, they did look like lumbering rain clouds at first, especially with a steady outpour of controlled exhaust to mask them. Electronically, they still didn't show on any scan. No one would know they were there unless they glanced up. This had to be a trap; she just wasn't sure for whom.

She opened the main comm, keeping her voice low and calm. "We have a scatter situation. Retreat to ships and blast off when full. I repeat, we have a scatter situation and need a full evac of this site immediately. Retreat to ships and bug out. Closest ship will do. We'll meet at evac point four. The others may be compromised. Don't wait. Go now." The chill building in her gut branched out to the rest of her body. There could be a rational reason for those ships hanging there. The screaming cold in her belly told her otherwise.

At the most, her people had a few minutes until the ships started firing. The other mercenary companies had to be unaware, judging by their continued prep for a ground battle that wasn't going to happen. But she couldn't do anything to help them; tipping them off could tip off the gray ships as well. She'd be lucky to get her own people out intact.

Deven jogged over and nodded to the lowering ships. "I didn't notice them. They've got an esper block up."

Vas stopped loading the command console. "They have an esper block?" As if they were expecting an esper? A high-level esper? Damn, this could be worse than she thought. Much worse.

"We can't do anything about it now. We need everyone off the ground five minutes ago. I have a bad feeling that we need to be airborne before they realize who we are." The unspoken command to go help the rest of their transport ships sent Deven running off with a nod.

The gray ships were hovering in place, but she knew it wouldn't take them long to move over if they noticed her people. A chill down her back told Vas those ships were looking for her people. Or her. There was no rational reason for her feelings, they just were.

The two smaller troop carriers got off the ground at that moment. Which meant they'd run out of time; the lift off couldn't have gone unnoticed. Whatever those lumbering gray ships were, they still would have to regain altitude before they could move over to Vas and her people. Even ships that huge could land on a planet with the proper equipment; they just couldn't maneuver worth a damn in atmosphere. Those behemoths were doing a controlled landing with the intent to fire upon the land below them. Instead of rising like she feared, they began opening fire on the troops below them. She made a note to find out who had been slaughtered down there. They at least deserved that. They'd come for a fair fight, and they weren't going to get that and it pissed her off.

Deven came back with twenty fighters in tow before she could finish trying to figure out the enemy ships and their maneuvers.

"Everyone else is on board. These were closer to us than their ships." The roar of the two final troop carriers blasting off threatened to drown him out.

Vas nodded over the noise and motioned toward the *Warrior Wench*. They got the rest of their people out. Now they needed to do the same.

Running, she and Deven led the remaining fighters onto the ship and entered the code to pull in the troop plank. They secured the extra fighters in a spare hold, making sure they were all strapped in before heading down toward the bridge. An explosion rocked the ground. The gray ships weren't on them yet. The explosions were heavy ordinance hitting a few leagues off, but the ships would be there soon.

"Mac, leave NOW," Vas yelled into her comm as she and Deven grabbed two emergency strap seats and secured themselves. Mac must have been waiting with his hand on the trigger. A split second later the ship threw itself into the sky.

Gallant-class cruisers could take off from a ground position, but they took a gradual assent. Too fast and the *Warrior Wench* would come crashing down faster than if those gray ships hit it.

Even though Vas didn't trust Mac with her money, she trusted him with her ship. Besides, she didn't have much of a choice.

The ship rattled and tossed as the gravitation of the planet fought with the attempt to break free. A few popping sounds told Vas repairs would have to be made, but so far no explosions foretelling impending doom.

"What were those ships?" Vas yelled over the strain of the engines as she hung on the railings. Both of them were strapped in, but at the rate they were being thrown around she didn't want to take a chance and end up with a broken neck if the straps broke.

He tightened his grip on his own railings as the ship felt ready to buck apart. "I have no idea. I saw the same thing you did."

"Damn it, this isn't time to be Mister Reticent. You've seen a hell of a lot more of this universe and things in it than I have. What were those damn ships?" She'd been in this business for twenty years, and right now she felt like a first-time novice. Her gut fought to come out, and not only because of the pull of the ship.

He stayed silent for a good five minutes, or at least it felt like five minutes as the ship bucked and fought its way free of the atmosphere. Finally he shook his head.

"I'm not sure, Vas. That's an honest answer. They weren't anything I've ever seen." He freed a hand from the rails to wave off her objections. "I'm being honest. I've never seen ships like those, nor ships that could do what those were trying to do in my life. But there are places I haven't been to in probably two hundred years." He sighed. "There are places the Commonwealth has never heard of. People who could have advanced to those ships had they wanted to."

The *Warrior Wench* stopped bucking, so Vas released her straps, carefully ignoring the way her hands shook.

"Fine," she said with a frown. She would have to count on him giving her what he thought she needed to know at this point. He didn't know those ships any more than she did. However, he brought up a good point; maybe asking some of her crew who were originally from outside of the Commonwealth would help narrow things down.

"Keep me updated if you think of anything. You don't know what might be important." She turned and made her way out of the bowels of the ship and up to the bridge. A few vents hissing into the ship's interior told her the *Warrior Wench* definitely hadn't come out completely unscathed. But as long as the tears weren't life threatening, they wouldn't worry about them yet.

"Gosta, did those ships do anything as we took off?" Vas slid into her chair, calling up as many images of the gray ships as possible. "Xsit, did all our transports make it out of the system?"

Xsit nodded, but Gosta's face became pinched in pain as he keyed in new images to be sent to her screen. "Only this."

The heavy ships wiped out the entire battleground in under five minutes. It was a good thing her transport ships got off before she did; not a single ship got off after the *Warrior Wench*. The lumbering gray ships had turned their sensors to the *Warrior Wench*. The logs indicated a low-level scan had been bounced off right after liftoff, but they hadn't launched an attack. Most likely they knew they couldn't maneuver fast enough to catch a Gallant-class cruiser with a lead on them.

The slaughter on the ground horrified even Vas.

"Keep recording. We need to send the data to the Commonwealth." She'd also be contacting the holder for this contract. Or she would have had they not most likely just been blown apart with their planet.

Vas turned as she heard a collective gasp, or imagined she heard it, from her command crew. "Yes, I know. Me sending something to them besides 'go to hell' messages." She studied the frozen images on her screen. "This isn't a normal fight. It's not one nobleman hiring a group of thugs to rough up the thugs hired by another. They were slaughtered. We owe it to the mercs who died down there to let someone know. There are dictates of battle for a reason. Those bastards just made themselves an enemy."

CHAPTER EIGHT

The bridge went silent as images of the slaughter on the ground held their attention. Vas let them watch; she believed in letting her people know what was going on. However, after a few minutes she cut it off. They also needed to re-group.

Right now she needed to get her people as far away from this system as possible. Since they were already doing that, and no pursuit had appeared, she felt it was safe to leave the deck.

"Gosta, I'll be in my ready room, if anyone needs me...." Vas let her comment trail off with a sigh as Terel came up the ramp to the bridge with Deven right behind. "Not again. Aren't I done with those damn shots? There are a few other things going on right now."

Deven frowned. "No, we're not done, and those ships didn't follow us. I told our troop transports to head to Home after they regroup. They'll be running scans to make sure no one trails them."

Vas gazed longingly at her ready room. Obviously these two weren't going to let her escape, and they'd joined forces to make sure she complied. "Please tell me we're close to being done?"

Terel smiled and stepped back to let Vas precede her down the walkway. "Soon, Vas, soon."

Terel then suspiciously found tasks for her med techs so it would just be the three of them.

"What's going on? I don't need another shot, do I?"

"Oh no, you need a shot." Terel's grin was feral. "But Deven found information which will speed up the process and get the rest of the poison out of your system completely. I needed a few hours to run tests on it though." She held up the evil needle, but the liquid in it this time shimmered gold.

"Wait on giving it to her for a minute," Deven said. "There's another thing I need to tell both of you."

"Like where in the hell you came up with a magic cure? How do we know it'll work?" Vas asked.

Deven pulled out a chair and swung into it. "You wouldn't believe me even if I told you, which for my safety and yours, I'm not. Take my word, it will work. But the person who gave me the antidote also examined your blood and said you were infected less than two weeks ago. Can you think of any reason anyone would have tried to kill you on your trip?"

Vas squirmed at more than the giant needle in front of her. She didn't think anything happened to her while she'd been gone. In fact, she knew nothing had happened, only a visit to Achaeon, a simple agriculture planet. So why didn't she want to talk about it? Fighting her own thoughts, she shook her head. "Nothing I can think of." She studied Deven's face. "Why do I think there is something else?"

Deven ran his fingers through his black hair. Vas took note; that was usually her response in dealing with him, not the other way around. "Because there is. There are blood trackers in your system. I didn't know such things were possible, but my source is thorough. In the last thirty-six hours you were infected with biological tracking nanites. Did anything else happen? On the station? In Skrankle's office? On the planet before you found me?"

"No," Vas said as an image came to mind. "Wait. A spacer slammed into me as I came back to the shuttle. But I didn't feel anything. He was probably just late for a job." The nagging image of the terror on his face got shoved aside.

Deven shook his head. "You wouldn't have felt it. We should go back to the station and see if we can find anything. Whoever did it wanted to be able to track you anywhere. My source said within a month there would be no way to get them out of your blood."

"Then we need to go back now. Terel, the shot—"

"Can't wait either." Terel said. "We have to get the poison out of your system. I'm not sure how this liquid came about, but it should completely clear the drell out of you. However, this shot doesn't go in your arm. Now, Captain, if you would bare your ass for me?"

 *

Vas's mind filled with wind that chased her and grabbed her. Terror ripped into her heart, her soul, and her mind. The winds from her home planet followed her, biting at her ankles, pulling her hair.

She couldn't let the wind inside her soul. Somehow she knew it would destroy everything if it got her.

Vas felt the scream in her throat as she fought herself awake. She thought she'd screamed out loud, but the lack of people kicking down her door told her she hadn't.

The dream had been horrific.

Vas was never scared. Ever. To be accurate, she hadn't been scared since the first night she'd snuck onboard a smugglers' scow when she was fourteen. Fear had swallowed her at the time, but afterwards life took away her capacity for being scared. She gave other people nightmares now. She didn't have them.

Vas lay in the luxuriously soft and deep bed, trying to will her heart to calm down long enough to go back to sleep. After a half hour she gave up and turned the lights on. She tried focusing on the dream itself to get her mind around it. The wind? Not even a child would be afraid of that. Without understanding what caused the fear, she couldn't fight it down.

Sleep avoided her and her dream made no sense. Slipping on her robe, she padded her way down to the mess hall. Food was a perfect solution to lack of sleep.

A vague shape stood in the mess hall, but the lights were very low.

"Vas?" Deven's deep voice seemed almost menacing in the darkness.

"Lights." Vas activated full lights before entering the room. She couldn't shake the chill invading her soul. The nightmare had gotten to her. Or rather the fact she'd had a nightmare got to her.

"What are you doing up?" she asked as she poured herself a cup of hot solie. Might as well wake up enough to get something productive done.

"I'm not sure." Deven sat near the view screen; he too had a familiar looking mug in his hand. "I couldn't sleep. Finally gave up and decided to get out of my room."

Vas pulled up a seat and laughed. "So who's in there now? Jasine? Llitrell?" She laughed even more at the look on his face. "Both?"

Deven's attempt at a wounded air didn't work very well. "I'll have you know, I do sleep alone sometimes. Most times in fact."

"But tonight?" She took another long sip as Deven drifted back to looking out the window. He smelled like sex; there was no way he'd been alone. However, she didn't know why it bothered her this time.

"So tonight I had a friend." He glanced at her long enough to frown, but then turned back to the view screen.

Vas scowled. He'd never had trouble discussing his sex life with her before. Oft times he'd go into great detail just to see if she'd leave the room. Now he seemed embarrassed. And she found herself not wanting to know who lay in his bed right now. More unnerving items to pile on to an already bizarre week. She shoved whatever was going on back into a dark corner of her mind. The thought that she may be jealous was more disturbing than her nightmare. Almost.

"Are you all right?" Deven asked.

She found she'd been staring into her solie cup. "Yes. No, I'm not." She paused, she felt strangely hesitant about telling anyone about the nightmare, as if she couldn't tell them. She fought past it. "I had a nightmare."

He pulled back in surprise. "I didn't think you dreamed, let alone had nightmares."

"I don't. I haven't had a dream since I was a kid. And no nightmares since then either." Vas felt an odd compulsion as she said it, as if the contents of the solie would be coming back up if she kept talking. Setting the cup aside, she took a deep breath and went on. She didn't let anything stop her, even if it was something in her own head. "Terror, pure terror. It makes no sense, but the wind tried to kill me."

He leaned forward and took her hands, pulling her closer as he rubbed them between his own. "You're freezing."

She let herself go closer to him; she wanted warmth and lots of it. "I don't know what the hell is wrong. I'm like ice." She looked up at Deven and gave an evil smile. "And I feel like I'm going to throw up."

Deven didn't flinch, but pulled her closer until she was almost in his lap. "I know. It's okay."

Vas almost jerked back, but his warmth felt so damn good. "Wait, what do you mean it's okay? What are you sensing?"

His chuckle stayed low. "The cuffs are still on, don't worry. It's just obvious that you're upset."

"So upset you'd keep holding me even if I puke?" Vas moved away from his chest far enough to see his face. She couldn't read his face as he looked down at her.

"I've held you when you're sick from drinking. Why not now? Who do you think usually keeps this mass of hair out of the way when you're on a bender?"

She pounded his chest. "Since I don't always remember those incidents I have to assume it's you." Her smile faltered. "But this is different. I don't know what in the hell is going on."

Deven reached around her then held her mug up to her lips. "You'll feel better if you drink something."

Vas took a long sip. It tasted different this time. The bitter solie she expected was sweet. Maybe it had cooled down too much.

"But I need to figure out what caused this." She paused as a yawn overtook her. "I can't be waking up in the middle of a battle zone screaming at nightmares."

"I know." He forced another sip down her. "And we'll figure it out."

"But," she said as another yawn overtook her. "Oh crap. What did you…?"

Deven smiled and gently picked her up to carry her to her room. She wouldn't be happy with him when she woke up, but she needed to sleep.

Moreover, he needed to think.

CHAPTER NINE

Vas woke up relaxed and tucked into her bed. Which was a very bad sign.

She rarely slept through the night, and never would have tucked herself in. It was a good night if she had a single sheet left on the bed when she woke up.

Then she remembered the nightmare from the night before.

And Deven.

"Damn him!" It took two minutes to pull the covers free. If Deven had thought trapping her like this was going to save him, he had another think coming.

She toppled to the floor the moment she tried to stick one leg into her flight pants. He'd drugged her too well obviously. But with what? Did the bastard carry sleeping pills on him now? She pulled herself up and sat on the bed to finish dressing and get her boots on. Quickly pulling her waist-length hair back in a ponytail, no time for a braid, she stomped out the door.

Terel rounded a corner right in front of her, and Vas was just enough out of sorts she couldn't stop from bumping into her.

"Drinking already?" Terel asked as she steadied her.

"No," she said as pulled herself away. "Deven drugged me last night. The bastard. Have you seen him?"

Terel changed direction and followed Vas down the corridor. "I haven't. Why would he drug you? What did you do to him?"

"Ha, already on his side, are we?" Vas shot Terel a glare. "He drugged me because I couldn't sleep." She held up one hand but didn't slow down. "I know how it sounds. He gave me sleeping pills when I couldn't sleep. However, he did it without asking me. I can't have a second-in-command who—"

"Anticipates his captain is too proud to admit she's having trouble sleeping and has a long day ahead of her so he gives her sleeping pills?" Terel laughed and easily kept pace no matter how fast Vas walked.

Vas stopped and turned to her friend. "It doesn't sound bad when you say it. But he can't go around drugging me at his whim." She waggled a finger at Terel. "You either. I am the captain, you know. A fact many people on this ship seem to forget." Satisfied that Terel was sufficiently chastised, even though she didn't quite look it, she continued her march to Deven's room. With any luck he was still asleep and she could give him hell before he was awake enough to defend himself.

A male scream of surprise down the cross-corridor ahead of them brought Vas to a wobbly run.

Mac bounced into her as she rounded the corner. A very naked Mac.

"What in the hell are you doing?" Vas jumped back. She was certain other mercenary captains didn't have to deal with the things she did.

At least Mac had the decency to look scared of her. On the other hand, he could just be extremely embarrassed. He was so red it was difficult to tell the difference.

Mac pointed behind him at a partially open door, which immediately slammed shut. "There was a misunderstanding. See Bathshea and me—well, she tricked me out here then locked the door. Like this."

Bathie's voice came through the door. "I told you if you slept with another woman, I would make you pay!"

"I don't want to know." Vas cut him off with a wave and stepped around him. "I really don't ever want to know. Just get your skinny naked ass out of my corridor and behind a closed door, any closed door, where it belongs."

Mac opened his mouth to defend himself, but Vas held up both hands to hold him off and resumed her stalking of Deven's quarters. "No, nothing. I don't want to know."

Terel rejoined her a second later.

"Please tell me he's heading toward his own quarters?" Vas asked softly, afraid to turn around.

"Yes." Terel kept her laugh down, but it was in her bright eyes. "He is not someone who should be running around naked. For any reason. I didn't even know you could get freckles down there."

"How did I end up with this crew? I mean really?" Vas asked the corridor in general.

"You picked us," Terel said. Her smile was just short of being rude.

"Don't remind me." Vas reached Deven's door and started pounding, then thought better of it. Why give the crew in the adjoining rooms a free show? Keying in her override, she let herself in.

Only to be disappointed. Deven had been there and he'd had company. But he and his company were long gone.

"Damn him!"

Terel took Vas's arm and steered her back to the corridor. "Excellent, so now I can get you down to the med lab like I intended."

"What? I don't need to go down there. You fixed it, right?" This wasn't how she wanted to start her day. Trying to recover from being ambushed by her own second-in-command, being accosted by another man who should never be without clothing, and now her best friend was dragging her down to her evil lab again.

"We don't know, do we? And we still don't know what those blood trackers are doing. Deven thinks he has them under control but we need to get them out completely. For that I need more samples."

Vas surrendered. She could fight armies, nations, even kingdoms. But her own crew? They just walked all over her. "Agreed. But afterwards we find Deven."

Fortunately for Deven, but unfortunately for Vas, she calmed down after an hour in Terel's lab. The blood tests hadn't taken long, and since she wasn't using that archaic needle, Vas didn't mind it. In truth she was fascinated by the blood trackers and had spent the last half hour examining them on a slide.

"I don't think they'll do flips right in front of you." Terel's voice cut into her observation, but Vas cut her off, still keeping her right eye on the scope.

"You never know. They are fascinating." Vas sighed and finally pulled away. Interesting or not, she had things to do. She'd confirmed Gosta had sent the alert on the attack at Lantaria to the Prime Council of the Commonwealth. The people who had hired them for the Lantaria job had paid enough in advance to cushion them for a bit, but in a week or so she would need to line up another job. In the meantime, she still needed to explore this new ship of hers.

Jumping off the lab stool, Vas headed for the door. "I'm going to go check out a few blank spots on the ship's schematics, see if any are spaces we can convert for storage."

Terel shut down the screen and turned to follow her out of the med-lab. "You mean places for smuggling?"

Vas pulled out a small pad with the ship's schematics on it and led the way toward the back of the ship where the two holochambers were. "You say smuggling, I say storage. We're storing items for transportation from one location to another." She frowned. "Maybe we'll have better luck smuggling than mercenary work. I'd still give a month's pay to find out who those damn gray ships belong to."

"Still no luck on anyone identifying them?" At Vas's shake of her head, Terel sighed. "That's not good. The council's lack of response isn't good either."

Vas stopped. She backtracked as an odd blank space appeared near one of the two holochambers. "Agreed, but not surprising. Personally, I would be concerned about unknown ships attacking a Commonwealth planet if I were in charge of the Commonwealth. Apparently, the council has their own agenda." She shrugged and tapped on the walls. The entrance should be right in front of her according to the schematics. "I warned them. If they're too complacent to get off their asses and do something, it's not my—aha!" She turned with a grin as a thin line appeared down the length of the wall. With a few more taps and a nudge, she got it open.

"Shall we?" She held open the door for Terel to go in first.

Terel ducked as she crossed the threshold. The opening was a bit shy of her six-and-a-half-foot-tall stature. Vas followed and was pleased when the hallway opened to a larger room. Depending on the rest of it, and where it came out, this might in fact be a likely smuggling candidate.

Terel tapped on her wristlamp as the light from the hallway faded behind them, and Vas did the same. It appeared to be a good-sized room followed by another hallway.

"Keep going?" Terel asked.

"Yeah, we should see where it cuts out. Maybe there's another room we can use."

Even with the wristlamps glowing from the cuffs of their uniforms, Vas almost smacked into Terel's back when the medical officer stopped suddenly.

"We've hit a glass panel." Terel held up her wrist to illuminate the plane. It was dark and coated with a shimmering substance. "I think this is it, there doesn't seem to be any more space…" Terel's voice dropped off as lights suddenly lit up the black space before them beyond the glass. The small room they were in was designed to spy on people in the holochambers below them. Considering this ship's former line of work, Vas could guess what they were spying on.

Terel and Vas stood back in the hidden room as the holochamber door opened. By mutual agreement both women stopped their conversation as Deven, stripped to the waist and holding two battle swords, entered.

"Now this, you have got to see," Vas told the doctor. Something would have to be done about this room. She didn't want anyone being able to pry into a private holochamber. Well, after this one time anyway.

Terel nodded, but Vas noticed she was keeping a close eye on Deven.

Not a hardship at all to do so, however. The man was disgustingly handsome, even more so dressed only in loose workout pants that hung low on his hips. His black hair was pulled back into a low ponytail. He queued up a sequence on the keyboard.

Vas knew this one immediately. It was one of his favorite fighting exercises.

Three hologram fighters appeared. All garbed in rough armor and clutching nasty swords longer than Vas's legs. She nodded in appreciation; not even she would have started so high in the workout.

Looking like an ancient prince from some exotic land, Deven bowed to the holofigures, and then took his stance. The figures didn't bother with a bow, but attacked with vicious intensity. Deven was a blur of golden skin and

black hair as he danced around the room. And danced
was the best term for it. Vas knew the man was graceful,
but his movements now were like some elaborate game.
He did what he intended to do regardless of the three
holoattackers before him.

His moves happened to put him within easy reach of
all three heads however and they were cleanly removed in
under a minute.

Deven continued his stylized moves, not even
bothered by the lack of opponents. However, the
computer didn't give him much of a break. Five more
attackers immediately appeared. Two each held a long
sword and short sword pair. One held two curved
daggers. The last two had a pike and a heavy long sword
that Vas doubted she could even pick up had it been real.

This time music joined the movements. An odd,
almost wistful sounding tune filled the arena, something
Vas had never heard in her life. It was gorgeous and
matched Deven's moves perfectly. Sweat glistened on his
skin as all five attackers moved in at once. Again,
Deven's movements were his own, not seeming to be in
response to those of his attackers. Having so many
opponents at once and fighting off so many different
types of weapons at the same time, even Vas would have
been hard pressed to hold them at bay. If she were honest
with herself, she probably couldn't do it. Not the first
round at any rate.

His moves were even more graceful, lighter, and freer
than before. His opponents might have been made of
light, but he was the one who moved like it. He wove in
between them, striking strategically as he flowed through,
leaving them staggering but not fallen. Vas would have
used their closeness to try to force one attacker to
accidentally injure one of the others, but Deven kept them
all separate. It was as if he just happened to be having
five different battles at the same time.

His movements were hypnotic and Vas found herself holding her breath as she watched. After five minutes, he dispatched the first, the pikeman, but it was more as if he hadn't wanted to kill the hologram rather than him not being able to.

She heard Terel's intake of breath as Deven did a round dive and came up, cleanly dispatching the two sword-and-dagger fighters in one long, sinuous strike. Vas saw the same look that was probably on her face. Complete awe. And more than a little attraction. Deven wasn't by any means Terel's type; she didn't date humans. However, no one could watch this dance without being swayed by Deven's charms. He moved as if in a lover's game; he just happened to be armed.

He drew himself up for another pass and quickly killed the remaining three holograms. The music in the room built and he held a pose as if waiting.

Vas studied her impressive second-in-command. It was really too bad she refused to get involved with one of her officers. And downright depressing that he was a telepath. Right now dragging him into her suite sounded like a damn fine idea.

Taking a deep breath, she forced her hormones under control. He might not always be one of her officers, but he would always be a telepath.

"Now you know why I keep him on board."

Terel raised one eyebrow. "Oh?"

Vas smacked her and winked. "His fighting skills, of course."

There was no way Deven could have heard them—Vas recognized the glass as a specialized soundproof composite—but he broke from his pose and nodded to the hidden room. With his arms out he bowed deeply. His grin told Vas he'd known they were there the entire time. Show off.

"Come on. Let's go," Vas laughed and she headed back to the door. "We don't need to build that one's ego any more."

She marked the exact location of the room entrance on her map panel, and then resealed the door as best she could. Gosta could secure it and block any viewing of the holochamber.

"You still thinking about Deven?"

Terel's words pulled Vas out of her thoughts. "What? No, where'd that come from?" She scowled at Terel. "I was thinking how we needed to block that damn room, or rather block the hidden viewing area. Why would I be thinking about Deven?"

"No reason. However your heart rate shot way up when he was out there."

"And yours didn't?" Vas didn't doubt Terel had been able to discern an increase in heart rate. One of the reasons her people made such great doctors was their incredible ability to pick up on physiological changes in others, regardless of the species. "Come on, you were focusing pretty tightly yourself. Deven's got a great body; it would be a crime not to admire it."

Terel folded her arms and peered down at Vas, something she obviously could do well, but usually didn't. "Nothing...else?"

Vas smacked her friend's arm, and then continued back to the command deck. "No, nothing else. He's great to look at, but he's a crewmember and telepath." She shivered. "You know how I feel about telepaths."

"You and your primitive views." Terel sighed and walked ahead to the lift that would take her back to the med lab. "Whatever you say. Don't forget to come back down to the lab tomorrow. I might have some more ways to fight those blood trackers."

Vas waved Terel off and continued down toward the command deck. Terel was imagining things.

The command deck was its usual controlled chaos. Gosta was up to his upper elbows in computer parts. Literally, his long sleeves were pushed completely back and his second elbows could be seen, something that rarely happened.

"What did you find?" Vas waited until she was at his shoulder before speaking.

"Damn it, Captain!" Gosta swore as he jumped a good foot in the air.

Vas tsked, and walked around him to her command chair. To be honest, she rarely sat in them much; they made her feel like a bull's eye for trouble. Even this one with its molding fabric and fancy design made her nervous. Maybe one day she'd design a ship with a command chair not in the very center of the deck.

"You know, Gosta, it's great how engrossed you are in your work, but we *are* mercenaries. You really need to pay more attention to what's going on around you." She leaned back and called up the specs. They were heading back to Tarantus IV's space station. Deven had mentioned some idea about checking out the pub she'd gotten her lunch at. Perhaps they could also see about finding the guy who ran into her.

He was reaching and she knew it. Vas didn't think they'd find a clue about who poisoned her there. Or who slipped those blood trackers into her. Whoever Deven's mysterious acquaintance was they didn't seem to think they were the same person. Which made sense. Why track someone down if they were going to be dead within thirty days?

Gosta continued to grumble. "I should think I wouldn't have to worry about it when I'm on the ship."

Vas didn't look up but threw the map panel directly at Gosta's head. A snap and a few swear words told her he'd caught it, but only barely. She didn't bother to hide her grin. "Getting better. You always have to be prepared. It's the only way to stay alive in this universe." She closed the navigation view screen. There was nothing to do on that front but wait until they got to the station. Hopefully they could at least find a short-term job there and it wouldn't be a total waste of time.

"Now, on that lovely little panel is a secret room, one right behind holochamber number one. I want it ready for cargo and it'll need to be better masked. If I can find it, inspectors can as well. Also, it views holochamber one. You'll need to block it immediately. Close the chamber until the work is done." She glanced around her crew. "Not that I don't trust some of you, of course." A few of the most likely voyeurs looked away quickly.

"Anything further?" Gosta leaned against his open console, looking almost smug.

"I believe so, yes." Vas studied him; he had something. "What? Did you find something interesting in your playing?"

"Interesting." He snorted and laid the map panel down. "You could say that. I'm getting closer to breaking the lock on the core." He frowned. "Whoever put it up was good. Really good. Far too good to have been working for Skrankle."

"Crap." Vas drummed her fingers on the arm of her chair, watching as the soft fabric filled each dent the moment her finger rose. "Which makes it all the more important we get it open, yes? Can you tell who did it?"

Gosta shook his head wearily as he closed up the console. Most likely he hadn't even gone to bed yet. "No, and that's almost as worrying as the level of effort they put into it. There was a very specific reason they put it in here. I am loath to break it until I know why.

"One other thing, I think I found a pattern with the parts." He uploaded another panel and brought it to her.

With a sigh she took the panel. "What's this?" It looked like a child's art project. Green lines circled around yellow dots and purple squares.

"That's the pattern." Gosta leaned over and tapped on the screen. "See here? These gray pieces are the parts of our ship. The lines are shipping lines, and dots are major warehousing planets."

She handed it back with a shake of her head. "What are the purple squares?"

Gosta was like a kid with a new shiny toy. "I don't know yet. But it's something."

She rubbed the heels of her hands on her eyes. Had she really only been awake for a few hours? Her brain felt as mushy as it had the night before.

"Great, Gosta, really great." She patted the tall man on his arm. "But I don't see the pattern." She raised her hand quickly. "I'm sure it's just me and my poor human mind, but if you say it's there, I believe you. You just tell me when you've got it all figured out, okay? I'm sure—"

A siren cut off her next comment.

"What the hell is that and someone shut it off!" Vas screamed to be heard over the blaring. It was as if someone had taken a standard proximity alarm and enhanced it by a hundredfold.

"Sorry, Captain." Mac's voice came out of the blessed silence, which followed the end of the siren. "This was the only emergency alert the system had. You need to get down to engineering, fast."

Vas started swearing as soon as she heard Mac's voice. "Why do I need to get there fast? And why in the hell does this ship have that...thing...on it? Gosta, pull that program ASAP, or at least make it civilized. Well, Mac? Why do you need me?"

"There's a body here. Or two. I can't tell."

CHAPTER TEN

"Gosta, you're with me." Vas ran toward the lift. "Xsit, find Deven, I'm assuming the klaxon hit the whole ship, but make sure he gets down there. Hrrru, find out if there have been any breaches. I need to know what we're dealing with." Her crew turned to her in shock. No one had ever gotten aboard the *Victorious Dead*, and the idea that there might be intruders on their current ship was foreign to them. "Now, people! We have a situation. Move it!"

Gosta jogged up behind her.

"Are you armed?" Packing her snub blaster already, she had freed two larger guns from hidden compartments in her command chair before she ran for the lift. She pounded the keys to send the lift to engineering the instant Gosta passed the threshold.

"No, I—"

She shoved one of the blasters at him. "I didn't think you were. When we get down there, stay behind me."

He took the weapon, but wasn't pleased. "There is no way anyone could have gotten on board. Mac was probably drinking."

"Possibly." She made sure both of her weapons were primed before she ran out of the lift as it opened on the last level. "Or someone got on when we were running away from Lantaria."

Normally she would have said that would be impossible, but she'd never had an evac like that before.

Vas slowed down her jog as she neared the partially open door for engineering. She should have told Mac to wait outside of the room so she knew there wasn't a surprise waiting.

Pointing to the door, she motioned for Gosta to keep to the other side. He nodded once and they moved into position.

Mac hadn't said they were under attack, but bodies didn't appear out of nowhere. In addition, knowing Mac, he may not have noticed if there was a person hiding.

Trading her snub blaster for the larger weapon, she slid up to the doorway, and nudged it completely open with her free hand.

"Don't come any closer. I'll shoot!"

"It's me." Vas sighed and pulled up the nose of her blaster. "Drop your weapon. Gosta and I are coming in."

Mac still had his own snub blaster out, but he holstered it as soon as she and Gosta came into view. "Needed to make sure. I was afraid there was someone down here and they were going to come back."

Vas shook her head; at least he called out before blasting his captain. "Where's the body?"

"Or bodies." Mac turned a weird shade of green. "I'm not sure whether it's one or more." He turned and led them toward the back of engineering.

On the *Victorious Dead* this section was mostly storage. This ship had extra equipment added but what exactly it did was something her engineering people would have to determine. From the dust blanketing the floor, no one had been down here in a very long time. Only a single set of prints went in and out. She sighed and sheathed her weapon. "Gosta, call off the security detail. We're fine."

"But someone's been murdered, Captain!" Mac pulled out his blaster again. "The killer could still be on the ship."

Vas stopped walking and motioned for Gosta to do the same. "Mac, how many sets of footprints do you see?"

He glanced around, scowling as it hit him. "Two. Well, one going back and forth." He holstered his weapon with a sigh. "Mine. I see my tracks going back and forth."

"Now that we know we're not under attack, could you show us this body? Or whatever it is you saw?" Vas studied the equipment they passed as a sullen Mac trudged further back into the room. Whatever this equipment was, it was new and huge. She'd have to get Bathshea and her best people down here immediately. Bodies aside, Mac might have made a valuable find.

She was determining if the new equipment should be sold as a lot or individually when she rounded the corner and stopped short.

"I give up. What is it?" Gosta finally broke the silence.

"This is a head, I think." Mac stepped back to let the other two come forward.

"It's definitely more than one. Either that or it's a mutant, or an unknown species," Gosta muttered as he paced around the pile of dead flesh before them.

"Okay, given the odds of it being an escaped mutant range from slim to none, what is it?" Vas stayed back. Death didn't disturb her—in her job she dealt with it far too intimately for it to do so. However, this pile of melted flesh and bone made her skin crawl.

"An excellent question," Terel said from behind them as she, her assistant Pela, and Deven entered the area. All three were loaded down with medical equipment. Deven still wore his workout gear. Had he been working out this entire time? His stamina was terrifying sometimes.

"Since I'm not the person here with the five or six medical degrees, I'm going to leave all of you to answer that question. Deven and Gosta, you're with me."

Deven glanced up from adjusting a spectral scan, and then arched his brow at Terel.

"If you don't mind, I could use him. We're likely to be down here for a bit." Terel didn't smirk, but Vas heard it in her friend's voice.

Vas glared at the room in general and her med officer and second-in-command specifically. "If it won't be too much trouble, I'd like both of you to come see me when you're finished." She started to head out then turned back. "Call Bathshea to come down and figure out what this equipment is when you've moved *that* out. I need to see what we have here. And no one touches any of the shiny machines until then."

"Any idea what we have in there, Gosta?" Vas asked as they left engineering.

He shortened his long stride to match hers. "The dead or the machinery?"

She punched in the command to call the lift. On her old ship the command panels were utilitarian, clean, chrome. Everything on this ship wore golden swirls and ostentatious lettering. Even on this level. As if any of the former guests would have been down in engineering. "Either. Both. I don't like mysteries, Gosta. I really don't. Yet more and more of them keep being dumped into my life. It's starting to annoy me."

"I wish I could say I solved some of them," Gosta said as he entered the lift after her. "However, I have no idea what that body was, nor the machines. And so far we don't have a clue as to who those ships were at Lantaria, or why they slaughtered a bunch of mercenaries." He frowned. "Actually, they may have destroyed the entire planetary population. I haven't been able to reach anyone on Lantaria since we left orbit."

She leaned against the smooth lift walls and closed her eyes. "That's not good. It's compounding the not good that already exists." With a sigh she opened her eyes. "Would having more people assigned to you help anything? I can take you off all command shifts. You can spend a few days solving some of our problems."

Gosta nodded. "A few folks in the tech lab might shed some light. But solving which thing?"

"I don't care." Vas walked past him onto the command deck. "I just want something resolved." She took a cursory glance at the crew. Nothing seemed to be going more wrong than usual. "I'll be in my ready room. Xsit, you have the bridge. Gosta, go recruit who you need and tell Hrrru to get back up here and take over nav duties." She palmed open the door. "Any more emergencies go to Deven."

She was able to spend a good three hours dealing with the stupid day-to-day paperwork that piled up with any large company. Considering the upheavals her nice, orderly world had been going through lately, the mundane work relaxed her.

Perhaps a bit too much.

The dream was more vivid than before, but still Vas couldn't see what was behind her. Only the wind ripping into her back as she ran. Sand the size of hail flew around her, obscuring anything else. A shape reached out, but whether to help her or hurt her she couldn't tell. She was too terrified to do anything except run.

An abrupt shaking freed her from the terror. But she came up swinging and flattened Deven before she realized who was shaking her.

Vas bounced back, shaking out her fist. She'd hit him hard and not well. Probably did more damage to herself than him. "Damn it, don't do that!"

"Tell me about it." He rubbed his jaw then got to his feet. It was impressive that she'd taken him down with a single blow. Of course, now her hand was going to swell up like a balloon. "You fell asleep on your console. When I came in you were twitching and whimpering."

She glared at him from the food dispenser where she got ice for her hand. "I do not whimper."

Stepping forward, he wiped the side of her face. His frown deepened. "You were crying."

A quick check in the small mirror near her dispenser validated his assessment. Any thoughts of what she had been doing fled her mind. Slowly it came back. She'd been working on forms, then the wind. The wind what?

"Damn it all to hell," she swore some more and wiped the wet marks away with her good hand.

"You had another nightmare, didn't you?"

She finally turned around. Denial was useless. He already knew, and he was her best bet to try and keep the rest of the crew from finding out. And for helping her find out what was causing it.

"Yes, but I couldn't have been out for long." She glanced at her clock. She'd been called down to engineering about four hours ago. "Not more than an hour."

Deven steered her back to her desk and her chair. "What do you remember?"

"The wind." She fussed with the wrap of ice around her knuckles. Terel was going to have to make sure there were no broken bones. "The sand. The terror. But no details. I have never, even when I ran away from that hellhole called home, felt that kind of terror." She rubbed her arms, but the chill wasn't external.

"Do you remember anything else? Even the smallest thing might help." He crouched down in front of her.

Closing her eyes, she tried to make her mind go back there. But to go back where? It wasn't a place. She couldn't focus on a location or item. She finally opened her eyes. "I can't remember it. The wind, a horrible wind, strong enough to shred flesh off bones. Sand, huge pieces of sand, stabbing and attacking." She flexed the fingers of her injured hand slowly; at least they moved. "Something else. This time there was someone there. Or something there. A presence. I couldn't tell who or what it was. Or if it was there to help or make things worse."

"Was the presence in your first dream?"

She let out a breath. "No. At least I don't think so. It felt different. I can't remember anything more."

"I could try and see if I can find anything."

"No!" She jerked back and glanced down to make sure his bracelets were in place. "I'm sorry, Deven. Your offer is sound. But I'm not ready. There has to be another way."

He nodded, and then stood up. "Let's first get you down to see Terel. Your hand is swelling up."

"If you didn't have such a stubborn jaw, I wouldn't have hurt myself punching it." Vas fought off the lingering tendrils of fear. She didn't have time to deal with this crap.

"I'll work on softening that for you."

"Please do."

Terel frowned as she moved Vas's hand back and forth. "How in the stars did you do this? Punching walls?"

"Beating up her second-in-command." Deven stuck out his chin as he spoke so Terel could see the darkening mark. He rarely bruised. He'd be a bit darker there for a short while, and then it would vanish.

"Why did you punch him?" Terel studied both of them, then unceremoniously pulled Vas over to the small synth scan machine. The looming pile of metal always gave Vas the willies. You stuck in perfectly good, but temporarily damaged, body parts and they came out packaged like someone's freeze-dried meal.

"Because his face got in the way of my fist when he woke me up." Vas scowled at Deven. She had planned to make up a story about her fist. She didn't want to tell Terel about the sleeping. Or the dreams. Damn Deven, he only kept his mouth shut when it was something she wanted to know.

"Keep your hand still." Terel positioned Vas's hand then stepped back as the machine took readings. "Since when do you sleep in the middle of the day? And you," she said as she turned toward Deven, walking over to examine the small mark on his jawline. "Why would you have thought it wise to wake Vas up? You're smarter than that."

Vas glared at Deven behind Terel's back. If he said anything about crying, she was going to space him. Hopefully that showed on her face.

He smiled at Terel. "Not sure. A moment of insanity I guess."

Terel moved away from her work. A thin, flexible cast now covered Vas's hand encompassing two inches past her wrist to her fingertips. She could move her hand, but not well. "I'd say you should be able to take it off in a week or so. The cast is a new poly. It'll become more flexible as it adapts to your body." She rocked back against a stool. "I suppose you want to know about our stowaway?"

Vas helped herself to a seat and nodded for Deven to do the same. She held up her hand before Terel could start. "Please tell me it's something cut and dried, not more mysteries, quandaries, or oddities."

"Sorry." Terel said. "The mystery deepens with our friend or friends. I am still running a program to separate out the tissue. I believe it was two beings, but they are so conjoined that I can't be sure."

Vas sighed and slumped backwards. "What do we know about it or them?"

"They're not human, or at least not completely. Which means they could be a member of any of dozens of species or cross-species." Terel hit the screen button on the computer and a clear image appeared hovering in the air before them. The blob didn't look any better on closer inspection. "They've been dead about six months. But the body mass was stored in some sort of liquid that both protected and disintegrated the tissue." She clicked a new button, and the image showed the tissue's decay. Terel moved closer. "As you can see here," she said while she waved at a red section of the image in the air, "this is heavily decayed. However, this section is preserved well enough to last for years. Decades even." Another section appeared.

Deven moved forward. "Do we know what killed them?"

"Or why in the hell they were in my ship?" Vas wanted answers. Weird treatment of the dead wasn't going to give her any of those.

Terel ignored Vas. "I think they, or it, was left in space. The tissue is similar to victims of hull breaches." She called up another series of images. All were more of the tissues and all, to be honest, appeared the same to Vas.

Not to Deven though. "I see what you mean. Those areas aren't right at all."

"Before you go into intense, and boring I might add, comparisons, can you give me a simple answer? To any of it?"

Terel pulled back from her study with regret. "Unfortunately, nothing beyond what I just told you. I have no idea how they got into engineering."

Vas rose to go. "We need to find out something, and soon. That floor had dust on it from at least a year. However they got in there, they weren't brought in through the door."

CHAPTER ELEVEN

They made much better time back to the Lucky Strike space station than they had heading out. The more Mac, Jakiin, and the two alternative pilots learned about the *Warrior Wench*, the more they were able to make her do. She might be a gilded tart on the outside, but inside she was pure fighter.

Which made Vas question the ship and Skrankle's possession of it even more.

Almost better than the discovery of a sublight power booster in the hull, Vas hadn't had any more nightmares during the trip back. Her sleep had been its normal sketchy self.

If she could only get rid of the vague, nagging feeling dogging her. The nightmares might have fled, but they'd left a mark. She found herself avoiding empty corridors. Being around her crew chased the demons away.

Unfortunately, they still didn't know who, or what, had been in the engineering section but they now knew what the equipment was. High-grade Starchaser parts. Starchasers being the Commonwealth's ultimate small gunship in a space fight. They made the Flits, single fighters that the *Warrior Wench* carried, seem like pop guns wielded by a five-year-old. The Starchaser ships themselves weren't on the *Warrior Wench*; Mac and Jakiin had spent two days tearing around trying to find where they might be hidden. However, while the ships weren't there, brand-new shiny parts were. Enough brand-new parts to make Vas and her crew very rich. That was, if it wasn't illegal to trade in Starchasers unless you happened to be a contracted official working with the Commonwealth. They were so dangerous to have that Vas had been ready to space the lot of them, but the greedy side of her made her settle for hiding them in a formerly hollow wall chamber. A few wall chambers actually; there had been quite a lot of them.

She felt secure with their hiding space as they radioed the space station for a docking berth.

"No one mention Lantaria. At this point we don't know what the hell happened. We went there, saw something was going on, and hightailed it out of there. But we do not tell anyone we saw those ships," she told her crew as they waited for the code to dock. It didn't surprise her that the Commonwealth hadn't contacted them after their reports, but their inaction did give her pause. Keeping their knowledge to themselves might be wiser for now. The events of the vid they had recorded of the slaughter joined the lurking tendrils of the nightmares. The low-level tension and fear lurking in her gut was something she hadn't felt since she ran away from home. However, fear had become a constant creeping ghost in her mind the last two days. One she'd be damned if she admitted to anyone.

Gosta glanced up from his nav screen. "Aye, Captain." His dull tone echoed his long face. He enjoyed mysteries, primarily because he could solve them quickly. The fact that aside from securing the locations of the other parts of the *Victorious Dead*, he hadn't been able to resolve anything didn't make for a happy Syngerin.

She leaned against his console. "You know, you could probably spend some time station side accessing the Commonwealth's database. We can't secure a line, but I know the space station has one in their library." Tossing a key card at him, she smiled. "I reserved you a slot for this afternoon for a few hours. Will that help?"

"Aye, Captain!" Gosta beaming was really more scary than reassuring, but it cheered her. Maybe he would find some useful information. Resolving some of these mysteries might allow her psyche to let go of the fear.

Deven followed Vas as she left the docking area.

"It's going to be really hard for me to get anything done with a teke lurking behind me." She tried to be insulting in a vain hope that he would get annoyed and shake off. No such luck.

"I'll leave the second you develop the ability to question people without them peeing their pants. Besides, they won't know." Deven held up his right wrist. His esper bracelets were covered nicely by a very ornate woven leather band. While still following the law by keeping his bracelets on, hiding them allowed him to function without attracting undue attention.

"I can't imagine that anyone at the pub put those trackers in me." She kept her voice low as they walked across the loading zone and into the station proper.

"Drinks, Captain? Your turn to buy, isn't it?" Bathshea cut in as she and Mac sauntered past them. Bathie *would* remember it was her turn. That woman could drink almost anyone on the crew under the table.

Vas glanced at Deven. Any chance she had at all of having some time to herself would only happen if she let him investigate that pub. Drinking would have to wait. "You might be right about that. However, I've got some errands to run. What say we meet back at four o'clock at the Hidden Cup? First round's on me."

The crew still within hearing range yelled in agreement, before vanishing to deal with their own errands. Vas hadn't given them time on the station when she'd picked them up. Gosta smiled and went down the long access way to the library. They needed to find a way for a complete library accessport to be put on her ship.

Too bad only Commonwealth service vessels could have them. Legally anyway.

"We might as well get it over with." Vas ducked down a small corridor that led to an older portion of the station. A pleasant thought hit her. "Actually, I think I could do with some fish, being as we're going there anyway. It'll be less suspicious if we order something."

Deven marred his perfect face by wrinkling up his nose. "I hate fish."

"I know." She whistled as she walked. Let him deal with it if he insisted on following her. Along with her recent case of nerves, her reactions to Deven were becoming disturbing. After over ten years of working together, she just now started imagining him in bed? She was actually worried about him when he took off on his own? In its own hellish way, the butterflies crawling around her stomach when he got too close were more cause for terror than the nightmares.

Pushing the annoying emotions aside, she turned down a narrow corridor that led to the main thoroughfare. "It's right here, looks like—"

"Like it's gone," Deven said.

An abandoned storefront sat where she knew the pub had been. All the other stores around it were exactly where she'd seen them. Or from what she recalled. To be honest she hadn't been paying as much attention as she should have been. She'd been lost in thought until the smell had caught her. The smell.

"Crap."

"You're sure it had been here?"

She ran her fingers through her hair. "Yes and even worse I just realized they were cooking fish, a lot of it. To get my attention."

Deven walked up to the storefront and peered inside. "Isn't that a little self-centered? They could have had other customers, you know."

"That's it. They only had one other. And he had meat, not fish." She walked up to the doors and pulled, but they were locked. Nothing of the pub remained. They must have taken over this storefront, did what they wanted to do, and then returned it exactly as it had been. "Damn it."

They could go around to the other storefronts and ask if anyone knew anything. However in this part of the station no one would admit to knowing their own mother if questioned by an outsider. "Your mysterious friend said the odds of someone using food to put those creepy things in my blood would be unlikely. What about the drell? Could that have been in the food?"

"I don't think the drell would work in food, but I don't know enough about them to be sure," Deven said as he dusted his hands off. "I don't suppose you noticed anything about the other customer when you were here?"

"No." A thought hit her and she turned and retraced the path she had taken when she left the fake pub and gone to get clearance for her flight. "I wonder if my friend had something to do with it."

"Friend?" he asked.

"My friend who did that nice body slam when I came out of the flight office." She pointed up at a crusty camera lurking in a forgotten corner. By Commonwealth law all stations had to have security cams. Whether they worked or not was another issue. But this one whirled softly and pointed right at the intersection where the guy had collided with her. "I think we might want to go pay a visit to the security office."

The security office was the usual small, dank, and awful common to all space stations. The clerk was a bit different however.

"What can we do for you, Captain Tor Dain?" The clerk sounded competent once Vas identified herself; his prone position on a small metal desk belied that. He hadn't opened his eyes when they announced themselves, but gestured at some chairs.

"Please make yourself comfortable. I'm a bit indisposed right now."

Vas and Deven remained standing. Much safer than the rusted mismatched chairs lined up against the wall.

"I need to check some cam data from a section in Old Port," Vas said.

"So does everybody." The human-looking security clerk rubbed the space between his eyes. "I can't let folks peep willy-nilly at things. There has to be protocol, you know. Requests must be done in triplicate and presented to the council. Probably could get it to you in the next month, maybe two." As he spoke, he let his left hand fling open.

She refrained from blowing the hand off in annoyance. Should have expected it though. The entire Commonwealth ran off payoffs. Usually intimidation worked to get what she wanted, but that wouldn't be a good idea in a station security office. Not if she ever wanted to set foot on another Commonwealth station.

She nodded toward the outstretched hand. If Deven wanted to stick to her on this trip, then he could take care of payments.

He rolled his eyes, but dug out some credit chips. The clerk didn't curl back his fingers until his hand almost overflowed.

"Could you at least sit up?" The clerk's prone position annoyed her.

At first she thought the clerk started choking, but after a few seconds she realized it was laughter.

"You wouldn't want me to do that." More gurgling. "The station keeps moving and my stomach with it. Still enough in me to do damage."

"Never mind." Vas took a step backwards to be safe. "Just tell us where we can get the camera data we need."

The clerk reached down and hit a small buzzer, and a gate against the far wall opened up. "There. Find what you need, but don't take anything. And remember, I didn't see you."

Vas nodded, not caring that he didn't see that either. Deven followed her in, pulling the gate shut behind him.

It only took a few minutes to find the right date and camera. She guessed that the clerk out front wasn't in charge of keeping things in order in here. As slovenly as the outer office appeared, the inner room practically gleamed.

Settling into a chair in front of the viewer, she called up the approximate time she'd been at the station office. A few more minutes of fine-tuning the camera image brought her to watching herself come out. It showed the man running down the cross corridor. He was peering at something in his hand, so wasn't looking up, and slammed into her. They couldn't see his face though. A humanoid, most likely male, but nothing else. That didn't provide any new information.

Pushing her out of the seat, Deven sat and took over controls, trying to narrow down the image of the man and the impact between him and Vas.

"Damn it." He swore after a half hour of adjusting. "I can't get a good look at his face."

She peered over his shoulder. "No, but what's that?" There was a small patch on the man's right upper arm. Blurred, like the rest of the image, but it had an odd shape, like an elongated diamond with wavy lines. Not a symbol she knew. However, something was familiar about it. "Can you pull in any tighter? I think I saw that somewhere, but larger."

"No, not only is the camera crap, their viewing system has got to be even older than me." Deven glanced pointedly around the room and then nodded at the screen.

"I agree." She smiled. Deven might be a telepath, but he also had very good unspoken communication skills. That was one of his vital characteristics for becoming her second-in-command. He had noted that there were no cameras in the viewing room. A copy of the file could be made without notice.

At her agreement, he pulled out his personal comm and linked it to the ancient viewer. All of her crew's personal comms had a few of Gosta's tricks added in. First and foremost, a high-tech data and image grabbing system. The section of vid-data they had been viewing could be copied in seconds.

As Deven finished his scan, she saw an image flash that she hadn't seen before. "Wait, freeze that. Go back half a second, there." Off to the far right of the view screen a tall thin being stood. Clearly not a human, but also not like any other species she knew. "What the hell is that?"

Deven palmed his comm device and peered at the image. The slight pause before he answered told her she'd have to question him later about it. "I'm not sure." He clicked off the viewfinder and put the data chip back where it had been.

She glared at his back until he turned around.

He sighed. "I'll tell you later. I don't think it's safe here."

"Okay, for now." She led the way out of the small viewing room and past the now asleep security clerk. "You're damn lucky I really need a drink. However, after the bar? You'll be covering that in detail."

"Agreed." Deven didn't sound happy, but he nodded and let her lead the way to the bar.

Vas stayed lost in thought the entire way wondering who would create such a setup like that pub just for herself. However, if the people who did it weren't the ones behind the drell or the trackers, what the heck were they up to? The more she thought about it, the more pissed she got. So she turned to direct some of that anger at another worthy target. Unfortunately, Deven seemed lost in thought as well. Most likely thinking of some good lies to cover whatever he saw on that vid. *We'll see about that.*

Many of her crew were already in the Hidden Cup by the time Vas and Deven arrived. Judging by their boisterous welcomes, they'd probably been there since they'd left the ship.

They went to the bar and ordered shots. "I'd also like a round for those morons in the corner." She pointed to her crew. Gosta arrived a few minutes later and joined Deven and Vas.

"Anything interesting?" She figured he hadn't found much or he wouldn't be here, but she asked to be polite.

Gosta's eyes almost glowed. Something that only happened when he'd been at a heightened state of interest. Either he had found something or he had a new girlfriend.

"Actually, yes." He shook his head to himself. "Not here. Better for when we're back on the ship." He patted his jacket, but didn't go any further. "Any news with you?"

"That should probably wait until we get back—"

"Hey, isn't that the *Warrior Wench*? By god, I heard she had come to port. Wonder if she'd like to conquer my bed?" A drunken voice cut her off. He was a big Syngerin, but where Gosta's tall, skeletal frame looked like most of his race, this man seemed to have obtained an unnatural ability to go thick and wide.

"Looks like a *Warrior Wench*-type gal to me, don't it boys?" A tall, dark-haired human who had walked in with him stared openly at Vas as he spoke.

She gritted her teeth for the first two taunts. *Just wanted to be able to have a drink in the bar with my officers.* Away from that damn ship and all the mysteries that were piling up. There would be no fights today.

"Wonder why she's still wearing all of her clothes though. Don't them wenches go naked?"

Even the first two jokesters shut up at the third's remark.

Vas slowly turned to face the new man. A good foot taller than her and clearly of Ilerian and human heritage. A disgusting and she would have said impossible, combination. Reaching back, she grabbed her shot glass. One slug and the fire burned its way down. Keeping an eye on the tall idiot with the big mouth, who, of all things, still laughed at his attempt to be funny, she handed her most noticeable weapons to Deven. "I'll be right back." She quickly downed his shot as well. Most likely they'd get kicked out after this, so she'd drink what she could first.

With a yell that her sand-miner ancestors would have envied, she leapt for the tall man. His laugh turned to a choke as her fist pounded his face sideways. "I KNOW you weren't calling me or my ship whores." Another swing and the idiot went down. "Oh come on. Two punches?" She tapped him with her boot, ready to turn away when the dark-haired human finally realized what happened and jumped toward her.

She swung out of his strike zone. "You have to be kidding." With one tight jab, she knocked the air out of the idiot. Then, she grabbed the back of his neck and jerked his head down as she brought her knee up, smashing his face. He crashed to the ground, out for the count next to his buddy. "Who taught you morons how to fight?"

"Me, bitch." The voice boomed an instant before two steel bands encircled Vas's upper body and lifted her off her feet. Fron stepped forward to help, but Deven held him back. Smart man.

Smiling at her second-in-command, she threw her head backwards as hard she could, stomping down at the same time into her attacker's shin. The crunch of his nose and shin were in perfect harmony with the bellow of pain that followed.

"Bring it on, boys!" The drinking hadn't been what she needed; it was this. Too much weird shit going on and not enough things to beat the crap out of. Luckily that thin cast Terel had slapped on her hand didn't slow her down at all. In fact, it gave a bit of support to her fist. Maybe she'd have Terel see if there was a military application for it.

Apparently, her taunters had been with a big crew, or made a lot of new friends quickly. Or Vas having so much fun made others want to join in. Three more guys came up swinging and bellowing.

The jackass who she'd just smashed in the face had bent down holding his nose, which of course made the blood come out faster. But it didn't stop him.

"Now you're going to pay!" He staggered forward, still obviously hurting from her attack on his shins.

"If I have to pay for this much fun, I guess it's worth it." She blocked his lopsided swing and struck up and out with her foot. She got him squarely in the chest and the crowd gasped as his ribs cracked. She also hit him with enough momentum to send him back toward the bar. "Deven, pay the man."

Deven downed a quick shot, then reached out and grabbed the man as he flung by. "Consider him paid." One punch and the giant dropped like a lump of meal.

Vas nodded and smiled to her second. The idiot Deven had taken down probably would have kept fighting until he'd injured far more than a few ribs and a busted nose. Having Deven take him out insured he'd live for another day.

With a returning nod, Deven swung out at another friend of the original punsters.

Vas smiled and dodged another flying fist. What a wonderful day. The rest of her company had held back, but when Deven dove in they decided to join. Soon they had a nice melee going that fell out the doors and into the station halls.

She found herself fighting next to Deven.

"You know, there's got to be a better way for you to relax," he said as he kicked an opponent in the head. The giant Garthian blinked slowly, taking a few moments for the information about its unconscious status to travel from the brain in his head to the brain in his tail. He finally collapsed in on himself like a folded bit of metal.

"But this is so much more fun. Not to mention much cheaper than therapy." Breaking away, she smashed a sneaky devil who was trying to creep up on Gosta with a chair.

"You have a mind doc on your ship. You're already paying her," he said.

"Your point is?" Laughing, she ran forward, using two downed Floxians as a ramp to leap up and smack a Silantian attempting to pin Xsit.

The fight lasted another ten minutes mostly because the station security circled it a few times before attempting to force their way in. Vas sidled up next to Deven as she saw the cops finally building the courage to start subduing participants. Fortunately, none of her people were out in the station itself. All were smart enough to stay inside the pub and away from the doors.

"What say we go find another bar? This one is becoming a little crowded."

Deven knocked out his opponent, wiping away a thin trail of blood from his cheek where an earlier Floxian had gotten a scratch in. "Aye, Captain." He nodded toward the bar keep who was standing off to the side wide-eyed and open-mouthed. "Shall I?"

Vas sighed. She felt bad about destroying the barkeep's place; she honestly didn't think it would have grown this big. Obviously more folks than just her crew were feeling tension. "Yes, and give him a bit extra. Times are tough and more likely going to get tougher." She always made it a point to pay for her messes, at least the ones that she or her crew were a major cause of.

However, it wouldn't do to have the fierce Captain Tor Dain worry about a civilian, so she usually sent Deven to go deal with them. He was subtle and quiet. The barkeeps came out okay, and her reputation stayed intact.

While Deven approached the stunned barkeeper, Vas glanced around to find her crew. All seemed to be mobile and most were nearby. But Xsit had now gotten a bit too close to the front door, "Gosta, go get Xsit for me, would you? I don't think we want to leave out that door."

Gosta came back almost dragging Xsit. She'd gotten her fighting face on and didn't want to leave. Her long bright orange trailing feathers that usually hung against the back and sides of her neck were fully extended. She would have made a fierce picture if she hadn't been currently cross-eyed.

"Let me stay, Captain! They keep insulting us!" Xsit bobbed and weaved which may have been helpful while fighting, but made things worse when Vas tried to subdue her. A drunk Xithinal was never fun to be around and often violently messy.

"Gosta, can you carry Xsit?"

"Not a problem. Shall we?" He scooped up the flailing Xsit, and then nodded to the barkeep.

The barkeeper motioned behind the bar where one of his waiters held open a side door. "Follow the corridor down and it'll spit out on one of the small cross streets. Take the left turn and you'll end up near the docks."

Vas nodded and led the way out. Who needed therapy when there were bar fights?

CHAPTER TWELVE

The barkeeper had been correct. A few twists and turns and they were on a small side corridor far from the melee and the Hidden Cup.

Vas turned to Gosta and the twitching Xsit in his arms. Vas didn't envy her; Xithinals had a powerful metabolism, one that worked horribly with any sort of alcohol. Drying them out was akin to a major drug detox for most species. "Can you take her back to the ship? Terel should be back onboard by now. She'll need to keep Xsit in lock-up for at least a day."

He nodded. "Agreed. I'll stay onboard." His grin almost made her want to follow him. "I have some things I want to take care of before we leave."

"Sounds fine by me." She shrugged; she'd find out soon enough what he was up to. Unlike Deven, Gosta kept a secret about as well as Xsit held her booze. She listened to a message on her comm that had come in during the fight. "Mac and Jakiin think they might have a job for us lined up. We'll be onboard after we see what they've gotten into now." Flying with her crew this inebriated and worked up didn't strike her as a good idea. However, neither did sitting in dock for half a day. "Can you take this lot with you? Tell Terel to give them an hour, then stims all around. I want everyone sober when we leave."

Gosta adjusted the squirming Xsit as he turned. "Where are we going?"

Vas smiled. "Good question. One I'm sure I'll have an answer for when I get onboard."

He nodded and bellowed at the rest of the command crew to follow him.

Vas turned back to Deven. "Mac said he left the directions for this deal of a lifetime on your comm. Where are we going?"

He flipped open his comm as he walked ahead of her. "Supposedly right around the corner. He said to go—" Deven stopped speaking and walking as he rounded the corner.

Vas sped up to catch up with him but she let most of the swear words stay inside her head for now.

"Oh. Crap."

Mac and Jakiin stood sheepishly in front of a pile of crates. The fact that no one else could be seen said that one way or another those crates were theirs.

"What did you two do now?" She resisted the urge to smack them, but she had to fight to keep her arm down.

"We found a great deal, but we had to agree to it before you could get back to us. They threatened to take it somewhere else—"

Vas held up her hand to cut off Jakiin's babbling.

"Is this legitimate shipping? Should it be out here in the corridor?"

Mac threw a cover he'd been clutching over the crates. "It's sensitive. It really shouldn't be, um, exposed." Luckily few people were in this part of the station.

"Damn it, Mac, you two took on a *job* without clearance? What the hell were you thinking?"

He squirmed and fiddled with the edge of the canvas. The crates weren't big, but they were large enough to attract attention. "They're paying me, us, I meant us, a lot of credits. They'd asked for me specifically, like they'd heard of me...." The flash of guilt in his blue eyes told her everything. He'd taken this job thinking it would be something small he could smuggle on. When the contact dropped a few hundred pounds of crates on him, he panicked and tried to make it a company job.

She pressed in close, not letting Mac move a bit. "What is my rule about private jobs?" Her voice stayed low, a feat in itself since she wanted to yell, scream, and beat the crap out of both of them. She maintained tight control over all of the jobs, smuggling or otherwise, that her company took on. Smuggling unknown items could be extremely dangerous, not to mention a potential trap. Unfortunately this mess was now hers since two of her crew had taken it on. She couldn't afford to dump it unless she never wanted to smuggle again.

Jakiin tried to scoot out of the way, but Vas pinned him with a glare, then tilted her head back at her immediate quarry. "Well?"

The freckles on Mac's face became much brighter as the skin around them faded. His Adam's apple had a stability problem as he searched for the right words. "No jobs or bringing anything on ship unless it's a job cleared by you."

"I couldn't hear you." She barely whispered, making Mac lean forward to hear her. Smacking him in the back of his head when he did so, she then grabbed his collar to keep him close. "You two are going to find a way to get this product onto our ship without notice, and you are going to give me a full report of exactly what is in it. I want scans, printouts, full information on who gets it and where we are taking it. I don't need to tell you," she said then turned her glare to Jakiin who had begun to fade to the left, "that neither of you will be receiving your cuts. And if I ever find out you two are even thinking of pulling this kind of shit again, I will space you both. I don't care if the president of the Commonwealth asks for you specifically." She stared down both of their terrified looks until they nodded.

She turned to Deven who had been using his comm to scan the crates. "Anything?"

He glanced around to make sure the corridor was still empty. "Fabric of a sort. Can't tell anything beyond that with this equipment. I'll warn Gon he needs to get a decom chamber set up for the crates."

Vas toyed with taking a chance and just leaving her pilots and their mess on the station. But she couldn't take that hit to her reputation. "Deven, stay with them and make sure they get this crap safely onboard."

At his nod, she turned and stomped back to the ship. On the plus side, at least they had a job. Because the fight on Lantaria should have taken a few months, she hadn't scheduled anything.

Back on the *Warrior Wench*, Vas made it all the way to her ready room door before anyone tried to even talk to her.

Bathshea finally risked her wrath. "Captain? The station had a message to relay. It's on a secure channel, so I forwarded it to your ready room."

"Thanks, Bathie. You going to stay up here?" Vas palmed open her ready room door. Bathshea might be the chief engineer, but she loved mucking it up on the command deck as well.

"If you don't mind." The dark woman flashed a grin. "I figure I can cover for Xsit for a while."

"That will work. Make sure Mac and Jakiin have their flight shifts covered by someone else. They'll be busy for a while."

Bathie nodded and went back to screening station traffic and comms.

Vas sighed as she shut the door behind her. Leaning against the door, she closed her eyes. After a few peaceful minutes, she re-opened them and glared at her desk. The flashing message sign ruined her mental escape attempt.

Secured messages were rare for her. Those being official dictates from the council or Commonwealth bureaucrats. When she received information that needed to be secured, it was usually information she had to secure *against* the council and Commonwealth.

It took a few minutes of digging around to recall her security code, then a few more to remember how to enter it correctly. Eventually the Commonwealth galaxy image appeared, rings of planets circling a large gas giant. Only a stationary picture though, someone like herself wouldn't rank high enough for an image message. Clicking the play button, she sat back in her chair.

"Captain Tor Dain, this is in response to your recent message about the events on Lantaria. Rest assured the Commonwealth is aware of the situation and has it under control. You are encouraged to forget about the last engagement and go about your business. Thank you for your concern."

She turned off the blank screen. Either the Commonwealth was more foolish than she believed or they were covering up something. Neither option was reassuring, but neither did either of them concern her. She'd done her bit when she forwarded the video.

In her gut she believed the unknown attackers were after her and her ship. She'd gone over Gosta's report on the other merc companies there and nothing stood out. All of them were smaller companies. The loss at Lantaria most likely meant the end for at least two of them. Rubbing the side of her face she pulled up the report again just to make sure nothing had been missed. A quick read told her nothing connected the other companies. She uploaded the entire package of all of the data on the event to a secret server she maintained, and then deleted it all from her own computer. Some might call her paranoid; she preferred the term prepared. In her experience anything unexamined could and would come back to bite her in the ass.

She thumped open the comm to the command deck. "Gosta, are Mac and Jakiin onboard yet?" Doubtful, but there was always a chance they'd move their asses for once.

"Gosta's not up here, Captain," Hrrru's soft voice answered. "Bathshea thinks he's in his lab. But I don't think the pilots are on board yet."

Vas thanked Hrrru and almost called down to Gosta's computer lab. Then she thought better of it. If Mac and the others weren't back yet, they had a bit of time. Gosta had been bursting at the seams about something. It would be a good idea to go down there in person and find out what he'd been up to.

The *Warrior Wench* had all of the labs, or offices, stuck away from the main quarters, and they were few in number. In the *Victorious Dead*, the labs were all part of the living area. While Vas admitted she enjoyed making a living as a mercenary, many of her crew had other interests. They enjoyed the mercenary life, wouldn't be in a company like this otherwise, but she wanted to make sure everyone had an opportunity to develop other skills and hobbies.

Information was Gosta's hobby. Vas often thought when he finally left the mercenary life he'd run an information center on one of the academic planets.

Surprisingly, the door to Gosta's lab was shut. He rarely shut it, preferring to share his information with any hapless soul who wandered down his corridor.

"Gosta? You in there?" She rapped on the metal door.

A clanging preceded the door opening, followed by Gosta sticking his head out quickly and motioning her inside.

"What are you doing?" Vas barely got inside when Gosta shut the door behind her.

"You're not going to like this. Well, maybe you will, but I didn't tell you before I did it...But I have a plan... It's not just for me you see—"

"Easy there." Placing both hands on his shoulders, she cut him off. Weird plans from Mac she expected, but Gosta? Never. Yet he babbled like a schoolboy caught stealing an upper classmate's speeder. "Now what did you do?" She gently pushed him back toward his desk and chair.

"I stole it." Gosta's long face looked ready to drag to the floor as he glanced up at her.

Vas removed a pile of documents from the lone other chair in the room and scooted it forward before she sat. "Why don't you start with what you stole, who you stole it from, and why you took it?" Unlike dealing with Mac, she knew Gosta would have weighed the good and the bad before breaking her rules. She trusted him not to have done anything against those rules unless he had a very good reason for it.

He stared at her for a few seconds, his eyes growing bigger. Then he turned to his computer and rapidly hit a few keys. "That."

It took the system a few seconds to load, and that alone told her it was something big. She really wasn't surprised when the Commonwealth Academic Symbol appeared along with the bold 'Property of the Commonwealth Academic Society' banner.

"You stole the library?" She sat back as the full catalog of information on this single machine scrolled past her eyes.

"Not all of it." He hit a few more buttons to end the constant scroll. "Just the important parts. It's only a copy, a link really. A non-traceable, non-breakable link coded to me alone, but really only a link." His face went from ecstatic pride at what he had in his possession to abject terror at what Vas might do to him about it.

His earnestness made Vas hold in her laugh. Not that it wasn't stealing, but even if caught the fine would be less than what Gosta made in a month during a normal job. Schooling her face to seem serious, she leaned forward and patted his arm. "Did you do it for the good of the ship and most of all to help your captain resolve some nasty mysteries which have been plaguing her lately?"

"Of course! I mean, it is for me as well, but of course!" He almost appeared insulted that she might imply he would keep knowledge to himself.

"Then all I can say is thank you." She rose to her feet. "Make sure you don't get caught. And report any findings to me." She froze halfway to the door. "Rather, any findings directly related to my problems. All others you can file."

Gosta grunted in response as his fingers flew over the keyboard. They'd be lucky to pry him out of here any time soon.

Vas smiled as she shut the door. With all the other drama invading her life, this was a nice surprise. Providing Gosta stuck to her final command and didn't feel the need to report all of his findings to her. She shuddered; that would be truly terrifying.

Deven was on the command deck by the time she returned. Mac and Jakiin were as well until they saw her coming and fled down the back corridor. Smart men.

"I take it we're ready to leave?" Settling into her command chair, she quickly called up their status. She didn't even care where they went. She just wanted open space around her. Maybe that attack at Lantaria was making her jumpy.

"We are." Deven gave a pointed look at Hrrru sitting in the pilot chair. "Mac isn't happy."

Vas gave the command to leave space dock. "Good. I really don't care. Do we have any info as to where we're going yet?"

Deven locked his arms behind his back in the almost military stance he often adopted. Even though he wouldn't admit to being part of any military in his past. "The Qualian system. The job is simply drop, get paid, and leave. Planet is low-tech and lightly populated. We probably won't even be noticed."

Her shoulders loosened as the commands and orders that would get the ship out into open space flowed around her. The fight had helped some with stress relief, but not enough. She turned back to her second-in-command. "Have you had a chance to look at our information?" Bathshea, Hrrru, and Fron were carefully not paying attention to their conversation. Which meant of course they were dying to know what was going on.

"Actually, I wanted to give it to Gosta. Shouldn't he be up here?"

"Gosta is ensconced in his lab. Which is why Fron has the nav seat. Figured getting him to try other positions would be a good idea."

Deven's eyes brightened when she mentioned Gosta's lab. He pretended to be all about sex and fighting, but there was a secret book learner in that fine body. She waved him off. "Go down and find him. You can see if he can find anything on our information."

"Captain?" Hrrru's hushed voice broke Vas out of her thoughts as she watched Deven stride off the command deck.

"Yes, Hrrru?" The star field on her view screen had completely removed the image of the space station. Thank the gods they were in space again. With a shake to clear her head, Vas turned toward the small Welisch yeoman. The Welisch had been bred for generations to fight in tunnels by a long-lost conquering race. Or formerly conquering, since the Welisch had risen and overthrown the invaders. Complete genocide wasn't pretty even when a race deserved it. Hrrru, like most of his people, appeared like a large pet: furry, soft spoken, and meek.

Vas figured he was one of the more dangerous beings on her ship.

"What's wrong?"

Short gray fur shimmied as he shook his head as he spoke. "Not wrong. But why does master Gosta have Graylian puzzle on his work panel?" Hrrru held up the panel Gosta had been trying to show her before. The panel with the weird circles and lines.

"A what what?" Vas had been lost in thought before the yeoman's call, but now she wondered if her ears were working.

"Graylian." Hrrru glanced down. He didn't enjoy the attention of others. "Small enclave of monks from home world. They live there now; but they came from the planet Achaeon. Chased out fifty years ago when the ruling prince overthrown." He waved a paw in the air as he got off track. "This looks like one of their ancient puzzle texts. Where did master Gosta get it?"

Vas walked over and took the panel. Maybe it would make more sense to her now as opposed to when Gosta showed it to her before.

"It goes this way, Captain."

The fact that she'd been holding it sideways and Hrrru had to correct her definitely indicated it hadn't suddenly started to make sense. "Thank you, Hrrru." She looked around the deck, but once her joy at leaving the space dock wore off, this part of the trip was rather dull. "I'll take this down to Gosta and see if he knew he had a Graylian puzzle. Maybe he's figured out what it means."

Hrrru bobbed his head and went back to his screens.

"Bathie, you have the bridge. If you need anything call me. Or Deven. Or Gosta. We'll all be down in Gosta's hidey-hole. Again."

The second trip down to Gosta's lab was uneventful, even if Vas did walk slowly to see if somewhere along the way she'd be able to figure out the linking of all the items on the panel. Or Graylian puzzle as Hrrru called it. Yet another piece of the master puzzle currently taking over her life. However, she was afraid some of the pieces were missing.

Alas, figuring out whatever clues were hidden on the panel wasn't going to happen in the short span of time between the command deck and Gosta's lab.

This time the door to his lab hung open, but only a hair's width. Deven's low voice could be heard asking Gosta a series of intense questions. By the time that Vas thought about sneaking up to eavesdrop, she knew she was already too close.

"Come on in." The tone in Deven's voice told her he knew who was out there. He had been talking about something she would probably like to hear about with Gosta, and he wasn't going to continue. Not only had her world become far more complicated as of late, it was also becoming more insubordinate.

With a sigh, Vas nudged open the door. "Hrrru had some questions about your panel. Or rather why master Gosta had a Graylian puzzle text on his log panel." She handed the flat disk to Gosta. Deven tried to peer at it but Gosta was holding it close as if he'd never seen it before.

"What did he call it? Graylian?" He peered at it as if for the first time. "I have heard of them, you know, I have." Shoving the panel into Deven's hands, Gosta's reed-like fingers dashed over his keyboard. An instant later Vas saw the fruits of his pilfered knowledge.

The large computer screen filled with text and images that continued to grow until Gosta finally forced it to stop. "Ah, Hrrru is a wise student to have picked out a Graylian puzzle." An image grew larger on the screen. Brightly colored lines and squares overlay a star chart. Far more complex and intricate than the one Gosta had found, but the similarity was there.

"I certainly wouldn't have seen it," Vas admitted. "I see it now, but glancing at the two things? I don't think so. Hrrru knew it immediately."

Deven studied the two separate images with a frown. "But why would the pieces of our ship be parted out in such a ritualistic manner? Can you check again that none have been installed anywhere?"

The clicking that followed was as much from Gosta's finger joints as the keyboard.

"No, see here," Gosta said as he pointed to each dot on the screen. "None of them are installed. They stole our ship, took it apart, and left all the pieces in an obscure religious pattern in space." He sighed and rubbed his long fingers across his face.

Deven rose and offered Vas his chair, when she refused, he stood as well. Vas could never figure out why her second-in-command would periodically pull out archaic chivalry on her.

"There has to be a connection. Vas, have you heard of the Graylians?"

"No, and I doubt a group of monks are going after me by hiding my ship in a puzzle. Besides, it's not much of a trick. We can see all of the parts." She waved at the screen.

Gosta leaned forward intently. "Unless that is the trick. In Graylian puzzles the obvious choice is usually the wrong one. Often the fatal one if my memory is accurate. But you are right, Captain. I cannot see them doing one of these this large, nor in space." He scratched one long elbow with his first knee in thought. "They were only dangerous to their own people. Those who chose to follow the religious path, but failed. Their ritual sacrifices were...inventive. They became even more isolated when they fled from Achaeon."

Deven frowned at Vas's intake of breath. "Why did you react to Achaeon just now? You didn't react to it before."

Vas shrugged. She'd been trying not to respond, but the coincidence was too strong. "It just hit me. That's where I went when I left last month. I was meeting a potential client about a job. Then I was talking to a seller about another base of operations. I might like a small planet on the side besides Home." The faces before her were unfairly judgmental. "Nothing happened. It was a simple trading trip. I lost track of time. There were some parties of some sort."

"You said it was a client." Deven's eyes narrowed. "And you never lose track of time. I think you swallowed a time piece as a child."

Vas waved her hands and paced around the small room. "It was a client and some trading...."

Deven grabbed her shoulder and forced her to look at him, then practically pushed her into the empty chair. Probably a good thing since the world was spinning and a dull drumming was threatening to take over her head.

"Vas? Look at me."

Deven's green eyes were enormous and dangerous. Why would she have someone so deadly near her? He shouldn't be so close. "Away. Too close. You're hurting my head." Black dots obscured her vision as she tried to pull back out of his grasp.

"I'm not causing the pain, Vas—"

"Actually, maybe you are." Gosta cut Deven off and Vas heard him tapping furiously at his computer keyboard. "She might be under a block. Something could be forcing her memories away from what happened. If so, any attempt to recover them will lead to pain or loss of consciousness."

Even with her eyes obscured by clouds of pain, Vas knew Gosta was thrilling in the search of what was hurting her. Or killing her. Again. This was really getting old.

"My brain is going to explode." Getting that sentence out was harder than the five weeks she'd been trapped on a desert island after a shuttle crash. "Make. It. Stop."

She felt cool hands on her cheek. "Vas, you have to release my bracelets. Now. Let me in there. If someone put a block on you, it will kill you. You've triggered it and it will keep shutting down systems...." Deven's voice dropped off as she opened her eyes. "Crap. You can't see, can you?"

Her eyes burned. She felt them open but saw nothing. The noise of the room was overwhelming her, pushing her mind deeper into her skull. Like a windstorm, but only in her head.

"Vas!"

Hands, too tight, far too tight, were shaking her arms. "Let me sleep." She struggled until she was sitting on the floor. The nice cool floor.

Cold metal pressed against her hand, and fingers fumbled her hand around the metal. Metal and hot skin. She tried to pull back, but the force of the other hand had her own pinned.

"Release the bracelets."

The words were faint. She wanted to ignore them. Sleep sounded so good now. But maybe if she gave in, the voice and the hands and the noise would leave her alone. "Release." She uttered the word, and then fled to a cocoon of darkness and silence.

Only to be rudely pulled back by a glowing presence in her mind. The unbearable light cleared and Deven's voice flowed into her mind. Words, arcane, mystical, and dangerous, flowed through her head. Why did she know they were dangerous? She didn't know how she knew, but she knew they were there to kill her. They chased her and pulled away the safe shelter. A part of her wailed as the words threatened to shatter her soul.

CHAPTER THIRTEEN

Vas fought for her life, fought against the words trying to swallow her entire self. They were inside her, in her mind, in her essence of being. They pulled and tore, ripping her away from the quiet peacefulness she sought.

As she fought to gather her tattered soul back around her, a slip in the onslaught of words appeared. A chink in the armor assaulting her mind. A moment of clarity.

The words weren't the enemy.

Deven's words were fighting the miasma that filled her mind. There were two parts. The most aggressive had laid there in wait since she had been attacked on Ghorlian Prime, the other was far older. Wait, she'd been on Achaeon, not Ghorlian…why would she have been on Ghorlian? The clarity faded…then rushed back in like sand filling a hole. She had been on Ghorlian. Making a deal for a huge job. One too good to be true. The bastards had taken her somewhere, but those memories were still shuttered. However, the fact that they existed, and that she had been kidnapped, those memories were free. Finally.

The freedom allowed her to help Deven's presence fight the encroaching darkness. She reached out and pushed against the shadows, looking for more answers that her mind withheld from her. Nevertheless, even with

Deven's telepathic assistance she couldn't push past the barricade in her head.

That her own mind had been used to block the truth from her almost pissed her off more than the idiots who tried to kill her with poison.

They took her ship, took her mind, then tried to take her life. They would have to invent new words for hell when she found the bastards behind this.

Disgusted at her own mind's ability to thwart her, Vas drifted toward consciousness.

To find herself cradled in her second-in-command's arms. She was surprised at how nice it felt. Not in a sexual way, but in a secure way. Although even in her weakened state, she had to admit it felt pretty damn good in a sexual way as well. Not enough for her to forget who he was, but good nonetheless.

She pushed Deven away. "I'm okay. At least my brain isn't going to leak out of my ears anymore. And I know that something happened while I was gone." As she said the words, she waited for that dark presence to swarm out of her mind and swallow her. A few seconds and nothing.

"I think, whatever it was, you broke it. I still don't remember much. I went to Ghorlian Prime for a deal." She frowned. Without knowing all the details it appeared that she had been an idiot for going to Ghorlian Prime. "This deal, whatever it was, obviously was nothing more than a trap." She held up her hand when Gosta looked ready to launch into data gathering mode. "No, I don't know where I went after that, or why they took me, or who they even are. Maybe you and your new toy can help me on that."

Deven helped her up into the chair, and for once Vas didn't fight him. That block in her head had been damn strong. If Deven had been a weaker example of his kind, she wouldn't have gotten out.

"You don't remember anything? Faces? What the deal was?" Deven frowned. "There was another block in there as well, one too old to be part of this. I couldn't see anything about it, but I think the new block cracked the old one."

Vas shuddered. She'd felt the edges of that older block, and she was pretty sure there was only one person and place it could have come from. Her older brother and her home world—a world where wind and sand storms could kill within minutes. However, he was dead and if she was lucky, so was her homeworld. "I don't remember a damn thing about the trip. As for a second block, there's not much we can do about it right now, is there?" At Deven's reluctant shake of his head, she went back to the current issue. If there was something else lurking in her head from almost twenty-five years ago, it could stay where it was. "We move on to what is happening now. We have to assume that the attack on me, my memories, and the missing *Victorious Dead* is all related somehow." She waved toward the computer. "Is there any way that database can combine things? Maybe see connections that we're missing?"

Gosta studied the screen he had up for a few seconds. "I don't know. Maybe with it I can at least fill in the pieces more." He finally turned toward her, worry unlike any she'd ever seen made his thin face skeletal. "Are you sure you're okay?"

Vas started to bravado it off, but stopped. "I'm going to be all right, Gosta. I've come out of worse scrapes."

"But not like this." His deep brown eyes were almost watery. "I've never seen anything go after you like this. You've always been the rock, the one thing in this company that stays the same."

For an instant Vas thought he was going to say *in this world*. He was clearly terrified. She'd always thought of her crew as her family, but she never thought about them thinking of her the same way.

"I have you and Deven, and this whole damn crew looking out for me. Whoever those assholes are, they don't stand a chance."

Gosta met her eyes with his own worried ones for a few minutes more, and then nodded. "Agreed. Whoever is doing this are assholes." Swearing was rare for him and the term sounded awkward. "And I will help you find new evil things to do to them when we find them." He paused, and reached up to a small shelf above his desk. "I was going to wait to give you this. It is not fully tested. But it might come in handy at some point." His face flared red in embarrassment as he tumbled a small, metal sphere into her palm.

"What is it?"

Gosta fluttered his hands and turned back to his monitor. "In theory it is an EM weapons buster. I have not named it yet. It could be used to temporarily disable blasters. Up to a class three, I would think."

Flashing him a smile, she pocketed the ball. Inventing things was his hobby, and about half of the gadgets even worked. Just not always as intended. She wasn't sure what good something that would wipe out her own weapons as well as her enemies could be, but she'd keep it.

"Thank you, Gosta. Okay, enough about me, did you two find out anything about our cargo or destination?" She poked Deven. "You know how I hate going into these things blind. Pretend I didn't almost die again and fill me in."

Deven went to the empty room next door to get another chair. He waited until he'd sat before finally turning to Gosta.

"We found what I think the seller wants us to find. It's nothing more than exotic silks, but they were from poisonous silk worms. Thus being used to make celebration robes for the Floxian magistrates."

"Which are illegal since at least half of the magistrates die." Vas rolled her eyes. "I say if they want to practice an odd way of population control through poisoned garments and their religious caste, more power to them." She rubbed the back of her neck; it felt like someone had shortened all of her neck muscles. "There's no danger to us from this fabric, is there?"

Gosta spun back to his data screen and happily clicked away. "No, Captain. The fabric has to be treated before the poisons become active. There's no threat to any of us."

She stretched as she got out of her chair. It wasn't just her neck; every muscle in her body suddenly felt two inches too short. "Mac and Jakiin are just damn lucky this one looks clean."

"You look like hell." Deven rose as well. "Your body is having a reaction to breaking down that command on your mind."

"Wonderful. Then if that's the case, I'm going to my quarters and trying to sleep. Deven, you have the bridge." She didn't know if it was because it was getting worse, or because he said it would get worse, but each step toward the door was like fighting through a swamp.

"Actually, Gosta, could you take the bridge?" He said from behind her.

"Deven—"

"You need something now or you'll not even be able to move in the morning. Gosta can babysit for a bit."

Deven took her elbow. Annoyingly, it seemed to be too much trouble to remove his hand. Which pissed her off even more. How could she control her crew if she couldn't even control her body?

"And don't even try to say you're fine."

Gosta came up behind them before she could come up with a response.

"I'd listen to him, Captain. He does know more about this sort of thing than even I."

Vas let the two of them lead her into the lift as if she were a thousand-year-old Ilerian godmother. "You two are worse than two little old ladies. Deven, you can escort me to my quarters. Gosta, you have the bridge." She glared at both of them. "But it was my idea."

Neither said anything but Gosta got off the lift in record speed when they hit the command level.

Deven stayed silent as they made their way to her quarters. Wise move for him.

"Now what?" she finally asked when they got to the door.

"I'll give you the best massage you've ever had." The look in Deven's eyes was definitely one that would do well in a brothel.

Vas backed into her door. "What the hell? Deven, this isn't the time—"

"It's the only thing that's going to work. Your mind and body are connected. Everyone's is. Your mind just had a catastrophic event take place, and now all those chemicals are rushing around your body kicking the hell out of it. The adrenaline release alone could make you immobile for days."

She tried to stretch to prove him wrong, but her arms felt like she'd been lifting heavy weights for a week straight. Thing was, she wasn't sure if she trusted herself if he started in on her body. She may not recall what had really happened during her month hiatus, but she was sure no sex had been involved.

However, she was damned if she was going to let recent events ruin her resolve where this sexy hunk of telepath was concerned. No teke had ever been in her bed and she was keeping it that way. She wished she could say the same about none ever being in her head, but she did not intend to let that number go up either.

However, he was also right about the massage. Just standing here was turning her back into a solid lump of metal.

"Okay." She put one hand on his chest as he grinned and started forward. "But nothing happens, do you hear me? You just make me relax, but keep all your other body parts to yourself."

He nodded and pushed open her door. "Whatever you say, Captain."

She ignored his look and shuffled to her bed. With an uncommon bit of self-consciousness, she stripped off her flight shirt and pants and eased herself on top of her bed. There was no reason for her to be self-conscious. She'd been naked in front of more than a few men, including Deven, during battles. Plus this was just a massage.

The minute his strong fingers touched her body, she knew why she felt awkward. If her body hadn't been tight enough to snap, she would have been sorely tempted to roll over and grab him. As it was it took a few minutes to force her body to not react to the long movements those hands were making. He carefully soothed her entire back, and then started in on her neck, deftly separating out the muscles and relaxing them one by one.

Why the hell was this man a merc? He could make fifty times what he made in a year doing just this, even more if he added sex.

A soothing haze filled her mind. As she relaxed further, her body began responding to his hands in a very different manner. Rolling over, she couldn't think of why she wouldn't want this man in her bed.

Reaching up and pulling him close, she kissed him and tried to return the sensations she was feeling. Deven held back, then leaned in and returned the kiss with an intensity she'd never felt before. Suddenly his hands were everywhere at once, and where his hands weren't his lips were. Her body had been almost too stiff to move moments before but now it needed to move, and it needed Deven.

Ripping his clothes off, Vas moved with an intensity unusual even for her to push Deven onto the bed beneath her. There was still a vague haze around everything, but it was soothing, not threatening. All she knew was that she needed him. She needed him inside her.

His hands went there first, teasing and taunting her, all the while the gray fog soothed any other thoughts. Pushing his hands aside, she climbed on top of him, her mind and body needing him more than she could believe. After a few moments, he flipped her beneath him, his eyes searching for something as his mind kissed hers. Their minds merged into one in an even more passionate reaction than the one taking place between their bodies. The climax was so intense that Vas screamed once, and then lost consciousness in a comforting world of gray fog.

CHAPTER FOURTEEN

Vas was actually having a nice dream, a lovely dream where a bevy of handsome men waited on her as she relaxed by a peaceful lavender sea. She could smell the brine of the water, almost hear the warbling of the local seabirds—when a klaxon roared through and shattered everything.

"Crap!" The sound had so pulled her out of sleep, that she'd thrown herself onto the floor of her quarters. Wondering why she was naked, she got to her feet and slid to the main comm stuck in the middle of the wall. "Vas here. What the hell is going on?" On a plus side, her muscles felt great. Deven's massage must have worked even though she didn't recall any of it. A small nagging voice starting pushing at her in her head, but she forced it away with Gosta's words.

"Captain, we've got a ship closing in fast. It's small, but won't answer our hails and could do some damage. I've gone into evasive maneuvers, but Hrrru can't keep up. It's changing course almost faster than we can." His voice was calm, but she heard the underlying fear.

"Get Mac up there now. Continue staying out of its way. And keep trying to raise the pilot or crew," Vas yelled into the comm as she threw her wrinkled flight suit back on. "If it's them or us, you'll have to blast it."

The silence told her he'd thought the same thing. Of course if that happened he'd probably go into seclusion for a month trying to purge his conscience of having to kill whatever idiots were on the ship.

"Aye, Captain."

Vas rolled her eyes as she palmed open the door. How did a mercenary company end up with so many non-violent types? And why in the hell hadn't she noticed before?

That thought was gone the moment she hit the command deck.

The ship was still coming at them, but either it had slowed down, or Gosta had overreacted about its speed. The *Warrior Wench* was easily staying out its way.

Gosta got out of the command chair as soon as she got on deck. "Report." She took her seat and called up the information they had on the ship. Raxilan-class, it was a small miner colony ship. Usually used for hauling ore. Probably had a crew complement of no more than four, five if they were friendly.

"We picked it up outside of the Deneb sector, didn't seem to be following us at first. Then about ten minutes ago it started closing in. It still hasn't responded to any of our calls. I even had the scrambler on in case they were outer world and didn't have a common translator. Nothing." Gosta punched in a few more numbers and the stats came in. "As it got closer we got this intel—single life sign, fading fast. The ship has enough raw ore to blow us out of the sky if it explodes anywhere near us. And it is tracking us with an automatic system. No pilot could have followed that tight, well, no non-teke pilot. And whoever is onboard is almost dead, so they couldn't be piloting."

Vas glanced over the data. Now that the ship was slowing down, the immediate danger was lessened. Still though, the thing was a bomb waiting for an ignition.

"Projections on when it will stop on its own?" She could pull back and order it blown to bits. It was too dangerous to be left out in space and the life signs were fading too fast for anyone to be saved.

But she didn't want to. The ship trailing them was another part of the growing posse of mysteries tracking her. If she blew it up she'd never know what part it played. Ore ships didn't go on destroy runs.

Gosta went to his own station, moving Bathie out of the way. "Within the hour. Whoever sent it after us didn't think we'd be able to outrun it. There's not enough fuel for more than forty-five minutes, an hour at the best."

Deven hit the deck at that minute, looking fresh and relaxed as usual, even though Vas was sure he'd probably been sound asleep. Something about him stirred the muttering in her head, and she roughly shoved it aside. Why did she have a very bad feeling she'd missed something? Deven had given her a massage and she'd slept. Nothing more.

"I checked, and there's no teke activity onboard. The sensors are clean." Deven seemed ruffled, not that anyone but Vas could probably tell. However, he was disturbed by something other than the ore ship.

"Someone took over a fully loaded ore ship, programmed it on a suicide run, and aimed it our way. I want to know why." Vas drummed her fingers on the arm of the command chair. Years of clean living and she got paid back with this. She sent a few nasty thoughts toward whatever deity was pissing in her bath, and then turned toward Mac. "Keep us clear. If it is on a suicide run it could still damage us from a distance.

"Bathie, monitor chatter around here. I know there isn't much in this sector, but chances are whoever sent that thing after us is keeping an eye on it. I know I would." Vas thumbed open the comm on her chair. "Terel? I'll need you to ready a team. Full suits. I don't know what's over there. We're going over as soon as its fuel is wasted."

She felt Deven's presence next to her long before he spoke. "Why don't I go with them?"

His closeness triggered whatever her head had been trying to tell her. Head and body both, she felt the flush start to grow and it was all she could do not to rip his clothes off on the command deck.

What the hell happened?

One full look in his eyes answered that question.

Son of a bitch, she didn't have time for this.

"I need five minutes with Deven. Gosta, get everything ready. Tell Terel I'll be down for my suit in a bit." She grabbed Deven's arm and jerked him toward her ready room. "Deven will be staying here."

Deven didn't put up a fight and stayed silent. Vas lit into him as soon as the door to her ready room slid shut.

"You son of a bitch, what the hell did you do last night? You know how I feel about *your* people." Vas was a rolling storm of emotions, with fear, pain, and betrayal being the strongest. She wanted him to feel some of them too. "You got into my head. You fucking got into my head and my body."

Deven wouldn't look up for a few moments, which would have given her food for thought had she been calm enough to listen. Bits and pieces of last night trickled into her mind. Her body and mind blending with his in a way that could only be unnatural. She'd never had sex like that in her life. And gods willing she never would again. It was all she could do to keep from running into her room and curling up and never coming out.

"It wasn't just me. You responded—"

"And you should have stopped me. Damn it, Deven." Vas folded her arms as tight as she could around herself. She'd trusted him. Completely trusted him.

"I didn't mean for it to happen." He held up a hand, his eyes meeting hers and staying there. There was a hurt there, and a softness. "Let me finish. I was trying to heal you as I massaged. I think I must have gone too deep with you mentally when I broke that block and the link was still there. Healing pulled us both into that." At her arguing glare, he went on. "A haze, do you recall a haze?"

Reluctantly she nodded. It was coming back, all of it.

"I saw it too, it was—" He tried looking for a word, but failed. "I can't translate it into any Commonwealth tongue. But it wasn't completely my fault. I was pulled in as well." He waved his hands between them. "Any residuals should be gone within a few days."

Vas turned away. The feelings were too intense. Part of her needed to have him right now. The other part needed to have him abandoned on some moon far away. As a child, she'd been kidnapped by extremists from her family's wind farm for two weeks. The extremists had all been high-level telepaths and thought nothing of rampaging through the mind of a child.

That portion of her mind couldn't bear to look at the man before her.

However, part of her felt the truth in his words. He hadn't been completely at fault. And the fact was she needed him if she was ever going to get her ship and her life back.

"We can't deal with this now. But tell me one thing."

"Anything." The sorrow in his voice softened her a bit, but she couldn't let him in.

"Could you have stopped it?"

He studied her and part of her felt the pull to go to him.

"Possibly. It wouldn't have been easy, but I might have been able to stop it." She'd never seen the level of pain in his eyes she was seeing right now.

"If that ever happens again, it will be your life." She put all the steel she had left in her in her voice and face. Not that she was certain she could kill Deven.

"Understood." He rose to move toward the door.

"I'm not done. You will switch schedules so that we are on opposite shifts until further notice. And stay away from me as much as possible."

"Understood. And I am truly sorry." Deven left the room.

Vas waited a few seconds, then took a deep breath, and followed him out. "So am I."

She had just changed into the heavy environmental suit she'd have to wear on the ore ship when Gosta called her.

"Captain, I think we're ready. The ship has stopped moving. Mac is keeping us as far out as he can, but I've got a tracker on it so it'll stay steady while the team goes over."

She buckled her grav boots, and then headed for the door, more than grateful that the ore ship was enough of a danger to distract her from Deven. "Have Terel and her team meet me at the shuttle. What's the status of the life sign?"

"Life sign vanished about thirty minutes ago. You still want full quarantine suits?"

"Yep, we have no idea what's over there. I'll be in the docking bay. Deven has the deck."

Vas made her way down to the docking bay before Terel and her people. While she knew Gosta would have scanned for any mechanical traps, they couldn't be sure of bio-agents. Hence the heavy environmental suits.

Once her final check was completed, she wandered over to the Furies. Deven and Jakiin had been spending some time down here, bonding as they worked on the rusting piles of space junk. To be fair, they were pretty damn impressive looking. All sharp angles and wicked looking weapons ports, it was clear to anyone these ships had one purpose: to destroy as much as they could.

She ran a gloved hand up the side of the third. Deven and Jakiin had been futzing around with the other two, but this one actually looked in better shape. It appeared to be a bit older than its mates, which wasn't saying much when dealing with ships that hadn't been made in over one hundred years.

"You too, eh?" Mac's voice broke her contemplation of the dangerous machine. "Jakiin has been spending way too much time around those things."

She turned with a frown. "I would have thought a flight junkie like you would be all over these."

Mac glanced at the ship but shrugged. "To be honest, they sort of disturb me. Too big to do what they supposedly can do and too damn old. Give me a Flit any day."

"We're ready." Terel, Pela, Divee, and Gon came into the flight deck loaded with equipment. Vas hadn't wanted the med team along for their ability to save lives; she wanted them in case there were any pathogens on board. Divee and Gon, both security engineers, were along for the same reason. She wasn't sure why Mac was there though.

"Mac, just why are you along on this? You know that ore hauler doesn't have much room. I really don't need extra bodies there."

"I'm playing pilot today. Deven pointed out that keeping someone in the shuttle while you all were on board might be prudent. Bathie hasn't heard anything on open chatter but if this was an attack we can't be sure that whoever set it up isn't still watching."

As much as Vas wanted to send him back just to spite Deven, she had to agree. It was even a little embarrassing she hadn't thought of it first.

"Then why are you still out here?" She smacked him in the back of the head. "That shuttle isn't going to do a pre-flight on itself, you know."

Mac jogged toward the shuttle in silence. Sometimes she thought there might be hope for that boy yet.

The others all got Terel's equipment on board and within minutes they were ready for launch. Vas opened a channel to the deck. "Deven? We're ready to go. Any last minute changes or intel?" It was easier dealing with him when she couldn't see him.

"Bathie hasn't picked up any chatter beyond normal. And nothing near us." There was a strain in his voice that she'd never heard before, but she shoved any concern for him aside. She couldn't deal with her own emotions right now, and she sure as hell couldn't deal with his.

"Got that. Vas out." She turned off her personal ship comms after making sure the ones on the shuttle were solid. Not that she didn't trust Mac to do a proper setup. Ah hell, who was she kidding, she didn't trust Mac. But he'd done his job this time. They approached the ore hauler without incident.

The ore ship didn't look damaged, at least not from the outside. Nor did it look old enough for age to have been a factor in a malfunction. Calling up the specs again she confirmed the ore hauler was only two years old. Called the Guppy for some inane reason. Assigned to the Ore Field Assessment and Survey Company out in the outer rim. Vas frowned. That wasn't anywhere near here. Nor would it have had to come out this far to pick up its payload. Ore was collected at least five planets closer to the rim than where they were.

She studied the ship through the view screen as they approached, but there were no clues there. The docking was tight and clean. She might not trust Mac on some things, but he was a damn good pilot.

"Everyone, cross check at least two other folks. Make sure all suits are tight. We have no idea what's on this ship and because of its freight we won't be able to tell if there's a bio-hazard until it's too late." Vas turned to check Terel's suit.

"You ready?"

Terel nodded then checked Pela's suit. "I think so. We should have every contingency planned for." They checked the rest of the crew, and then Vas called up to Mac.

"Mac, we're ready. Open the doors. Keep them locked until we are ready to come back though. No sense exposing more of the shuttle than we need to."

"Aye, Captain."

"Come on, boys and girls. Let's see what's here." Vas palmed open the latch. "Oh shit..." She froze and slowly raised her hands. A wide-mouth blaster rifle had been inches away from the door when she forced it open and was now aimed clearly at her head.

CHAPTER FIFTEEN

"Look, we're sorry. We didn't think there was anyone alive." Vas said with her hands up and prayed her team behind her was doing the same. The gun's muzzle was less than two feet from her head, the sight lamp on it blinding her to anything beyond. "We don't mean you any harm, but you did try to ram my ship."

There was no response, but the gun didn't lower either.

"Terel, I don't have a scrambler on this suit, and I really can't put my hands down to get one. Can you power one up? I'll try again."

Terel didn't answer, but a soft whirl of the translation device told Vas she'd done what was asked. Vas repeated everything she'd just said and the scrambler spit it out in fifteen different base languages. Obviously those weren't the only languages in the known universe, but all of them were root languages. Between them they covered more than ninety percent of the known population at least in a rudimental fashion.

Judging by the lack of movement from the gun, this person must belong to that ten percent that wasn't covered.

"Damn it." Vas lowered her hands a tiny amount to see if there would be a result. Nothing. "I need ideas, people."

"Hold on. Let me check something." Terel kept her voice low and soft. Even though the person on the other end of this blaster wouldn't understand, they might react to tone.

A soft chime indicated Terel had turned on her life signs scanner. What was she doing, checking to see if there were others they missed? Even if this person was alone there was no way they could charge him or her.

Hands on Vas's shoulders pushed her arms down. "You can lower your arms. Our friend here isn't going to shoot anyone." Terel stepped around and took hold of the blaster rifle and switched off the sight lamp. "At least not deliberately. Although we should probably disarm him carefully. It might still go off."

Vas wiggled her shoulders to get the kinks out, and then motioned the rest of the team forward. It took a few minutes for her eyes to see something other than spots.

"Damn me. He's frozen there?" Once she could see, it was clear her 'attacker' had been frozen in place. Face, hands, and neck were black and brittle. Even his flight suit appeared ready to shatter off of him.

Terel scanned some more. "Yes, but I don't understand how. There's an atmosphere in here, an odd one, but it should be breathable. But leave your suits closed please." Terel added that for Vas's benefit; she was always trying to get out of environmental suits faster than the doctor liked.

"No worries, doc. Suits will stay on until you say. Can we move him? I'd really like that weapon discharged and secured somewhere."

Gon moved forward. "If you don't mind, Cap't, I'd be fine with lowering him down and seeing to the gun." Gon was a Garthian, and his accent and rumbling voice always reminded Vas of farm country on an ag planet. But he was also the best suited to dealing with frozen beings. Garthia had been known to go through cycles of freezing that lasted years.

She moved out the way and let him lumber past. With a gentleness that was surprising due to his size, he carefully laid the frozen body down and began working on the blaster. Finally, he broke the hand and removed it that way.

"Sorry, Cap't. Tweren't another way to get it." He opened the casing to take out any rounds, and then looked back up at her. "Whoever he were, he went out firing. There aren't any charges left."

Vas turned back toward the space lock, but there were no telltale burns indicating he'd discharged his weapon that direction. In fact there were no burn marks at all. "Great, yet another mystery to haunt my sleep."

"Did you say something, Cap't?" Gon asked.

She waved him off. There was no reason for the entire crew to know how bizarre her life was becoming. "Nothing, just talking to myself. Terel, you're with Divee and me. Pela, stay with Gon. Get our friend here in a full decontamination suit then put him in a decon storage locker. We need to take him back and see if there are answers we're missing. I don't want to take any chances here. Let's go see what else is on this damn ship."

Vas moved forward cautiously. The ship had tight quarters, and she really didn't want any more surprises. Granted the only person who was supposed to be on here was dead, but she'd heard of pirates masking life signs in abandoned ships, and then attacking those who came after it. As a sometime pirate herself, she'd never pulled that stunt, but she knew others who would. The passageways were narrow and low. Good thing Deven had stayed behind; as it was, Vas was having to duck with the added height of the environmental suit. Deven was about three inches taller than her.

An ore hauler wasn't designed for looks, comfort, or speed, just hauling huge amounts of rock from one end of the galaxy to the other. However, this one was in worse shape than any she'd seen. The lights were off; most

likely they had been cut to a bare minimum to feed
whatever had been done to the engines. There was no
way a normal ore hauler could have reached the speeds
this one did, even for a sprint. Someone had clearly
adapted it to become a bomb. Now the question was if it
was after Vas, the *Warrior Wench*, or just any poor sap
who came through this part of space.

A low, repeated noise, not part of the ship's
functioning, could be heard down one of the
passageways. Vas held up her left hand and clenched her
fist. The two behind her froze instantly. With a nod she
slowly walked down the short corridor following the
sound. A dim light glared unnaturally in the dark from a
doorway that was cracked open.

After checking to make sure Divee and Terel were still
standing guard where she left them, Vas nudged the door
open.

The cabin was small, its tiny space taken up by a
narrow cot and a rickety metal desk. The muted sound
and light were coming from a small computer screen
embedded in the cabin wall. The image was broken and
obviously stuck in a loop. Then the static image cleared
and a delicate brunette appeared. She held herself regally
although she wasn't anyone Vas recognized. She spoke
common perfectly, but there was an accent, odd and fluid,
that Vas couldn't place.

"I hate to put this on you, Ghassil, but there's no one
else. I can't get out there in time. You've got to—" The
image scrambled again, the voice nothing but garbage,
then it came back.

"—arrior wench. She'll be in that system soon—"

Vas swore as the image and voice went completely
into undecipherable gibberish.

Damn it. Whomever that woman was she had ordered
this ship to attack the *Warrior Wench* and worse, she
knew where they had been going.

Vas tapped her comm. "Divee, can you come in here?" After a second thought she added, "Terel, you too."

She fussed with a few more pads and buttons, but the same loop repeated without any new data. A rustling announced someone behind her. Vas stepped back from the system and waved Divee forward.

"Can you pull that computer and its memory out of that wall? I need everything you can save."

The slender human man nodded. "Yes, Captain Tor Dain. I can see what can be salvaged from the wreck. I will endeavor to obtain all of the information you need." He gave a slight bow, a lock of jet-black hair falling forward inside his suit.

"Good man." Divee had been with her for four years, yet he was still as formal as the day he arrived. Vas gave a mental shrug. He was damn good at computers, almost as good as Gosta, and a formal tech wasn't a bad thing. Just odd. "Terel, stay with him until he gets the machine free. I'm going to keep searching. If I'm not back in ten minutes, call for Gon and send him out after me."

Vas sighed and raised a gloved hand the instant Terel's mouth started to open. "No, you can't come with me. I don't think anyone is here. However, if there is, they may not like Divee stealing their computer system. I need you here."

"I wasn't going to ask that." Terel folded her arms, or tried to. The suit made them too bulky to do it effectively. "I was just going to ask if you would like Divee to pull the main computer logs once he gets this personal one out?"

"Right." Vas knew Terel hadn't been about to say that at all. She was the biggest mother nag of the entire crew. "But that is good thinking. Divee, please ransack and pillage as much technical information from this ship as possible. Then return to the shuttle." She nodded and went back down the corridor to rejoin the main passageway.

Ten minutes later Vas had finished prowling around the abandoned ore carrier. The entire ship had clearly been ill-used and without a regular crew for a while. She guessed it hadn't hauled ore regularly for at least a year. The hold was completely full, but it had dust on it. Obviously the ship had been taken with a full load quite a while ago.

All of the corridors had the same smoky residue as the main hallway. Vas had rudimentary science equipment with her, but not enough to tell what it was. Scraping off a sample she sealed it in a case and slipped it into her pocket. Another mystery for Gosta to solve.

Terel and Divee still weren't back when she made her way to the shuttle, but Gon, Pela, and Mac were having a fine conversation. A conversation that stopped when she came into view.

With a sigh, Vas stepped past them and peered into the shuttle. The decon case was sealed nice and tight. "Good work. I didn't find anyone or anything else. Have we heard from Terel and Divee?"

"Ay Cap't, they radioed that Divee had pulled as much equipment and data as possible. T'were heading back a few minutes ago," Gon said.

Vas nodded and stared into the dark looking for them. This place was dead. Very cold and very dead. She suddenly didn't want to be there anymore. She rubbed her arms, but the feeling intensified. They needed to leave now.

"Terel? Come in. Where are you?"

"Almost there, Vas. Divee may have found a port system with more data."

The feeling of needing to leave was almost overwhelming. Coldness crept up her gut toward her throat. "Cancel that, get back now. We have to leave." She turned to the others.

"Get ready, Mac. The second they get on board we take off." Another wave of fear overtook her. "Lay in a course straight out as far from this thing and as fast as you can."

"Terel, damn it, where are you and Divee?" Vas refrained from yelling, but she did push Pela and Gon into their seats and double checked that the decom chamber was secured.

"We're here, Vas. What's the hurry?" Terel's headlamp came into view as she spoke.

Vas motioned for them to get in the shuttle. "Can't explain. Just get in and get buckled." She pulled shut the docking door. "Now, Mac." She barely had time to get in her seat before Mac disconnected the link with the ore hauler and blasted off.

They were about three minutes out when an explosion slammed into them and sent the shuttle into a spin.

CHAPTER SIXTEEN

"Mac, were we hit?" Vas yelled into the comm as debris and loose equipment bounced around the shuttle. She'd gotten everyone secured, just not all of the packs. Luckily, the important things were locked down. It would still be damn useless if she or one of her crew got knocked out from an unsecured scanner. "And get us stable!" A pulling on her harness told her that the inertial dampers were off as well.

"I'm trying!" Mac yelled back. "We weren't hit directly, at least not by anything big. This is from the explosion." A second later the spinning stopped.

Vas pulled on her harness. Some of the pressure was still there, but it was returning to normal.

"How did you know that was going to happen?" Terel sat across from Vas, and it was clear the doctor was itching to do a full examination on her to find out that very answer for herself.

"I didn't know it was going to explode." Even as she said it aloud, Vas knew she had known. Not exactly what was going to happen, but that something was. Specifically, something very bad was going to happen. Far stronger than her normal gut instincts, this was almost a command. Which was almost as disturbing as the fact that they'd been three minutes away from being space dust.

"I did know something was wrong," she finally admitted both to herself and to Terel. "I have no idea how, but in those last few minutes I knew something was horribly wrong."

"Maybe you've been hanging around Deven too much and it's catching," Terel said. After a few moments, she laughed. "I'm kidding. Telepathic abilities aren't contagious."

"I know that."

"Right. Then why did a look of terror flash across your face?"

Terel had her there. However, there was no way in hell she was going to discuss the disaster of last night with anyone, not even her best friend. She didn't want to know what secrets lurked in others' brains. Ever.

She gave Terel a shrug. "Anyway, somehow I picked up on something. I just knew we had to get out. Call it highly honed skills of too many battles." She flipped open her comm. "I presume the ore hauler is destroyed?"

"Yup." Mac's distracted voice indicated he was still fighting the shuttle over something. But he was too good of a pilot to let it win.

"Are we going to have to call for someone to come get us? Or is it fixable?"

"Captain! It's always fixable." Mac was clearly insulted that she would even imply such a thing. "I have never lost a ship yet and I don't plan on doing so. We should be ready to rendezvous with the *Warrior Wench* in a few—" A pinging cut him off. "Hello, what's this?"

"Mac? Was that an alarm?" Vas was ready to take her chances with the shuttle's internal stability and remove her straps to go to the front when he took too long to respond.

She was just loosening her buckles when he came back on the speaker.

"Sorry there. We've got a visitor who wants to make sure we're all right. She's asking if we need help." Mac laughed at something only he could see. "And I'd say let this lady help me anytime."

Another sense of foreboding hit Vas, this motivated by knowing Mac's taste in women. "Is it a pretty brunette with an odd accent?" The woman who had ordered the dead man to charge the *Warrior Wench* hadn't said she wasn't in the area, just that she couldn't get here in time.

"Ah, you know me too well, Captain." Mac said. "She said she can pick us up—"

"Cut communications with her. Now." Vas unbuckled the restraints, and then made her way to the command portion of the shuttle. The heavy boots in the suit kept her stable, but the systems clearly weren't working properly. It took her longer than intended to get to the front.

Mac turned toward her from the pilot's chair. The screen was still up but the volume cut off. The face growing more animated in her silent speech was the woman who had ordered the dead man to attack her ship.

"I said cut the connection. And get a hold of Deven. I want the *Warrior Wench* here as soon as possible. Do we have any maneuverability in this bucket at all?"

Mac rocked back in his seat as she reached forward and cut the contact with the woman. "She's just trying to help."

"Get Deven now." Vas tapped the dark screen. "That woman sent a message to the corpse on that hauler, a message as to where we would be. And she called us by name."

Mac winced, but called up Deven. Vas started speaking as soon as her second-in-command appeared.

"Deven, there's a ship closing in on us. They were the ones who sent that ore hauler on its attack vector and most likely the ones who just detonated it. I need you to get here now."

"That ship is closing in on you too fast. We won't make it in time if they decide to go after you. You'll be in weapons range in less than five minutes." She heard him bark commands, but she knew his judgment on ship abilities was never off. If he thought they couldn't get there in time, they couldn't.

"Jakiin and I have two of the Furies up and ready to fly. A Flit wouldn't hold against that cruiser closing in on you, but they might."

She swore to herself. She didn't trust those rusting antiques, but judging from the information she was gathering on the cruiser heading toward them, he was right. The *Warrior Wench* only had eight of the small fighter Flit ships onboard, and that wouldn't be enough to go after a cruiser.

"I hate to say this, but go ahead. Have the *Warrior Wench* close in as quickly as she can, but get those rust buckets of yours out here."

"Aye. Hang on, we're coming." Deven cut off, leaving Vas to stare at the ship closing in. The flashing red comm light indicated the cruiser was still trying to contact them.

"Captain, are you sure that's the woman who ordered the attack?" Mac said his hand far too close to the flashing comm button for Vas's comfort.

Reaching around him, she turned the comm to deny and the flashing stopped. "Yes, I'm sure. I know it shocks you to learn this, but beautiful women can be evil too. I saw her and heard her. She knew where we were going to be and when." Folding her arms, she glared at him as she saw his hand twitching toward the button.

"I know beautiful women can be evil. I work for you don't I?" Mac's face flashed red the instant the words were out of his mouth. "Not that you're evil, or that I think you're beautiful. I mean you are, beautiful that is, but I don't think of you that way."

Vas laughed at his attempt to save himself in spite of the situation. "I think you should just shut up now. Don't worry, I know what you mean. Or rather what you are attempting to mean. Have Deven and Jakiin launched yet?"

Mac gave an audible sigh of relief as he turned to the console. His fingers flew over the keyboard and an image of the two Furies heading toward them appeared.

"Excellent." Vas stayed back.

The Furies took up position in front of the shuttle. After a few more minutes Mac got the shuttle's systems back up. The cruiser was just entering target range. First one Fury, then the second fired up weapon systems. The cruiser reduced speed, but didn't stop. Nor did she fire up her weapons.

Vas let out a breath. She had no worries of the *Warrior Wench's* ability to keep that cruiser in its place, but she really didn't want to see if the two Furies could take it down.

After a few tense moments, both Furies powered down their weapons.

"Deven, what the hell are you doing? Just because she's not flashing weapons doesn't mean she's not planning on it," Vas yelled at her second in command. "She's still moving forward in case you hadn't noticed."

Deven's face appeared on their screen, the odd-looking Fury pilot equipment closing in around him. "I know that. I also know who she is. She wants to meet on the *Warrior Wench*. Can the shuttle move now?" There was a tone in his voice, one that told Vas she wasn't going to be happy. Not that she was already. How in the hell did Deven know and trust someone who'd sent a bomb after her ship?

"We're not meeting anywhere. I heard her issue orders to the idiot flying that hauler, orders that mentioned us and told him to get to us first. Yes, this shuttle can fly, but I'm not turning my back on her."

The lead Fury, most likely Deven, pulled back closer to the shuttle. He often did that, his piloting mimicking what he would do if he were standing there. "Vas, I trust her." There was an almost palatable pain in his voice and face now. "I don't want to discuss it over the air. I don't know how secure these things are given the current situation. However, I trust her at this point. We need to hear what she has to say."

Vas let an army of swear words tumble around her head before she spoke. The question was did she still trust Deven? As pissed as she was at him, the answer still was the same—she did. She wasn't happy about it, but she trusted him in matters of the ship and crew. "Damn it, Deven, you and I are going to have a very long conversation when this is over. Escort her in. I want you and Jakiin on either side of that cruiser. Blow her out of the sky if she steps one toe out of line, friend or not." Vas nodded toward Mac. "We'll come in from behind." Not that the shuttle had any weapons to speak of, nothing that would even make a cruiser think twice. However, Vas didn't want that damn ship behind her.

Both men knew better than to argue at this point. Deven silently moved with Jakiin into flanking positions, and Mac fired up the engines to follow the cruiser in. Vas was satisfied, or almost. She flipped open a comm to the *Warrior Wench*. "Gosta, get a small security detail to the docking bay. Deven and Jakiin will be followed in by a shuttle off that cruiser. Make sure it only has one life form on it and that it docks in the security section. Escort our guest to my ready room and keep her there."

"Aye, Captain," Gosta responded. If he wanted to ask more, he managed to hold back his curiosity.

With a final glare at Mac just because he needed it, Vas went back and resumed her seat.

The flight back was brief, and her crew stayed out of her way to the command deck. Since they followed everyone else in, Vas was the last one to get to her ready room. Deven, Gosta, and the striking brunette were all chatting quite comfortably by the time she got in.

Luckily none of them had dared to take her seat. With a nod to the two men and a glare at the woman, Vas slid into her spacious chair. She took her time getting settled, then turned toward the woman.

"So do you want to tell me why you ordered that corpse in my hold to charge my ship?"

The woman's smile made her even more mind-numbingly beautiful. Vas could see she would get whatever she wanted from men, or women who fancied women, regardless of the species.

"Well, Vas—might I call you Vas?"

"Captain Tor Dain will be fine."

Again the flash of beauty, this time in a nod and grin. "Understood. Captain Tor Dain. I think you misunderstood my command. Although to be honest, I'm not sure if the person you found was my man Ghassil. I'd like to check the body if I could?" Something must have shown on Vas's face for she sat back a bit. "In a while then. Once you've heard me out."

"Why don't we start with who you are and why you knew where this ship was? We're a registered mercenary ship in case you hadn't noticed. Last time I checked our travel paths are private." Which was one of the few benefits of being a legit mercenary instead of one of the rogue ones. The rogues got more money, but they also ran the risk of the Commonwealth smacking them down like a fly. Moreover, there was no protection of their movements.

Deven leaned forward. "Actually, I'd like to make the introductions if I could. Vaslisha Tor Dain, this is Marli. We've been friends for a very long time." He paused, looking carefully at the woman. "Over one hundred years."

"What? She's like you?" Vas reached for the blaster in her desk out of instinct, but held off grabbing it. *Crap, another long-lived telepath?*

"It's okay, Captain. I'm not like Deven, and I assure you I'm not a telepath. And in a way, we have met." Her grin was softer, more real than before. "Or at least I've met your blood."

Vas rocked back in her chair and studied the ceiling for a few seconds. Well, she'd wanted to know about Deven's mysterious friend, hadn't she? She just hadn't realized it would be a beautiful woman with a command cruiser and a rampaging ore hauler.

"You're the one who gave me the antidote to wipe out the last of the poison and found those trackers. Thank you." Vas nodded to the woman. "But that still doesn't address your man trying to ram a highly modified ore hauler into the side of this ship."

Marli steepled her fingers in front of her face as if weighing what to say. "He wasn't trying to charge your ship; he was trying to stop the ore hauler. It was automated with some program we couldn't crack, he intended to find out who had rigged it, why, and if he couldn't disconnect the command, to destroy it. He'd been on it for the past three days trying to find those things out. I last spoke to him thirty-two hours ago. He never answered my last hails."

Vas got up and paced. Sitting and thinking didn't go together for her. "How did you find out about it, and why wouldn't you just warn us?" She turned to Deven, "Did you know about this?"

He shrugged and raised his hands. "Not until I opened the comm and ordered her to back off when I was in that Fury." He turned to his friend. "They fly very well by the way."

Vas swore. "They came from her too?"

"I'm glad." Marli beamed a smile that bounced around the room. "I figured if anyone could get them running you could. Although I do admit I didn't think they were going to be used against me."

"If you had told me you were now in possession of a command cruiser I would have been more prepared. That happened recently I assume? Or did you just have it waiting for you?"

Vas watched the banter then raised her voice. "Okay, back on track, folks. Original question, how did you know where we were and what that ore hauler had planned?"

"I was tracking you." If she was embarrassed at all about her actions, Marli certainly didn't show it; her warm brown eyes were sincere. "Those blood trackers are easy to follow if one knows how." She raised a hand as both Deven and Vas spoke at once. "Your blocking is working. Whoever the person is who got them into your bloodstream, they can't sense you. I can because I coded to them when Deven brought them to me."

Vas seriously thought about getting that blaster after all. As if her life wasn't messed up enough at this point she had this woman to deal with?

Luckily, even Deven didn't look happy about that. Maybe he didn't completely trust this exotic woman.

"Marli, you didn't tell me—"

"I know I didn't, darling." She cut him off with a pat on his cheek, as if he were no more than a child. "But sometimes I have my own reasons." A delicate frown crept across her face. "However, I really need to see if the body you have brought back is my man. He was a good person." For a brief moment Vas thought she saw sorrow and an age far older than this woman could possibly be. It vanished in an instant.

"I still need answers." Vas folded her arms and leaned forward. "Whoever you are, you're following us, or me, for some reason. According to you, someone else was as well, and they were the ones behind the attack."

"Yes. Can we see the body now?" Marli rose so gracefully Vas could have sworn she floated to her feet.

Deven rose as well. "I hate to say this, Vas, but you might as well talk and walk. She's even more stubborn than you." He rolled his eyes and slid open the door.

"Trust me, I know how stubborn both of you are, let's just go see the body. Marli can fill us in as we walk."

Vas thought about arguing, but she wanted to know who the dead man was as well. Instead she left the room, and then dropped back to Gosta. "Can you stay up here on the deck? I don't think her crew would try anything with her on board, but I don't completely trust her. She's not telling us anything."

Gosta nodded, and then ambled over to the command chair. "I'll call you if anything interesting happens."

Vas smiled then caught up to the other two. "Now, about why you were following us?"

"She is tenacious, isn't she? Reminds me of a younger you." Marli's comment was for Deven, but her smile was for Vas. "Or a very much younger me." She studied Vas for a few moments while they waited for the lift.

"Very well, if you are like me you'll want it blunt. You deserve that much. Someone poisoned you with the drell, yet another someone wanted to track you through your blood. Both are extremely rare and unusual things by themselves, together they are unheard of. I wanted to see who was trying to make you a pawn and who was trying to remove you from the game." She tossed back her long hair and leaned against the wall of the lift as it lumbered down to the med level.

"About a week ago, not too long after Deven left, I heard rumor of a stolen ore ship. Actually one of the pirates living on the same rock I was visiting got stone drunk and was bragging about his latest job. Stupid idiot fell into my lap telling me he'd programmed an ore ship to go after some silly brothel barge and had been paid obscenely for the job." She gave a light shrug of her slender shoulders. "I broke his neck after he told me all he could."

Vas was the only one surprised by the comment. Marli looked like a pampered aristocrat, but those delicate hands and heart were obviously much harder.

"After I found out the trajectory, I called up the *Scurrilous Monk*, my ship's name by the way, do you like it?" The switch from cold, matter-of-fact killer to proud ship momma was swift.

"It's unique, I'll say that. Do I even want to know how you got that name passed through?" Deven laughed as he led them off the lift.

"Probably not, but I do love the name. Reminds me of old friends." The vicious grin that followed made Vas almost want to ask for the story behind it.

She did find herself laughing along with Marli. She couldn't help it. The woman was even more outrageous than she was. "Okay, I like the name. But if you could get your man on the ore hauler, why didn't you just shut it down?" Actually she knew the answer, probably the same reason she didn't blow it out of the sky when she first found out about it.

"I needed to know who was behind it. Well, I wanted to know. The idiot in the bar was useless even before I snapped his neck. The programming on that hauler was highly detailed. There was no way to shut it down short of blowing it up. At least no way we could tell from the outside. Ghassil was my weapons expert. He thought he could find a way to disarm it. The rest you know." Marli halted before the med lab doors, almost hesitant to go in.

"Maybe it's not him?" Vas asked with a gentleness that even surprised her.

Marli flashed a sad grin, and then pushed open the lab doors. "I'd like to think that, but I can't see how he could have gotten off of it. The ship picked up speed the day after he got onboard and I couldn't catch up."

Deven had already called Terel, so she had the decon room up and running. She was in a full safe suit on the inside, the blackened husk clearly on display.

Marli walked up to the window, and pressed one hand wide against the pane. She held it for a few seconds then turned back to them. "It's him."

Vas moved forward to get a look at the man who'd died trying to save her ship. Most of him was a blackened husk. Terel would be able to tell more after the autopsy, but his cause of death was destructive whatever way he died.

Terel was slowly peeling his uniform off, when a flash of fabric caught Vas's eye. She tapped the glass to get Terel's attention, and then finally found the room comm. "Hold up a second. What's that patch?"

The man's arm was mostly burned through, but his upper shoulder was relatively untouched. An elongated diamond symbol filled the fabric on most of his upper arm.

"Deven, look at his arm." Vas pulled him forward, as Marli turned to look as well. The frown marking her lovely face indicated that the uniform wasn't hers.

"That looks like the one on the vid." Deven shook his head. "But that man was taller."

"What man?" Marli turned back. "What is that? Ghassil left my ship wearing one of my uniforms. That's not it."

"Terel, can you bring in a scanner? Get as close to that patch as you can."

She frowned at Vas. "It would be just as easy to take it off. I'm not going to autopsy his clothing." With a small knife, Terel carefully removed the patch. "Let it go through a complete sonic cleansing. I still don't know what he died of or what that weird air inside the ore ship was."

"How long?" Vas could see something was going on between Deven and Marli. The brunette might have been telling the truth that she wasn't a telepath, but she was communicating with Vas's second-in-command somehow.

"Now." A small ding came from the left of the windowpane, and a sealed packet popped out with the patch, newly purified, inside. Deven grabbed it and put it in one of his inner pockets.

"Wow, didn't that take a few hours on the *Victorious Dead*?" Vas hated that this ship could do so much more, but the fact was, the flouncy thing was loaded.

Terel's sigh said she didn't like speaking ill of the *Victorious Dead* either. "Yes, it did. However, these systems are state of the art. Now do you three need anything else?"

Vas took the hint and started herding the other two toward the lift. "No. Just make sure to prepare the body for burial. He'll be going back with his captain."

Marli didn't say anything, but she caught Vas's eye and nodded her thanks.

CHAPTER SEVENTEEN

Vas let Gosta stay in command until the next shift change. She also let Deven go say good-bye to his friend. Marli hadn't been able to find the answers to any of her questions, so she decided to take her dead crewman home.

A light rap on her ready room door instead of the usual buzz pulled Vas out of her thoughts. She wasn't one for introspection or deep study. One of the reasons that even though she liked science, she wasn't very good at it. She preferred to go in, take charge, and blow up whoever or whatever needed to be blown up.

"Come in."

She closed her computer screen when Deven entered. Along with pondering the pile of crap her life was becoming she had been looking for another merc job. Deven had suggested they wait until they knew more of what was going on.

Vas wanted a job to keep her mind off things.

"Interesting friend you have there." Vas nodded toward the seat in front of her. As pissed as she still was at him for his actions of the night before, she couldn't stay mad. Not with everything else in her life going to hell. He was the closest thing she had to a true confidant, even closer in some ways than Terel. She'd pocket away that anger at him until life became normal again.

Deven took the seat and leaned back into it with a sigh and closed his eyes. For the first time in the years she'd known him, he actually appeared tired.

"That's one way to put it." He kept his eyes closed.

"Want to tell me where you met her? Or why she knows about more dead race shit than even you do?"

Deven rubbed his forehead and temples with the heels of his hands. "I was afraid you might wonder about that." After a pause he opened his eyes and leaned forward.

"I have to tell you something. Something that you may or may not believe and something that could get both of us killed instantly if it got out." He studied her face, almost as if he was looking for answers. Or something else. Finally he made up his mind.

"Marliress is an Asarlaí."

Vas burst out laughing before she noticed his face had gone still. "You're kidding. Come on, Deven. Don't mess with me right now. I have no idea what in the hell you are, because you won't tell me. Nevertheless, you'll tell me that your sweet little brunette friend is a member of an ancient super race? An ancient, *dead*, super race, I might add?" She reached into her desk drawer and grabbed a flask of Hydriang fire ale. Holding up her hand to stop him from speaking, she took a deep swig. The burn down her throat felt numbingly good. "Okay, explain."

"This is serious, Vas. Marli is immortal. She's been around for over ten thousand years."

She studied his face for a few minutes, then sighed and took another long burning drag of her flask. Damn, half of it was gone already. She set it down carefully.

"I have had a month taken from me, my ship stolen, been poisoned, and people are dropping out of the sky in ships I sure as hell have never seen. I have mysterious fused bodies appearing in my hold. And Starchaser parts that will be a slow death for any of us if we're caught with them." She rose and stood in front of him, then grabbed his face with both hands, peering deep into those fathomless green eyes. "Do not add to my problems."

"Vas—"

She shook his head. "No. Don't do it. I seriously have no idea what is really going on with you and your friend. I'm thinking I don't want to know." She moved his head up and down in forced agreement with her, then let go and patted his cheek before making her way back to her chair. There was one happy point: the odd physical pull toward Deven was gone now. Her new sport of extreme drinking probably had something to do with it.

"I don't want to know." She drained the flask. Very odd, it used to hold so much more than that. "I think you should go do whatever it is you should be doing. Let Gosta keep us on course for wherever it is we have to drop Mac's shit at." She bent down to rummage through her desk for anything else flammable. Thank goodness she'd stocked her ready room when she first moved in. It was good to have priorities.

"You're still here." She popped her head back up from her rummaging and glared at Deven. Somehow in her searching she'd ended up on the floor. She narrowed her eyes. "I told you to stay away from me. Before was different, you had to be here. Now you don't."

"You're getting drunk." Deven scowled. "And you're on the floor."

"Yes, I am on the floor. And no, I am already drunk. No 'getting' involved." She leaned against the wall behind her desk. "Except for you getting out of here. Now."

Deven waited to see if she would change her mind. When all she did was continue pulling on her new flask, he gave up and let himself out. Vas drank for entertainment, never out of some emotional need. At least she never had until now. He really hoped what happened the night before hadn't compounded this new drinking binge. He hadn't been lying when he'd said he had been pulled in as much as her.

Shaking off his thoughts, he nodded toward the command chair. "Gosta, make sure no one bothers the captain when the shift changes. She's still in there, but it won't be pretty if someone disturbs her."

"Aye, Deven. I'll make sure the next watch understands." Gosta unfolded himself out of the chair and caught Deven in two strides. "I thought you might want to know that your friend's ship tagged us before she went to hyperspace. I took the liberty of ordering a team to go disengage the bug, but haven't sent them out yet."

What are you up to, Marli? That she was following them for altruistic reasons either now, or a few days ago when she put her crewman on that death ship didn't even cross his mind. Marli was pure Asarlaí, regardless of how many decades she'd gone without seeing any of her kind. Asarlaí saw altruistic behavior as weak. Still, having her know where they were might come in handy.

"Wait on that." Deven motioned Gosta closer. There were only two other crewmembers on deck right now, but a small crew spread gossip all the faster. "Keep an eye on it, and an eye out for her ship. I want to see what she's up to. Just don't let any of the others know, especially the captain."

Gosta pulled back, and shook his head violently. "I can't—"

"She's under a lot of pressure right now. Trust me." He glanced back to Vas's ready room. "It's for the best."

Gosta's face gave the most hints of his mixed heritage when stressed. Right now he looked like one of the long thin bugs his distant ancestors evolved from. He cast a furtive look at Vas's ready room, and for a moment Deven feared he might have asked too much.

Taking a deep breath, Gosta turned back to face him. "Aye, Deven. Things have been weighing on her. She protects us. It's right we protect her sometimes." With a nod he strode back to the command chair and settled back in.

Deven allowed himself a sigh. Maybe breathing room and a few secrets were all he could do for Vas at this point, but he had to do something. Satisfied that Vas would stay undisturbed in her room—she sure as hell wasn't coming out for a while on her own—he went to his ready room. He'd borrowed a high-end data scanner from Gosta, but hadn't had a chance to look at the film they stole from the space station's security.

Actually he'd forgotten about it.

That was a disturbing thought. He didn't forget things. Ever. That was a problem for someone as long lived as himself; over four hundred plus years he had more than enough things he'd like to forget. However, nothing ever got lost, drifted away, forgotten.

Until now.

Pulling out the chip containing the stolen data from his comm, he opened the scanner and dropped it in. The images were clear and crisp, a welcome sight after the muddy mess he'd viewed in the station. Whatever was wrong with the machines back on the station at least it wasn't on the recording end.

He watched as Vas came around the corner, noticing that she wasn't paying attention at all when the tall man ran into her.

Vas was always on watch.

Deven replayed the scene again. It hadn't been clear in the station, but her look was one of content obliviousness. She had plenty of time to move before the man hit her, but she hadn't been paying attention.

He followed Vas's gaze—she was looking right at the faint outline of a tall, slender glowing form. While he'd seen the outline before, he hadn't been able to tell what it was. He also didn't see that Vas was looking right at the shimmering form. That she had been as surprised as he to

see it when they were at the station was almost as
disturbing as the image.

Swearing under his breath, Deven adjusted the clarity.
The image was impossible to focus on, almost as if it
hadn't really been there. With even more creative swear
words, Deven tried a few more filters. He stopped
swearing in shock when the image finally cleared. It was
a hologram. It would have been visible to anyone in the
area, but on film it was ghostly.

It was an Asarlaí.

And it wasn't Marli.

CHAPTER EIGHTEEN

Deven seriously contemplated joining Vas in her ready room and getting brain-killing drunk. He knew what Asarlaís looked like even before Marli's little peepshow at her home. His people were possibly the only ones left in the galaxy who had accurate images of the true Asarlaís.

As far as he knew, and as far as Marli stated, she was the last Asarlaí left.

Fussing with the image didn't help any. It was clearly an impossibly tall and skinny man, with long silver hair, and faintly glowing red eyes.

He couldn't decide which was worse, the fact that there could be another one of them alive, or that Vas was staring at the image like a long-lost lover. If that man who slammed into her hadn't done so at that moment, he had a nasty feeling she might have tried to approach the hologram.

There was nothing more he could tell about the hologram, at least not now. If he trusted Marli, he'd contact her and ask her.

Since that wasn't an option, or at least not one he was ready to deal with yet, he turned his focus on the young man with navigational issues. Human or one of the human offshoots. Probably about Mac's age but shorter. Stocky build, thatch of black hair flying behind him as he ran. He was looking back and forth between something out of range behind him, and a small object in his hand. Unfortunately, neither were clear on the vid.

The flight suit was unique though. Dark blue and skin tight, the badges on the arms were like nothing he'd seen before. The main one was the elongated diamond shape they'd pulled off Marli's crispy crewman. He pulled out the patch from the dead crewman, and blew up the image on the scanner as far as it could go.

He didn't need the computer system to tell him the two were a perfect match.

The edges weren't solid, but marked to look like it had been carved out of glass instead of fabric. The one in his hand, although purified by the ship's systems, was smoky from whatever had charred the crewman. However, he could still see the image on the stiff fabric.

Focusing in, he managed to capture a clean shot from the man on the vid. The language on the badge wasn't one he was familiar with, but running a computer search would translate it.

The language wasn't Asarlaí. Deven let out a breath in relief at that.

The language on the badge belonged to an obscure outer rim world. Mostly kept to themselves. Separatists that wanted to pretend they weren't part of the Commonwealth, but kept using their services nonetheless.

The home planet was called Rilliania. Population hovering around four million on a planet large enough to handle far more. Deven frowned as more information came up on the screen. Their population had faced a huge boom in the last hundred years. Usually that indicated a major change in tech, but if the Rillianians had such a surge they weren't telling anyone.

He wasn't surprised when a scan of the crew database revealed no one from Rilliania. He'd never met anyone from there, and the reports listed them as extremely planet bound. Hard to meet a people if they won't let anyone on their world nor come off it themselves. He scanned again to see what races or cultures had contact with the Rillianians.

He rocked back in his seat, surprised and hopeful as the screen flashed the only outside race the Rillianians allowed on their world. Wavians. Out of all of the peaceful, calm, helpful races available in the Commonwealth, this neurotically isolated world only made contact with one of the most vicious species in the Commonwealth.

Flarik had been in hibernation since they'd left the Tarantus IV station almost two weeks ago. While he was certain this wasn't as long of a sleep as the moody lawyer had been hoping for, it should be enough to keep teeth in check when he woke her up. Had they actually fought on Lantaria, she would have been woken long before this anyway.

He loaded the information he had on the badge into a panel and left his room.

He stopped short for an instant when he saw the next shift was already in place. Had he really been in there that long? Gosta should have had a few more hours. He nodded at Nariel sitting in the command chair. "She still in there?" He asked with a nod toward Vas's shut ready room door.

Nariel bowed her head slowly. The mind doc was a Silante and every movement was languorous and graceful. "Aye, or at leassst according to Gosssta ssshe isss." Her grin revealed tiny perfect fangs. "I haven't sseen her come out."

"Excellent." Deven made his way across deck to the lift. "I recommend you not let anyone in to disturb her. No calls either." He tapped the comm clipped to his hip. "If you need me call my private comm." He turned as the lift doors opened. "Oh and I'd advise everyone to stay clear of her if she does come out."

Nariel gave a low chuckle. She wasn't afraid of Vas, one of a few crewmembers who wasn't. However, she did find her captain's antics amusing.

"I'll look forward to it then." With a wink, she turned back to watching the screen in front of her.

The late shift was sparsely manned, so there was no other crew out and about. Low-level floor lights guided him down the crew quarters into the furthest corner. Flarik must be very happy with the *Warrior Wench*; she'd not been able to get as far away from the rest of the crew as she'd wanted when she'd joined them on the *Victorious Dead* five years ago. However, this ship had far more crew room than their missing one. Deven walked past empty quarters for a good minute before he hit her room. Flarik said that the noise from the regular crew was distracting for her hibernation. Deven knew there was more to it than that. Wavians rarely flew with non-Wavian crewmates for a reason.

The smells of the other races made them think of prey.

There was a popular series of fictional horror vids made of a race not unlike the Wavians who in a half-doze ate the rest of their crew before they even came out of hibernation.

Deven buzzed the external comm once. He figured it might take a while to pull Flarik out of her sleep, but slow and steady awakenings were better than a sudden one. Especially with someone like Flarik.

He almost fell into the room as the door slid back and a confused, but extremely awake, Flarik glared at him. She stuck her head out past him, her long neck extending to clearly see down both ends of the hall. Then she cocked her head and pulled him inside.

Deven tumbled in, his eyes blinking in the dim light.

"Sorry, did not expect a guest," Flarik muttered as she bustled further into her lair. "Lights up." The illumination increased to an easy level.

The room before him was a mess. Wavians preferred cozy, nest-like quarters, so the reconstruction of the original furniture and features wasn't surprising. The condition of the new creation was.

Clothing and fabric from the original furniture was flung all over, bits of fibresteel and plastic littered the floor. Flarik vanished further into the room and came back wearing a heavy green robe. She perched on one of the piles and nodded.

"Why are you here?"

"Are you all right?" It wasn't what he'd intended to ask, nor possibly the best thing to ask a Wavian, even one who'd been his shipmate for five years. But she looked so out of things he was concerned.

Flarik glanced around her quarters with a wince. "Fair question. Very fair question. I believe I am now. But something was wrong, very wrong." Her eyes were bright. "I had a dream, one that penetrated my hibernation. There was an ancient evil on this ship."

Deven set himself down on one of the more solid piles. He didn't think Wavians were telepathic, at least not on a scale he'd ever heard. And when she was in hibernation it took an explosion to wake her. However, something had reached into her mind through that instinctive sleep.

Something at the same time that Marli had been on board.

Carefully making sure no nuances of what was going through his head came out in his words, Deven leaned forward. "Did you see what it was?"

He wasn't careful enough; the shrewd lawyer bobbed her head. "So something did happen. Something, or someone, was on this ship who shouldn't have been."

"A number of things happened while you were asleep." Maybe he could dodge around this, but he knew that somehow she had felt Marli's presence.

Flarik rose to her feet, and rocked back and forth, a hunting stance she used when facing a challenge. "Perhaps so. However this was a unique person." She glared at him as if it was his fault. "I did not dream it."

Wondering where his ability to keep things hidden from others had vanished to as of late, Deven let out a sigh. "No, I don't think you did. There was someone on board." He'd already told Vas, how much worse could it be if Flarik knew? Besides this might be the only way to engage her help on this. "There was a woman on board. An Asarlaí in disguise. Vas knows, but no one else can."

Flarik's golden eyes locked on to him so intently he knew why the fictional horror vids had been so popular. She was terrifying.

"An Asarlaí. Alive. Here."

"It's a long story, but yes—"

"You let one of them aboard this ship?" Flarik started shaking and rocked back until she hit the pile of fabric behind her. In a very un-Wavian movement she tumbled onto the pile and sat there.

He'd never seen any Wavian, much less Flarik, who was unique even for her species, be so visibly unnerved. If he didn't know better he would say the lawyer was terrified.

"Is it gone now?" Her voice was low, her feathered chest rising quickly as she took in short tight breaths.

"Yes, she's left." He debated calling for help, but that would cause problems for both of them. "Are you going to be all right?"

Flarik rocked for a few moments, her eyes shutting slowly as she nodded. However, whether the nodding was toward him or herself he wasn't sure. Finally her outer lids opened followed a few moments later by her inner ones. Her golden eyes were their usual predatory self when she stared at him.

"I was taken off balance by the news that not all of the monsters we thought to have destroyed eons ago are dead." She rose and tightened the robe around her. "I will ask the captain for an extended leave. It is my duty to remove this last beast."

Deven ran his fingers through his hair. This wasn't turning out well.

"Flarik, I understand that the Wavians suffered during the time of the Asarlaí. Many races did. But this one is different. She's working with us."

"She? Is she your mate?"

Deven fought back his initial choked response. "No. However, I have known her for over one hundred years. She has no ill intentions toward your people, or this ship." He hoped. Truth was he trusted Marli to be Marli, nothing more.

Tiny feathers that covered Flarik's head ruffled forward. "Who are you to have known an Asarlaí?" She spit the word out with more venom than a Kjarion pit viper. Clearly the history of the Wavians had not forgotten the Asarlaí.

"That's really too long and convoluted to go into now." He fingered the panel in his pocket next to the patch. He pulled the panel out and held it up. Maybe if he could distract her she'd let things lie for now. "Do you recognize this language?"

Flarik switched to lawyer mode and looked like she wouldn't let the interrogation go, but a chance glance at the image on the panel pulled her attention and she whipped it out of his hand.

"Where did you get this?" If anything, she was more pissed off than she had been about the Asarlaí. "Do you understand what this says? This is blasphemy. Where did it come from?"

Deven pulled out the burnt patch. "From an image of someone wearing a suit with a patch like this."

She hissed and refused to touch the patch even though it was clearly sealed. "The evil came from that. Was the Asarlaí wearing it?"

He put it back in his pocket for safety. "No. However, someone working for her had been wearing it when he flash froze to death. She claimed he hadn't been wearing it when she last saw him." He waited until the feathers on her head settled down. "What does it say?"

She fixed him with a tilted glance, her golden eyes narrowing. "I do not think I like you visiting me, Second." She arched her shoulder to release the tension she'd been holding, and nodded at the panel. "However, it is as you say, for the good of our ship. That badge states that the Asarlaís are gods that shall rise again out of the ashes and resume their place as the godhead. But more disturbing is the language it is in."

"Rillianian?"

"Yes. Which I presume is why you brought it to me. The Rillianians and my people have been compatriots for thousands of years." She nodded slowly. "They stood with us when the Asarlaí atrocities began."

"How much contact with them have your people had recently?"

She flung the panel at him and stomped back to her bathroom. "Not as much as we should have had, that is clear." She quickly came back out completely dressed and perfectly groomed. "I will not hibernate again until this is resolved. The Asarlaí may not have been whom I sensed. However, I will address the issue of her, and you, after we have solved the other issues."

Deven followed her out of her chambers. Middle of the sleep cycle or not, Vas was going to get a wakeup call.

Luckily, it was just Nariel and Divee up on deck when the battle began.

"Stop pounding, or by the goddess I will blow you away through this damn door!" The sound Vas made wasn't really a yell so much as a bellow.

"Captain Tor Dain, it is vital that you open this door. We must speak now." Flarik was calm, or so she appeared. However, Deven saw the feathers down near the base of her neck start to ruffle up. Nariel was studiously engrossed in reviewing the previous day's logs, most likely for about the fifth or sixth time. Divee was starting to take apart a perfectly good console. The thin human was the only one on the ship with almost as much skill as Gosta. Anything he took apart he probably could get back together.

Gosta. The man wouldn't appreciate being wakened hours before his sleep cycle ended, however Deven didn't think he had much of a choice. At this point it was a contest to see whether Flarik would tear the door open before Vas blew a hole in it.

"Nariel, call up Gosta. No, wait. Go get him." At Divee's panicked look he added, "And take Divee with you. Tell Gosta we've an emergency and need him now."

The mind doc looked ready to offer her assistance, then thought better of it and nodded. "Aye, Deven." An instant later she and Divee fled the battleground.

Deven took a deep breath and turned back to the combatants. Right now a drunken merc captain and a pissed-off, sleep-deprived, Wavian lawyer were probably the deadliest combination in this region of space.

The feathers on the back of Flarik's neck were completely up now. "You must take action. It is your duty."

Vas's responding comment was too garbled to hear, but Deven thought it was, "Fuck my duty." He really hoped Gosta got up here quickly. Things were going to get a lot worse if he had to intervene.

"What did you need?"

Deven spun at Gosta's breathless question. Thank god on this ship of drama kings and queens they had Gosta. "Good man." Deven clasped the taller man's shoulder and propelled him toward the captain's ready room.

"Condensed down, we need to get into Vas's ready room. Preferably before she and Flarik destroy the door."

The thin navigator took a deep breath and squared his shoulders. "Aye."

The two combatants were down to snarling at each other in low phrases through the door, so the clicking of his multi jointed legs sounded harsher than usual.

"Captain? It's me, Gosta. Deven and Flarik are very concerned."

Noises came from the ready room, but they were too low for Deven to hear. Gosta however clearly could hear them.

"No, Captain, I don't believe they will go away." More muttered sounds followed by a burst of laughter from Gosta. "No, nor do I think they will drop into a vat of boiling oil, hang themselves, jump out an airlock, or get you more Hydriang ale."

Again the sound of muttering followed, and then Gosta took a step back from the door. With a click it unlocked and slid open. The woman who stuck her head out was not the Vas Deven had left a few hours ago. Her glorious red hair stuck up in haystacks, writing styluses could be seen in two knots hanging off the right side of her head, and the entire left side of her face had weird indentations where she'd clearly lost consciousness at her desk.

"You all have two seconds to get your bony asses in here before I lock it up again." However, it didn't look like she would be doing anything quickly as she slumped against the doorframe.

Gosta helped Vas up and was arranging her at her desk when Deven and Flarik entered. Deven shut the door, after a quick nod toward Nariel and Divee who had trailed Gosta to the bridge. They could resume their normal low-key shift in peace.

Deven immediately went to the small food dispenser in the corner of her ready room. Vas rarely used the one on the *Victorious Dead*, far preferring the galley to the limited supplies found in the ship-wide dispensers. But desperate times called for desperate measures. "One solie, dark." The small box-like machine gave a soft whirl and a cup appeared filled with the pungent brown drink.

"Drink it." Deven sat it down on her desk, and then pulled forward a chair.

She glared at him petulantly.

"You know, it's really hard to take you seriously when you have writing styluses growing out of your head." Deven leaned back in his chair and folded his arms. He wasn't going to even try to get this started until she'd taken the edge off her bender.

Vas glared some more, but she did reach up into the mess of hair with a wince. "Damn." She reached into her desk and pulled out a small signal mirror, then grimaced some more. "I'll drink the damn stuff. But I'll have you know I was perfectly justified in my drinking. My life is filling with unexplainable shit." She took a long sip of the steaming drink, her shoulders lowering as it worked its way into her system. That a stimulant was acting to relax her spoke volumes about her current state. "Shit, by the way, that none of you have helped get rid of."

"I have been in hibernation, Captain." If Flarik was upset about the previous battle of wills, she gave no indication now. Her clawed hands stayed folded neatly in her lap. "However, had I realized what was happening, I would have forgone my sleep."

Gosta fiddled with a flap on his tunic. Finally he glanced up. "I may have found something, but you're not going to like it."

Vas stopped trying to untangle her hair and looked at him from under a chunk of it. "Go on."

"The attack from that ore ship may have been prompted by the monks. I believe that I underestimated the Graylian monks and their puzzle."

If Flarik's neck could have turned a full one hundred and eighty degrees it would have. "What? You've invited Graylian monks on the ship as well?"

"No, of course not. They don't leave their home world…wait, as well as what?" Gosta asked.

Deven winced. "I told her about Marli."

"What?" Vas almost spit out the sip of solie she'd just taken.

"That captain who came to get her crewman? What about her?" Gosta glanced around the room in confusion.

"Why don't we save that for later?" Deven motioned for Gosta to continue and Flarik to sit back in her seat. "Now about the monks and their puzzles?"

"Yes, well…I realized that one of the pieces of our ship wasn't more than a slight nudge off the track to the meeting with Mac's buyer. So, I entered that in as a precursor to the data on the planet for Mac's drop when we left the space station." He leapt to his feet and jerkily paced the small ready room. "It was my fault. I know how seriously the monks take their puzzles. They use normal ones as a test for their initiates on their home planet. But we weren't sure you see—" His earnest face flitted from one to the other; his hands worked themselves into knots. "We didn't know if that was a real Graylian puzzle or simply a fluke. I mean, no one has ever heard of a Graylian puzzle in space." He gave a nervous laugh.

"The idea is insane. Or was. Until now." He deflated back into his chair. "The monks have great penalties for initiates who try to solve it out of order. They view it as cheating." He shook his head in a quick jerking manner. "They have our ship parts in specific locations that follow the initiates puzzle. I was trying to go after the nearest piece, but it wasn't the first in the puzzle. I believe they sent the ore ship after us as a penalty."

Vas threw back her head and laughed, a good sign the solie was working to clear the alcohol out of her system. "Don't be ridiculous. Some planet-bound monks light years from us sent out an ore ship to ram us? We could have blown that ship out of the sky even with its increased speed. The only reason I didn't was because I'm sick of the mysteries around here." She continued to shake her head, only stopping when she saw the looks facing her.

"What? You three really think Graylian monks sent a trap for us. Because we didn't follow their little plan?"

"Yes." Gosta's answer was simple.

Flarik frowned. "I didn't realize Graylian monks were now involved. Clearly my hibernation was at a bad time. I must agree with Gosta. If the monks have set forth one of their puzzles, they will fight any attempt to break it. One must adhere to the proper order."

Deven waited until Vas looked his way, and then just nodded once. If Gosta had found a true Graylian monk puzzle, and the pieces of the *Victorious Dead* were the goals, then he was surprised they'd only sent the ore ship. Graylians were peaceful unless it was anything revolving around their religion.

"Captain, I agree the Graylian puzzle work is important, but I wish to discuss the Rillianians. I don't believe that we can—" Flarik was working up to a full verbal attack when the comm buzzed on the desk.

"Vas, we've got a problem."

Terel's voice was high, a sure sign of stress. Not to mention she was never awake this late, or early, depending on how you looked at it. Vas held up a hand to hold off Flarik and answer Terel. "What is it?"

"Pela just woke me. She was doing an inventory. Blood samples from all of the crew are missing, your blood vials with the trackers are missing, and our corpse is gone."

Vas frowned. "Marli took him back with her."

"Not that one. Someone took the body or bodies we found in the storage room."

CHAPTER NINETEEN

Vas swore and told Terel they'd be down there in a few minutes. Then she folded her arms and glared at Deven. "Any reason to think this wasn't your friend?"

The look that crossed his handsome face told her he'd made the same connection. Hell, he'd probably made it before she did.

"No. I hate to say this, but Marli is involved for her own reasons. I won't speculate at what they are, but I don't think she'd harm this crew."

Vas leapt to her feet. She'd resented the solie he forced on her at first; wallowing in a drunken stupor had been liberating for the first few hours. Now she was grateful. "You don't think she'd hurt this crew? What if you think wrong?"

"Well, she did plant that tracker on the hull." Gosta winced as soon as he said it and pounded his forehead. "I'm sorry, Deven."

"She did what?" Vas couldn't believe this. "And you didn't want me to know?"

"I told Gosta not to tell you because you were busy drowning in a vat of booze." Deven turned and headed out of the room. "It's not hurting anything, and it's better to let her think she got away with that than some of her other tricks."

"Did you know about the body snatching as well?" Vas was going to have to rethink trusting Deven with her ship and crew. What the hell game was he playing?

Flarik stood near the door, her patience clearly thinning. "I understand there is a crisis of sorts in the med lab. If I am needed, I would like to get there before it is time for me to feed." A flash of that mouth full of tiny daggers reinforced her request.

"Agreed." Vas wasn't afraid Flarik would try to make her an entrée, but if she was disturbed enough to make the comment, they really shouldn't keep her waiting.

It took only twenty minutes to catalog all that had been taken. DNA samples from each crewmember were gone. The bodies, Terel was fairly sure there were two, and that they had died in a very similar way as that of Marli's crewman, had been taken so cleanly the protective covering was still intact. The only thing left of them were the files she had hidden deep in her backup computer.

No damage had been done. No one had seen anything. They were just gone.

"When would she have had a chance? You were with her the entire time, right?" At Deven's nod, Vas continued her tirade. "Then how could she have gotten them out?"

"Not in that tiny little suit." Mac winced as Vas smacked him in the back of the head.

"Why are you here again?"

Rubbing the back of his head, Mac frowned. "I was the one who noticed the bodies were gone. I should have some stake in them since I found them, you know."

"You came down to look at the bodies." Vas glanced around. "Okay where is she?" Gosta, Deven, Flarik, and Terel were all she could see but Mac wouldn't have come down here for nothing.

Such a pale face really shouldn't lie. He flashed bright red before he even opened his mouth. "I don't know what you're talking about—"

Vas whapped him in the back of the head again.

"Ouch!" He resumed rubbing his head and took a calculated step back. "Okay, I might have been showing one of the girls—"

This time Terel hit him.

"You're bringing dates to my med labs?"

"What is it with you people and the hitting? No, it wasn't a date. She just said she thought it was cool about the bodies and all and since I found them."

Vas rubbed her forehead. The headache slam back from her bout of drinking was creeping in early. With help from Mac. She'd have to get something from Terel before her brain started leaking out her ears.

"Just go, Mac. Thank you for telling us the bodies were missing. But go." She lifted an eyebrow at Terel's glare. "And I wouldn't suggest using the med lab for show and tell anymore."

Argumentative by nature, Mac opened his mouth to defend himself. Flarik, who had stood back since they got to the med labs, made a clicking noise with her teeth.

Mac was gone an instant later, all protestations gone with him.

Vas caught Flarik's eye and noticed a smile. The Wavian may have more of a sense of humor than she gave her credit for.

Unfortunately, even after Mac left, they didn't come up with any answers. That the Graylian monks were somehow involved was now a certainty. How they managed to trigger an attack against the *Warrior Wench* when she went after a piece out of their ornate order was completely unknown.

Terel was going to pull apart the limited data she had on both the bodies found in the hold and Marli's late crewman to see if there were any connections. Marli clearly took the extra bodies for a reason.

Vas made her way back to her ready room with Deven and Gosta dragging behind. Flarik had given up and returned to her quarters to try and sort things out. Getting her and Gosta together to brainstorm would have been ideal, but she needed to figure things out with the Asarlaí in the equation first. Then she'd work with Gosta and leave that part out.

"So, gentlemen, I believe the question is where do we go from here?" Vas asked as the door slid shut behind Deven.

"I think the same as before. We have to lay low until we get a handle on things." Deven pulled up the most comfortable chair in the small room and threw up his feet. Vas realized he probably hadn't slept in over twenty-four hours. "There are too many players involved." He held up a fist, flinging up fingers as he counted. "Whoever took the ship. Skrankle. Whoever poisoned you. The owners of that fake pub on the space station. Whoever slammed into you." Vas thought he gave her an odd look at that, but he went on quickly, adding his other hand. "Plus, the ambush at Lantaria, the bodies, the Starchaser parts, the ore ship, Marli, Graylian monks, and Rillianian idiots."

"Okay I missed the last one. I assume it has to do with why our erstwhile lawyer was swearing about them under her breath when she left us." Vas frowned. "I thought her people got along with those xenophobic nuts."

She felt a pleasant flush when Deven appeared surprised. That was something that almost never happened.

"How'd you know that?"

Even Gosta was startled but at least he didn't say anything.

"I am the captain, people. It's my job to know who on my crew are friends. I'd always understood those two races were supportive of each other."

Deven ran his fingers through his hair and stretched, fatigue etching a few lines on his face. They'd probably have to wrap this up soon or she'd have him sleeping in her ready room.

"They may have been. But according to Flarik that's not going to last." He pulled out the piece of fabric. "It took some work, but I made a readable copy. Flarik said it's from some Asarlaí-worshiping cult. The Wavians believe the Asarlaí were the worst abominations in the history of the galaxy. She was not pleased that a world her people trades with is worshipping them." He flipped the patch to Vas then got out the panel with the image from the vid.

She studied both for a bit, frowning as she realized he only had the image of the man who hit her, and the patch from his uniform on the panel and not the entire clip. She was going to have to bug him about it when Gosta wasn't around. He didn't need to see any more infighting than he already had.

"Gosta, can you see what, if anything, you can find on this group or cult?" She flipped the panel and saw Flarik's translation on the back. "Use these terms, and stick to connections with the Rillianians."

He stood, taking the panel and patch. "I take it I'm off watch shift again?" He wasn't even paying attention to her answer as he peered at the item in his hands. Clearly he'd be happily ensconced for a few hours.

"Yes, you'll be covered."

The door shut on her last word. To be honest he probably hadn't even heard her.

"Now why in the hell would an Asarlaí want those bodies and the DNA samples?" Vas pushed Deven back into his seat as he attempted to follow Gosta out. He might fall asleep in here, but she needed some answers first. She went to her desk as a thought hit her.

"Hold off on that. Could your friend have done to you what had been done to me? You know, erase those memories?"

"No, of course not. I would have noticed." His comment lost steam as he clearly gave it some thought. His creative swearing told her his answer.

"Two weeks ago I would have said no. Over the years I didn't think of her as an Asarlaí, but more of an equal."

Vas waited but he'd drifted off in thought. "And two weeks ago you realized...?"

"Sorry. I realized how very much she and I aren't equals. She could have wiped my memories with a thought. Hell, she could have had us all help her carry them out." He leaned forward and held his head in his hands. "This isn't good. We need to take that tracker off our hull."

"No, your first instinct was right. This just confirms that she can do whatever she wants." She tapped the computer in front of her. "I did notice one thing though, but I didn't want to mention it in front of the others. The computer in the lab where the bodies were was on. I had its information sent to me, any searches in the last twenty-four hours. Terel's too fastidious, and none of her people would have left it running."

"I didn't even see you do it."

"See? Not all of us need pretty mind tricks to pull something." She flicked up the transfer information as Deven came around behind her. "Hmm, the ship's systems? Why would she pull up...hello?" Vas froze as a series of screens unfolded to reveal an entirely unknown system running in the ship, directly below the hold where the body and Starchaser parts had been found. She clicked around until the entire system schematics spread out before her. "A particle mover."

"What?" Deven leaned forward, and then pulled back with a deep breath. "Oh. One of those."

Vas spun on him. "What do you mean, 'one of those'? They're completely theoretical. Something that can take apart things, weapons, people, anything, and mash them into the tiniest of molecules, then send them from one place to another? That only gets a 'one of those'?" She folded her arms and glared. "I suppose your people use them all of the time. Whoever they are."

The look on Deven's face made it clear he didn't want to discuss his people. However, he obviously recognized this highly secret bit of tech. The inner circle of the Commonwealth council might be used to the concept; normal merc captains certainly weren't. And their seconds shouldn't be.

Without answering her, Deven reached around her and began flipping through the screens. His look grew darker the more he saw.

"Damn it, what is it?"

He tapped the screen with a frown. "That thing is fully functional. And it also has Rillianian writing on it."

CHAPTER TWENTY

Vas swore as Deven pointed out the various components. It was carefully hidden but they would have found it eventually.

The system was informally called a particle mover. A bureaucrat with no imagination named it ten years ago when the rumors about such a machine started. Vas shuddered. There was no way anyone was going to tell her that was safe.

Now as a weapon it had potential: aim it at your enemy, move their particles, and just don't reassemble.

"I recognize that look," Deven said. "You're planning world domination again."

She laughed in spite of herself. "Not exactly. I already have a world. Now, galaxy domination might be interesting." She tapped the screen. "I think they are missing a hell of an application. Make it smaller, more mobile, broaden the beam? A dream weapon."

"Wouldn't work, at least not yet." Deven went back to his seat and settled in. "Yes, my people do have something very similar, and no, they haven't been able to make it mobile or have a broader range."

"Pity." She sighed and shut down the screen. She'd let her eggheads play with it; she had enough of them on the ship she might as well use them. Personally she couldn't see a big use for it unless they wanted to move the

Starchaser parts off ship. Most likely the particle mover was as contraband as the Starchaser parts. Even using it would end them up with far too much Commonwealth attention.

"Why aren't they after us?" she said out loud as her thoughts wandered.

"Who? I think we have enough people after us right now, don't you?" Deven leaned back and shut his eyes.

"The Commonwealth." Vas threw a stylus at him but he batted it away without opening his eyes. "Come on, *this* is a pleasure cruiser? Currently under ownership by a mercenary crew and it just happened to have come loaded with Starchaser parts as well as top-secret tech?"

"Un-huh." Deven didn't open his eyes. "They don't know. Or the parts and tech weren't theirs. Or they can't touch us."

She looked up sharply at his last comment. "What do you mean they can't touch us?"

"I don't know, Vas." His voice was fading; he wasn't even trying to stay awake anymore. "But they didn't even check out Lantaria. One of their worlds was attacked and no one came. What does that tell you?"

She thought about it. Honestly, she'd briefly thought about it before, but it was usually a good thing when the Commonwealth wasn't shoving its protuberance into everyone's business. Now that she thought about it, there were fewer visits to distant planets and ships listed in the Commonwealth databank in the last few months. Less red tape for getting things approved if it meant a bureaucrat was going to have to leave the inner planets.

"What does it mean?"

"I have no idea." His words were so slurred she didn't even know if he got them all out.

"Fine." She rocked back in her chair. Damn, she wanted to ask him about the video but he was done for. Granted, he had the disgusting ability to sleep anywhere. She swore there had been times in war zones he not only slept standing up but he also never dropped his weapon. But even he had limits.

Which left her alone with her thoughts. Not a place she liked to visit often.

The buzz of the comm saved her from an extended trip.

"What ya need?" She probably scared the hell out of whoever was calling. For some reason her crew didn't like it when she was bored.

"Captain, ah, Gosta wanted me to tell you that before he went down to his lab he programmed the nav system to head for Mnethe V. He said we have a drop?" Xsit chirped. Usually Vas felt the small Xithinal was too perky for first shift, but being as she herself was wide-awake it didn't bother her this time.

"Great. What is our ETA? Oh, can you notify Mac and Jakiin and tell them to get their delivery ready? This is their baby."

"Aye, Captain." Xsit trilled her version of a polite laugh. "We should make orbit in less than an hour."

Vas studied her sleeping second-in-command. Left alone, he could probably get a good few hours nap. She debated waking him as payback for bringing Marli into this. However, he just looked so damned sweet in that chair.

She really was getting too soft.

"Go ahead and have Klaxitia oversee Mac and Jakiin's prep. Deven's out of commission for a bit."

Xsit signed off.

Which left Vas with the chore of who was going to go down planet-side for the trip. With a sigh she pulled up Mac's original list. He, Jakiin, and Bathie. The sigh grew heavier.

She flicked open a private comm to Gosta. "How's the search going?"

"I still haven't found anything. There is a lot of information to sift through. This will take time, Captain, you can't believe that—"

"Easy there, Gosta." Vas laughed. "I'm not checking on your progress."

"Thank goodness, I will be able to find—"

"I'm calling you off your search for a bit."

"Captain? I thought this was a priority?" He sounded like a small child whose favorite toy had been yanked from his grasp.

"This should just take a few hours. I need someone to ride shotgun on Mac's little trading adventure and Deven's out cold. I want you to go down instead of Jakiin. I don't trust him and Mac together. Take Divee and the triplets too. They can help move the product faster." Vas sat back and ran over her modifications to Mac's original plan. The drop seemed straightforward. There was no reason for any of her more serious people to go along.

"Aye, Captain." The annoyance at being removed from his beloved research was lessened. "I completely understand. I don't trust them either. Does Jakiin know he's not going?"

"Nope, you get to tell him. Mac too. They should both be moving their stock down to the landing bay."

"Aye. I'll call if there's a problem."

Vas smiled as she cut the call. Gosta wasn't happy, but he was the best person for the job. Even though this should be a simple drop and run, Vas didn't trust simple things anymore.

Vas was in the gym exorcising some demons when Xsit patched in a call from the planet. About time. They'd gone down three hours ago, and even with the wanderings that often followed these types of jobs, they should have been finished before now. She reset the anti-grav weights, grabbed a towel, and opened the comm.

"Vas here."

"It's Divee, Captain. He sounds upset."

"Patch the call through." Vas frowned. Why was he calling and not Gosta?

"Captain, we have a problem." Divee's voice was faint, as if not wanting to talk too loud. "The buyers aren't here, and um…one of the cases broke open."

Vas swore. She knew Mac and Jakiin couldn't set up a smuggling run right. Every time she let those two boys try something responsible, it bit her in the ass. Now the buyer was missing. And if the tone in Divee's voice was any indication, something very bad was in those crates. Which meant they weren't what they originally scanned as. Which meant it wasn't just Mac and Jakiin's mess anymore.

She hated when people lied to her about what she was smuggling. It was simple: she ran a clean ship, and she had an almost 100% success rate in terms of getting cargo safely intact to its destination without the Commonwealth being the wiser. All she asked for were a few simple things. No people, no live animals, no drugs, and no explosives or arcane Asarlaí-based archeology. And no damn lying.

"I'll be there in ten. That's as good as I can get. Keep whatever it is under control and if the buyers do come to pick it up, stall them until I get there." Vas said.

"Aye, Captain." The obvious relief in Divee's voice didn't boost her spirits any.

She called Deven and was pleasantly surprised when he sounded awake. She'd left him in her ready room the entire time.

"Something has gone wrong with the wonderkids smuggling operation. We need to get down there before things get worse."

"Do we know what happened?" From the slight catch in his voice he was probably jogging down to his quarters for a quick change.

"No, but the buyers are AWOL, the boxes broke open in a bad way, and Divee called me."

"Crap. Who else do you want?"

"Terel, Jakiin, and you two." Vas pointed to Gon and Walvento who just happened to be passing into the gym at that point. The heavy Walvento looked surprised; as the ship's master gunner he rarely went off ship. Nevertheless, he shrugged his massive shoulders in agreement. "I've got Walvento and Gon." She smiled at the two men then pointed at the gym and shook her head. "I need every one armed and ready to drop in less than ten minutes. Oh, and get Bathie up on the bridge. She's got command while we're gone."

Vas clicked off her comm. Deven would get the others together and Walvento and Gon had already run back to their quarters for their gear. She paused before she headed down the corridor to her quarters, and then tapped into the command deck comm.

"Xsit? Close off the storage bay where the cargo was stored. Depending on what our friends had us carrying, I may need to have the storage area quarantined."

Drugs and Asarlaí artifacts were always her biggest fears. When she'd first started traveling on a smuggling ship as a girl, she'd seen a ship come into dock with the entire crew exploded from the inside out. They'd been carrying a messed up street drug and it got into their air vent.

Vas grabbed her weapons and slipped on some heavy pants and boots. She went back for a flak jacket after a second thought. Better to be prepared. Her weapons were easy: three blast pistols, a long range snub gun, and a brace of knives.

She got to the shuttle bay to find all of her team there before her. Good sign. She filled them in on what she knew as they made the planet drop.

Vas and the others made their way through a thin clump of trees to Mac's drop point with their blast pistols drawn. They kept the shuttle at a distance, in case something went sideways. This planet was listed as low-tech, but not enforced, and she wasn't going to risk her life or that of her crew, to abide by the inhabitants' sensibilities.

There was a clearing up ahead, but Vas still couldn't see any of her people.

However, she could hear them.

No yelling, no gunfire, no screaming. Nevertheless, some very odd noises and a few voices talking low.

Vas and Terel entered the clearing first. Terel moved ahead to scan the area, with Deven and Jakiin going around the outside of the clearing to see if anyone was lurking. Gon and Walvento stayed back with the shuttle in case someone had to go for help.

An interesting tableau spread out before them. The crates from the ship were in the middle of the clearing. The seals were clearly visible on all but the one furthest away. Immediately Vas saw what happened. They'd stacked them too high and the top one had tumbled off and cracked its lid on a rock. Which wouldn't have been a problem if there had been silks and tapestries in there like the manifest said there were. Like their sensors had said there were. Instead there were piles of a strange dust. Damn it, next time, if there was a next time, she was prying open every last crate.

Mac was the first of her people she saw. He was lying on the ground, still at first, and then he rolled around. Then he snorted and grumbled. Then rolled some more. Divee was sitting as far from the group as possible. He nodded to Vas, but didn't appear willing to move closer.

The triplets were down on the ground with Mac, but not moving. Gosta was standing closest to her and Terel.

Vas nodded to Mac and the others. "What the hell is wrong with him? With them?"

Terel shrugged and tapped her screen some more, but her face was becoming more concerned the more she saw on her screen. Vas wasn't sure but she thought she heard swearing under the doctor's breath. Something rare enough to have Vas contemplate pulling out another weapon.

"The box had a Rillianian stamp inside, but Mac couldn't read it. He's stalking a turtle," Gosta finally said. He pointed to the four people on the ground as if giving a lecture.

"He's what?" Vas watched Mac and the other three with him. Now they were all doing the same roll, grumble, and snort maneuver. Maybe she didn't hear right. She didn't know what they were doing, but she was pretty sure no turtles were nearby. Unfortunately, she wasn't surprised about the Rillianians being involved.

"He's stalking a turtle. But the problem is that he thinks he's a grunge beetle." Gosta said sagely. "Of course anyone can tell he's a turnip. Clear as day. Turnips, the lot of them." He folded his arms and studied the people before him.

Vas pulled back and took a good look at Gosta. She'd file his comment about the Rillianian stamp for later. "You too? Damn it, Terel, what's wrong with them?" Vas took a few more steps back, trying to distance herself from Gosta. She wanted to push him toward the others, but didn't know if whatever caused this was contact-born or not.

Terel reconfigured her med screen. "I don't know, Captain. They scan fine."

"Terel. Are you kidding me? *Look* at them!" Vas pointed to the group, five people in various stages of hallucination.

"I'm telling you they scan fine. Too fine if you ask me. There's nothing—" Terel swore as her scanner beeped. "Damn it." She held off answering Vas, but called back to the ship. "I need a full dose of Glincin for at least five people, possibly more. The area the crates were in needs to be level four decon. Clean it tight and we might need tranq guns." She cocked her head at Vas. "Unless you happen to be armed with non-lethal force?" At Vas's confused headshake, Terel continued into her comm, "Yes, tranq guns. Have someone take them to the drop zone. Do not walk them in."

"Terel, if you don't tell me what the hell is going on...." Vas glared at the doctor.

"At least one of those crates has Pericdin dust in it. Mac and the others on the ground were probably dealing with the busted case, so it's hit them the hardest. Gosta is just starting to show the symptoms. Divee may have been exposed, or may have stayed clear enough to avoid it."

Vas didn't wait. She whipped out her gun again as soon as she heard the name of the designer drug.

"You can't blow it up. Not with everyone around." Terel actually stepped forward and lowered the barrel of Vas's gun. "I know how you feel, and I feel the same. But we have to get the infected out and into treatment, and keep the rest of us from becoming exposed."

Vas swore but put away her gun. "I get to blow apart the people who are responsible for this." She held up a hand to stop Terel's response. "I get to blow up something. What do we need to do anyway?"

Terel plugged some more information into her scanner. After a minute or so she appeared happier. "If we can get them to the ship quickly, clean them up, and give them lots of counter agents, they should recover in a day or so." Vas noticed she left off what could happen to them in a worst-case scenario.

"The trick is going to be getting them to the ship." Terel studied the area. "The breeze probably carried the dust. It's so fine it would disburse easily. It shouldn't cause any problems just yet, but a full water drop over the area after we get our people out should do the trick." Terel frowned as she continued looking around.

"Where's Deven?"

"He was coming around the other side, since we didn't know what was—" Vas stopped at the increased concern on Terel's face. "What is it?"

The doctor started walking around the outer area. "Telepaths do not react well to this stuff. Extremely not well." She thumbed open her comm. "Deven? Stand perfectly still. Wherever you are, do NOT move." She flipped the comm and called the ship without waiting for his response. "We're also going to need a level-five stunner and hazard suits for everyone. We can't spend the time to walk to the drop point, so send someone with them. Just make sure they are suited up."

Vas fought to keep from grabbing Terel. She trusted the doctor and could understand that sometimes things had to be done immediately, but she also knew she needed to know.

"What the hell is going on? We didn't need suits before but we do now?"

Terel looked uncomfortable and her brow added a few more wrinkles. "Espers have an odd reaction to Pericdin dust. It affects their strongest urges, their most finely honed skills. And it works outward."

"What do you mean? Just tell me what this crap could do to him." Vas folded her arms and glared.

Terel sighed. "Not only to him, but to us. Each esper has specialized skills, areas of the mind they control better than others and that they are strongest in. On Pericdin dust those skills, talents, drives, whatever you want to call them, are turned outward to an extreme. If he's been exposed he'll be projecting intense drives to anyone nearby until we can get him completely subdued.

And there's no way those esper bracelets will be strong enough to stop him."

"What are Deven's skills? Being a pain in my ass?"

Terel scowled. "No. His two strongest areas are sex and fighting. He's odd that he has two. Most espers only have one. But both are particularly strong. If he got exposed to that dust and starts projecting, we're going to have the galaxy's largest orgy followed by the galaxy's fastest mass slaughter."

CHAPTER TWENTY-ONE

"Oh shit." Vas hit her comm. "Deven? Where are you? Don't move. Just tell me where you are."

Silence answered her. "Jakiin? Are you still with Deven?"

At first she thought he was gone as well. He finally responded, but his voice was low.

"No, Captain. He started acting strange." He paused. "I think he was going to kill me. He challenged me to a duel."

Vas let out a breath. Well, that answered which was going to hit first. "How do you feel Jakiin? Feel like killing Deven?"

"Captain! I wouldn't kill him. He's just so wonderful."

"Oh shit, both are hitting at the same time?" Vas turned toward Terel for some answers but the doctor just shrugged.

"Okay, Jakiin, I need you to go five hundred meters away from the clearing. Do you hear me? Five hundred meters straight out. Keep hiding from Deven. He's wonderful yes, but you can't go near him." Silence answered her. "Jakiin? Crap. Answer me."

"Sorry, Captain, he's getting closer. I think he's following me."

"Jakiin? Run." Vas said. She knew Deven was fast, she was hoping Jakiin was faster. "Go away from the clearing as far and as fast as you can. Don't stop, don't think, just run."

"But, Captain—"

"Damn it, that's an order. Run!"

A crunching sound followed by fading footfalls told her he'd done as she ordered. Of course it also told her he'd dropped his comm. She had no idea why he took that off, but at least he was running. Hopefully, he could keep running until they could get help down here.

Terel clearly wanted answers, but she had to check on the others. "Walvento? Gon? Check in. Has another shuttle dropped yet?"

"Not yet, Captain, but I think the buyers might be here. An armored lander is rolling this way."

"Damn it. When Mac recovers and Jakiin has stopped running I swear I'm going to chain them both to the outside of my ship." Vas said it more to Terel than the man on the other end. "How far out? Have they seen you?" If this were a real drop pick up, the land transport wouldn't be armored. The people coming toward hers weren't friendlies.

"Negative, Captain. We've got long range on this shuttle, but they'll see it and us within a few clicks. No sign of an extra bird for us."

Vas closed her comm again. "Terel do you have any tranqs in that kit? Anything we can knock our people out with? We can't wait."

"The only things I have are in hyposprays. If I get close enough to use them, I'll be compromised."

Vas grabbed the med kit and flipped it open. "No, you're the only one who can get us out of this. I'm walking them in." She waved off the protests. "Who else is going to get us on the ship? There's an armored land transport coming in hot. Our second shuttle hasn't landed yet. We need to knock them out and get out of here. Now."

There was pure panic on Terel's face. She didn't improvise well. "We can't. You'll be exposed. And what about Deven and Jakiin?"

"I'll have a little time before I start being affected, right?" Vas loaded a hypospray too slowly for Terel, who grabbed the rest and loaded them as they argued. "Jakiin is a really good runner. He'll keep going until we can get him. And landing a shuttle in front of Deven should cut him off long enough to get them both."

Terel finally gave up arguing and nodded. "Move fast. Divee, how are you feeling?"

"Freaked out, doc. Can you fix them?" Thank the stars Divee's voice sounded normal.

"See? He can help too." Vas reopened her link to Gon and Walvento while Terel filled Divee in on what was happening. "Okay, boys, change of plans. One of you call the *Wench* and see what the status on the second shuttle is. If they are on their way, fill them in. We need you to take your shuttle and try to scare off that armored lander, then come and drop over near the clearing." She took the hyposprays from Terel.

"Terel will fill you in on the rest. You take your orders from her for the rest of this mission," she paused, "no matter what I or Deven say. Understood?" The responding affirmations made her smile. Nice to know they took orders to disobey her so well. She nodded once to Terel then ran into the clearing. If she moved in fast enough and stayed upwind she could keep her exposure to a minimum.

Gosta had now joined the others on the ground as his own hallucinations robbed him of the ability to stand. Typical Gosta he was still trying to analyze things even though his ability to reason was shot. He was trying to describe what he was seeing, but his words made no sense and were rapidly degenerating into other languages.

Vas placed the hypospray against his neck, dodging as his hands flung out. He waved once more then his eyes rolled back. Tucking the used spray into her waistband, she jogged toward Mac.

Who was trying very studiously to dig his way through the planet. His nails were bloody and even his mouth had dirt in it. Pushing his hair aside, and clearing away a few clods of dirt, she shot him with a fresh spray. The triplets were easier as they had stayed together and not tried to fight the effects of the drugs. They'd returned to a semi-conscious state and she thought about not giving them shots. Then she thought of the trouble three drugged former heavy worlders could cause in a shuttle.

With a shudder, she quickly hit all three just as blaster shots rang out in the distance. She froze. Had they come from the shuttle or where she'd sent Jakiin? She'd been counting on Deven's old-fashioned honor to work through whatever the drug was doing to him and make him go after Jakiin with something other than firearms. Had she been wrong?

Returning fire coming from the left reassured her it was the shuttle. An instant later she saw it hovering its way toward them.

Vas automatically reached to tap her comm, and then she realized they were probably communicating with Terel. But it had only been a couple of minutes; she wasn't affected yet.

"What's our status?" She waved as Divee nodded her way while he ran to Terel and the shuttle.

"Gon and Walvento damaged the lander, but the chatter indicates there are more hostiles on the ground coming in." Terel paused as static broke in from the shuttle. "They said that a mid-sized, unmarked cruiser has chased two generational ships into the atmosphere. The *Wench* is holding back waiting for orders. Our second shuttle didn't get off in time so I told them to stay put."

Vas laughed. She'd make Terel a military commander yet. "Tell, crap...." She paused as a wave of fog took over. Who did she leave in charge of the *Warrior Wench*?

An image of a laughing woman flitted through her head. "Tell Bathshea to protect those generation ships. We have to assume the ship chasing them is...." She fought to keep focused but keeping her thoughts on track was getting harder. And when did she sit down?

"Stay where you are, Captain. Gon and Walvento have space suits on. They'll come and load everyone. I'll tell Bathie to save those ships. Just sit this one out."

Terel's voice seemed very far away. Then Vas realized her comm was a good foot away from her. Reaching for it, she fell over and decided to lie there. She didn't feel the effects as much lying down. And the grass was nice. As she drifted off, a strange thought rode through her head. Something she'd read about this damn drug. She grunted as she fought her way through a pile of green worms about five feet long that she was pretty sure weren't really there. Eventually she got to her comm.

The worms had almost covered her when she got the comm open. "'erel... stims. Use stims...to get the worms off." She thrashed, trying to clear her head. "No. Stims. Fight drug. Stims." She leaned back. She knew she needed to fix something, but the worms wouldn't let her think. They invaded the flex cast she still had on her hand and turned it into a giant flower. The comm started speaking to one of the worms so she threw it. A minute later it became Terel in a haz-mat suit.

"Captain?" The doctor's face was awfully big and there was a worm running through her head, Vas tried to reach up to swat it but fell back. "Damn it, Vas, this is hitting you too fast. I don't know if stims are going to help. It's not a medically approved treatment. And with the amount I'll have to use, it's going to hurt like hell."

Vas watched the pretty colored words come out of the worm's mouth but didn't understand them. Then the worm held up a long, thin, glowing stick.

"Stims."

Vas tried to tell the worm to use them. Whatever they were, stims would help. Something. "Stims."

"Aye." The worm leaned forward with the glowing stick and stabbed her with it.

At first coolness spread through her body, then it turned to fire.

Vas screamed as every nerve in her body burst into flame at the exact same instant. She felt her body arch uncontrollably, and then slammed her back to the dirt.

"Damn it, that fucking hurt!"

"Good to see you too."

Terel's voice was nearby and Vas forced her eyes open. Halos of brutal light surrounded everything. However, the worms were gone and her mind seemed to be her own again. Of course everything still hurt like hell.

"Ya know, just because I tell you to do something stupid doesn't mean you have to do it." She shut her eyes again. The world was too bright.

"Actually you were right. Stimulants can offset Pericdin dust for the short term. If they don't send you into cardiac arrest when they first hit that is. We'll still need to flush your body of them, but you should be okay for a least a short time."

"How can you call this okay? I've never been in this much pain in my life." Vas forced her eyes open to glare at Terel. "My hair hurts!"

The doctor reached down a gloved hand to help her up. "You're well enough to complain, aren't you? We've got Mac and the others in the shuttle. Jakiin is still on the run; Gon's tracking him with the shuttle scanner. Deven's far enough behind to keep him from affecting Jakiin much, but we need to get them out of there. The lander did have buddies; Walvento thinks we have about a half hour before they get here."

Vas turned away and threw up. "Side effect of the stims, I presume?" She reached into Terel's med kit for a bandage to wipe her mouth. "What about those two ships that were being chased?"

Terel took her arm and led her toward the shuttle. Vas was in too much pain to argue or fight back. "Bathshea says the cruiser pulled back when she got closer. Our ship seriously outguns it, but the cruiser hasn't left the system completely. She says it seems to be waiting."

"Probably for its friends down here." Vas shook her head, a near fatal mistake. She grabbed the side of the shuttle and waited for the world to stop moving. "Okay, tell Gon to lift off. Let's get Jakiin and Deven first, and then deal with what's going on in space." She forced herself to look around for something to put Deven in, but there wasn't anything. "Will knocking him out stop his broadcasting?"

At Terel's terse nod, Vas slid into her seat and managed to buckle herself in. But not before she grabbed another hypospray.

"You can't be serious." Terel tried to grab it, but Vas had recovered enough to keep it from her.

"How else are we going to get him up here? Or Jakiin for that matter." She held out her other hand. "I'll need another one."

The shuttle began to lift off, when a thought struck her. "Wait, what's the safest way to destroy that crap?" She pointed out the window toward the crates in the meadow.

Terel sighed and put a second hypospray in Vas's hand. Then tapped the comm to the pilots.

"Drop fire suppressant foam on the crates. Then fire a low-yield torpedo once we're a hundred meters up."

Vas smiled and patted her friend's hand. "See how much nicer it is when you're reasonable?"

She watched through a window as bright green foam shot out from the bottom of the shuttle, engulfing the entire meadow. It quickly hardened and pulled all of the molecules of the drugs, crates, grass, and dirt into one neutralized lump. Gon raised the shuttle higher and Walvento fired off a single shot. The tableau before them went up in a fireball.

As the shuttle rose, Vas saw two more armored landers closing in on the meadow.

She doubled over in pain as a slight movement shattered every neuron in her body. "Can't you do something? We don't have to worry about it wearing off in a few hours, because I'll be dead long before then."

Terel's look wasn't as kind as Vas thought it should be. "That, my dear captain, is why stims are not the detox of choice. And no, you can't have anything for the pain. The stims are masking the Pericdin but it's still in your bloodstream. You won't die from it, but you'll want to. I could knock you out?"

"And miss nailing Deven with a hypospray? No way." Vas let her breath out and wrapped her arms around her torso; not moving helped.

Terel frowned as Vas checked the charge on her snub blaster. "You don't have a stunner or a tranq gun. Are you going to shoot him?"

"If I have to. I may not have a choice, and I'll try not to hit anything vital. I am fond of him, you know. But we have to get him to the ship, and he has to be unconscious when we do it." She gave a lopsided grin. "I'll aim for a leg."

"I'm sure he'll be grateful," Terel said with a shake of her head.

"Captain, Terel." Walvento addressed both. "I'm closing in on Jakiin and Deven. Looks like they're running out of energy."

Vas loosened the strap on her seat and made sure the hyposprays were secure in her waistband. "That'll make my job easier. Walvento, lower us down in front of them as tight as you can safely get. Divee, get out a long-range blaster rifle. When I open the hatch, I need you to try and keep our boys from running to the sides. Don't hit them."

She raised a hand of caution to the slim man. "Only I get to do that."

He didn't say anything but calmly readied the weapon and took up his position. The shuttle hovered and began to descend. The engine was amazingly quiet for this size of machine and as they dropped, Vas swore she could hear yelling outside.

She turned to Terel right before she opened the door. "How long before his telepathic issues hit me?"

"Immediately. In fact, I'm ordering Walvento to raise the shuttle until he's knocked out."

"Good idea." With a wince, Vas slammed open the hatch and dropped the five feet to the ground. She fought throwing up again as the world jumped up to meet her.

"Shit!" She bounced to her feet as quickly as possible, not taking the chance that Deven or Jakiin were close and homicidal. Or worse.

The dusty ground was covered in scuff marks. The guys had been here but taken off. A few well-aimed rifle blasts from the shuttle above pointed her toward the left.

Keeping her snub blaster in her right hand, she gingerly jogged that direction. She better find them and get them taken out fast; she didn't know how much more of this pain she could handle. That is if she still hoped to have her brain intact afterwards.

She hadn't gone far when she noticed Jakiin hiding behind a tree. The land was sparsely covered, but clearly he had run into the small clump of trees ahead. And since his back was toward her, she had to think Deven was in there now. Turning to wave at Divee to make sure he saw her going in, she pulled one of the hyposprays free and readied it.

She felt silly holding a hypospray in one hand and a gun in the other, but she couldn't chance Deven overpowering her. She hadn't been kidding about shooting him. He hadn't admitted he was immortal, or anything like it. However, he was well over two hundred, and she knew of very few races that lived that long naturally. Besides, she meant it about aiming for a leg.

Jakiin wasn't paying attention to her at all, engrossed in something in the trees beyond him. Vas was almost to him when he finally turned around. Even racked in pain, she was still faster than him and used the butt of her blaster to knock him on the back of his head. Confusion filled his face, then his eyes rolled back in his head, and he tumbled to the ground.

Vas shot him with the hypo just to be sure he stayed unconscious, then dragged him into the open area so the shuttle could come down and get him. Squaring her shoulders she marched toward the trees.

And was completely unprepared for the sight in front of her.

Deven was very actively engaged with four large, elephantine, women. In ways she didn't even think possible. Even though the sight was in no way arousing, Vas felt her loins tighten; Deven's gift was hitting her. Fighting to keep from ripping her clothes off and working her way to her second-in-command, Vas gritted her teeth and pushed the first two women aside. They were Ellines, a race normally not sexually compatible with humanoids. The thought of that was enough to hold off the urge to sexually attack Deven long enough to get the hypospray in his neck. He glanced up with the saddest expression she'd ever seen, and then folded over one of the large, gray women. The women all looked surprised, then tumbled to the ground unconscious as Deven's influence over them cut off.

Vas pulled him free of the Ellines, but couldn't get him very far. Gosta was right; Deven was heavier than he appeared. He shouldn't be projecting. Terel said he wouldn't project if knocked out. But looking down at him all she wanted to do was wake him up and have sex until one or both of them died.

Dropping to her knees, she fumbled for her comm. "Terel. Didn't work." Neither did her voice, so raspy and dry it sounded like someone else. "Knocked Deven out, still projecting."

She let the comm slide shut as she gently pushed his dark hair from his face. He really was beautiful. A loud noise forced her attention away from the lovely man.

The Ellines were rising and fixing their uniforms. They looked bewildered, but clearly no longer affected by Deven's projections. They didn't even look like they really saw her or Deven. Which was much safer all around. Vas didn't doubt who would win in hand-to-hand combat between her and four Elline guardswomen. Considering the insignias on their uniforms, they had been on patrol when Deven found them. They silently left the clearing to return to whatever their previous task had been.

"Oh crap." Vas slid down next to Deven.

A horrible whine exploded next to her head.

Her comm lay on the ground, hopping a bit as the buzzing made it jump.

Tracing the outline of his mouth with her finger, she grabbed the offending item to fling it away, but something stopped her and made her open it.

"Vas, you have to get clear of him. I can come down, hit him with another hypo, but you have to get clear." Terel's voice was tinny and vague, but Vas caught one point.

"No, not going to leave him."

She thought she heard swearing, but she didn't care. A down thrust of air caused her to look up. The shuttle was now hovering over her. A pair of small projectiles came down. She threw herself over Deven to protect him, but they were just hyposprays.

"You have to hit him again." Terel's voice sounded so far away she could pretend she didn't hear her.

Vas ran her hands up and down the amazing body before her. She didn't want him to sleep; she wanted him to wake up. She wanted him to do to her what he had been doing to the Ellines.

"No, want wake up."

More swearing followed, and finally a man's voice was on the comm. "Captain, if you use the spray he'll wake up."

"Divee? Is that you? Why don't you come down here too? More fun."

"I, uh, can't right now, Captain. But if you give him those sprays he'll wake up for you."

Vas pouted. She wanted someone to touch her. Now. Grabbing both sprays, she shoved them into Deven's neck.

Suddenly the world slammed back into focus and she rocked back on her heels.

She adjusted her clothes. She hadn't gotten them off but she had been getting there. "Thanks, Divee. That worked. Terel, we need to get Deven to the ship without him exposing others. He was having sex with Ellines." Not only were they physically very different, Ellines weren't the most gregarious of species. As a whole they worked as bodyguards for the lesser species. Of course in their eyes everyone was a lesser species. That Deven had been able to manipulate them into an orgy was one for the record books. And a scary testament to his abilities.

"That's not good. Nor possible, I would have said." Terel's voice was distant as she rustled around the shuttle. "I think we can put him in the decon chamber. It'll have enough air inside it to get him to the ship without exposing the rest of us."

CHAPTER TWENTY-TWO

Vas rubbed her arm as Terel's assistant, Pela, removed the cuff and the plexi-cast. It had taken longer than she'd hoped, but shorter than she feared. An hour after getting the shuttle back on board, her system was free of the Pericdin dust. The stims were still in effect however, although they were dying down to a dull buzz. Pela assured her the effects would be gone in a few hours.

The rest of her ground crew was still unconscious. But at least they'd gotten everyone on board safely. Deven required two more hypo sprays to keep him down, and Terel finally resorted to a low-level anesthetic drip when she found him and an assistant about to rip off each other's clothes. The fact that he was doing everything by touch and still had his eyes closed was possibly more disturbing than he and the Ellines.

"Can I go now? Bathie's been calling down here every five minutes. There's something going on with those generation ships." Vas said.

Pela glanced over to Terel, who frowned from where she checked on Jakiin. Finally she reluctantly nodded.

Vas hopped off the medical cot and crumpled to the ground. She quickly pulled herself up and waved off the medical staff. "Damn it. It's those stupid stims. My joints still aren't working right." She walked to the rest of her ground crew just to make sure they were resting peacefully. If she glowered at Mac and Jakiin as they slept, it was perfectly justified.

"Call me if you need me. Oh and I'm sending Hrrru down here. He's neutered and won't be affected in case sleeping beauty breaks his bonds."

"Deven's under enough sedation to knock out an army." Terel said.

Vas shook her head. The doctor hadn't felt how strong he was. If she had her way, no one would be in here with him. Her reaction was clear enough for Terel to get the point.

"Send him down. He's telepathically numb, so in case Deven wakes and is still sending; Hrrru can run for help before we kill each other."

"Hrrru's numb?" Vas frowned. She prided herself on knowing things about her crew, so how could she have not known that? A numb soldier could be invaluable during certain missions. They couldn't be swayed by any telepathic attack. She could easily find ways to increase their asking price in future fights with someone like him in her company.

"Yes, and he doesn't want anyone to know. Actually a growing percentage of the Welisch are numb. Each generation there are more. Unfortunately, their priests see it as a curse and refuse to let outside medical professionals examine them. We've kept his secret."

Terel's pointed look said it all. Vas sighed at the lost imaginary money. She couldn't use him. Like having a great throwing knife but being told it had to stay in a case. "Understood. I won't say anything."

Shaking her head at a planet half-filled with fighters who couldn't be affected by telepaths and yet being unable to touch them, Vas made her way slowly to the bridge. The fire in her body from the stims was dying down, or she was just becoming more used to it.

Bathie and Xsit were in a low conversation with Divee when she got there.

"You sure Terel cleared you?" Vas asked Divee as she approached. Although he seemed to have managed to stay clear of the dust, she wanted to make certain anyone who left that sick bay was completely free of it.

Divee paled a bit, and then nodded. "I'm able to return to work, Captain."

"Oh for the love of...Divee, I don't want you." Vas noticed that he'd been staying as far from her as possible on the flight up, but hadn't made the connection. "Trust me. Deven could make an Ilerian mate with a Wavian. Not pretty and they'd both probably die during it. But he could have made it happen."

He nodded but he still watched her warily.

"For crying out loud, just go down below and oversee the cleaning of the storage area. Make sure they didn't miss anything." She turned from him and pretended to examine the records on the screen by her command chair. She turned around after a few minutes.

"He'd better get his head together soon. I have a far greater reason to be freaked out than he does." She laughed as she caught Bathie's expression. "You know what I mean. Now what's this about the generation ships? Didn't that thing stalking them leave hours ago?"

The smile left Bathie's face. "Aye, Captain, it did. And it's cleared the system. However, the generational ships' guards all left before they got to this system. They don't have any protection and they are unarmed."

Xsit lifted one feathered eyebrow in mimicry of Deven. "They have asked for protection from you."

Vas almost missed the chair she was sliding into. "What? I'm a merc. You told them that, yes?" She scowled at the shrugs from both of her officers. "They're generation ships, not refugees. Tell them to go to one of the inner worlds and hire more guards."

She pulled up the record of the ship that had chased them in. The firing had all been to herd the ships it was chasing toward the planet below; not to destroy the ships.

At least they'd stopped whatever plan they had the moment they registered the *Warrior Wench* in orbit. Most likely pirates.

"They *are* refugees. They bought those ships when their world was destroyed." Bathie was serious now. "They were from Lantaria."

Vas closed her eyes and thudded her head against the headrest of her command chair.

Bad idea. Even heavily padded it still pounded the back of her skull into her eye sockets.

"Crap."

"Exactly."

Vas turned toward the new voice. Flarik had come on deck. As a rule the Wavian didn't spend much time on the command deck. But not only was she here, she was wearing a flight suit like the rest of the crew. Very disturbing.

"We can't abandon them." Xsit's voice was passionate. She'd had a few hours to get into the idea.

"There is this as well." Flarik came to the side of her chair. "I understand this image is tied in to many of our problems." She held up a panel with the elongated Rillianian logo on it.

"This was on the ship chasing the refugees." Flarik expanded the image of the aggressive ship until Vas could see it on the bow.

"When did my life become so screwed up?" Vas ran her knuckles over her eyes. Yup, that hurt like hell too. Maybe she should give up this life, take up farming.

"I give up." She turned back to the communications station. "Xsit, notify whoever is leading those two ships and ask them where they are trying to go. We'll protect them as much as we can."

Xsit bobbed. "That is one of the problems. They do not have a place they can go."

Vas appealed to Flarik, but the Wavian just stared stoically. Bathie refused to meet her eyes.

"Fine. We can take them to Home. They can have that tiny continent in the far south. We can erect barriers around it to keep them away from our people. However, I need all of them checked out. Just what we need is a terrorist to cap off a perfectly nasty couple of weeks."

"Thank you, Captain." Xsit chirped to herself as she contacted the lead ship. Bathie went ahead and contacted the guard at Home to let them know they were bringing folks in. Flarik had obviously just come up for the information about the ships, so with a nod, she left to go do whatever it was she did.

Vas let herself get lost in the field of stars on the main screen. She wasn't used to bringing non-crewmembers to her planet. Hell, she wasn't used to helping people. She made a living out of other people's disagreements, wars, and stupidity. Helping wasn't part of her life.

Yet here she was, helping two full ships of total strangers and offering them a chunk of her very private home. With all that had happened to her in the last month, helping these two ships was more disturbing.

The fact that there were refugees from Lantaria was also upsetting. She really should interview them and find out what they knew. The Commonwealth had blown her off about her concerns of what had happened to the planet; they wouldn't have sent any support for the survivors.

She tapped open the comm. "Flarik? I need to borrow you for a bit."

"What is it, Captain?" She couldn't have been that involved yet; she would have just gotten down to her rooms a few minutes ago. However, the terse tone was still there. Clearly she wasn't finding anything useful, or rather wasn't finding what she needed to get the Wavian Empire to attack the Rillianians. Vas knew that Flarik had her own motives at this point for helping. Hopefully the two goals would follow the same path for a while yet.

"I know you're busy, but I need you to go interview some of the survivors on those ships. Bathie is running a full manifest on everyone who is on board. You can pick the most likely candidates from the list."

An audible sigh escaped over the comm. "Aye. Is there anything specific you want to know?"

"Yes, what they saw when those ships attacked." Vas paused; Flarik had been asleep during the entire episode. "You have seen the vids, correct?"

"Of course."

Vas didn't let her laugh creep out over the comm. The two words sounded like she'd tossed a mortal insult at Flarik. Of course, being both a Wavian and a lawyer perhaps she did. Both prided themselves on being prepared and informed to the point of obsession.

"Find out what they remember, how many ships escaped, and if they have an idea of who did it. Anything would help at this point. We have to assume the slaughter of that world is tied into the rest of this mess somehow." She tapped her finger on her teeth in thought. "I'm going to try and contact the council again. I can't believe the Commonwealth would just walk away like this."

"Very well, Captain. Flarik out."

Vas got up to head for her ready room, then turned back to Bathie. "Can you check on the rest of the folks in the med lab for me? Let me know once they've regained consciousness."

She nodded. "Oh, and Grosslyn says you'll owe him a vat of ale for dropping these folks on him like this. At first he couldn't understand why we're adding more troops." She laughed. "Took him almost a full ten minutes to understand that these weren't fighters, and another five to figure out that we were giving them land."

"Eh, he'll survive. He's too set in his ways." Grosslyn managed her planet when she wasn't there. Which was about ninety-nine percent of the time.

Vas went to her ready room and slid the door shut. The stims were starting to wear off and the searing pain in her joints and muscles was being replaced by a rock-like stiffness.

Settling into her chair, Vas connected to the inner worlds system that would eventually get her to a Commonwealth flunkie.

After making the connection request, she went over to the food processor and ordered up a sandwich. Those stims had played hell with her adrenaline system. Knowing the lovely bureaucracy behind the heart of the Commonwealth, she figured she had at least a half hour before they'd pick up her call.

She almost dropped her sandwich when her computer beeped that the call was being answered. Holding the pieces of her sandwich together, she ran for her desk.

"Captain Tor Dain?"

"I'm here."

"Expeliar Curellen here. You had an urgent matter?"

Vas swore. They responded in less than five minutes, and with an Expeliar? She'd expected a low-level clerk, not a high-ranking official. "Thank you, Your Excellency. I was concerned about the attack on Lantaria last week. My ship has recently come to the assistance of some of the refugees."

"Lantaria? I wasn't aware of anything wrong there." He paused as he glanced down at a screen. "We have on schedule that you were involved in a job there with three other mercenary companies. According to this you should still be fighting."

She'd wondered if they had done anything with her previous very long report. Obviously not.

"Expeliar Curellen, unknown ships attacked the merc companies with us. I believe all were lost. I didn't see any of their ships get off the ground." She paused, waiting for him to say something, when he didn't she added, "And we just found about two hundred refugees. They claim Lantaria was destroyed."

"I see." His tone grew cooler. "Do you have any proof, Captain Tor Dain?"

What the hell was he getting at? She'd said she'd seen the attack.

"I was *there*, Your Excellency. The ships that attacked were planet killers, huge, unmarked, but they knew their business. We only got away because we weren't in the fight zone when they started." She wasn't sure what was happening, but something was very wrong. "We tried to contact Lantaria after we escaped. There was no response."

The silence on the other end was chilling. Finally a click indicated that the Expeliar had muted her call, someone else had to be in the room with him. Another click brought him back.

"Where is the *Victorious Dead*, Captain Tor Dain? We do not show your ship on the grid." His voice dropped. "Where are you currently?"

Vas's heart rate jumped without the extra boost from the stims. She had reported the full change of ownership of the *Warrior Wench* before she'd even picked up her crew. She'd reported the *Victorious Dead* as inactive at the same time. How in the hell could someone as high up as an Expeliar not have that information?

While she was trying to figure out what was happening, he added another question. "And where did you say you saw those refugees? We'll want to find them and make sure they're safe."

Vas took a steadying breath and backed away from the comm. Something was very, very wrong. A quick check of the line confirmed that it was connected to an inner Commonwealth call. But that didn't calm her any. Warnings in her mind all but demanded she sever the call immediately.

"They were heading in-system. They said something about the Novia system." She picked something plausible, difficult to search, and in the exact opposite direction of where they were heading. She knew she didn't want the person on the other end to know where the refugees or her own ship were, even if she had no real reason why. "They were in trader ships, about four or five, slow moving."

Again the click as she realized he was conferring with someone near him. They didn't know where she was, and they didn't know she was in the *Warrior Wench*. If she bounced the line when she cut it they couldn't reconnect. At least not easily. Vas swore as she realized Gosta was most likely still unconscious. Divee might be able to do a good enough block to keep them from being traced.

She cut the call.

"Xsit? Get me Divee, stat. And do not, under any circumstances, accept any calls from the Commonwealth."

"Captain?"

"Don't ask, just don't. And I need Divee now."

Vas cut the comm and paced her small ready room. She'd never spoken to an Expeliar in her life. They were a cadre of the ruling elite, third tier from the top. There was no reason her general call would have been routed to one such as him.

Unless they were waiting for her.

Wishing she had recorded the conversation, she frantically grabbed a stylus and pad and wrote down everything she could remember. There may have been things she missed. However, far worse than the recent goings on was the thought that someone in the Commonwealth's upper tiers knew who she was, and was looking for her, her ship, and those refugees.

The door chime rang. Hopefully it was Divee; right now she needed a shield around her ship and those refugees. Crap, what if someone else knew who was in those generational ships?

"Come in," she yelled then waved at Divee to sit as she called Flarik.

"Flarik, I need you to make sure no one on those ships contacted anyone, especially anyone in the Commonwealth. And you need to find out who they've been in contact with since they left Lantaria. And tell them no outgoing messages to anyone until I say otherwise."

The pause before she answered told Vas that Flarik really wanted to ask questions. However, the lawyer was too smart to do so on an open comm. "I will come find you when I get back on board." The closest she would get to, "you'd better tell me what's going on" that Vas had ever heard.

"Thank you." Vas said, then turned to the thin man waiting for her. "Divee, I need you to hide us from the Commonwealth."

CHAPTER TWENTY-THREE

Divee's gray eyes grew large and his mouth seemed to have a mind of its own. A silent mind of its own. He finally broke free. "Might I ask why?"

"No. You may not." She softened her tone at the look on his face. "Not yet anyway. I just had a very odd conversation with a Commonwealth bureaucrat, and I think it's best we lay low."

"Are we...." The look on his thin face was almost painful. He was loyal to the end to her and the company, but he was also possibly the most law-abiding citizen of the Commonwealth that Vas had ever met.

"No, we are not going rogue." She knew what he was afraid to ask. She shuddered. Rogue mercs had been becoming rarer over the last five years. Rumors were that the Commonwealth had been silently removing them, preferring to control all mercenary companies, however indirectly. However, no proof had ever been found.

"We are simply avoiding them for now. I believe there may have been something compromised with the clerk I just spoke to," she lied quickly. Looking at the thin lines of concern that marred his face, she came to a decision; Divee might need to be transferred back to Home for a while. She didn't doubt his loyalty to her, but she couldn't take a chance on his loyalty to the Commonwealth interfering.

He looked like he decided it was best not to think about things too much. "I believe I can shield us. Do you want us off the grid completely?"

The Expeliar had said he couldn't find them on the grid, but that was because he still believed she and her crew were in the *Victorious Dead*. She contemplated just having Divee leave things as they were on the grid. She shook her head at that thought. It was the council of the Commonwealth she was dealing with, not some backwater rubes. It wouldn't be difficult for that bureaucrat to find out where she was.

"Yes. I know it's dangerous, but we need to be off-grid completely at this point. We don't know who was behind those gray ships at Lantaria, or who they were aiming for. We have to protect ourselves," she paused, "and the poor people in those ships."

For a team of mercs, her crew was a huge bunch of softies. Divee's face crumpled at the mention of the refugees. She might not have to bench him after all.

"You're right, Captain. If there is any question, we must protect those people." He rose to his feet, every inch the former aristocrat he was rumored to be. "I will have all of us completely blocked immediately. No one shall be able to find us."

He quickly left to go about his business, leaving Vas to marvel about her choice in crew. Maybe it wasn't them who were going soft, but her.

They could start heading toward Home the instant Divee said they were blocked from the grid. Well, once they were blocked, and Flarik and Bathie gave a clean bill for those refugees, that was.

She ate half of her pathetic sandwich in two bites, and then opened the comm.

"Terel? How are they?" She'd asked Xsit to keep her updated but it had been her experience that her version of ready and her doctor's version of ready were two different things.

"Still not ready to return to duty, Captain." If the tone of her voice hadn't let Vas know Terel was annoyed, the use of her title would have. So be it.

"That's not what I asked. I need to talk to some of them."

Terel's sigh was loud through the comm. "Which ones?"

Vas grinned. "Depends. Who's awake?"

"Jakiin is probably in the best condition. In fact," Terel paused as she muttered to someone in the med lab, "you could have him. He's beginning to annoy me." The last was said lower, but Vas was certain Jakiin heard it.

"I was hoping for my second-in-command."

"He's still out. Vas, there's no way I'm letting him regain consciousness until I'm certain everything is out of his system. You'll need to be without him for a little while yet."

Vas wolfed down the rest of her sandwich. "Send me Jakiin then. I have some things to ask him." She almost signed off, and then flicked the comm open again. "How's Mac?"

"He's almost ready, not completely conscious, but I can send him up in a few." Terel signed out and Vas went to the deck. With nothing really going on she didn't mind leaving Xsit in charge. Too long would be bad. Xithinals as a whole didn't like being in charge of anything. They were flock creatures and vastly preferred that others lead the flock.

Xsit had been slumping over her console, staring forlornly out at the stars when Vas came onto the deck. She perked up immediately.

"Captain, good to see you. Nothing to report."

"Thank you. Has Flarik returned from those ships yet?"

Xsit pulled up a small screen with the internal information. "Not yet. Bathie should be back up on deck soon though."

"Captain?" Divee's voice cut in over the comm. "I believe it is done." There was a hesitance in his voice that Vas didn't like to hear. He was talented enough to be Gosta's equal, but his constant self-doubt weakened him.

"It either is or it isn't, Divee," she said. "Which is it?"

The pause on the other end told her he was still far too unsure of himself. Finally he came back on with a cough. "It is. We, and the refugee ships, are blocked from the grid."

Vas settled into her command chair with a smile. "Thank you, Divee. You can return to cleaning out the smuggling space."

She turned at the sound of steps, expecting her missing pilot. There had been more than enough time for Jakiin to make his way up here. But it was only Bathie.

"I checked and cross checked them all. The refugees are safe, and they're what they say they are." Bathie settled into Gosta's chair with ease. One advantage of so many smart crewmembers is that they weren't relegated to only one position.

"Thank you. You didn't happen to see Jakiin wandering the corridors, did you?"

Bathie shook her head, blond hair staying in perfect place. "Nope. Ya want me to go get him?"

"No." Jakiin was probably hiding from her hoping something else would pop up to take her focus off him. The way things had been over the last two weeks she'd bet he wouldn't have had to wait long. Vas sighed and opened a ship-wide comm.

"Jakiin, get up to the command deck immediately." She shut it without waiting for a response. Even though Flarik was working on their lineup of mysteries, she figured she could work on one end of them.

Those damn crates.

She had no way of knowing if the crates were a deliberate plant, meant to do something to her and her ship, or simply property of stupid drug runners. A month ago she would have chocked it up to stupid drug runners. Now, she couldn't let anything go by without questioning it.

Come to think of it, how did she know that things hadn't been this messed up before and she didn't see it? Maybe her missing time and the taking of the *Victorious Dead* hadn't been the start of it, but a part of a longer pattern.

"Oh, my head." She closed her eyes and sat back in her chair. The backlash from the stims was fading, but the pounding in her head seemed to be getting worse.

"Are you all right?" Bathshea asked as she ended yet another communication with the folks on Home. Grosslyn really wasn't taking the addition of two hundred refugees well and continued to harangue Bathie.

"No." Vas waved off the engineer as she saw the look of concern. "Ah, there's one of the problems now."

Jakiin came slowly down the corridor leading into the command deck. He looked like a man taking that long final trek to an airlock funeral.

As well he should.

"Come on, boy, I don't have all day. I'm still recovering from that shipment of yours."

Jakiin winced, and the gills on the side of his neck, normally not visible, fluttered briefly. A sure sign he was seriously distressed.

"Tell me how you and your partner found out about this shipment. Considering that you wouldn't have known we were going back to the station so soon, I'm thinking it was a lucky thing you found something so quickly."

Jakiin slowed down to a stopping point just outside the reach of the command chair.

As if that would protect him.

"I could still shoot you from here, you know." Vas folded her arms and glared at the unlucky pilot. Well, self-inflicted unlucky anyway.

"What?" He jumped a foot back, the veins in his pale face standing out like green roads on a map.

"I'm just saying that staying out of physical striking range of someone with a blaster at her side is fairly stupid." She motioned for him to come closer. "And might piss off the person holding the blaster."

Looking even more like a dead man walking, Jakiin stepped forward but kept his head down.

"Where did you and Mac find out about that shipment?"

"Mac found it when we were leaving the docking bay. A woman came and asked us if we wanted a quick job. She said she knew of Mac by reputation and only wanted to hire the best."

Should have known. The only thing worse than Mac's love of schemes was his weakness for the female flesh. Any female flesh. Vas motioned for Jakiin to go on. She didn't trust herself to say anything.

"Mac asked her if it was dangerous, or drugs, or any of the other things you don't allow on the ship." His red-brown eyes were earnest as he finally glanced up. "She said it wasn't."

Vas wrapped her hands around each other so she didn't grab his throat. "And what was to stop her from lying? Crap, Jakiin. You two took on a job without checking, without clearing, and based on the client's say so? I don't know what to do with you two, seriously." Her fingers flexed with the need to smash his head into the arm of her chair. Finally she shook it off. "I don't suppose you got anything worthwhile in terms of who she was?"

Jakiin took an involuntary step back, shaking his head. "We have the contract...but Mac didn't know if it was real or not. He tried looking her up after we left the space station and he couldn't find her."

Vas closed her eyes and counted to ten. Deven kept insisting that trick would work to calm her down. Peeking open an eye, she realized she still wanted to strangle Jakiin. She tightly shut the eye and resumed counting.

She'd reached one hundred and fifty when a coughing interrupted her.

"Captain?" Jakiin's voice was little more than a squeak.

She didn't bother opening her eyes. "Yes?"

"Are you all right?"

"A better question would be if I can keep from blasting you out an airlock long enough for Mac to get up here." She couldn't believe this. If the two of them were brighter, and hadn't been with her for the last eight years, she would have thought they were agents for whichever deity was trying to ruin her life.

Still keeping her eyes closed, she flipped open a comm channel. "Terel? Is Mac on his way?"

"I'm shoving his ass out the door as we speak." From the tone of her voice Terel was almost as pissed off with the pilots as Vas was.

"Send flyboy to my ready room. He needs to be up here before my ass hits my ready room chair." With a deep breath she opened her eyes and nodded to Jakiin.

"You heard that. I'd think you'd be waiting for me outside of my door."

Jakiin's eyes went huge, the red coloring overpowering the brown. With a nod he all but ran for the door in question.

Vas really didn't take joy in terrifying her crew. Well, okay, to some degree she did. But only the ones who deserved it. After the pranks they'd pulled recently, Jakiin and Mac deserved it. But they'd always just been opportunistic, not criminally stupid. Until now.

She was just sitting down, glaring at Jakiin for the hell of it, when a loud thump hit her door. Amazing, for once Mac almost made it on time.

"Come in."

The door slid open as Mac was straightening his strawberry blond hair. He flashed a grin that suffered a quick death. Ducking his head, he slunk into the empty chair next to Jakiin. The door slid shut before he made it all the way into his seat.

"Okay, I'll make this simple. I'm asking myself why I haven't spaced you both right now. But I'll give you two a chance to get out of this." She steepled her fingers in front of her face. "Someone played you both for idiots and almost caused untold havoc and possible death for most of this crew. You both massively disobeyed orders. You took a smuggling job on your own, without checking it."

She paused, as Mac looked ready to argue. She raised an eyebrow and cocked her head. He wisely folded his lips as if biting them and shrugged.

"As I was saying, you boys screwed up big time. Mac, Jakiin said you tried to track the woman down who hired you. How far did you go?"

Mac appeared as if he was still waiting for permission to talk. Finally he decided it was better to respond. "I tracked down the name she gave us, and the name of the company she said she was working for. Well, I almost tracked down the company she said she worked for. By the time I realized she was a dead end, we were being chased by that ore ship." He took a deep swallow. "And I forgot."

Vas stared up at the ceiling, willing the thin metal tiles to give her the wisdom to deal with morons. "Lucky you, you get to continue that search now. I want you to find out...." Her conversation faded as Mac stared at something behind her.

The image from the screen capture of the man who'd slammed into her on the space station was still up on her back screen and had captured Mac's attention. Deven hadn't sent the rest of the data disk up, but he had forwarded her that image in case she knew him. She hadn't, but had left it up in case it jogged something.

Mac still hadn't said anything, but hit Jakiin's arm to get his attention. Both sat there staring for a few moments.

"How did you get his picture?" Mac said and kept his eyes on the image.

"If you have him on camera, don't you have the woman as well?" Jakiin blurted at the same time.

"You two know him?" Vas watched them both carefully.

"Aye, Captain. The image is grainy, but I remember him. He was with the lady who hired us. The woman with the dust. I'd recognize that uniform, even if I didn't know the face." Mac spoke with a certainty he had been lacking moments before.

Vas clicked the image to make it a bit clearer. "What else did you notice about the uniform?" She didn't want to lead them into recalling something that really hadn't been there.

"That thing on his arm." Jakiin finally found his voice as he waved at the still image. "You can't see it very well there. But it was this weird long diamond shape."

Mac nodded slowly. "Yeah, I remember that. I know most ship patches, never seen that one before. And the lady had the same symbol on her necklace. Real expensive too, something definitely upper tier."

CHAPTER TWENTY-FOUR

Vas swore. The man who slammed into her was tied into the gang who'd gotten those drugs on her ship. Which meant it wasn't a gang at all but yet another tie to the Rillianians and possibly the Graylian monks. She still wasn't sure what was going on, but the knots were all starting to point one direction.

So much for sloppy drug smugglers. When they'd seen the Rillianian stamp on the inside of the box, she'd pretty much figured that theory was dead. However, she'd still held a sliver of hope for it, one that just died.

She needed to get the rest of the vid from Deven once he was clean and conscious. Maybe there would be something else to jog her two pilots' memories.

"I don't suppose you have any other information?" She spun around and fixed them both with her best glare. Jakiin flushed his gills after a few moments and Mac just looked like he was going to be ill.

"No, but we could continue to see if we can find anything about that company she said she worked for?" Mac said with a pathetic attempt at a smile.

Jakiin nodded.

It wasn't lost on Vas that neither of them had asked again about how she had that image.

"Yes, you'd better." She glanced from one to the other. Their mistake had been just that, a mistake.

Potentially catastrophic in scope, but not one they came to completely on their own. They were set up. Someone was looking for them because they were on the *Warrior Wench*.

"I want you both to find this woman, somehow, somewhere, find her. And write down everything you remember of your encounter, starting with the instant your feet hit the gang plank." She raised a hand as both started to rise.

"Separately. I need you two to work apart. No, it's not a punishment," she added as both pairs of eyes went wide. Although separating them more often might cut down on problems. "I need to see what each one of you remembers. If you're together one might influence the other's memory. It's vital we know everything."

"Aye," both said in unison, but neither rose to their feet this time.

"Dismissed." Vas held back her grin; she might have actually gotten through to them.

With an almost military nod to her, both turned and left.

Vas turned back to the still image. "So what secrets are you hiding, my friend?" When no more tidbits of information came forth, she got up for some mint tea. The herb was soothing and cleared her head. She also swore it could heal. One of the few traditions from her home planet, mint tea was used for everything from curing sick children to ending droughts. She'd never had the nerve to ask Terel if it really worked. She didn't think she'd be happy if the answer was no.

Sipping her tea, she tried to sketch out the series of events. Until she knew different, she had to stick with her missing time as the start point. Try as she might she couldn't get past the blocks in her head to find out what had really happened. She really needed to let Deven try, but she couldn't. It was completely illogical, especially considering the stakes, but she couldn't let him prowl in her head. Not again.

Whoever took her felt she wasn't going to come back, so that was party one. She drew a line on a huge pad and labeled it. Party two was whoever had tried to poison her, she marked off that cluster. Party three was whoever put the trackers in her blood. The groups could have overlapped; there didn't have to be three. Something big was happening. Something that she felt she could just see the edge of. Her mind was putting pieces together, when her door buzzed and almost sent her through the roof.

"Damn it! Come in!" she yelled as she sorted out her papers.

Flarik entered and silently slid into one of the chairs. She watched as Vas gathered her scattered things. "Is everything under control, Captain?"

"Not yet, but it will be." She toyed with how much to involve Flarik. The Wavian was a member of her crew, granted, but she was also a Wavian lawyer. Her reaction to the Rillianian threat had been disconcerting and eye opening. How much of a help she would be to Vas and the crew if she found a way to go after the Rillianians herself was a good question.

"We need to retrieve the *Victorious Dead* pieces." Flarik said.

Vas studied Flarik over the rim of her mug, waiting for the insightful portion of her comment to arrive.

When nothing more followed, Vas sat her mug down.

"Yes, I was aware of that actually. However a few things have popped up to distract us from our goal." Had they not let Flarik sleep enough? Usually the lawyer was the brightest of the bunch.

"Now. I believe we must start immediately. Once we have captured the first piece, we can take our time collecting the rest." Flarik rose to her feet and paced within the small room. "The monks are working with the Rillianians. They are using our ship in a training ritual."

Vas watched for a few moments. She'd never seen Flarik distressed enough to pace. Then Flarik's words sunk in.

"Training ritual? As in they are going to blow up my ship?" She'd heard of the Graylian monks' rituals. They were obsessive and often very bloody.

"I believe so. Maybe not right now, but eventually. However, if we can capture the first piece, it will slow them down extensively. They cannot complete whatever ritual they are trying to do without the first piece." Her grin was one her brutal ancestors would have admired. "And if we refrain from going after the other pieces for a while, it will drive them mad. Utter chaos."

"I like the sound of that." Vas knew that sometimes a full frontal assault wouldn't work in a battle. The one she apparently was fighting against the monks and the Rillianians was such a one. "While I don't understand their obsession with ritual and order, I understand being able to use it against them. If this will throw them off a bit, we might be able to figure out what it is they are training for. And stop them. Do you know how far the first piece is?"

Flarik nodded. "I have cracked their puzzle, at least the first part. It's not more than a short hypergate hop from here. Down in the Solaris system. We can be there in a day."

Vas knew they needed to keep moving and get another job. Both of which were being compromised by having to stay hidden from the Commonwealth until they figured out what was going on.

However, not having retrieved any of her ship—Gosta still hadn't been able to break through to the core yet—was chapping her hide. That it would throw her enemies into chaos was just a bonus.

"Agreed. Tell Bathie to lay in the course, and let's go get part of our ship back."

After a few hours of flight, Vas wasn't sure what she had been expecting. But it wasn't the ugly lump of plaststeel hanging in space before her.

"What did they do to my ship?" She sank deeper into her command chair as they closed in on the mass. If Gosta's readings rang true, this blob was part of her ship. Of course she really hadn't counted on them destroying the pieces, and then hanging them out in space.

"That's not the piece." Deven peered up from the console he'd commandeered once they came out of the hypergate. "The piece of our ship is inside that."

Terel had finally given him a medical release after some more badgering from Vas. There was no evidence of what happened on the planet on his handsome face, but he didn't look like he wanted to talk about it either. Which was fine with her.

The fact that part of her ship was inside the mess before her made Vas a little happier, but she was still confused. And pissed.

"Why? Did they really steal my ship, chop it up, coat it in refuse, just to leave it out in space in some twisted puzzle?"

"Yes." Hrrru nodded as if she'd asked a genuine question.

The earnestness on his face kept her sarcasm in check. "Thank you, Hrrru. I suppose what I meant to say was, why me? Why my damn ship? But that's not going to be answered today." She spun toward the rest of her crew.

"Ladies and gentlemen, and I use those terms loosely, how do we get our ship piece out of that?" Part of her had to admit the monks had been amazingly creative in their use of space junk. The thing before her looked like a trash ball. Anyone who accidentally came across it wouldn't even scan it for salvage.

Gosta squinted at the main screen as his fingers flew across his console keypad. "I think we'll have to take the entire thing with us." His frown and squint both deepened as he typed commands even faster.

"There is most likely a clean way to get the pieces out, but with what we have to work with out here, I can't see how." He stopped typing. "We need to send it to Home and let them try to pry it out on land."

Vas stared at the piece of melted and warped refuse before them for a few minutes then finally sighed. She did have plenty of people stuck at Home without anything to do. This would keep them busy until she found a job for them.

"Xsit, call Home and have a team come get this. Tell them to bring heavy haulers and a few of the smaller fighters. We'll stay here until it's loaded, but I don't want them to be unprotected in case someone comes after them." She wasn't sure how closely these monks were watching their training exercise. However, if they were behind the ore hauler, she had to figure they were watching something.

The mini-armada from Home appeared with remarkable swiftness. Obviously boredom was getting to her fighters.

She also had the ship's complement of Flits out patrolling, and kept all of the weapons ports open. But no one tried to stop them.

The captain from the Home armada wanted to know if they should go after the rest of the pieces in the puzzle, but Vas told him no. While her instinct would be to get all of the pieces as soon as possible, she was willing to bow to Flarik's expertise in this. If she felt just taking one and leaving the others for now would cause more mayhem, so be it.

CHAPTER TWENTY-FIVE

The next day started with no answers to any of her growing pile of questions, but at least they had a job. Deven barged into her quarters at some hideous hour to tell her they'd received a rescue job. Family cluster group, not more than a few hours away. Vas thanked him, then rolled over and went back to sleep.

She should have realized something was up when he never called her as they got closer.

"Damn it, Deven, you said this was a job. Not a mercy mission." Vas swore a few hours later as she stared out over the ten raggedy-looking population ships below her as they came out of the hypergate. She should have checked his data, the bastard.

"This is a job." He folded his arms and looked down at her. Quite a feat when she was only a few inches shorter than him and she currently had her flight boots on. "I'm paying us."

"You don't have enough to pay for what I think you're asking." She ran her hands over her face. "We need real work, not guard duty. You can't come up with—"

"Captain, we just received a transaction. Non-traceable, but it's for eighty million credits." Xsit's voice went into the upper register with the amount. That was more than they pulled in during an entire year. Where the hell had he come up with that money? No place he'd tell her, of that she was certain.

She stared at him in silence for a good three minutes, and then finally shrugged. "Since you're hiring us, what's the job?" She wasn't going to fight about this here, but she was going to find out what the hell was going on before they did anything with those ships.

"They are our job. And the folks still on the planet. There's a war going on, but many of the people are refugees from outlying worlds who came here to hide." He pulled up a map of the largest continent. "The fighting should be here." He pointed to an area not far outside a densely populated area. "But it's here." He tapped another area further down near the equator.

Vas studied the screen. There was no way a professional mercenary company could have mistaken the two areas. Which meant someone was after the refugees.

"Where did you say they were from? Lantaria?"

He shook his head. "I don't think that many people made it off that rock, we may have the only survivors back on Home. These are from the Sicila system, two of the larger moons. The moons were destroyed two months ago."

"What?" How in the hell had she not heard about something that big? Part of being good at her job was knowing what was going on in the Commonwealth systems and beyond. Yet moons were being blasted apart with no word in the space lanes?

"Someone or something is destroying smaller outlying worlds, and it's been going on since before Lantaria." His eyes were as flat as his voice, but Vas knew that masked fury. She couldn't blame him. Two months? Yet the Commonwealth had done nothing? She'd never been a huge fan of the Commonwealth, but she respected the way it protected its people. Until now.

As much as she'd like to walk away from this, she knew they couldn't. She couldn't. Something was changing in her more than just going a little soft and having feelings for Deven. Besides, Deven's money had already been transferred.

"Shit." Vas said, and then opened a ship-wide comm. "I need a landing crew to get to the shuttle in the next ten minutes." She turned back to Deven. "We get in, get the ones still on the planet, then lead the whole bunch out of here." She jabbed him in the chest. "But not Home. There are a few thousand people out there in those ships, and I'm not flooding my only refuge. We can find that moon you said Marli has been hiding on."

"She's not going to like it."

"I don't really care. That's as good as it gets right now." She turned to finish her orders for the ground crew. Low-tech planets were interesting in that they called for weapons that required more skill than pulling a trigger. However, when her goal was to get in and out as fast as possible, they were a pain in the ass. And she'd have to play by their rules. She couldn't take the risk that it was the entire Commonwealth selling these people out. She didn't need to lose her merc license.

"Make sure those population ships can hold the people from the planet. We're not taking them in our ships."

"Already done." Deven's smile told her he knew she'd give in on this. And he most likely knew it wasn't because of the huge sum of money he'd thrown at her. Well, mostly it wasn't.

"You're making me a fool." She got in his face and spoke low enough that none of the rest of the crew could hear.

"No one thinks you're a fool." The look in his eyes was gentle but that just made her want to smack him more. "Maybe this is who you're meant to be."

Vas held his gaze for a few seconds then stalked off. "Go to hell." She didn't really mean it, and she swore she felt his eyes bearing into the back of her skull. She'd bet all those credits that he knew she didn't mean it either.

It took surprisingly little time to get a full landing crew down to the planet. Well, as full of a crew as Vas could gather from her command staff. Since Deven had originally said this was a cleanup mission, she'd only counted on twenty fighters. Given the new situation, she'd been able to add another fifteen, but more than that and the *Warrior Wench* would be dangerously undermanned.

What had her jumpy was that while there were definitely a fair amount of fighters in the refugee zone, there were no warships in orbit. There should have been at least one cruiser out there lending support, but Gosta continued to report nothing beyond the mammoth population ships full of refugees.

The area of the fighting was rough, the terrain far too mountainous for a clean pickup. Vas scowled at the mountains as she flew the shuttle in. Close enough to be a major problem if enemy troops were hiding in them, far enough to be a pain in the ass to go check out.

The city before them had clearly been abandoned long before any fighting took place. Buildings showed new scars from primitive mortar rounds next to already crumbling buildings. Which made sense. Easier to take over an area if it was already discarded. The refugees had probably been welcome to the place.

"Since you're our client, what do we know about them?" Vas asked as she watched her crew unload. "Did the locals accept them?"

"I know what you're thinking, but yes, from the reports I gathered, the local population welcomed them. This part of Asterlia is extremely underpopulated and the refugees were willing to pay a fair amount."

Vas sighed and buckled on her sword. "So it's not the locals, and we have about eighty people still to get off planet." She poked him with her fist. "Paying fees or not, you owe me for this. We're not a rescue barge, you know."

Deven nodded, but Vas could tell he wasn't sufficiently cowed. He never was.

The rest of her crew was armed and ready, so they jogged into the town. The dangerously silent town. In Vas's world, silent was rarely ever good.

The city wall had once been made of a light yellow brick, probably not more than five or six feet high, which indicated a low level of aggression between neighbors. Most of it was little more than golden dust now, blown apart by something far heavier than a low-tech planet could produce.

Not good. That reinforced that whoever did this was not part of the merc companies fighting to the north and didn't care who knew it. The penalty for bringing high-tech weapons to a designated enforced low-tech world was brutal. The fact that whoever was behind this did it without a care chilled Vas almost as much as the continuing silence did.

"Be careful, people," she said as her team prepped to spread out. "I want a full recon in groups of four or more. If you lose sight of one of your team, come back to base. There is something very wrong here."

Vas nodded to her three and they slowly moved out. The stillness of the place crawled along her spine. A crunching of rubble followed by the high-pitched whine of a pair of arrows was the only warning. With a warning yell to her people, Vas flattened herself to the ground. The arrows thunked into the broken building behind them. Her two archers leapt to their feet, ready to fire back. For moments no one moved, the wind lifting the rubble was the only sound.

"Show yourselves," Vas yelled as she dusted off her knees. "We've come to take the refugees off planet."

"Captain Tor Dain? Isss that you?"

The extended "s" sound relaxed Vas's shoulders. She knew that Silante voice.

"Carrix? You old bastard, what are you doing ambushing proper mercs?" With a nod to her archers, she sheathed her sword. Carrix was a mercenary captain of a small company of Silantians. While single species companies weren't common, some worked extremely well.

Carrix had one that did.

A rumble of ruins slid down about twenty feet from where they were standing. Moments later five short, dust-covered forms came out. Vas's frown grew even deeper. Two were limping badly. It took a hell of a lot to make a Silantian limp. And they usually stayed in much larger groups. Keeping an eye on Carrix and his four-member team, Vas scanned the ruined buildings lumbering around them.

"Please tell me you brought more people than what I see." Carrix stopped in front of her, letting the man he was helping slide to the ground. Silantians were a small reptilian-based race, not more than five feet in height. However, what they lacked in height, they made up for in bulk, and their short powerful legs served them well.

Vas glanced around again, but still saw nothing. "We have another thirty spreading out. What the hell happened? Where are your people?"

The small captain before her was clearly exhausted, another thing she didn't think could happen to Silantians. His golden slitted eyes held hers. "It's a trap."

Vas had her sword out before he drew another breath, but he grabbed her arm and slid her weapon back. "Easy, old friend, the trap was already sprung. Although it may have been you they were after. They didn't seem happy to see forty Silantians swarming the town."

"Should we be standing out here?" Vas held off from responding to his grab of her sword hand. She and Carrix went back to her first merc job. That, and Silantians had a different concept of personal space than other races.

Carrix's residual gills on either side of his neck flittered in embarrassment. "No, we shouldn't." He shook his head. "Forgive me. We've been trapped down here for a month, and my mind is not functioning." He turned and led all of them into an enclave of crumbled buildings.

Vas motioned for two of her people to stand guard but stay behind shelter. Normally she would trust Carrix to have some sort of guards, but she had a sinking feeling the four with him were all he had left.

The main room he led them into was collapsed, but the next room was clear and had clearly been home for the five Silantians. Vas held her tongue until Carrix got the two injured fighters settled. "Damn it, Carrix, what the hell is going on?"

He sighed and patted a rough stool next to him. "In a viper's egg, I have destroyed my company. We answered a call for help thirty days ago. There is a sanctioned action in the far north." At Vas's nod that she knew that, he continued, "We received a plea. None of the companies fighting to the north could or would come down, and the plea was from a group of Silantians on board some slow-moving population ships. The ships are still in space, yes?"

Vas nodded. They'd checked them out. Were they not legitimate?

Her concern had been clear on her face, and Carrix patted her hand. "Do not worry; they are not the ones to fear. They called out legitimately asking for help for the people still trapped here. They had no way of knowing they'd already been slaughtered."

"When?"

"Before we got down here. That much is known. We were attacked by unknown forces the moment we set down. We pushed them back into the mountains, thinking we were going to save the people trapped here. They doubled back and laid a trap." His eyes closed. A look of exhausted sorrow filled his scaled face. When he opened his eyes, the gold had faded to a light green. "My company was butchered in that first day. I only could save these. Before reinforcements could come down, a pair of unmarked ships blew the *Guardian* out of the sky."

Vas heard Hrrru's intake of breath behind her. She'd kept him with her since he was the calmest of the three she had, but even he couldn't help but react. Carrix's ship held over 250 people and had often worked together with Vas's company.

She wanted to extend her sympathy, but the Silantian way was to mourn their dead only after they had been avenged. "Do you know anything about the ships that attacked? There's nothing out there now but the refugee ships."

"Not much I am afraid. Their attackers hit without warning. There was very little my people could say before they were destroyed. I would tell your Gosta to be on extreme alert."

Vas nodded, and thumbed open her comm. "Gosta, Carrix is down here. His ship was destroyed without warning. Gather the refugee ships as close as you can....." She paused, ten slow-moving population ships against something that could blow a heavy cruiser to bits. "Belay that. Have six Flits escort the refugees out of here. Now. Take them to Home and make sure to have them go through enough jumps to throw off anyone following. But get them out of here and stay on red alert." That would only leave a skeleton crew on the *Warrior Wench* but she didn't have a choice.

"Aye, Captain." Gosta's voice was clear and calm even though she knew he too would have been shocked by the destruction of the *Guardian*. "There is a pocket of plasma not far from here. Shall I move to it? The shielding on this ship is unlike any I've ever seen, we can safely stay there for some time. And it will help mask us from sensors should they come back."

Vas glanced at Carrix, but if he realized that pocket was most likely the remains of his ship, he gave no response. Most likely he knew full well what it was.

"Aye." She turned to Carrix. "Did they happen to mention if the ships were gray unmarked heavy cruisers?"

"Yes, two of them. You have dealt with them before?"

Vas sighed. "Yes. They destroyed Lantaria." She clicked her comm back on. "Gosta, it's the gray ships. Get close to that pocket as soon as the Flits and the refugee ships have gone through the gate."

After a few more security commands, Vas called Deven and the others. She wanted them to continue their search, but they were now searching for hostiles, not potential victims.

"Did you recognize anything about the ground troops?"

Carrix rose and helped one of his injured men drink some water. Both were probably not going to survive.

"No, they have on heavy black atmosphere suits." He turned and held her eyes. "They didn't say anything except for one order. They demanded to know where the *Victorious Dead* was."

Vas had been sipping out of her canteen and almost choked. "What? They asked for my ship?"

"Demanded," Carrix said. "I told them they could go to hell."

"Damn it." Vas clicked open her comm again. "Gosta, they came here looking for the *Victorious Dead*. Make sure your codes are scrambled. Only call down when you have to. Otherwise maintain comm silence."

Gosta's response was a crisp affirmative, then a few muttered comments about missing ships.

Vas smiled. She knew she wasn't supposed to hear that part; clearly her navigator was more than a bit frazzled. "I'll keep my end open, you just listen and record. Just don't respond unless it's desperate." The recordings from her comm could be important if they didn't make it out. She contacted Deven and asked him to warn the rest of the teams. She also suggested they regroup into teams of eight.

"What did Gosta say about looking for the *Victorious Dead*? His speech was too fast for me to hear." Carrix said.

Vas flashed her old friend a smile. "You shouldn't be listening in on other conversations, old man." She trusted Carrix and his people but she couldn't be sure that their base wasn't compromised. They'd clearly left it more than once. If those gray ships and their mysterious black-suited fighters were looking for the *Victorious Dead* instead of the *Warrior Wench*, let them.

"He was being his usual smart-ass self. Don't worry; he'll keep my ship out of sight." She should just grab her people, Carrix's people, and flee. The instant he'd mentioned the gray ships she knew it was too late. The only reason they hadn't attacked yet was probably because they were trying to confirm it was the *Victorious Dead* out in orbit. Which meant her people were already targets.

She rose then went to the back of the room. A pile of golden brick rubble showed where a wall had once been. Beyond that was another, larger room. Part of the ceiling had crumbled, but it would hold her people.

"Deven, we need to pull back and get back on the shuttle. Call back all groups and meet at my location."

"Aye, Captain. We haven't seen anything, but there are too many ruins to check. I'll—"

An explosion rocked the building as well as knocked out the comm signal. Vas was flung to the floor as more of the unstable building tumbled around her.

"Crap, what was that? Deven? Report."

"Gon here, Captain Vas." The deep rumbling voice filled the airwaves, but still cut in and out. Whatever the blast had been it had physical destruction as well as EMT after-effects. "We're near the outer rim of the town. Someone has destroyed our shuttle."

Vas rubbed her face. She hadn't thought someone would be able to hack through their system to drop the shuttle's shields that quickly.

Unless they'd used enough fire power that they destroyed the shields instead of hacking through them.

She almost called Gosta, but the fact that he hadn't contacted her with the destruction of the shuttle confirmed what her gut was telling her.

At least one of the gray ships was up there right now.

CHAPTER TWENTY-SIX

"Damn it. Gon, get your people back here. Do not go near the shuttle wreckage under any circumstances. Lock into my location and get back here as fast as you can. The hostiles are here and in space."

It seemed like hours, but was most likely only minutes before the rest of the teams came in. But not Deven's.

"Gon, did you see any of Deven's team?" She knew he picked up a second team, but they should have made it by now.

"No, Captain Vas, I have not seen him." The giant man turned back toward the entrance. "I'll go get him?"

Vas almost laughed; no doubt he'd probably pick Deven up and put him over his shoulder. At least that was the tone of his voice.

She'd glanced outside when she let Gon's group in, still a few hours from nightfall. Deven would have called if it had been safe, or he could have simply found something and gone to track it down.

"No, we wait. He knows where we are. If he doesn't show up soon, we'll go out for him." She turned to her people. "And no comms. From here out, we assume the enemy can hear us."

"It is generous of you to stay and die with us, but how do you intend to leave?" Carrix had been silently sitting in the corner. However, he'd obviously heard everything.

"We'll find a way. Our enemy, whoever in the hell they are, isn't as on top of things as they appear." She nodded up to the ceiling indicating the sky above them. "Things aren't what they—" Her words were cut off as another explosion rocked nearby, this one clearly ground based and far too close to their hidden location.

Vas counted her limbs from the gravel-filled pit she'd been flung into then called around for the others. "Is everyone okay?" The responses varied in tone, but all reported positively. She was heading for the doorway when rapid weapons fire echoed through the tight buildings near them. Damn it. How could they compete with high-tech weapons when they only had bows and swords?

A memory of something Gosta had said about the newest toy he'd invented trickled into her mind. Swearing to herself she scrambled to her pack and dug through it. She hadn't paid much attention to Gosta, but it seemed he thought his toy could knock out tech weapons for a period of time. Of course he wasn't completely sure for how long, nor how far it would reach. Nor if it even worked.

She said thanks to whatever deities were listening when her hand hit something small, round, and cold. "Ha!" She triumphantly pulled out the sphere and sprinted toward the entrance.

"Vas, what are you doing?" Carrix yelled at her as she leapt over piles of debris.

"Leveling the playing field."

The two people she'd left in the front were gone, hopefully hiding. There was still no sign of Deven and his people. She didn't want to use Gosta's toy until the enemy was closer, but at the same time, she might not have that luxury. If she waited too long the enemy could blow them away without ever getting close.

The dust from the previous explosion still flittered in the dusky air, and she found herself fighting to keep from coughing. Ripping part of her undershirt off, she made a mask over her nose and mouth. While it kept out most of the dust, it didn't block the sudden stench of death that rose up as the wind changed. They must be downwind of where Carrix's ground team had been ambushed.

Vas breathed through her mouth as well as she could. She didn't know what she was waiting for, but this gizmo of Gosta's might be their best hope and she didn't know if it would work more than once. If it worked at all.

The sound of people running hell-bent toward her location bounced down the empty road.

Followed by the very unwelcome sound of blasters.

Vas let out a breath and set the command on the small sphere. Now she wished she had paid more attention to Gosta when he had been babbling about this thing. The only thing she remembered was that she didn't have to throw it. Just set it, and then watch as all the blasters died.

God, she hoped Gosta was as good as she thought he was.

Pushing the final sequence she watched the people running toward her, some of Deven's people, but no Deven. Behind them ran about twenty ominous black suits calmly firing but herding more than trying to kill.

A wave of light burst out of the sphere. She almost dropped it out of surprise, but she hadn't felt anything.

The bastards in the suits did, however.

Their blasters locked up. A moment later the ones in the front exploded, taking out the people holding them as well. Unfortunately, it only took out a dozen; the rest threw their weapons away too fast. Vas stepped back as six of her people dove for the building's doorway.

"Where's F'vain and Deven?"

"F'vain got taken out by those bastards. Deven sent us here and tried to draw the bulk of them away." Mac swore as he wiped dust and blood from his face. "It was useless though. Too many of them followed us."

Vas looked back out where the black suits were retreating. She knew they wouldn't be gone for long. Just long enough to load up on low-tech weapons. She stored Gosta's sphere back in her bag. She'd have to give that man a promotion one of these days.

"Carrix, we need a better place to fight. This is too damn small and there's only one way out."

The small reptilian smiled at her from where he attended one of his dying men. Dead men actually. Both had passed away and he was administering last rites, or whatever their religion followed.

"Do you think I am a fledging?" He nodded toward the back wall. "All is not what it seems."

Frowning, Vas walked to the back. What was the old lizard babbling about? There was nothing here except.... Pushing aside what appeared to be a solid wall of rubble she saw it opened to a cavernous room. The fake wall was actually a mimicking fabric. Perhaps the room beyond had once been a ballroom, royal chambers, or warehouse—the original purpose of it was long lost. Whatever it had been, it would be a decent place to defend. Normally she wouldn't choose to fight in a building, but she didn't like the odds against them outside. Clearly there was something or someone that gray ship in orbit wanted alive otherwise they would have just started blasting when they destroyed the shuttle. Their orders had changed since the attack on Lantaria.

She was just getting her and Carrix's fighters in place when the black-clad fighters broke through an outer wall. They did it without tech unless you counted the suits themselves. Yelling commands, she settled in for an ugly fight.

Deven swore when he heard the explosions. Clearly all of the hostiles hadn't followed him. He grimly studied the bodies surrounding him. At least he'd taken out some of them.

He started to pick up one of the blasters laying near a fallen enemy, when a light flooded the area and all of the blasters gave a high-pitched whine. Swearing, he threw it and dove behind a pile of rubble. An instant later all of the weapons exploded.

Crap, he could have used those. However, judging from the direction of that light wave, it may have been something from Carrix's people.

Deven heard the fighting up ahead, but there were no sounds of blasters so whatever had blown up the ones near him must have destroyed them all. He easily found the group of buildings they were fighting in. It surprised him that no one was on guard, then realized they were either dead or had fallen back to the others.

It took a moment for his eyes to adapt to the dark inner room, but eventually he saw the only ones here were dead. Two Silantians, laid out too peacefully to have fallen in this fighting. Three black suits crumbled to the ground, not so peacefully. No one from the *Warrior Wench* yet. Stalking forward with his sword out, Deven entered a large room. At least thirty black-suited warriors were fighting his people. Vas was surrounded by at least three and couldn't seem to keep up with them.

Something was very different about these fighters. The ones he'd destroyed outside were good, but not like this. These people were speeding up even as he watched, flashing throughout the room.

Vas wasn't going to make it.

Deven ducked as a flung blade missed him by inches. He couldn't afford to worry about Vas. If he were killed it would do her no good.

Regaining his balance, Deven swung his sword up just in time to block an impossible shot to his head. He thrust back, only gaining a small bit of breathing room. There was no way whoever was in that suit could move like that. It wasn't real. The person flipped over its own shoulder, then turned to strike down one of the Silantians. Two Silantians swarmed the attacker, but couldn't hold it off for long. With a yell, Deven leapt into the fray, slicing as he went. He had never felt so helpless in his life. At least not when he had a weapon in his hand. These people in the black suits were fighters beyond the ability to imagine. He would think they were AIs but their movements were too fluid, too adaptable, for artificial intelligence.

"Deven, behind you!" Vas yelled from across the room.

Deven swore again and ducked. That suit of armor had gotten in behind him before he'd even seen it. Or had it? He swore as the realization hit him. He hadn't noticed the small devices they were wearing at first, but he saw them now.

"Vas, they've got scramblers. We need to have the ship send a block." Deven leapt at the new aggressor. Yelling it across the room probably wasn't the most strategic way of communicating. If their attackers had translators they knew what was coming next. But at this point Deven's only goal was to get as many of their crew out in one piece.

The fighters were fast, but they were also using a highly illegal technology. Scramblers could affect time in small doses; just enough to move in on a victim before they could tell you were there.

"Shit." Vas yelled back. "Gosta, you heard the man. Aim some blocks down here or you're becoming the new captain the hard way."

A low-level hum filled the room. Their attackers didn't react at first, then one by one the company was able to start taking them down. The black suits noticed that.

"There is no way in hell I ever want your job." Gosta's voice came out over the speakers. He was broadcasting to the whole company. If Vas didn't care who heard, neither did her navigation man. "That gray ship is moving in closer. Should I engage?"

Vas dodged and sliced down two attackers with a stunning leap and a quick sword hand switch. Deven took a second to admire her. He might be the better swordsman in terms of technique, but no one could out-fight Vaslisha Tor Dain when she was in the moment.

"Negative, Gosta. That ship is off limits." Deven said back over the comm. That ship would massacre the *Warrior Wench* if she came out of that plasma pocket.

"Just stay ready. We may have to try that new tech we got." Vas yelled.

"Vas, we haven't even tested it." Gosta never called her Vas unless he was really upset. Even with his teke powers blocked, Deven could tell the navigator was really, really upset. Not that he blamed him. The idea of transferring cargo via that particle mover wasn't too bad. His own people hadn't been too far away from such tech when he left. But living people?

Looking around he realized they might not have a choice.

With the scramblers disengaged, the company held their own, but they were still outmatched. This fight couldn't go on too much longer if they wanted to get out with anyone still alive.

Hrrru went down as he lost against a pair of the black-suited fighters. "I think you're right, Vas," Deven yelled as he sliced through two of them to reach the downed man. Hrrru was still breathing, but barely. The sword had missed both of his hearts by inches.

"Okay, Gosta, whatever you have to do, do it. Get Flarik to help. She may know the tech. All of our team plus...Carrix." Deven heard the sorrow in her voice as Vas realized the remaining Silantians hadn't survived. "We need evac now."

"Aye."

It was amazing how much anxiety could be conveyed in one word.

Sorth and Gellio both collapsed as their attackers brought them down. Gosta and Flarik would need to move fast or there wouldn't be anyone to save.

Carrix and Hrrru vanished. The Silantian captain had been guarding the injured Hrrru and they were closest to the edge of the fighting. Deven really hoped they'd made it to the ship.

To his right, two more of the ship's company vanished. The black-suited fighters fought harder as their foes were taken from them. That there were fewer to fight wasn't helping the remaining ship's company. Jakiin got pulled away just as three black suits were closing in.

"Faster, Gosta, or you'll be pulling corpses."

Deven didn't want to panic the man, but they weren't going to make it.

Gosta didn't respond, but the next pair went faster. Clearly he was stuck with only two at a time but he was increasing the turn-around.

Vas swore as she was pulled up with Mac, leaving Deven and Gon. The huge fighter unfortunately was close to six of the black suits and he stumbled as they literally launched themselves at him. Deven saw him go down but had his own group to hold off, and an instant later light filled his vision and his senses went inside out.

He floated for what seemed like eternity. Briefly, he wondered if perhaps it hadn't been Gosta who pulled them out but the gray ship. Or maybe the machine hadn't worked at all. Eventually the light faded and colors and sounds slammed into his head.

"Deven? You in there?"

Deven cringed at the loudness, but eventually opened one eye. Vas's very concerned face hovered above him looking like an angel. He tried to reach up to her, but his arms weren't working.

"I think so." An attempt at lifting his head forced him to shut his eyes again. "What happened?"

"The machine doesn't work well with telepaths. I'm just speculating mind you. Gosta's running a full diagnostic, or as full as he can with illegal equipment." Flarik was somewhere over his right shoulder, but he didn't look to find out where.

"Does it feel like your faculties are returning?"

That was Terel, somewhere down in front of him. Eventually he was going to have to open his eyes again. Taking a deep breath, he willed his head not to explode.

"I think so. I guess it's a good thing my people never went ahead with work on a machine like that." This time the world wasn't nearly as bright when he opened his eyes. Whatever happened it was fading blessedly fast.

"He'll be fine." Vas grinned, and then nodded toward Terel. "Call me if anyone needs anything. Otherwise we have to get out of here immediately."

Deven reached forward to grab her hand. He pulled her fingers back as she started to leave. "Wait, what about that gray ship? It was up here, wasn't it?"

Vas's smile turned feral. "Aye. That 'was' being the important word." She shook her head in admiration. "I doubt we'll be able to pull this trick again, but Gosta used our new toy to transfer some gifts directly into their engine room. Right through their shields as neat as you please. They exploded about ten minutes ago." She put a finger over his mouth as a million questions fought to the surface.

They'd blown up one of those monster ships?

"Ach, like I said, we need to get out of here quickly. The escort Flits didn't get the rescue ships more than a few jumps out before running into trouble. They had to turn back or risk being destroyed; they barely made it out of an ambush. They should be back here within a few minutes. Then we run. I have a feeling this area is going to become very crowded very soon."

CHAPTER TWENTY-SEVEN

Vas smiled to herself as she sat in her command chair. The look on Deven's face when she told him about the gray ship was almost as good as seeing it explode a half hour ago. Almost.

Thanks to those bastards, they'd lost eight people. Gon and Hrrru were still in recovery, but Terel thought they'd pull through. Still, they'd survived when the odds were horribly stacked against them. She'd invited Carrix to stay on board, but he just asked to be transported back to the planet near the merc companies in the north. He knew one of the captains, a distant relative, and could get a ride back to their home world after the fighting.

"Gosta, if those refugee ships are ready, we need to make our way to the hypergate. I want to hop a few times in case our friends decide to track us."

He flipped the main screen so it looked out toward the gate. "Aye, Captain. They all report ready. Slowest one is a class two. We'll have to keep that pace as we change gates."

Vas sighed. There was nothing to be done about it. Deven had promised the refugees that the *Warrior Wench* would get them out. And now that she had them, she had to admit she wouldn't go back on her word either.

"Understood. Get us out of here, Gosta."

The engines engaged rapidly and pulled forward into the hypergate. Vas watched the nav screen on her small computer at her seat. The codes were good and the hypergate opened cleanly. She held her breath as the slowest ship almost looked like it wasn't going to make it, but it cleared before the gate shut. There weren't any ripples on the nav computer that indicated any more gray visitors had hit the sector, but Vas didn't relish having to go back for a missing ship.

The first three hops went cleanly, and Deven had recovered enough to return to the command deck after the third one. That was a very interesting side effect of the particle mover; it clearly completely disabled telepaths for a brief time. Something she'd have to keep in mind.

Vas ordered Gosta to swing as random and as far as he could on the jumps. She went through all this trouble to save these people; she didn't want whoever was after them to find them easily. Nor to find her ship.

"Captain, I think we may have an additional problem," Gosta said from his console.

When he didn't elaborate, Vas prodded him. "Well? The ships are all sticking together right?"

"That's not it. They're holding up. However, I left a tracking buoy at the last planet. Flarik suggested it while you were on the planet, I agreed." His voice quivered a bit in defense, but when Vas didn't yell at him he continued. Actually she thought it was a great idea and was punching herself that she hadn't thought of it.

"More gray ships?"

"No, that's the thing. It's a Commonwealth ship. Three of them actually." His pause told Vas she really wasn't going to like his next part. "War-class cruisers, all of them."

Vas hadn't told Gosta about her blocking of the Commonwealth trackers, but he most likely had seen it once he returned to his station. What the hell was going on? A single War-class cruiser could have easily wiped out the *Warrior Wench* and all of the refugee ships. To have three show up that quickly was terrifying.

"Noted." For good or ill their path was laid out. For now at any rate. She flipped open the ship-wide comm. "Attention. Until further notice we are staying clear of any and all Commonwealth ships or transmissions. Evidence has indicated that there is something wrong within the hierarchy itself and we need to avoid it." She was about to close the comm line and deal with the faces on the command deck when Divee's earlier fear came back to her. "And no, this does not mean we're going rogue. We're just staying out of whatever mess is happening. If you believe you cannot continue in such a fashion, notify Deven and we'll find a way for you to get to Home."

"What?" she said to the command deck after she closed the comm.

"Could you at least warn me before you declare war on the Commonwealth?" Flarik asked from her new console. "The legal ramifications of such an action will be enormous." She'd never wanted to be on the command deck before, but now she'd taken up an unused science station almost permanently.

Vas rose and turned to face the entire command crew. She briefly filled them in on her encounter with the high-ranking official. It spoke volumes that none of them interrupted her.

"Now we have three War-class cruisers showing up immediately after we blow up one of the mystery ships. I don't think it's too paranoid to think something very wrong is going on with at least part of Commonwealth. Hopefully it's just a fringe element, something they can deal with quickly." She faced them all with a grim look. "But it's not a chance I think we can take given the recent actions. Do any of you disagree? My offer of leaving is open to *everyone*." She met Deven's eyes long enough to let him know that included him.

Mac finally broke the silence with a nervous laugh. "Sorry. I think I speak for us all, but we're not going anywhere, Captain. You think we need to hide from the Commonwealth, we hide."

Vas was actually touched by the loyalty on his face. He was a huge pain in the ass, but his heart was solid. The same look was reflected on the rest of her officers' faces.

Deven shook his head. "You really think you could run this barge without us?"

"I don't know what I was thinking." She laughed and took her seat. "Gosta, lay in the course for the next jump. I want at least four star systems between us and them, whoever *them* is."

Gosta's response was lost as the ship made a horrible grinding sound as it entered the hypergate.

"Damn it, what just happened?" Vas yelled loud enough to be heard over the screaming klaxon. "And someone shut that damn thing off." Her last command came out far too loud as the screaming machine stopped right before she finished. Travel within the hypergates was usually disturbingly uneventful. Whatever was wrong with this one must be pretty nasty to cause that kind of rattling.

"Are the rest of the ships still with us, Xsit?" Deven called as he ran to the nav console to help Gosta.

"Yes, but the captains are all calling in. All of them had the same jolt we did." She gave a worried chirp. "Worse, the smaller ship is having thruster problems now."

"I need answers, people." Vas tried scanning the system logs but there was nothing that should have triggered such a reaction. She switched her scan to the gate, but the system looked okay. Waitaminute. "Crap, we're being pulled off course. Something is pulling this hypergate stream out of alignment and dragging all of us along too. Damn it, it's changing destination. Gosta?"

The ship groaned and rattled as whatever was happening to the hypergate put horrific strain on the shell. If something the size of the *Warrior Wench* felt like it was going to shake apart, she hoped the smaller ships even survived.

Gosta pounded his console. His eyes were huge when he glanced up. "I can't break it, and I can't see where it's pulling us."

Flarik's fingers moved with lightning speed as she followed the same connections Vas had. She swore, or at least Vas assumed it was swearing and not praying, under her breath. Vas joined the Wavian and tapped her shoulder.

"I can see it now. However, this shouldn't exist. It's a supergate, or rather we're being pulled toward a supergate." Flarik tapped a shaking claw at the screen. "In theory supergates can bend space to the point that inter-dimensional travel can exist. The hypergate we went in was tied to something much bigger. It's dragging us to the location of the supergate on this screen."

Mac tried to compensate for the pull, but the most he could do was keep the ship intact. "That's insane. Nothing can be that big. The power it would take would be—"

Vas had been paying attention to Flarik's screen, but she turned toward him when Mac cut himself off. His eyes were locked on the main screen, his jaw slack. Vas spun.

"You mean something like that?" Deven said grimly.

The hypergate path dropped them in an unknown section of space, at least it wasn't on any screens Vas had ever seen before. Smaller klaxons rang throughout the ship as the adjustment of hypergate travel cut unexpectedly short.

In front of them was the biggest gate she'd ever seen. Ten War-class cruisers could fit through it at the same time without a problem. Whatever material it was made of emitted an eerie glow that filled the command deck. The only thing more terrifying than it was the cluster of gray ships in front of it.

CHAPTER TWENTY-EIGHT

The klaxon that Vas was hearing way too often blared again as one of the smaller enemy ships barely adjusted in time to avoid them. Why in the hell would any ship veer that close to an opening hypergate?

"Damn it. Get us out of here now, Mac." Vas tried counting the gray ships but they were changing formation. From what she was seeing on the screens, the massive supergate in front of them had only been at half power when they were dragged her. It powered down too fast for her systems to gather much information. However, she made sure every single data-gathering piece of equipment was aimed at the mess before them. If there was any information there, she was going to get it.

"We're still not moving, Mac. Code up that hypergate and get us the hell out of here. Tell the refugee ships to high-tail it the second we get the gate open...." Vas trailed off as what had stunned Mac was flashed to the main screen. The gate they had just come through was dead.

"Vas...."

She waved Deven off. "I see it. Later, one of you really smart people will tell me how in the hell we and ten little tagalongs made it through a busted gate. Now, someone find us another way out."

"There isn't another way, Captain. We have to get that gate functioning again." Flarik in lawyer mode was nothing against Flarik in pissed-off former engineer mode. She was typing in commands so fast the feathers on the back of her hands appeared ready to burst into flame.

"We have a bigger problem." Deven switched screens where two of the gray cruisers had maneuvered themselves in between the refugee ships and the dead hypergate they had somehow come in through. The refugee ships huddled closer to the *Warrior Wench*, but Vas had a feeling it would only be minutes before they were completely cut off from both the hypergate and the supergate. Considering they were in unknown space, the option to flee in hopes of finding another gate was useless. On the plus side, the gray ships hadn't started destroying anyone yet.

"Not to be a pessimist or anything, but why circle us like this? They could blow us all out of the sky at any moment," Vas said.

Flarik glanced up from her rapid commands for the hypergate, moving over a bit to let Bathshea at the twin console. "I would say they want something from us. Or the ships with us. No one attacked them at the planet. And when they tried to flee, the bastards only blocked them from escaping."

Vas ran her hands through her hair. "Damn it. We have no idea what they're up to, but we can't let them trap us here. Bathie? Any luck?"

"Between Flarik and me we can eventually get that hypergate up. It was shut at this end. Clearly our friends didn't want to be interrupted. I'd say that however we got here, they didn't intend it. I don't think they expected us. And the fact we made it through could be why they aren't blasting us." She looked around the deck. "We need time to get the hypergate back up before they change their minds."

Mac turned paler than normal as he watched the twenty or so massive gray cruisers slowly lock in position. "But how in the hell are we going to get to the hypergate even if we fix it? We might bust through, but only with heavy damage and there's no way any of the refugee ships would survive."

"I'm working on that." Gosta's lean face was tight as he ran programs trying to find ways to disable the gray ships and their smaller support cruisers. Even a temporary solution might let them all get out. He swore as one of his attempts came back negative.

"We can't try my trick from before. The ships are shielded in such a way to block the particle mover. The one I destroyed must have gotten word to them before it exploded."

A hit rocked through their own shields and Vas tumbled to the deck. The strike hadn't been meant to destroy, but it was far too close to the engines for peace of mind. "Suggestions, people. We just ran out of time. They know this ship is the only threat. They're going to keep us here until they get what they want." Her eyes stayed glued to the screen as she picked herself up. The gap between ships was growing smaller. Soon there would be nothing but a ring of gray around them.

Deven had been ominously quiet. "Vas, I need to talk to you."

Vas started to shake him off then saw the look in his eyes. She joined him in her ready room.

"Deven, we don't have time—"

"The Furies. We can use them to blast through the ships once the hypergate is up again. We can clear a big enough space so that all of the ships get through."

Vas shook off the chill that climbed up her spine. "That's not an option, Deven. There are other choices."

"What would those be?" Deven pinned her arms. "We're out of options, Vas. With the refugees we've got way too many people to get out and a tiny hole to do it in.

I can make that hole bigger. We have no idea why they haven't slaughtered us already. But you and I both know what will happen when they get whatever it is they want."

His dark green eyes seemed lighter now, a tawny gold that she'd never seen before circled the iris. She checked his bracelets. Was he trying to use his teke powers? Against her? However, the links on his wrist were still solid.

"There has got to be another way. Gosta said—"

Deven cut her off with a finger across her lips, an oddly gentle gesture considering the situation. "Gosta isn't going to find another way out. We've got three Furies, at least two that we are certain work. Jakiin and I can do this. Two well-placed strikes from the Furies and you can get everyone out."

Vas couldn't meet his eyes anymore and pulled out of his grasp. "Everyone but you and Jakiin." She'd lost people before, people she cared about. It came with the job. But this was different. This was Deven. She wasn't sure exactly how she felt about him, but she'd counted on him always being there.

Deven reclaimed his hold on her and forced her to look up. "We might live, you know."

Vas felt the lie even as it left Deven's lips. "For a damn telepath, you're a lousy liar." There must be dust still in the air vents from the hit they took; her eyes were having to blink far too much. "I can't let you. I should go. You and Jakiin aren't the only ones who can fly those monsters."

"No. Your place is to get everyone out." He lightened the mood with a playful smile. "If the ship was sinking, then you could stay. Otherwise, it's the second's option to go out with a bang. You don't have a choice. They'll close the hole completely in minutes. Then they'll just circle around picking off the ships one by one until they get what they want." He met her eyes.

"I can't sense much, but they have some sort of powerful telepath or a teke-program on at least one ship. They *will* get whatever it is they are after."

Vas rocked back and stared up at the ceiling. Damn dust. With a quick wipe at her eyes she forced herself to look at Deven again. "What code will you send when you're in place? The timing will have to be perfect."

Deven nodded. "I'll radio a Cattera code. They won't know what it is. You can have our ships as far away from the opening as they'll let you. You'll have to run like hell after we clear the space. They'll get the blockade back up in no time."

Vas nodded, suddenly not trusting herself to speak. She tried anyway. "We, I...."

Deven smiled and brushed his knuckles along her cheek. "I know." With the smile still on his face, he pulled her close and kissed her. Gentle at first then with an intensity that would only be matched by the explosion he was about to cause.

Vas allowed herself to be swallowed by it. By the time she surfaced, he was gone. Dashing aside the remains of tears, she ran to the command deck and threw herself in her chair.

Bathie's hair was plastered across her forehead with sweat. "We've got the hypergate up. Well, as close to up as it's going to get. I'm keeping the energy readings below their sensor level so they don't realize it, but one word from you and we have a gate."

"For about ten minutes." Flarik didn't look much better.

"Xsit, contact the other ships. I need all of them to pull back from the area near the hypergate on my mark. They need to get as close to us as possible." Vas entered in her own command codes. Once Deven sent the Cattera code, her ship would back up out of harm's way. She had to think for a minute on what she needed to tell the other ships. Deven invaded her thoughts. Vas banished the thoughts. She had no time for anything right now.

"Gosta, after Xsit signals the other ships, I'll need you to send a private beam to their captains. Use the tightest clearance you can. We're not sure what the enemy can pick up or not. The ships need to pull back to us, but be ready to run for the hypergate immediately." She waved her hand as Gosta looked dangerously ready to ask a question. "No. No questions. We have one shot, and one shot only." Vas took a deep breath and willed her voice to stay steady. "Just make sure everyone is ready on my command."

The tension and fear that had filled the command deck minutes before was replaced by hope and focus. That was good; if they were all focused on the task and the timing, they wouldn't notice certain things until too late. It would be best if she was the only one on board who knew what was about to happen for as long as possible. She knew Deven would be able to mask the departure of the two Furies. No one would have seen or felt the lumbering, but deadly, ships disembark. No one but her. Even though she knew she couldn't have really heard it, she swore she knew the instant the ships left the landing bay.

It seemed like only seconds had passed when Vas got the Cattera code. Shoving the lump in her throat aside, she slammed the instruct code in and yelled at Mac to pull the *Warrior Wench* back as far as he could. A few tense seconds passed but the rest of her impromptu fleet did the same.

Everyone was focused on their tasks, so no one noticed the first explosion a few moments later. They noticed the next one though.

"Captain, there's a major firefight taking place near the gap between the ships," Xsit said. "I think they may be trying to close the space."

"No, they're not closing the gap." Vas's voice was low, but she knew her crew heard her, it wouldn't take them long to make the connection. "Gosta, did the captains get your orders? When the gray ships closest to the gap in front of the hypergate explode, we go through. They'll close ranks in no time, so everyone has to get out together."

Gosta turned toward Deven's empty chair and cocked his head. Vas gave a curt nod in response. The sad look on Gosta's face told her he understood. Vas was grateful. If Gosta knew, it might make it easier when the inevitable happened.

"Aye, Captain. The ships are ready and await your mark."

Vas didn't respond as the firefight of the two Furies and the gray ships grew even bigger. She didn't know how long Deven and Jakiin could hold on, nor how much damage they could inflict before they went. But she knew if there was any way at all they could save the rest of them, those two would.

Minutes later, she felt the first Fury explode an instant before she saw it. They had already disabled or destroyed four of the gray ships, and the debris glowed around them. The explosion of the first Fury knocked out two more. The second Fury exploded an instant later taking out six more ships.

CHAPTER TWENTY-NINE

Vas gripped the command seat and bit her lip to keep the emotions out of her head and face. "Go! Gosta, send the command. We have to run. Any ship that can't make it will be left behind. I don't think our guests are going to like us very much at this point."

The look on Gosta's face made it clear that he knew what those two explosions had been. He got the refugee ships in line and in seconds all of them were fleeing toward the hypergate.

The *Warrior Wench* escaped through the opening of the destroyed gray ships after all of the others. For all of her bluster, Vas couldn't let anyone be left behind, not after what it had cost to get them all out.

Xsit spun as her sensors picked up the Furies debris. Vas knew there were no life signs. She had already checked.

"Captain! Those were our Furies!"

"I know. Xsit, tell the refugee ships to stay on the heading." Vas turned toward Mac. He wasn't the sharpest of her crew, but it wouldn't take him long to realize who had been on those ships. He was focused now on maneuvering through the debris, but Vas nodded at Terel to stand near him. More muttering was heard in the command deck as more people picked up on Xsit's observation.

Vas finally opened a ship-wide comm. She had wanted to tell Mac and a few others privately, but she couldn't have people distracted. Even getting away from the trap didn't spell safety for them, not by a long shot.

"Attention." Her voice sounded odd in her ears as she addressed the crew. "Those explosions you saw, and the firefight that preceded it, were two of our own using the Furies to grant all of us the chance to live. Deven—" Her voice caught as something hard and rock-like formed in her throat. "Deven and Jakiin gave their lives to save our company and those refugees out there. It is up to us to make sure that their lives were not lost in vain. We will deal with this loss when we are free. We aren't free yet."

The entire command deck was silent. A part of her soul curled up and died.

Xsit shook. "But, Captain... Deven? Jakiin? Couldn't they—"

"Have survived that?" Vas steeled her voice. Right now she couldn't be soft or she would fall apart. She finally realized what had been affecting her these last weeks. Deven. Bloody stars below, she had fallen in love with Deven. She crammed that horrific thought as deep into her head as she could.

"No. They couldn't have. And I, *we*, don't have the luxury right now of grieving a single individual, or even two. They died to save those refugees and us. We owe it to them to get everyone out alive."

"Captain, we've got another problem." Gosta pointed toward his screen as soon as she got close. "It looks like they're trying to reopen their supergate."

Vas swore as she watched the screen. The refugee ships were at the hypergate, but could only go through slowly. There was no way all of them could get through before that supergate opened. Who knew what was going to come through it, but with their luck it would be more gray cruisers. At this point, even one more could destroy everything Deven and Jakiin died for.

"Tell the refugee ships to keep going through the gates. We're going to have to hang back. Once they get through, they need to go to the Zarlan system, but make a few hops in case someone is tracking them." She turned back to the large screen.

The two remaining heavy gray cruisers were still hanging back, but the smaller ships were moving closer to the refugee ships. "Mac, move us toward those two ships over there." Two of the destroyed enemy ships were leaking enough plasma to blow up half of the quadrant if even a pop gun went off. No one would be stupid enough to risk firing on them there. Neither could the *Warrior Wench* stay there for long, but they'd cross that bridge later. Mac silently moved the ship into position. Vas knew he was hurting too. Jakiin and Deven were two of his best friends. Nevertheless, none of them had time to grieve.

They needed a new plan. The two remaining heavy cruisers were moving closer. Any advantage the *Warrior Wench* had gained by destroying the smaller ships was going to be lost quickly. They needed to stay here to defend the refugees' backsides until right before that supergate opened. Xsit pulled up the recorded steps it went through when it closed; she could reverse it and get their opening sequence. The *Warrior Wench* would know when to move.

"How much heavy ordinance do we have left?" Vas was exceedingly grateful that the *Warrior Wench* had been stocked with even more ammo than her beloved *Victorious Dead* had been. However, she feared that even those advanced stores might be gone at this point.

The gunnery officer turned to her with a slow nod. "We're okay. We were mostly using the lower grades once the cruisers backed off. The heavy stuff seemed a bit overkill for the smaller ships."

Vas smiled. That was her gunny, most cautious weapons person ever known. That resolved one issue.

They had enough to hit whatever came through that supergate right at the apex of the transfer. That should destroy anything trying to come through, not to mention shatter the supergate itself. In theory. The problem was, they couldn't even try with those two gray cruisers coming after them.

Judging by the slow pace of the sequencing, the supergate was going to take at least another few minutes to open, which was most likely why the heavy cruisers were now coming closer. Clearly whatever had held them back before ended once the Furies took out three-quarters of their ships. They would blow the *Warrior Wench* out of the sky the moment they left the plasma bank.

Something was going to have to hold off those two cruisers.

Vas turned and ran toward the docking bay corridor as a thought hit her. "Xsit, when that supergate signals pre-opening I need you to tell Gosta. Gosta, run the *Warrior Wench* as close to that supergate as you can without risking explosion. Fire everything we have at that supergate once the event horizon is breached. Blow those bastards out of the sky." Vas saw her gunny go white. The idea of throwing everything at anything was foreign to gunnies, especially hers.

"But, Vas, those ships will nail us the minute we break free of this pile of radioactive mess."

Vas stopped. She couldn't just run out.

"I know." She looked slowly into the eyes of each one of her deck officers. Her family. "I'm going to take the last Fury and ram it down those cruisers' throats." She was the only person still onboard who could fly a Fury so at least she knew there'd be no arguing. "Hopefully they'll have a healthy respect for it after the damage Deven and Jakiin caused their fleet. If I can hold them back long enough without engaging, I will." She left it unspoken what would happen if they decided not to back off from a single ship, even a Fury. "I want you to follow the refugees to Zarlan, stay there for two days." She forced a smile that tried to encompass everyone. "I will find you."

Vas turned away quickly and ran down the corridor toward the fighter ships. She'd sworn at Deven when he'd brought the Furies on board. More than a few captains felt the monster ships were cursed. But he might have very well saved all of them by his actions.

Vas had gone through the ships when Deven wasn't paying attention. This third one had some cosmetic issues, but was solid. Cursed or not, they were amazing ships and grand examples of overkill in warship design.

Saying a prayer to any deity who decided to listen, Vas threw on a flight suit and climbed on board. The Furies weren't designed by humans, or even humanoids. They were an ancient design of a lost race, one that had been futzed with until they could accommodate humanoid shapes. Still, everything was just a tad too big. Made Vas feel like a little kid caught in the grownups' vehicle. She finished buckling herself in and prepped the launch sequence. No matter how much she loved commanding her ship, she still loved the thrill of a one-person fighter. The excitement of the dock doors opening to the vacuum of space, the stars practically daring her to come out and play. This was what she went into space for.

The final check held clear and she keyed in the launch sequence. She almost stopped it when it looked like someone else was down in the bay, but then the shape she thought she saw vanished. None of her people would be stupid enough to come down here, and anyone who was deserved to be flung out to space when she launched.

She wasn't sure what she was expecting, but the Fury handled the launch with amazing smoothness. A stab of sorrow hit her as she immediately wanted to call Deven and tell him. What had he thought when he and Jakiin lifted up? Roughly shoving aside those thoughts, Vas spun the ship and headed away from the *Warrior Wench*.

They only had minutes before that supergate opened. Hopefully she could keep the heavy cruisers out of the way that long.

Suddenly the ship rocked. Well, it seemed like it did. In fact it was holding course, but two Flits shot by it making it seemed like it had rolled.

"Who in the hell is that? Get your asses back to the ship now." Vas might not know who they were, but that gold trim could only have come from the *Warrior Wench*. Who in the hell decorated fighter ships?

Two more Flits burst out, joining the first two just to the sides of her.

"Answer me now or by all that's unholy I will blow you apart myself." Vas swore.

"Aw now, Captain, you wouldn't want to do that. These are mighty pretty ships." Mac's voice was not a huge surprise.

"Goddamn it, Mac! Take these others back now. I don't need you out here. You can't hold against the cruisers."

"We aren't going to try." Mac's voice was smug. "And just what are you going to do to us if we don't go back? Blow us up? Put us in the brig? Sorry, can't do that, cuz we're out here."

"Vas, you need them." Gosta's voice broke in from the *Warrior Wench*.

"Damn it, you too, Gosta? Doesn't anyone follow my orders?" Vas kept heading toward the cruisers. She didn't have time to waste. And the rest of her crew knew that.

"I'd follow you to hell and back, Vas. We all would. But you've got more to handle than just the cruisers." Gosta pinged over an image. "We got this right as you launched."

The faint comm image showed a group of short-range flyers. Yet another heavy cruiser was on its way toward them, and this one still had its single-person fighters.

CHAPTER THIRTY

Mac's voice cut in. "You didn't really think I would let you go out in a blaze of glory by yourself, did you?" His voice was clear, but Vas just hoped he wasn't feeling guilty for not having been the one who went out with Deven. Mac was by far the best pilot they had. He might be trying to convince himself that if he had been the one who had gone out, Jakiin and Deven would still be alive. Of course, the fact that he had no idea how to fly a Fury wouldn't stop him from feeling he could have saved everyone.

"Mac," Vas started to say something to make him feel better, but couldn't think of anything.

Mac cut her off. "Besides, if you try to chase us back we'll all get blown to bits."

Damn him. As much as she wanted to force him to go back, she was glad he was here. And she couldn't go after the cruisers *and* fight off the twenty or so fighters who were winging their way toward them. Normally she would say the four Flits next to her couldn't either. However, she had a guess who were in the other three. "I assume we've got the triplets here with us?" There were a few other pilots who were almost as skilled as Mac: Deven, Jakiin, herself, and a set of triplets from the Gyolin providence. They were truly terrifying when in the zone and judging by Mac's confidence, that was who was flying with him.

"Aye, Captain!" All three answered instantly. Suicidal nut jobs, they sounded happy to be out here facing certain death. Actually, they probably were.

She shook her head with a sigh. They had a job to do. Hopefully they'd all make it out. But she had long ago stopped worrying about those under her command. She couldn't do it in their line of work if she wanted to stay sane. Well, she thought she'd been able to.

"Fine. Mac, you have command of the triplets. Just hold off the fighters long enough for Gosta to blow up that supergate when it opens. No heroics." Silence echoed back. "I mean it, you four. If you do anything to deliberately get yourselves killed I will hire a witch doctor to bring your shades back and keep them in a jar. Am I understood?"

The 'aye captain' that followed was tight and loud. Mac didn't have the same beliefs as the triplets, but he went along with it. The triplets' religion was very specific in dealing with the afterlife. They weren't afraid of what would happen to them in this life—they were terrified of what someone might try to do to them in the next one though. Knowing as much as you could about your crew came in damn handy sometimes.

"Excellent. Now, ladies and gentlemen, we have a job to do."

Vas gunned her engines and charged the approaching cruisers. One held back, perhaps waiting to see if the first one could handle her ship. Or its captain recognized the Fury before the forerunner did.

She fired a volley to make sure they understood completely what they were facing. No other ship around fired like a Fury. And with good reason. When Furies broke down, their firing mechanism was the first to go. Usually resulting in massive loss of life.

The approaching cruiser halted. Mac and the others shot off past her to engage the enemy fighters. Too bad they were only outnumbered eight to one; the enemy fighters wouldn't last long.

She stopped firing and slowed down. As much as she craved to engage the cruisers in battle, to fully feel what this Fury could do, she knew she couldn't do it. She had to keep them held here for just a few minutes longer. As long as they were focusing on her, they might not notice what the *Warrior Wench* was maneuvering to do. Actually, judging by the loose way they guarded their gates, they must not have had someone blow one up before.

There was a first for everything.

Light flashes to her left told her that Mac and the others had engaged the smaller fighters. She just prayed they were focusing on what she would do to them if they got themselves killed and kept the dramatic fighting to a minimum. Although, she felt the four out there probably had a better chance of surviving than she did.

The two cruisers still held back, one sending what had to have been two of its last fighters out to meet her. They had to be kidding. They were afraid that she could take down their cruisers so they sent out single fighters?

With a few choice swear words for idiotic cruiser captains, she moved toward the fighters. Their course had them heading for the *Warrior Wench*.

Vas was just about to open her guns when something made her stop. Deven had been her voice of reason many a time and it was as if he stepped in now.

Holding back, she set up every scan the Fury could send at the two enemy fighters. At first nothing, standard across the board. Then one little light pinged red.

Hidden explosives. The Fury's computer systems cut through the electronic masking they'd laid on the ships. The two fighters were actually on autopilot with no one on board. They were also fixed with enough explosives to wipe out the *Warrior Wench* and anything else within a hundred specs. Most likely a combination of low yield explosives that could get through the *Wench*'s shield.

"Gosta, those fighters heading toward you are bombs. Obviously our friends aren't worried about blowing up their supergate from the outside. Make sure you fire *inside* the opening when it happens. It's going to be the only way to shut it."

Gosta's voice came back thin and scratchy. Either the Fury's comm system was breaking down or more than likely the cruisers were scrambling communications. "How...stop...contact."

Vas swore and rekeyed a message through the board. Hopefully it would get through. "Stay where you are. I'll take them out." And pray the shields on the Fury held, she didn't add. "Keep with your mission." Gosta was going to need all of his remaining weapons to take out that supergate.

Vas thought about telling Mac, but he and the others were fully engaged with their fighters. There would be no way for any of them to break free. Not to mention the shielding on the Fury would be a hell of a lot more than what was on the Flits.

The shielding.

Working furiously, Vas keyed in a sub-space code. One that should break down the shielding on the two fighter ships heading her way. What she was trying wouldn't work if there had been real pilots onboard; they could re-code their shielding before she could get in. Her proximity alarm went off as the fighters closed in. She had plenty of time to move the Fury out of their way, but she couldn't do it if she wanted to get through their shields. The klaxon sounded faster now as the ships came far too close.

"Yes!" Vas sent the code. Tense seconds went by as she spun the Fury out of the direct path. She couldn't get far away but hopefully she'd be far enough.

The explosion sent her flinging about the cabin, sure the Fury wouldn't hold. A second one followed that spun her in the direction of the cruisers. She'd gotten both of the fighters, but wasn't sure if there was anything left in the Fury to fight off the big ships.

The cruisers didn't think she had anything left. Both moved forward slowly, but they moved forward. A screeching filled Vas's head-set. Finally, she oriented her ship and self enough to realize it was Mac screaming at her.

"Damn it, Mac, I'm all right. Stick to your own fight, and let me worry about mine."

Vas cut the comm system. It was a distraction for her and Mac. One they couldn't afford.

Hopefully, she was right. She flipped on the outer guns only to find they were jammed. The explosion of the two bomb fighters had wiped out half her firepower.

The cruisers dropped speed as she got power back to the systems. They had no way of knowing how much of the Fury was still operating, but with the systems coming on they had to know she was still in the fight.

Swearing at the Universe in general, Vas squeezed off a round from the inner guns. The outer guns would have been more impressive but with them out, she'd just have to go for quantity over quality. She decided to make an example of the forerunner and sent all of the aft torpedoes toward it. Judging by the lights on her console it looked like they all fired. In typical Fury fashion the ship rocked like a beast when the shots fired, but they got off.

And made it through the cruiser's shields and slammed into its left side, taking out a landing bay and what appeared to be its weapon array. "Woooo!" Vas yelled, forgetting her own comm was off. The Furies had a reputation for being able to slip through many ships' shields. Their potential instability offset that advantage, but when you didn't have a choice, you took what you could.

An explosion from the left drew her attention. Three of her fighters were hovering over the fourth. The ship hadn't made the explosion, but if three were trying to protect it, it had to be seriously damaged. They were limited in what they could do to fight the remaining enemy ships and still protect the dead Flit. Vas's systems couldn't scan through all the debris, but she had to assume that the remaining three pilots could see a life sign in the fourth ship and that only the ship was dead, not its pilot.

Even though it had felt like hours, the supergate behind them was just finally reaching its apex in the opening sequence. Since both the uninjured cruiser as well as the remaining fighters were ignoring it, Vas assumed they hadn't figured out what the *Warrior Wench*'s real goal was.

Crap, four enemy fighters were breaking away from the ones engaging Mac and the triplets. They were heading right for the supergate.

"Damn it, break off. Two of you have got to get those ships. They can damage the *Wench* before the supergate opens."

"But, Captain," Glazlie cut in, "we can't leave Mac."

Vas took a deep breath. She was losing way too many people she loved on this trip. Someone would pay. However, right now she had to save far more than her favorite rocket jockey. "Go. You have to stop those ships. Now."

Vas cut the comm as the second cruiser started to edge forward. Apparently the fact that the first cruiser had only been damaged, not blown out of the sky, was giving its captain balls.

Vas would take care of that little problem for him or her.

"Go now, all of you. I'll cover Mac once I take care of big, bad, and ugly."

Silence followed and Vas was afraid the triplets wouldn't follow the command, but an instant later, the three Flits raced toward the enemy fighters.

Vas hoped that Mac had the common sense to play dead. She couldn't take the time or chance to warn him. But if what she was going to try didn't work, neither of them were going to survive anyway.

She spun the Fury around. Parts of what she really hoped weren't important pieces flew around the cabin at her rapid move. She kept Mac's dead ship behind her as she charged the injured cruiser. The undamaged ship was too far away to stop her, but its rapid change in direction, away from them, told her the captain had figured out what she was going to do. Perhaps his balls had started to shrink up.

Damn it, if that supergate doesn't open soon we're all fried. Vas held course but kept her screens up to track the action behind her. Mac still hadn't moved. The supergate past the *Warrior Wench* opened, just as the triplets caught the renegade fighters and blew them out of the sky. The three Flits broke formation, breaking off around the *Warrior Wench* to stay out of firing range.

The supergate opened, the clear shimmer indicating something was coming through.

Vas stayed on course for the burning enemy cruiser, but started cutting her speed.

Behind her, Gosta fired everything he had at the ship emerging out of the supergate. The explosions rocked even the enemy cruiser that was trying to make its escape.

Vas had to fight for control as the Fury spun on the concussion wave. She regained maneuverability and blasted away from the burning cruiser, only to have to dodge as Mac's dead ship was flung past her.

"Damn it, Mac, are you alive? Say something." She flew after his dead ship.

"You told me to shut up." His voice was weak, obviously disoriented, but still his usually petulant self.

"Are you in your suit?" She had seconds to pull this off before his dead Flit would slam into the burning cruiser.

"Yeah, but—"

"No buts eject now. Damn you to hell, Mac, eject NOW."

A normal Flit or fighter could never have picked up a single person at this distance, but thank god for Mac, the Fury was anything but normal.

Vas saw a tiny speck eject from the Flit. Without waiting for confirmation of what it was, she coded the Fury to grab it with a tractor lock and dump it in the hold. She gunned the ship as far from the burning cruiser as it could go. Another concussion wave rocked the Fury as Mac's burning Flit slammed into the cruiser and exploded.

Vas thumbed the storage compartment. "I hope to hell you're back there, Mac."

"Just what would you do if I wasn't? Glue me back together?" Mac's voice echoed oddly in the Fury's storage area. "Damn it, that was close!"

"Hey, you're still here to bitch, ain't ya?" Vas made sure the storage area was secure and hadn't taken any hits. "Stay put. There's not enough room in the cabin for both of us. I have one more ship to check on, then let's see if we can make it back before this Fury decides it's had enough of us."

The enemy cruiser that Mac's ship had hit was still busy dying; explosions rocking it from inside and debris was spreading outward. However, it was the second cruiser, the last one still intact, that Vas was worried about. Granted, it had moved away from the fighting, but not enough for her comfort. It could still charge forward and attack the *Warrior Wench.*

Vas punched the Fury's engines and shot forward. Because the outer wing guns were still jammed, she was limited to what charges were left in the smaller inner wing weapons, but a quick check told her it was enough to at least cripple the cruiser.

The cruiser was holding in place. She could almost imagine what was going through that captain's mind. His fleet was gone. Whatever big, bad, and ugly they had been waiting for to come through that supergate was now floating around in tiny pieces along with the remains of that supergate. Most likely he was torn between revenge and getting the hell out of here.

He waited too long to make up his mind.

Vas thumbed the launch controls, dumping everything that was left in the Fury's inner guns into the side of the ship. At first she thought it hadn't worked, then a chain of explosions, following the length of the cruiser, burst into space.

"Let's get out of here." Vas said to Mac then turned the Fury around.

Mac only grumbled from his place in the storage area, but Vas took that as an agreement. The last cruiser was burning quite nicely behind them as Vas gunned the Fury as much as she felt safe. Pieces of the supergate and the massive cruiser that had tried to come through were spinning around the debris of the earlier fight. At least that part had worked.

"Now that is a sight for sore eyes," Vas said then chuckled to herself that she was actually glad to see that garish *Warrior Wench* design.

"What is? I can't see anything down here." Mac's whine told her he was okay.

"Our ship. She's intact."

"Gosta? Come in?" Only static met Vas's hail and coldness grabbed her heart. Had the explosion from the supergate done damage she couldn't see? Now that she looked closer it was clear that the *Warrior Wench* was listing. And the three Flits were still circling outside the landing bay.

"Damn it, Gosta, you better be okay." Vas tried again, and then flicked the channel to reach the Flits. "Glazlie? Huglin? Marwin? Are you guys okay? Have you been able to reach the ship?" She clicked back. "And I have Mac in my cargo area. He's cranky but in one piece."

"I heard that!" Mac yelled from the storage area.

"I know you did." Vas yelled back and sent her message again. Was no one left?

"Captain, good to see you." Glazlie's voice was scratchy with static but most likely that was the fault of a billion tiny pieces of what used to be a supergate.

"Can you reach the *Warrior Wench*? Are you all okay?"

"We're fine, but no, I haven't been able to reach them, nor get the landing bay open." More static cut her off. "But it looks like the rest of our ships got through the hypergate."

Vas studied her screen. That was good and bad. Good for the refugees, bad if the *Warrior Wench* wasn't functioning.

"I'm going to move in closer." Vas moved the Fury as close to the *Wench* as she could.

Damn it, they had to have made it. The ship didn't look that bad from the outside, even up close. But she was starting to list even more.

"Gosta, Xsit, anyone. Come in." She opened the hail to hit all personal comms as well. "Anyone, this is Vas calling anyone on the *Warrior Wench*. Is anyone picking me up?"

The silence that followed almost made her throw up. At least they'd gotten all those refugees out of here. Damn it though, it just wasn't fair. Vas started pounding on the console as the events of the last hour—was it only an hour? —caught up with her and dragged her under. Damn it all to hell! First Deven and Jakiin, now the entire crew?

"Captain?" A faint voice echoed from her open comm. "Vas? Is that you?"

Vas wiped her face, surprised at the wetness she found. "It's me, Terel. Are you guys okay? I can't get anyone on the command deck comms."

"We're okay, battered, and the ship is going to have to limp somewhere safe for repairs. Gunny is having a fit at no weapons and in enemy territory. But we're okay. Gosta's trying to replace the comm system with one he stole from a Flit. Should be enough to get us along. Bathie and Divee are trying to get the stabilizers back on. And the engine will only hold hyperspace for about ten minutes at a time, so we'll have to do short jumps." Terel paused. "Did you all make it?"

Vas thought at first that she was asking because Mac's ship was gone, but then she realized if they'd been blind since the supergate exploded they couldn't possibly have a clue as to who was out here. "We made it. Mac's lost us a ship, but he's in one piece."

"I heard that too!" Mac yelled from the back again.

"And again I don't care!" Vas yelled back.

"Who are you yelling at?" Gosta's voice was a very welcome sound. "And you guys can come in at any time; we've got commands for the landing bay back. The ship will need to sit like this for a bit longer, but you can land now. She won't be doing any unexpected moves."

Vas glanced up as the triplets headed for the bays. Obviously the comm was completely working again. She reached back and pounded on the storage wall. "Hang on, we're going home."

Mac gave a reply that was luckily mumbled. Well, it was lucky for him it was mumbled.

It was a bit tricky to get into the landing docks because of the list, but at least the ship wasn't bouncing around. The triplets were all waiting behind the blast glass when she shut off the engines. All three ran forward as the outer doors shut and pressure was back in the hanger.

Vas released her seat and climbed out as well. She almost forgot to release the storage door but a pounding reminded her.

"Ouch!" Mac swore as he tumbled out.

"Why in the hell were you leaning on the door?" Vas helped him up. He was filthy; obviously his ship had been on fire before she got him. However, his bright blue eyes were very cognizant. And pissed.

"How was I supposed to know that was the door? I was just the tagalong!"

He would have continued his tirade but Glazlie ran up and engulfed him in a hug, a hug far more than just shipmates would imply.

Vas left the hanger. There was too much that happened today for her to sort it out now.

"I expect you to meet me on deck, Mac." She'd give him a few minutes with his friends.

Her energy faded as she walked to the command deck. She knew she needed to deal with Deven's loss, but she didn't have time. Or she didn't want to make time. Funny how she could still imagine what Deven would say. He would say she was dealing with physical issues to avoid the emotional ones.

And he would be right.

Nevertheless, the fact was they still had a lot of physical issues to deal with. She didn't have time for grief yet.

The command deck wasn't a total mess, but wires were everywhere and at least two consoles were gone. Some of it appeared to be self-inflicted and judging by the swearing she heard behind one console she could guess who did it.

"Can we get out of here yet?"

Gosta popped his head around the raised console. "Does it look like we can?" He shook his head. "Sorry, Captain. I'm still having some trouble patching together enough of a system to get us through the hypergate.

Whatever was in that ship or the supergate fried just about everything."

Vas took her seat, and then turned to Xsit. "Has anyone checked to make sure the hypergate is still even functional?" They'd gone far beyond the original estimate that Flarik thought she could keep it working.

Xsit chirped and ducked to run the scan. Things must be bad if Xsit was down to chirping. But she'd always had a serious sweet spot for Deven, and unlike Vas she wasn't as good at blocking her feelings.

A loud chirp got everyone's attention a few moments later; Xsit peeked up with an embarrassed look on her face. "Sorry." The rrr's came out as a trill, and Xsit coughed, then tried again. "I'm sorry. I didn't mean to startle anyone. The gate is still up and working." She clacked her beak. "I'm not sure how long that will last though. It took some damage from the explosion as well."

Vas put her head back against the headrest. She had no idea how long before the enemy would come back. She had to assume there were more of them who were not at whatever this rendezvous had been. She toyed with trying to reclaim part of the Furies, but they were literally shattered, and any larger portions were in the radioactive spill from the dying ships. Besides, Deven and Jakiin were dead. Bringing back their bodies, or parts of them, would only make things worse.

She knew the *Warrior Wench* had a full complement of escape pods. In theory if enough pods linked together they could trigger a hypergate and at least ride it for a few stops. Which would mean leaving the *Warrior Wench* behind. That wasn't a plausible idea. So what was?

"Got it!" Gosta shouted, but swore a second later. "Almost. Damn it. Wait, we're back, but we have to run now. Jakiin—" Gosta closed his eyes as he automatically shouted the dead man's name. "Mac, get us to the gate. I don't care where it goes, just get us out now." He nodded over to Vas. "We have minutes before the system crashes."

Vas nodded. "You heard the man, Mac. Let's leave this wretched galaxy."

Mac nodded tersely and hit the codes in. The ship lumbered a bit—whatever patchwork repairs had been done to stabilize her, they weren't completely holding. But it moved. They made it through the jump.

True to the estimate from Xsit, they couldn't stay in the hypergate stream for more than ten minutes. The first jump, Vas tried to push it, but the ship started to rip itself apart. She kept their jumps to no more than eight minutes after that.

Because they had to keep their jumps so short, it wasn't until they'd gone through about twenty, that Vas agreed to have them lay in command for the system the refugee ships were meeting them at.

The refugee ships had made it intact and a thorough scan of the system indicated no other ships in the area, so Vas instructed them to head for Home.

"We've got this now." Flarik's voice was unusually gentle as she came to Vas's command chair.

Vas knew she was right, they were fine now. Nevertheless, she didn't want to leave the command deck. The fighting and the massive number of hypergate jumps they'd made had allowed her not to think. The crisis was over for now. Now would come the thinking.

She held off answering Flarik as long as she could, but the crew was starting to look at her in sympathy. Damn it, she couldn't break down in front of them.

"Thank you, Flarik. You and Gosta have the deck. Mac, call me the instant anything odd comes our way, or when we get to Home."

She made it to her quarters just as Mac sped them into the next hypergate. The soothing hum of the ship as she used the hyperspace links relaxed the knots in Vas's neck. Which wasn't a good thing as they were about the only thing still keeping her emotions in check.

She held on until the door was shut and locked behind her. Flinging off her flight jacket, she did something she hadn't done since she was nine and her brother betrayed her to a bunch of telepaths. She threw herself on her bed and cried until she fell asleep.

CHAPTER THIRTY-ONE

Mac rarely obeyed orders, and judging from the time she'd been asleep, he hadn't changed. Vas swore as she looked at her wrist piece. She'd been out at least three hours, far longer than it would have taken to get to Home.

Which meant Mac disobeyed her yet again, or they weren't safe.

"Gosta, where the hell are we and why wasn't I called?" Vas rolled herself out of bed and shrugged into a clean flight suit.

"Because I told him not to." Nariel's voice was far more clipped than usual. Her sibilants were clean. "We're safe, don't worry. I can come down there or you can come to my office."

Vas ran her fingers through her hair. She didn't have time for this. "Nariel, I know what you're trying to do. We can deal with this later."

"I come down there, or you come here."

"Now wait a—"

"You gave me an order when I first came on board. Do you recall what it was?"

"This isn't the time—"

"You said, and I quote, "If at any time I feel that anyone on this ship, including you, is not able to function, I have the obligation to lock them up until such time as I believe they can return to duty." Her voice softened.

"Vas, I know you are hurting. This entire ship is hurting. We need to deal with it now. You need to be able to help them through this."

Vas stared at her comm. What kind of mercenary had a mind-doc who could overrule the captain? She shook her head. A healthy one. She'd seen too many mercs crumble by not taking care of themselves and their crew physically and mentally. Giving Nariel and Terel overriding control to look out for her and the crew was one of the smartest moves she made. And one of the reason they lost so few crewmembers.

It was, however, a pain in the ass.

"Come down here." She tried to pull her quarters together a bit. No reason for the mind-doc to have more to deal with.

An hour later neither Nariel nor Vas was truly happy, but Nariel was willing to leave her alone. Which was about the best she could hope for. They'd lost three others besides Deven and Jakiin, plus the eight they'd lost on the planet and the ship was still limping. The good news was that the refugee ships had all made it…to Home.

Vas drummed her fingers on her command chair when she was told the news. It wasn't as if they had a choice. Their contact for the ships didn't have directions for Marli's secret hideout. Hhssion, her supply clerk, had stayed aboard the largest refugee ship. He had given them the way to Home.

"Ya know what? We'll deal with that later. They can stay put. If Hhssion sets them up and works it out with Grosslyn, I have no issue with it." She stood and studied her command crew. The command deck was still in pieces. They should head to Home for repairs. She just wanted to take a few more precautions before they potentially gave away their last safe spot.

First she needed to say something. She flipped open the comm so it went ship-wide. "I know our recent loss has hit all of us hard. But know that our crewmates died saving us. Saving this ship, and those lives sitting at Home. Deven and Jakiin went forth fully knowing they weren't coming back. Likel, Johannis, and Ti didn't know it, but they were fighting for all of us when they fell at their posts just the same. Same with the eight we lost on the planet. We're not safe yet, but when we are, we will grieve, laugh, and remember the fallen. To the victorious dead!" The last was echoed throughout the ship.

With a deep breath she shut off the ship-wide comm. Now to follow through. "How many more jumps can we make before we're stuck?"

Gosta's head bobbed as he ran calculations in his head. "Probably no more than four or five."

"Which is it?" Vas softened the question with a smile. "Do we jump that fifth or not?"

Again the bobbing. Gosta finally shook his head. "No. We've already jumped six more times since you left the deck. Four more we can clear. That would put us at thirty total since we fled. Another isn't worth the risk."

"And anyone that can find us after that many jumps already knows where Home is," Bathshea said softly. She had been sitting in Xsit's seat since Vas arrived. Most likely the emotional Xithinal was in Terel's care.

"Agreed." Vas resumed her seat. "But first I need one more sweep of the ship, inner and outer. We need to make sure not the tiniest speck of tagging is on us." Gosta had suggested a hypothesis on how they were pulled into the dead gate that flung them into the gray ships: Marli's tracking beacon. He wasn't sure why yet, but something about it had opened the gate. Vas had a bad feeling it was due to some sort of Asarlaí tech built into the tracking beacon. Unfortunately, she couldn't tell Gosta that. That Asarlaí tech opened a closed gate again tied the Asarlaí-worshipping Rillianians into the gray ships. Vas added it to her notes, and copied them all to Flarik's personal computer.

She turned to Bathie as another thought hit her. "Can you have a crew scan the Fury and the three Flits as well? I seriously doubt anyone out there had time to tag us during that fight, but you never know. Their tech is beyond us. Oh and, Mac, go space your flight suit."

The squawk that answered was reassuringly normal. "What? Why? Do you know how long it takes to break one of those in just right? I took that thing everywhere!"

"Don't really care, flyboy," Vas said. "That suit was out there, they could have bathed the entire area in trackers. Dump the suit." She sighed. "You can have one of the *Warrior Wench* flight suits." The ship had come with a limited number of extremely high-end flight suits. Vas had been holding them back so there wasn't a knock down fight for them.

Mac's face went skeptical. "Really? I thought you weren't letting anyone have those?"

"Well, if you don't think you deserve one...." Vas shrugged.

"No, no, no! I'll take it." He grinned. "Thanks, Captain."

"Get fitted once we've finished our hops. I have a feeling we won't be staying on Home long." Vas nodded to Gosta and Flarik. "Can I speak to the two of you in my ready room?"

Both followed her in silently and took their seats. Vas took a breath to settle herself. The talk with Nariel had helped but the fact was, it was going to be a long time, if ever, before she got over Deven. This had to be done.

"I need a new second-in-command. Normally I would wait a bit but we have to consider ourselves at war. Therefore, we can't wait. You two are the most likely candidates, so I wanted to start with you."

Neither appeared comfortable with her words, but Flarik looked almost ill.

"Captain, I respectfully have to decline. I would not be a good choice."

Vas kept her face neutral. She agreed completely. However, she also knew that with someone like Flarik, that admission had to come from her. This way she'd support whomever Vas chose.

Gosta now looked completely ill. Unfortunately for him, he was the best choice.

"Captain, I—"

Vas came around to the front of the desk and held his gaze. "I know you don't want this. No one wanted this situation to come up. Nevertheless, you're the best choice. People listen to you, Gosta."

The two bobs in his neck wavered up and down a few times before he spoke. "But I can't enforce things. People may listen to me, but they don't...fear me."

Vas turned her look to Flarik, someone people did fear. She didn't have to say anything.

"Do not worry, Gosta. People *do* fear me." She ruffled her head feathers and put her most predatory look on. "I will make it clear that not listening to you will make them answer to me. Between us, we can make a serviceable second-in-command."

Vas smiled. It turned out even better than she'd hoped. With Flarik backing him, Gosta would be able to take control should something happen to her.

"Thank you, both of you." Vas went back to her chair and checked her computer. The scans of the ship were still running. They had time to resolve a few more things. "Now we need to put things together and fast. Who in the hell is behind this?"

Gosta relaxed. "I believe there is more than one group. With different yet somehow connected objectives." He glanced at Flarik. "The Rillianians, the Graylian monks, and the gray ships. I believe they may be working together. But I'm not sure to what level. We have to assume the gray ships are from somewhere far outside the Commonwealth."

"Do we know what they are trying to accomplish? Where is the Commonwealth on this?" Vas turned to Flarik. "Did we find out who those ships were that entered Mnethe V space just as we left? Did we get anything from them?"

Gosta bowed to Flarik to go first.

"They belonged to the Welischian consulate. The ambassador has a small fleet under her flag. They are Commonwealth, but only stick to outer rim."

Vas swore. "Which puts them with the Graylians most likely."

"There's more," Flarik added. "They were reported destroyed two months ago in a mysterious accident. And at the same time, two of the larger Graylian monasteries were abandoned."

"Damn it. They could belong to anyone now, but my money is on those monks. Did they see us leave?"

Gosta watched his screens again. "I don't think so. Xsit tracked when we picked them up on our scanners. They shouldn't have seen us unless they did a log search of the gate."

Which they could do if they were still Commonwealth. However, unless the entire system had gone bad, three 'destroyed' ships couldn't use any known codes to search a gate. At least that was good news.

"As for the Commonwealth itself, it's unclear. The person you spoke to may have gone rogue and still had channel access. Or it could be deeper." Gosta said. "But unless you want to go to the Commonwealth home worlds, we can't get close enough to any of them to tell."

"No, we'll stay away from that option. We'll maintain blocking until I have reason to feel otherwise." She looked at her two officers. Both were clearly exhausted. She'd had time to collapse. Whether they wanted to or not, they needed it as well.

"The scan still has some time to run, and Mac and I can get ourselves to Home. I want the two of you to both go talk to Nariel." She waved off both complaints before they could be launched. "No options. I did it. You two do it. Then to your quarters. Get some rest, meditate, whatever. I have a new challenge for you."

She flicked up the computer screen and turned it toward them. They'd gotten some hopefully useful data on their mysterious gray ship friends during the fight. "I need you both to analyze this and look for weaknesses. Also look at anything we gathered on their ground troops." She shook her head. "I should have tried to bring a body back with us. We don't even know what species they are. Deven," her voice caught just a little, but it was getting better, "Deven scanned some data of them on the planet. It's in the system too. Report back when you find something."

CHAPTER THIRTY-TWO

Two months later they were still no closer to finding solutions. The data from the gray ships proved nothing except they weren't from this galaxy. A confirmation of what they already suspected, given the tech the ships had used.

They'd made it to Home for repairs, and aside from a brief sighting of Marli's ship on one of their hops, hadn't run into anything dangerous or troublesome since then. Vas thought of trying to flag down Marli to tell her about Deven. However, the *Scurrilous Monk* seemed to be leaving the system very quickly and Vas didn't want to get in her way.

Whatever was going on within the Commonwealth was growing. Nothing official, but the channels for the outer rim planets indicated fewer contacts between the council center and the outer rim offices. It was as if the Commonwealth was closing in on itself, not caring what worlds on the rim were being lost in the process. If this was how the Commonwealth died, it died with a whimper, not a bang.

The unprovoked attacks on small outer planets continued and Vas and her crew found themselves running more refugee rescue missions. The pay was next to nothing. Most often it *was* nothing. However, there weren't any other real jobs in the outer rim, and Vas didn't want to go further into the Commonwealth center to look for work. Thanks to Deven's last job, they were going to be solvent for a long while.

They'd broken the Graylian monks puzzle completely thanks to a bedridden and bored Hrrru. So far they'd recovered two more of the pieces of the *Victorious Dead*, which had been hauled back Home to be dug out of their trash coating and then stored. Flarik had allowed them to pull in a few more pieces to try and help build morale, but she still felt that leaving at least some out there would be best. The monks were obsessive and by taking out the first three pieces in their ritual training exercise, Vas and her crew had effectively shut down their training completely. She had no idea what they'd been training for, but given the recent events, she had to assume that stopping it was a good thing.

Vas had fallen into a routine: find out where the next piece of her ship was, see if any refugees needed help, and try not to think about Deven.

It had been going fine until she had a very vivid dream of him and woke up almost screaming his name.

"Damn you, get out of my head." Vas's people often carried on conversations with the dearly departed, it was one of the few traditions she'd kept when she'd fled the barren rock she'd grown up on. However, talking to his shade didn't get the dream out of her head. It was far too passionate to leave quickly. "Bastard," she said as she shoved the dream into a dark corner and got dressed to go to the command deck.

They were en route to the fourth part of the ship, when another attack on a small moon colony prompted a detour. That many of these attacks occurred within the systems containing her ship pieces couldn't be a coincidence. Why these gray ships were destroying harmless worlds was another unanswered question. So far the ships were avoiding any of the more heavily defended planets on the outer rim.

Vas was just leaving her room when a klaxon sounded and an impact jolt slammed her into the wall and she tumbled to the ground. She picked herself up and ran to the lift. They were going through a small gate, rarely used. Had it exploded?

The command deck was in chaos when she reached it. Gon was in the pilot's chair, and while he had some flying skills he wasn't nearly as good as Mac. The ship was surrounded by huge pieces of debris.

"Where's Mac?"

"He's off shift right now," Gosta said as he rapidly made some adjustments on his console. Gon was fighting to keep up but another piece of debris hit their shields. It was smaller than the first but the impact was still clear on the screen.

"No offense, Gon, but get Mac up here now!" Vas threw herself into her command chair and called up the specs. They'd managed to come out of the hypergate right into what used to be a small moon and the remains of a population ship. A quick scan indicated no intact ships were in the area.

Mac must have been awakened by the first jolt. He was half-dressed as he ran onto the command deck. Gon gratefully cleared way and took over another console. Mac got them clear of the debris field.

"So who were we supposed to pick up? Please tell me they weren't on that moon. Or ship." Vas scowled at the screen showing the shattered moon.

"Refugees from Zario, attacked a few days ago." Gosta paused as his sensors brought in more data. "They were probably not on the moon, neither it, nor the planet it was circling were suitable for life, but that ship was theirs."

Vas slammed her fist down on her console. The gray ships had never gone after refugees this aggressively. Not since Mnethe V.

So why chase them down and attack them again?

"Do we know anything about them? Zario's a simple ag planet. Why would they want to slaughter them?"

Gosta ignored her question but pointed at something on one of his screens. "I'm actually picking up life signs on that planet." He glanced up. "It was abandoned a few centuries ago. Not enough water to support life."

"How many?" Maybe they had gotten off the population ship before it was destroyed.

"Not many. No more than forty or so. We could easily fit them in a shuttle to get them up here. Just long enough to drop them off somewhere else." He added the last defensively. He knew how Vas felt about strangers on her ship.

She pondered the screen before her. A support ship from Home could be sent out, but she had no idea if the ships who did this would be back or not. This was something new for them. She needed to get the innocent victims of this oncoming storm safe. It was what Deven would have wanted. She let herself have a small smile at that thought. Deven would be proud of the work they'd done in the last two months. His credits from that last job had gone toward setting up another refugee planet to take the pressure off Home. Much to Grosslyn's relief.

"Do it. Contact them and tell them we'll be down with a shuttle. I want you, Terel, Flarik, and Nariel there along with a support team. We're going to scan these people carefully before they come onboard. Understood?"

Gosta smiled then quickly dropped it. "Aye, Captain. We should be ready to go in half an hour."

The refugees were right where they were supposed to be, not that there would be many places to hide. The landscape was covered in rubble, rocks, and refuse, but nothing taller than a small child.

The leader was a small older man of mixed heritage, appearing to be part Xithinal and part Silantian. An odd combination to say the least, but clearly harmless. Most of the people with him were even more so. Old people and young children, though no babies. Judging by their lack of belongings, they'd obviously been rushed off their home world quickly.

"I am Bhotia. Thank you for helping us." He was gracious in his greeting, but kept looking over his shoulder.

Vas took his hand. "I am Captain Tor Dain. Might I ask what you're looking for?" Her team spread out as they began interviewing and scanning the refugees.

"Something here has been hunting us. Ten of our people have been attacked since we were forced to flee down here."

Vas pulled out her blaster and nodded for the rest of her team to arm themselves.

"How long ago? Is it nearby? What kind of beast?"

Bhotia shook his head, his neck folds old and mottled with age wobbled with the movement. "They were taken three days ago. I am not sure, but I believe it may be a diflin gaul."

Xenobiology wasn't her field. "Terel, have you heard of a—"

Vas's question ended in a scream as out of nowhere a mass of weight, claws, and teeth slammed into her and tore open her left side. She swung around and got it off shortly, but the brute was huge and was easily three times as heavy as she was. Her first blaster had been ripped out of her hand on impact, but she grabbed the other from its holster and fired point blank into the thing's scaled chest. She heard the others shooting at it as well. The creature dug into her a few more times before it finally shuddered and collapsed on top of her.

Yelling and screaming pierced the air as Vas fought to stay conscious. After what felt like hours the pressure on her torso lifted and the animal was rolled off of her. Terel dropped next to her feeling for broken bones and doing temporary closures on the gaping holes. Vas winced as stabbing pain flooded her when she tried to speak.

Terel shook her head. "Don't. Your right lung is punctured. I can fix it, but we have to get you on the ship." She looked over her shoulder and her frown deepened. "Damn it, Bhotia says this isn't the only one. We've got to get everyone out of here."

Without waiting, Terel slid a hypospray into Vas's neck. Vas tried to fight back. She didn't want them just loading everyone on the ship. But darkness crept along the edges of her vision. Suddenly a new form appeared on the edge of her sight. Reaching out for her.

Deven.

CHAPTER THIRTY-THREE

Vas swore as the world went sideways. She had to stay awake. That was Deven. She knew that was Deven! The part of her that was still rational pointed out that her former second-in-command had been blown apart two months ago. However, he looked awfully good for a dead man. The drugs wouldn't let her keep her eyes open and she felt them roll back in her head. Damn it.

Gosta watched Vas twist as they transferred her into a medical bed on the *Warrior Wench*. She was barely alive from the injuries and yet she was fighting the coma drug like a tiger. He could serve with her for a hundred years and still not figure that woman out. She finally started to lose consciousness, her eyes focusing on something far beyond him. "Deven," she muttered, then was out.

Terel turned toward Gosta. "What did she just say?"

Gosta felt a sad pang well up. He never knew if Vas had realized how she felt about Deven. However, Gosta knew. "She called out for Deven." He frowned as a dark thought hit him. Some cultures felt you saw the dead when you were dying. "Tell me the truth, how bad is she?"

Terel's face crumbled. "Not good. That beast shredded her up inside. A traxliann gaul shouldn't have been there."

Gosta frowned. "Agreed. We didn't lose anyone, but it wasn't for lack of that thing trying."

Terel fixed more long-term tranqs for Vas. "No, I mean it really shouldn't have been there. And Bhotia claimed it was a diflin gaul. Those could survive on such a world, but they're smaller, more scavengers than predators. This one is a traxliann gaul. They're water creatures. This planet is too dry. If we hadn't killed it, it would have died in a day."

"So how long had it been there?" Vas had tasked Gosta to resolve her growing collection of mysteries. She wasn't going to be happy to find out yet another had appeared.

Terel soothed Vas's forehead as the stronger drug kicked in and slowed her heartbeat. "I'd say no more than a few hours. It couldn't last more than a day in that environment. Someone didn't care, nor did they care that it would be obvious this wasn't a natural attack." She tapped her chin in thought, her humming going up an octave. "You brought the body on board, right?" At Gosta's nod she continued. "Make sure to keep it in secure storage. I'm going to check and see what else we can find out from it."

Gosta nodded, then went to the medical comm. "Gon, make sure to keep that monster in a cool bin. Terel will need to conduct studies on it."

"Aye, Gosta. Not sure why she'd want to. But I'll go back and secure it."

"Do you need me for anything else?" Gosta hated to leave his captain, but in this area he knew his presence wouldn't help. Besides, perhaps he could use his library and find some answers.

Terel glanced up and blinked owlishly. Obviously she had already dismissed him. "No, we should be fine." She reached for his arm. "I wouldn't mention the captain calling out for Deven to anyone. Even her, unless she remembers, which I doubt she will. She needs to let his shade rest, even in her heart."

Gosta nodded sadly. "Agreed."

"Deven?" Vas was obviously losing her mind. The shape in front of her looked just like her second-in-command. Rather, her *late* second-in-command. The man turned around. He wasn't wearing a shirt, just low-slung loose white pants. New spider-like scars covered his torso. His face was mostly left untouched except for a few thin scars on his right cheek that ran from the corner of his eye to his jawline. He was standing in a bank of fog; actually, they both were. She couldn't see anything except him.

"Vas? Oh, gods." The man who looked like Deven took two steps forward and grabbed her arms. With an intensity Vas really didn't think one would feel in the afterlife, he kissed her until her knees went weak. Literally. He had to catch her before she went down. Again, something one wouldn't think would happen in the afterlife.

"So it was you? Or rather it is you." Vas's thoughts were jumbled even to her. She knew she wasn't awake.

"Am I dead?" she asked the stunning apparition before her. If so, at least she was going to have good company.

Deven steadied her feet. "No, but you're not far from it or I wouldn't be reaching you like this." His green eyes bore into hers trying to search for something. Finally he shook his head. "It's no use. I can't read you on this level."

Vas glanced down at his wrists automatically. "Your bracelets...."

"Were destroyed when the Fury blew up," Deven said without regret.

"So then you are dead. However, I may not be. Yet. But you are." Vas nodded. "Of course you are. You're a figment in my dream. My dying dreams, if figments can tell those things." She started looking for a way out. Maybe if she found her way out of wherever here was she'd regain consciousness.

Deven ran a finger down her cheek, smiling when she leaned forward. "Trust me, I'm not a figment. And Vas, I am alive. Don't ask how, I can't tell you. But I came back from the explosion."

Guilt hit Vas hard. Deven and Jakiin had survived? And she'd left them?

"No. Don't feel that way. I was dead. Sadly so was Jakiin, and he's gone. I stayed dead long enough that even Terel would have had me buried if you had retrieved what was left of my body." He put a finger over her lips. "I can't explain how. I'm not sure myself. Nevertheless, I am alive. You just have to find me. But first you have to live." Frustration deepened the new scars on his face. "I can't tell what's wrong with you though."

Vas rubbed her arms. She couldn't stop looking at Deven. Deven. Her Deven. "I think I fell in love with you." Crap, oh crap. That was not what she meant to say. Ever. Even if this being before her was only a bit of her dying mind.

Deven's eyes went wide, and then he pulled her close again. "I thought so too. I mean, I felt that way too. Still do. I didn't think you...."

Vas stiffened her arms to hold him back. "Okay, let's not go there. I'm dead, dying, or about to get that way. You were dead for quite a while apparently." Her eyes narrowed. "Waitaminute. That time that Terel almost buried you. You really were dead, weren't you? Not in some healing coma?"

"Yes, I was dead. What could be called dead. For most people."

"No, not what *could* be called dead. Did your heart stop?" Vas waited until he reluctantly nodded. "Then you were dead."

"And you aren't yet." Deven shook her. "Vas, what is going on? What was the last thing you remember?"

Vas racked her brain. "I was in the infirmary. Gosta and Terel were there. Terel...damn it, Terel knocked me out again. She needs to stop doing that."

"It's for your own good."

Vas waved her hand at Deven, pacing around the vague space. It really was like nowhere, vast and gray with nothing to show top from bottom. "So she keeps saying. But that's not it. Something else...." Vas snapped her fingers. "That last group of refugees."

"The Mnethe V group? What about them?"

"No, not them." She stopped pacing and peered at him. "You do realize you've been dead two months, right? We kept picking up refugees and relocating them when we could. It wasn't to honor you or anything, just seemed like the thing to do. Things are getting weirder out there. More dangerous, and not in a good way."

Vas drummed her fingers on her chin as she tried to get back on track of the elusive memory. "That was it. We were going after a small group on Hkjsg. You know how I hate desert planets, but that was where they got chased to so that was where we went. Anyway, when we found them, they claimed they'd been stalked for days by this monster, a diflin gaul they said.

"Then this thing lunged out of nowhere. Huge monster. Reptilian skin, long snout, odd little legs. But it could run faster than anything I've ever seen that wasn't a machine." A shudder racked her. "I didn't even have a chance to get off more than one shot, and that was after it was on me. It was trying to feed on me when the others killed it."

"How long did the refugees say it was chasing them?" Deven's eyes were intense.

"A few days, why?" Vas couldn't figure out what was making him so worried.

"Vas, diflin gauls don't sound like what you described, but traxliann gauls do and they can't live on a world like Hkjsg. Anything more than a day at the most and they would die. Someone planted that thing there to go after you. And those refugees had to have been in on it."

"I've got to wake up."

Deven nodded, his eyes deadly now. "Yes, you do. And you've got to live."

Vas waited a few moments, but nothing changed. "Okay, so what do we need to do? I'm still here and while you are literally a sight for sore eyes, those refugees might be taking over my ship as we speak."

"Our ship." Deven corrected with a smile. "I don't know. Even in my rather long life I've never communicated like this with someone. I've no ideas on how to get you back there; I'm not even completely sure how I was able to call your spirit here."

A loud buzzing sound overtook his words and Vas felt herself being pulled away. Deven didn't seem to notice at first then smiled. "Save yourself, save the crew. Then find me."

"You didn't tell me where you were," Vas screamed as he became smaller and smaller.

"I don't know." The response was faint but clear.

Vas was still swearing when she woke up.

CHAPTER THIRTY-FOUR

"Damn him all to hell!" Vas swore as her eyes opened to her room in the medical suite of the *Warrior Wench.*

"Damn who? And I'm glad to see you're feeling well enough to swear." Mac's dry voice came from out of her range of vision, but a turn of her very stiff neck showed him. He looked like he hadn't rested or bathed in a few days.

"You've been watching me?"

Mac flushed. "Well, yeah. Terel has you on camera, so she should be here in a few minutes. But I wanted someone to be here when you woke up."

"Don't you mean *if* I woke up?" Vas grinned as the look on Mac's face told her that wasn't far from the truth.

"Okay, maybe. Thing is if you woke up, I wanted someone to be here. You've been out for forty-eight hours."

Vas tried to prop herself up but her entire body was encased in steel, or so it felt. She couldn't move anything more than her neck and hands. "Why am I so stiff? And why didn't you at least take time to bathe?" Mac and his clothing were a bit ripe.

"You're stiff because of the meds Terel had to keep pumping in you to keep you alive. We almost lost you twice." Mac tried to look offended. "And I was willing to sacrifice hygiene to make sure you didn't wake up alone and this is the thanks I get?"

Vas smiled and eventually Mac dropped his wounded expression.

"So shouldn't Terel be here? I'd think if she'd lost me twice she'd be anxious to see how I was faring since I'm now awake."

Mac frowned. "I would think so, too. She was fussing over you like a mother glock with one chick until I finally chased her out a few hours ago."

"And she hasn't been back?" Vas frowned and glanced at the camera. Its beam was on, meaning it was recording. It wasn't like Terel to leave any seriously injured patient alone for any length of time, especially someone like the captain.

Vas motioned for Mac to move closer. "Is there a microphone on too? With the camera, I mean. Are they recording sound?"

Mac started to speak, but Vas just mouthed, "Nod yes or no."

Frowning, Mac nodded.

Vas swore and pulled him as close as she could with her stiff limbs; at least she was able to move a bit now. "I need you to disable the camera and the microphone. But I need it to look like something just went wrong with the system."

Mac pulled back, looking with growing concern at her face. "Wh—"

"Don't ask, just do. I'm serious, Mac. Have you ever known Terel to leave a patient alone this long?"

Mac swore. "No."

"Then I need you to do what I asked, quickly. Don't draw attention to your moves." Vas almost let him go then pulled him back. "Wait, lock the doors first. Is there anyone else in this portion of sick bay?"

"No," Mac said. "The others were bandaged up and sent to their rooms."

"Okay, lock the outer doors if the rooms inside still look clear, then this one. If you see anyone, and I mean anyone, only lock these doors."

"Vas, you're scaring me. What the hell is going on?"

"No time. Go." Vas let him go. Damn it, she hadn't come back in time. When she first woke up she thought her whole encounter with Deven had been a wishful dream. A fantasy brought on by a too close brush with death. But Terel would never have left her alone for any length of time, even with Mac on guard.

Mac came back from the outer rooms, and then locked the doors they were in, and ducked behind the wall the camera was on. A flick and the recording beam died.

"Outer rooms were clear. I could hear people down the corridor but they sounded a ways away and I couldn't tell who it was. I've locked everything I can." He folded his arms. "Now can you tell me why the hell you had me cut us off from the rest of the ship?"

"First, help me up." Vas tried to move and got her upper body off the bed before she crashed down. "Damn it. Look for something to fix this. Terel's got me so full of pain blockers, I can't move."

"Vas…." Mac looked ready to argue, but then gave up and went rummaging through the medicine. "This should work, but you're going to hurt like hell."

"If what I think is happening is actually going on, that's the least of my worries." Vas nodded when Mac didn't move. "Now, Mac. We don't have much time. Those med seals won't hold for long once they realize we're on to them and in here."

"See, that's the problem, I don't know who *they* are." Mac tried to hold his ground, but finally gave in and pulled a hypospray out of the medicine cabinet.

Vas winced as the hypospray did its job far too well. Her entire body caught on fire as pain flooded every nerve.

"Son of a bitch!" Vas's scream echoed in the small room. Panting, she wiped away the tears as her body adapted. The pain still raged but once the first shock was over it was almost bearable.

"The 'they' I was talking about are the bastards who have taken over our ship. The ones we brought on board."

Mac rocked back. "The refugees? How in the—why would they and how would they take over our ship?" He peered at her closely. "And just how would you know about it since you were trapped down here and unconscious?"

Vas squirmed. It wasn't going to be easy to convince Mac. Hell, she wouldn't believe him for a second if the roles were reversed. "It's hard to explain. However, the refugees used that damn creature that attacked me to get on our ship without being scanned. The thing that attacked me couldn't have survived on that planet."

"Maybe it was a mutation?" Mac's look wasn't good. If Vas couldn't convince him that they were under attack, he was going to unlock everything and run straight into the pirates taking their ship. Irony was a bitch. Her crew had done more than a bit of pirate work in their day, but this was the first time on the receiving end. However, her crew wouldn't have stooped to such low tactics to take a ship.

"You really think that someone is hanging out with a climate controlled tank of them, letting them out every day or so? So they can harass a bunch of refugees from a planet that was destroyed?" Vas sat up gingerly. The pain in her back was horrific, and spasms echoed every move. At least she could move. "Come on Mac, think about it."

Mac frowned. "But why didn't Gosta or Terel figure it out?"

"They might have." Vas frowned as fear for her friends grew. It was one thing to be lost in battle, another to lose people on your own ship. "When was the last time you saw either of them?"

Mac thought about it. "I probably saw Terel in here about five hours ago." He looked at his watch and swore. "Actually probably more like ten hours ago. I must have fallen asleep in here. She was finally setting up an autopsy on that gaul. I haven't seen Gosta since we brought you in." Mac winced, and then ran his hands through his hair. "He was going to get the refugees settled in."

"Damn it, there are times I hate being right." Vas forced herself to sit up through the pain that flashed all over her body. Hopefully once her nervous system got used to handling the pain again it would become bearable. "We have to assume the entire ship is compromised by now. What do we know about the refugees? Or rather the bastards pretending to be refugees?"

Mac started pacing. "Not much. We know what they told us: running away from a destroyed planet, big silver ships came out of nowhere. They claimed to be from Diloxi, small population, low-tech. The idea of them taking off in the generation ship we found the remains of was plausible."

"They described the ships?" Vas fretted. She didn't remember them describing the ships. Had she even paid attention to their story? Great move: walked right into a trap and handed over the keys to her ship. Most survivors they met got out before the ships actually arrived, or else they didn't survive.

"Yeah they did. Sounded just like the ones at that ambush at Lantaria and the ones at the supergate." Mac paused. "Why are you looking at me that way?"

"Because I don't think you wanted me to stand here stark naked in front of you and I just realized who's on our ship," Vas said as Mac hastily turned his back as she reached for some medical garb to wear. Even just getting dressed was a new exercise in pain. "It's the Graylian monks, or some group of Rillianians, or both. They haven't been able to catch us, so they snuck on board."

She slapped Mac's ass as she hobbled to a cabinet looking for any type of weapons. "You can turn around now."

"But how did they know we'd be here?" Mac was slower than usual today. He must have been napping a lot.

"Not hard to figure out how to catch us. We've been doing good will trips more than our own jobs for the last two months." Vas swore and stumbled over to another drawer. Didn't Terel have anything useful here?

"It's been kind of nice, sort of a tribute to Jakiin and Deven," Mac said softly.

"You don't have to get defensive with me. I'm the one who ordered the runs." Which was weird in and of itself. Emotions or not, the amount of time they'd burned rescuing small refugee groups was something the old Vas would have laughed herself to death over.

She took a deep breath. She needed to tell someone and right now Mac was it. Wasn't going to be easy by a long shot, but if something happened to her she wanted someone else to at least know about Deven.

"Mac, about Deven," Vas said and took another couple of slow breaths. There was no way to say it without sounding crazy. And she couldn't even tell Mac how Deven did any of it since she still had no idea.

"He's not dead." There, she said it.

Mac's face softened and the closest thing to compassion that Vas had seen on his face appeared. "Of course he's not, Vas. He still lives on in our actions." He reached forward to comfort her but Vas smacked him away gently.

"No, he's *really* not dead. Jakiin is however. Really dead. But Deven is alive."

"How could Deven have survived that? And how could he have survived and Jakiin didn't?" Disbelief warred with hope on Mac's face.

Vas shrugged. "He didn't survive. He died. He just didn't stay dead." Vas waved her hands at Mac. "I don't know how, he wouldn't tell me. Deven isn't completely human regardless of how he looks."

Mac stepped away a good two steps. "Deven died, but isn't still dead, and he told you things? After he died, things?"

Vas schooled her face to look very serious and not the least delusional. "Yes, he spoke to me while I was under those drugs. No, no. I don't know how, nor do I think I was just dreaming. He's alive. Again. Somewhere."

Mac looked like he was fighting to believe her. "Okay, so you're saying that Deven contacted you while you were in a drug-induced coma to warn you about the refugees who are actually these idiots who have been chasing us all over the galaxy. Said idiots have now taken over the entire ship except for us."

Vas nodded. "Yes."

"All of that and all you'll say is 'yes'?" Mac walked around the room swinging his hands. "How am I supposed to believe you? You could be totally delusional. You did almost die, you know."

"Yes, you told me. Twice." Vas wasn't going to push him. She didn't even know if the two of them could re-take the ship. But she did know there was no way in hell she could do it alone.

"Shit." Mac finally stood in front of her. "I have to believe you, don't I?"

"Pretty much. If you want to live. I have a feeling our pirates don't realize we're down here or both of us would have gotten a rude awakening." She spun as a thought struck her. What would she do if she'd been caught by pirates? Hide as many of her people as possible. "Check the sensors. Are they up?"

Mac muttered to himself about captains who couldn't check their own sensors but he looked it up. His whistle gave the answer. "Nope, they've been down for at least ten hours, maybe longer. Whoever did it caused a catastrophic cascade failure in the main system. It'll take weeks to get it back up."

"That's our Gosta. They probably did get him first, but he was able to crash the system before he was subdued." Vas refused to think that any more of her people were dead. At the very least the pirates would keep them to sell as slaves. Dead, they had no value. Vas smiled for the first time since she'd woken up. "We may not be the only ones free then. Our first goal is to get weapons, then figure out some way to tell our crew from the pirates, if they're using shape-shifting tech, they may be able to look like anyone. Oh, and figure out how many of them there are, how heavily armed they are, and how best to take them out."

Mac sat back down on the chair he'd been on when she awoke. "You're kidding, right? "

Vas smacked him in the head. "Do I look like I have room to kid? I can barely stand, and if I go back on the pain meds, I can't move. It's you and I until we can get some of our own people back. Unless you think you and I can take this ship back by ourselves?" Vas folded her arms and glared.

Mac ran his hand through his spiky hair and reluctantly stood up. "No, boss. I'll start in the outer room looking for weapons." He shrugged. "Terel always managed to get weapons when she came back here, so she must have a stash."

"Good thinking." Vas tried to ignore the running stabs of pain that followed her every movement, but it wasn't easy. Each time she moved a new pain snuck up and whacked her. She pulled up the secondary computer systems and began looking for a back door. Unfortunately, as complicated as the under layers of an advanced computer system were, it wasn't enough to distract her mind completely.

Deven was alive.

Part of her wanted to shout with glee, the other wanted to scream in fear. What was he that he came back from the dead at least twice? She'd done a close study of the scans on the remains of his Fury, and it had haunted her for weeks. There couldn't have been much left of him to recover. If the explosion hadn't destroyed him, the radioactive debris would have.

Maybe it wasn't he. Maybe this was all some delusion? A dream from being too close to death herself? Even as she thought it, she knew that wasn't it. Deven was real. His presence in her head or wherever they had been was far too disturbing not to be real.

Which left her with the issue of having to figure out how she felt about it. She'd dealt with his death. It had taken awhile, but she'd been able to repress it. Of course he would be the first one to point out repressing it wasn't dealing with it. But she was going to apply the same tactic she'd used in dealing with his death to his life. Who the hell knew what was going on between her and Deven, but while her ship was being run over by bastard pirates with religious leanings was not the time to be thinking about it.

"Ha!" Vas muttered out loud as she got the nasty questioning inner voice to shut up.

"Did you find something, Captain?" Mac stuck his head inside the doorway.

Vas turned back to her computer quickly. What was wrong with her? Her focus sure as hell wasn't holding up. "Actually, I," she paused when the search she was running pulled up the specs she needed, "yes I did." Thank gods; she didn't want to explain her issues with Deven to anyone, least of all someone like Mac. She fought off the shudder that caused.

"How good are you at Alterian programming? This ship originally belonged to them."

Mac shrugged. "I had some in flight school, but I'm—"

"Perfect." Vas cut him off and offered him the chair in front of the console. "You've got more than me. I found the sub-system. You tell it to find a way to locate our people, but only on this computer. Better yet, load it on one of the handhelds. Tell the system to lock out all others." She patted his shoulder then went into the outer room. "I'll go find the weapons."

Vas heard Mac swearing as he typed, but at least he had a clue as to what to type, which was more than she had.

Mac was right; Terel always went here instead of her quarters whenever Vas ordered her to go out armed. She prowled around the lab, flinging open doors at random.

"Captain, I think I found some of them," Mac yelled from the inner room. "The system is still unable to access some of the ship. Either it's a side effect of Gosta crashing it, or else it's something the pirates did when they tried to undo Gosta's work. I'm trying to cut through, but only partial luck so far."

Vas sat back on her heels as she hit another weaponless cabinet. She was glad that Mac found a way to track her people, at least some of them. However, without weapons there wasn't a lot she could do. If there was a time she needed a powerful telepath on her ship this was it.

"That's great, Mac." Vas rubbed her eyes. As neat as the med lab was, obviously there was still dust. "Keep trying to break through. Get as much intel as you can."

"You okay, Captain?" Mac's voice sounded like he was getting up.

Vas wiped her eyes some more. Stupid dust. "Stay in there and find more of our people. Once I find Terel's

stash we'll have to move fast. I can't guarantee they don't
know we're here."

The chair squeaked as he sat back down, and his voice
was subdued. "Understood."

Maybe there was more to Mac than she had thought.

Swearing to herself about the weapon situation, she
pried open a locked cabinet labeled hazardous materials.
She kicked herself for not thinking of that cabinet first.
Terel kept her hazardous items in a completely separate
lockup.

"Yes! Mac, come here. Do you think this will be
enough?" she yelled as she pulled out enough weapons
for a small army. Just who was her peace-loving doctor
planning on arming?

"Captain!" He ran forward, storing as many weapons
on his person as possible.

"Easy there, bucko." She pulled a heavy-duty artillery
rifle out of his hand and put it back in the cabinet. "We're
on a ship, remember? *My* ship. No heavy weapons. I
don't want to get it back full of holes." She put a sword in
his hands. "And try one of these. You really aren't half
bad." She didn't know when the *Warrior Wench* had
become *her* ship in her head, but it was there now. It was
as much a part of her as the *Victorious Dead* had been.

She laughed. He looked like a kid whose daddy just
told him he was a good boy. Then she grabbed as many
small, edged weapons as she could hide on her person,
finishing up with another of the smaller curved blades
that worked out well in confined quarters, and a Mark
Three blaster very similar to her own. If anyone was
going to end up shooting her ship, it was going to be her.
But only as a last resort.

"Now, where are our people? Closest group that's not
attended by the pirates first. We'll gather people then
work our way up toward the command deck."

Mac ran back into the inner room and came back with
two comm tablets. "I uploaded it to both in case we get

separated. But it looks like at least six people are in the lower weapons tanks. Probably a good place to start."

She cringed. Probably an excellent place to start. The weapons tanks were not a place sane folks would go to linger. If her folks were there, they were hiding. "Good idea. Were you able to pull up the brig?"

"Not yet. We may just have to see who's in there when we get there. I don't think we can take a chance on leaving the search running."

"No we can't. Another very good point." She pulled out one of the smaller caliber weapons and fixed a silencer on it. "Terel can bill me for a new computer." With a nod Vas went back into the inner lab and blew away the computer they'd hacked into. Either they'd find enough of her people to take back the ship, or they'd fail. Leaving the computer up would just be another way to help the pirates.

"Okay, flyboy, let's see how good of a hacker you really are, lead on." She palmed open the door and slid partially around it. No one was in sight, so at least that was holding up.

Mac grinned at being allowed to take point and slipped out into the hall.

CHAPTER THIRTY-FIVE

Vas heard people down one of the side corridors and froze. Mac reacted a few seconds after she did but still managed to stay out of sight. From the sound there were just two, one of them sounding like one of the frail old women they'd pulled off the planet. Or rather sounded like a surprisingly hale, hardy, and younger version of one of them. They'd used glamours of some sort, something high-tech enough that the scan before they landed hadn't revealed it.

At least her ship hadn't been taken by a bunch of old people and children.

Vas fingered her curved sword and toyed with ambushing them where they stood. Problem was she couldn't be certain it was just the two, and if she was honest with herself she was in no condition to take on anyone at this point.

Mac turned, clearly thinking the same thing. With a frown, Vas shook him off and nodded down the way they were going. There would be time to take out those pirates when they had more fighters. Besides, she didn't want them tipped off.

Mac continued moving toward the stairs; they couldn't chance the lift. The lower weapons chamber was only two flights down. Unfortunately, those were the longest two flights Vas had ever limped down. Clearly Terel had done some major surgery while she'd been out floating around talking to Deven, but there were still plenty of things wrong inside her body.

The door to the weapons locker was sealed shut, a perfect hint someone was inside. Fortunately, the pirates didn't know that.

"Could you tell what species was down here?" Mac had been able to separate out their people based on the bio signs stored in the computer, but Vas hadn't thought to ask who might be down here.

"No," Mac said. "I couldn't get it that refined, just which were our people. But I think we know who's probably down here."

She nodded. Flarik, Xsit, and any other of the warm-weather species. The lower weapons locker was kept uncomfortably warm to keep the weapons-grade plasma in a controlled setting, primed for firing. Now the question would be how to get them out.

Vas limped around Mac and pounded on the door. Sometimes the simplest way was the best. "It's me, people." If any of the pirates were down there they would have fired on them already. No one in their right mind would hide in a weapons chamber.

A few more poundings brought a crack in the door followed by the muzzle of a snub blaster.

"It's Mac and me. We need to get our ship back."

The door opened wider and a clatter was heard. An instant later Xsit's thin form slammed into her. "Captain!"

Vas held her breath as pain engulfed her. Mac carefully pried the excited communications officer off.

"The captain is still injured, go easy. She should be in pain-med-filled peace right now."

Flarik, and rest of the snub-nosed blaster, appeared as the door opened further. "Yes, just how are you able to move, Captain?"

"She had me take her off her pain meds."

Vas glared at her pilot. "I can answer for myself, you know. It doesn't matter," she added as she handed out more snub blasters and swords she'd brought from Terel's supply. "We have to get more people free, and then kick these bastards off our ship."

Flarik informed her of what little she knew. Xsit had been coming back to the deck from a break when she heard the pirates take over the command deck. She'd run until she literally hit Flarik. Their section of ship hadn't been searched yet, so they were able to find four others and hide. The only thing they knew for certain was that all of the refugees had been under glamours that were dropped quickly after gaining access to most of the ship.

"I still don't know why they didn't come after us though," Flarik said. "A good scan or two should have shown us."

Vas readjusted her weapons after unloading so many. "We think Gosta sabotaged the system before they got him. He'd better be able to put it to rights quickly when we get my ship back though."

She turned toward her new partner. "Okay, Mac, we need to get a few more people before we go after the pirates, and get more intel. Where next?"

Mac flashed a smile at being asked his opinion, and then checked his comm pad. "I'd say the holosuite we blocked off. Or rather, that weird room behind it." He tapped the screen. "Looks like there are four of our people in there. However, we'll have to be careful. It looks like three of the pirates are in the holosuite."

Vas checked the power level on her snub blaster, made sure her sword hung loose, and nodded. "Let's go retrieve some more of our people, shall we?"

The trip to the room behind the holosuite wasn't difficult. The pirates clearly felt secure in the fact that they had control of the ship and didn't appear to be running patrols. Vas questioned their laxity. She never would have been this relaxed unless she had the entire crew in the brig. They'd met her and Flarik, yet they weren't concerned that they were missing? The Graylian monks might be great on the psychotic religion front, but they weren't so good at battle plans. Unless they were waiting for something.

The small room was locked as well, another clear sign their people were still inside. But unlike the previous time, she couldn't just yell and pound on the door. She needed someone to pick the lock.

"Mac? I've got a job for you."

He pulled back in shock when she explained what she needed him to do. "But why would you think I could—"

"I have your juvenile records on file, Mac. We don't have time for this."

Glancing at the others, as if this was going to change something about him in their eyes, Mac hovered over the handle and tried tumbling the lock.

After a few tense minutes, a slight click, followed by the popping of a seal, told them he made it.

Followed by a low-voiced, "If you take one step or call to your friends I'll blow you away right here."

Vas stepped closer so she could be seen. Mac was so close to the door whoever it was probably couldn't recognize him.

"It's me. You're about to blow up Mac."

"Captain?" Pela said as she flung open the door. "Sorry, Mac, nothing personal, you know." The assistant medic patted Mac's arm as she pulled him aside then quickly looked down both ends of the corridor. "You need to get in here, but I don't think we can fit everyone in."

"No, we need to re-take the ship. I just wish I knew who in the hell was really behind this. It must be the monks, but I'm not sure if anyone else is involved." Vas said.

"Bhotia, or whatever his real name is, is in the holosuite. I think he's setting up a torture chamber in there."

"Shit." Vas turned to Flarik. "Do you know if they've been searching the ship?"

"I don't think they have. Which is extremely odd, wouldn't they make sure they have us all?" Flarik said with a nod.

"Unless they don't care. I need to see what they're setting up before we go after them." Vas tried to think of a scenario where one didn't care if the people whose ship you'd just pirated were still running about. Nothing good came to mind.

She turned to Flarik and the others still in the hallway. "You all go to Bathie's quarters and lock yourselves in. I'll be back as soon as I can. If I'm not back in thirty minutes, assume it's up to you to get our ship back."

Mac and the others nodded. Then he checked down the hallway to make sure it was clear, and they vanished.

Vas followed Pela into the small spy room. The triplets were already there, but were silently watching the tableau before them. Bhotia, or whoever he really was, stood in the middle of an ancient-looking shrine, wearing a Graylian monk's robe. Clearly the setting was something he'd programmed into the holosuite himself. Two of his henchmen stood near the door as he slowly walked around his creation. Horrific torture devices, some even Vas couldn't figure out, filled the rock-strewn room.

"Cover your eyes." His voice was lower than before and accented strangely. His two guards both nodded and covered their eyes with dark fabric pulled from their uniform pockets. Uniforms that were very familiar. Vas was glad she'd sent Flarik away with the others; she had a feeling those Rillianian patches would have sent Flarik into berserker mode.

After the Rillianians finished tying their blinds on, Bhotia raised his arms and began chanting. A moment later a being appeared in the center of the room. Impossibly tall, with long silver hair that flowed to mid back, the male; it was clearly that, peered down at Bhotia with contempt in his red eyes.

"Why have you called me?"

"We have found them, great one. The ship you spoke of, we are on it. The sacrifices are ours." The look on his face proved whatever Bhotia was, sane didn't fit in his worldview. "We follow the great rise of the Asarlaí. All we ask is to serve."

Vas almost jumped at the name. So that was what Deven's friend really looked like? Maybe it *was* his friend; there was no rule that a glamour had to stay the same sex. Whoever it was, they weren't on the *Warrior Wench*. Not yet. She knew it was just a hologram even if the guards were made to think their god stood before them.

"You will be rewarded once the Realm has risen again. We are still recovering from our last encounter with the ones you hold. Our fleet was severely damaged by the unclean powers they were able to use against us."

A thin bead of sweat trickled down Vas's back. So the Asarlaí, or whoever was pretending to be them, were the creatures in the gray ships. Part of her mind screamed at the impossible nature of that idea. After all, the creatures in the black flight suits from Mnethe V hadn't been near as tall as this being in the holosuite. But there was no way around it. They'd only destroyed one fleet: the gray ships.

"Captain, I think there are pirates coming down this corridor. We may need to leave." Pela whispered.

Vas kept her eyes locked on the hologram before her. "Not yet. We may never get another chance like this. Stay close to the door though." She knew she was risking all of their lives. There was a good chance the pirates had finally started looking for the missing crewmembers. But she needed to get any details she could. Providing they survived getting their ship back, she needed to know just what they were up against.

"Yes, master." The worshipful look on Bhotia's face was just a hair short of madness. "We will bring them to you immediately. We will take them through the hypergate, to your awaiting justice."

The Asarlaí smiled benevolently. Or it would have been benevolent if his fangs didn't gleam so much. "I was wise to choose you. You may sacrifice them after we have questioned them, and find the one we need. For the Realm." He gave a tight nod.

"For the Realm." Bhotia mimicked the nod, but dropped to his knees as he did so.

"We go now." Vas pushed the triplets to move, but horror had them frozen. "It's a hologram. For now. If we don't regain the ship quickly, and avoid being dragged through their hypergate, that thing down there will be real. And I don't want to be a sacrifice to anything, do you?"

That moved them.

Pela stood in silence next to the door, her blaster out, but she didn't seem tense. "They went by quickly, but I don't think they were looking for us."

Vas cracked the door and checked the corridors. The way to Bathshea's quarters was clear.

"It's me." She kept her voice and knock low, but they had to move fast. Their only chance was to retake the ship before Bhotia got it through a hypergate. Who knew how many Asarlaís were waiting for them.

Mac opened the door and Vas told the rest of them what they'd seen. She didn't mention Deven's friend. It was far too complicated at this point, besides she felt that if Marli had wanted the ship, she would have already taken it.

"We don't even know if it was an Asarlaí," Vas added as she finished.

Glazlie shook her head with a worried frown. "We know what they look like, Captain. That was one." Clearly, there were more than a few races who kept the memories of their old nemeses alive.

"That was a *hologram* of one. Other people know what they look like too. They could have easily faked it. The point is, real Asarlaí or not, those bastards have my ship, have our people, and plan to do something very bad to us. We can't let Bhotia get this ship through that hypergate." She passed out the supply of weapons she'd taken from Bathie's locker. The huge stash was one of the reasons she'd picked this room; Bathie was always well-armed.

"Mac, have you been able to see the brig on that thing?" If she was pulling this kind of job, she'd have all the crew locked up tight, but there was always a chance Bhotia wasn't playing the same game she would. Actually, she probably would have sent the crew into space in communications-disabled life-pods. But then again, she wouldn't be bringing in an entire crew to be tortured by some dead race of psychotic megalomaniacs.

No matter what she had to do, there was no way she could allow this ship and crew to be brought before that thing she'd seen in the holosuite. Most likely Bhotia wasn't stupid enough to leave the self-destruct program in place. But that didn't mean she didn't have other options.

If she needed to, the Flits and the remaining Fury in the docking bay could be armed and commanded to fire from a single button hidden on her command chair. While in the bay. It was a secret option she always maintained on the *Victorious Dead*, and had added it to this ship almost immediately. No one, not even Deven, knew of it.

There was no way these bastards were getting this ship out of this system. She had no wish to die, but she knew enough of the Asarlaís history that being brought before them would be far worse than death.

Mac swore softly to himself as he tried to hack into the ship's damaged system. He'd tied into the computer in Bathie's room, linking it with his small command panel to pull up his makeshift locator. The screen lit up, then crashed.

"Damn it, I can't get in, no matter what I do."

"May I?" Flarik took the control panel in her clawed fingers. "I've found that sometimes if you do this." Turning the panel around in her hand, she gave it a sharp rap on the edge of Bathie's desk. An instant later a scratchy-looking but functional locator appeared on the screen. Flarik handed the machine back to Mac with a small smile.

"Why, Flarik, I never knew you were so tech savvy." Vas shook her head, more at the looks of awe on the faces around her, than Flarik's actions. Although she'd admit Flarik would probably be one of the last people she'd expect to do the 'hit it until it works' routine.

Maybe this crew was rubbing off on the Wavian lawyer as well.

"Aye, that worked. I can see the rest of the crew; they're all in the brig." Mac said.

Vas looked around the small room. They had ten people against forty or more insane religious zealots. Normally she'd say the odds were in their favor except for the whole religious madmen issue.

"We need to make a plan, get our people out, get our damn ship back, and track down the bastards behind this. We don't need to know anything more about their plans except that we can't let them open a hypergate. Under no circumstances can that happen."

Vas studied the group before her. Mercenaries by nature were fighters, however they weren't suicidal. This very well could turn into a suicide run and she needed to be sure they were aware of it. And willing to follow through if need be.

Flarik stepped forward, her collection of bladed weapons far less noticeable than the others. Then again, she carried her best weapons on her at all times. "I think I speak for all of us when I say we agree."

Vas would like to think that Flarik's grimace and the noticeable flexing of her clawed fingers didn't make a difference in the responses of the others. Nevertheless, they did all nod in agreement very quickly.

Her plan was simple; they didn't have enough people to be exotic. They broke up into two groups to stay hidden better and re-grouped at the brig.

That there was no interference in the corridors was not comforting. Yes, it was clear from the hologram that the pirates were under orders to bring in the crew alive. It sounded like the Asarlaís wanted someone on the ship, but they weren't sure who.

Vas had a bad feeling in the pit of her gut that she knew who.

That bad feeling was reinforced when she did recon to get a better idea of who was guarding the brig.

The corridor leading up to the brig was empty. Again, a disturbing rather than comforting situation. Where in the hell was Bhotia's crew?

Vas continued to creep forward, slowing even more when she saw four silent pirates outside of the brig double doors. Two men and two women, all were humanoid and looked Rillianian. Nevertheless, their blank stares as they faced forward were eerie.

All of them had blades, not blasters, and one of them....Vas let a swear word slip out before she bit her lip. One of them was her brother.

CHAPTER THIRTY-SIX

Vas slid back out of sight of the guards. Her brother. Here. Her *dead* brother.

How in the hell could someone who died years ago with the rest of her unlamented family be standing in front of her brig?

Sure that she was imagining it, Vas took a small mirror she'd grabbed along with her weapons and held it so it would view the brig doors.

Her palms grew so sweaty she had to pull the mirror back to her before she dropped it.

It was Borlan. He was older, a lot older. She'd only gone back home once after she ran away. A quick and painful visit that confirmed what she'd always felt: she had no family. But he looked just like their father. Thick red hair cut in a severe paramilitary style, sharp blue eyes, and the unmistakable Tor Dain chin.

If there was ever a time Vas needed Deven, this was it. She didn't know how Borlan survived the supposed destruction of their home continent, nor why he was here with Rillianian scum. And she had no idea how to deal with it.

"Captain," Flarik spoke from beside her. That Vas hadn't even noticed her approach wasn't a good thing. "You've not moved for over five minutes. Is there something wrong?"

"I...." Vas's mind froze. The worst thing was, there was no love lost between her and Borlan, never had been. Fifteen years older than her, he was the one who was watching her as a child while their parents worked. Protecting her when the band of telepaths kidnapped her and kept her hidden in the desert. She later realized that it hadn't been an accident that she'd been taken under his watch.

"Oh fuck it all to hell." Vas kept her voice low as the implications started rolling in her brain. "Flarik, I can't explain it right now, but that red-haired son of a bitch out there is my brother. I need you to kill him first."

Flarik pulled back as if struck. A slight hiss escaped through her teeth. "Your hatch-mate? I thought you had none?"

"This isn't the time for it, but I didn't. He and my whole damn family died fifteen years ago—or so I thought. He's connected to the Rillianians, and may have been back when I was a child." Which could mean he had insight into what had been done to her. Vas took a few seconds to weigh keeping him alive to get information about her past. Her true past. The one Deven hinted about being hidden under some block in her psyche. Nevertheless, the danger her brother was to her and her crew while alive was bigger than that. "He needs to die, and he needs to be killed before I can do anything else. I'm not sure I can face him." That was possibly the hardest sentence Vas had ever uttered, but it was true.

Flarik studied her carefully, reading nuances in Vas's face and bearing that only a Wavian would understand. Finally, she nodded. "Agreed. If he has your fighting skill, and has been working with the Rillianians, he is too dangerous to live."

Vas motioned for the rest of her crew to come forward. They had to take the guards out quick.

"Do you want a blaster?" Vas held hers out, but wasn't surprised when Flarik frowned at it.

"No. A family member should be dealt with the correct way. The old way." She nodded toward the brig corridor. "However, if you wish to shoot the others as I kill the traitor, please feel welcome."

With that Flarik raced into the corridor, her movements too fast to be clearly seen.

Vas rounded into the corridor a few feet ahead of the rest of her crew, her blaster firing to take out the closest guard.

Nothing happened.

Bhotia had activated a dampener of some type on the ship. It was a good thing her crew had edged weapons as well as blasters.

"Swords out! Blasters won't work," Vas yelled to her crew as she threw away her useless firearm and charged the three guards.

Flarik knocked Borlan down and was using her claws against his sword. In close quarters the claws would win, but Borlan was far more skilled than Vas recalled.

The other guards were almost to Flarik when Vas hit them. She'd leapt over Flarik and Borlan to knock two of the guards to the ground. The pain from her wounds ripped through her, but she still took them down.

By the time she turned, Mac and the triplets had killed the other two guards. Surprisingly, Flarik was still fighting with Borlan.

Flarik wasn't losing by any means. Borlan was dead; it just hadn't reached his brain yet.

But there was still enough of him left alive to recognize Vas. Hatred filled his ravaged face.

"Bitch. You were supposed to have died. I betrayed my gods to make sure you died. You—"

The rest of his words ended in a gurgle as Flarik's claws ripped out his throat.

"Captain?" Mac looked between Flarik rising to her feet, Borlan's bloody body, and Vas. "Did he know you?"

Pela smacked him in the back of his head. "He was her kin. Can't you see that?"

Actually considering the damage Flarik had caused, Vas was surprised that even someone like Pela could tell. But she nodded slowly.

"We don't have time for that now. There will be guards on the inside as well, and we should assume they probably know we're here. But aside from that one," she kicked toward Borlan, "these didn't seem to be trying to kill us. Hell, they weren't even very good at defending themselves. We can work on the assumption that the rest of the pirates are under the same orders." She chanced a glance at Borlan, and a shudder went through her. He had been good once, or so she thought. She'd idolized him until he hadn't saved her from the telepaths. She waved the others on. His secrets died with him.

"I think I can crack the doors." Mac waved his modified command panel. "But you're not going to like it."

"Mac, I need those doors open. I don't care what you need to do."

"Seriously?" Mac glanced around at the crew surrounding them. "I have witnesses."

Vas folded her arms. "Yes, whatever you need to do, just get these doors open before the people inside call for reinforcements."

Mac shrugged then ran some wires into the door lock and through his command panel.

An instant later, the double doors slid open.

And so did every door in the corridor.

"What the hell? Mac, what did you do?"

"What you said. I opened the door. Actually, all of the interior doors on the entire ship. And no, I have no idea how to close them again. The system kinda shorted itself out."

"Kinda?"

"Well, that was actually my plan. Shorting them out caused them to go into emergency mode…and you don't really care, do you?"

Vas let out a long sigh. "Not really." The problem of all of the doors being stuck open would be dealt with once they got their damn ship back. Even if Mac had to re-set each one individually.

It had only been a few seconds since he sprung the doors, but Vas was still surprised when no guards jumped in their face.

"You two, with me. Rest of you hold back." Vas pointed to Flarik and Mac as she pulled out both swords and crept into the brig's main room.

The room was empty, but meals and drinks were scattered about as if left in a hurry. Vas silently motioned everyone forward.

Yelling was heard down the cell corridor. And the unmistakable sound of sword on sword told her fighting had started. Vas broke into a run. She'd counted on the orders to bring in her crew alive to keep everyone safe. Had Borlan not been the only one who ignored that?

She skid to a halt as she finally saw the combatants, or what was left of them. Gon was pushing the last guard off his sword.

"How did you get out?" Vas asked as she counted noses. Most all of them were roughed up to some degree, but it appeared that everyone was there.

"I have no idea," Gosta said. "The guards were getting weapons out when all of a sudden, the brig doors opened."

Vas spun toward Mac. "You even opened the *brig*?" Maybe she found someone to apprentice under Gosta and his hacking skills. "Never mind. They're out and the guards are dead."

"Thank the stars you're all alive. We feared the worst," Terel said as she saw the people with Vas, then she frowned. "You shouldn't be out of bed."

"Good to see you too, Doctor." Vas engulfed her friend in a hug then pulled back with a wince. "If something happens to me, ask Mac to tell you what I told him." When Terel started to interrupt, she shook her off. "Not here, not now. Once we get our ship back." She turned to her crew and saw they were busy arming themselves with as many edged weapons as could be found.

"We've been boarded by a band of Graylian monks with Rillianians along for good measure. And they're Asarlaí worshippers. They are trying to keep us alive to get us through a hypergate to their Asarlaí masters. I think that's why there's a dampening field of some sort blocking the blasters. That's an advantage for us: we don't want them alive." Vas spoke to Terel but her eyes were on Flarik.

Flarik nodded to the crowd. "I recommend that everyone here let me kill as many as I can to allow me to work the anger out of my system." Her bright eyes hit everyone in the room.

Vas shrugged. She didn't care who did the killing as long as those bastards died. "Agreed. However, it would be best if we can take Bhotia alive. I need more answers. Under no circumstances can we let this ship get through a hypergate. We must destroy the ship before that happens. They will torture all of us."

Once the rest of the crew were armed with swords, knives, and daggers she sent strike teams throughout the ship. Unlike the pirates, she took no chances. Ten members of her crew she kept with herself. They marched down the primary corridors to the command deck. They met little resistance since the few fighters they found couldn't hold against trained mercs.

Which was another disturbing thought that Vas filed away for later: why send in troops that couldn't hold their own with the weapons they were forced to use? More than once she'd seen a pirate reach for a blaster that wasn't there. Unfortunately, none of them stayed alive long enough for her to ask. At first she just thought they were horrific fighters, and then she realized they were poisoning themselves with some sort of capsule embedded inside their cheek, as they were overwhelmed. She recognized the distinctive bite, grimace, and crumble to the ground maneuver from other campaigns.

"Terel, stay back and pull some of these bodies aside for examination. I want to know what they're killing themselves with as soon as possible." Neither she nor any of her crew were showing signs of ill effects, but there were suicide drugs that could take the offensive once they'd done their original job. Better to be safe than sorry.

Terel nodded, and Pela went to find contamination suits. Vas grabbed Terel before she followed. "There's another body I need you to look at."

Terel nodded. "The man who looks like you that's in a pile near the brig doors? I already planned to unless you gave me express orders to leave him alone." The look on her narrow face indicated that she dearly wanted to know who the body was.

"He's a relative I didn't know was alive. But I have a lot of questions about him."

Terel nodded. "Understood. I'll keep Gosta back with me to help with the poisoned bodies. Be careful up there, Vas. They aren't playing a war you're used to."

Vas shook her head. "Tell me about it."

After catching up to the rest of her people, she crouched next to Flarik. "Anyone between us and the bridge?"

"Nothing." Flarik's eyes narrowed. "This is most unusual, Captain. They must know we are out here by now."

Vas peered down the empty corridors that led to the command deck. "Actually, they may not. Mac said Gosta destroyed the ship's communication systems, all of them.

When the main comms go down they cause havoc with personal comm systems as well. We can't talk to our people, but they can't talk to their people either."

"That is probably true, although their tactics in such a case are inferior. We shall destroy them without complication."

Vas hid her grin behind her hand. Flarik was so matter of fact. There was simply no way in her worldview that inferiors could get the best of her. Having seen enough lag-rats take down prey fifty times their size on her home world, Vas didn't share the sentiment.

"Let's just be prepared for the worst, shall we? We have no idea how close Bhotia is to a gate."

Flarik nodded, then motioned that she would take half the fighters to the other side of the command deck.

Vas waited until she figured Flarik would be in place, and then stormed the deck. There was no way to sneak onto the command deck, and one glance at a nearby screen told her they were out of time. They were approaching a hypergate. The warnings flashing on the main screen told her the codes weren't in yet, but Bhotia was minutes away from taking her ship and crew to hell.

Bhotia had taken over her command chair, but appeared calm as his people rushed forward to defend him. Gon was almost to the pirate nearest Bhotia. Vas wasn't sure how the big man had outsprinted the rest of the crew, but he somehow had. Bhotia ignored his own man then tilted his head and gazed steadily at Gon.

"You cannot stop the march of our Gods." Gon's feet no longer moved and he crashed to the decking. His face contorted in pain as his body slowly froze from the feet up. His breathing became ragged and harsh.

Divee ran through the pirate he had engaged, and then rushed forward as well. Vas saw him look up at Bhotia only for a second, and then he too crashed to the ground.

Within moments six of her people lay on the decking, their lives slowly being taken from them as their systems shut down.

"What in the hell?" Vas tried calling her people back. "Don't look in his eyes. Don't even look *at* him. Back off, all of you!" Obviously whatever special talent Bhotia had, his flunkies didn't. Vas ran her sword through another fighter and leapt forward to reach Bhotia. She made it but stumbled and landed on the ground. Her eyes met his accidentally as she scrambled to her feet.

His eyes were a flat gray-green, not at all like the ice blue ones found in the average Graylian. An instant later all thoughts of any color fled Vas's mind as the whirlwind of her nightmares slammed into her head. The sandstorm in her mind came from Bhotia, but whether he was the source or just the carrier she wasn't sure. The force of the wind and sand dropped her to her knees, and she fought to stay conscious.

"My masters and I do thank you." As Bhotia spoke, a roaring filled the command deck and everyone but Vas was dropped to the ground. "I had been cautious before. We were not sure of the force they were seeking, but you have presented yourself to me. I see you are the one they wanted. I no longer need to be careful with the others."

Vas fought to look to the sides to see if anyone was alive, but no one, not even the remaining pirates, moved. Klaxons echoed throughout the ship as life support crashed everywhere but the command deck.

"Yes, I'm afraid the others are dead. My masters wanted them sacrificed and I have done so. I will absorb their energy to give to the ones who rule all." His eyes had become red and no longer even the least bit Graylian. He was somehow channeling his Asarlaí masters and they were drawing out the life force of her crew through him.

Vas fought to move, but the sandstorm in her head locked her into place. If she could just get to her secret control button, the one that would set off a chain explosion in the landing bay...

"Dear, dear." Bhotia spoke as his mind smacked her to the ground. "That won't do. You can't blow up my pretty ship. And I need time to drain the sacrifices properly." He reached under the arm of the command chair and pressed her secret code for destroying the fighters. Vas almost collapsed when nothing happened.

"If it's in your mind, I will take it. You can't hide anything from me. I control you. In fact," he smiled and motioned her to the navigator's chair, "you will be the one who enters the code for the hypergate."

Vas fought, willing her broken body to just die before it completed its task. But as if it was someone else, she watched as her hands entered the gate code and the hypergate to hell opened before her.

CHAPTER THIRTY-SEVEN

Vas couldn't even cry as she heard the horrific gasps as her crew's lives were pulled from their bodies. Entry into the hypergate hadn't affected Bhotia's slow destruction of the people left on the ship, but it had freed part of her mind. He must not have enough power to maintain his killing of the crew, controlling the hypergate through her, and keeping control of her mind.

A small corner of the storm inside her skull cleared and Vas pushed at it. There was one person who could have stood up to Bhotia's mind attacks. Her mind grabbed hold of the memory of Deven and held on tight.

Slowly, the sandstorm in her mind died. She cancelled the hypergate command codes, not caring that to do so mid-entry could rip the ship apart.

Somehow Deven's strength was in her memories of him, like a voice in the back of her mind guiding her. It allowed her to push Bhotia back. Well, Deven and something else. A power flowed through her like a windstorm from her home world, filling the spaces the sandstorm had scoured. With a focused thought, she regained control of life support and the klaxons silenced. Terror threatened to engulf her anew at what she was doing. How she was doing it was something she'd deal with later...much later. Never, if she had her way.

Bhotia realized he'd lost control of her and the ship and ran forward to physically stop her, but he froze when he got a good look at her face.

His mouth twisted in a silent scream, and the red coloring drained from his eyes.

"What are you doing? You can't exist!"

His words made no sense to her, but his terror emboldened her and chased away some of her own fear at the power flowing through her. There was still some sort of telepathic link between the two of them, so she grabbed the connection and forced her way into his head. All those years around Deven had taught her more than she knew. Her power wasn't coming from Deven, but how to use it was.

However, where Deven had been a calm green sea, Bhotia was a storm-wrecked swamp. It took a few seconds to get past the crazed ramblings of an insane mind, but she finally started picking out a few coherent bits.

Long streams of Commonwealth ident and shipping codes, and worse, ways to break them, fled past her mind's eye before she could take hold of them. However, there was no mistaking what they were. And where they came from—the inner circle of the Commonwealth itself.

From another mental stream, the orders to take the *Victorious Dead* came through. It was granted to the monks as the spoils of a war to come. A brief image of Skrankle, drooling as he signed the contract to disassemble her beloved ship, flitted through her mind. These images were lightning clear, focused by Bhotia's complete terror at her being in his mind.

There was something else, something bigger. While he hadn't kidnapped her, he had been directly responsible for poisoning her with the drell. The self-proclaimed God of Biscuits, Jeof's clearvac-ravaged face appeared as Vas saw him through Bhotia's eyes as he telepathically planted the seeds of her destruction, and gave Jeof a small hypospray. Throughout all of the images stood the being they'd seen in the holosuite, the Asarlaí, and behind him an armada of gray ships.

She tried to push deeper, but he was slipping away. Suddenly, the image of the sandstorm reappeared and not from Bhotia's mind.

He was trying to overwhelm her consciousness and fight back, but the sandstorm was coming from her own mind in retaliation. That was the final snap of any sanity the man had left.

The sandstorm was somehow connected to her childhood. Whatever it was, it literally scared the wits out of him. Even the thought of his master's wrath wasn't strong enough to hold up against this.

Babbling incoherently, Bhotia shoved himself away from her, finally breaking the connection with Vas and pushing her to the floor. He was across the command deck in an instant.

Vas knew she had no chance to get him. She had nothing left; just breathing right now took all of her will. And none of her people had moved yet. She had no idea if they were alive or dead.

With an unintelligible scream, Bhotia dove for the emergency hatch. Normally there would be an escape pod there, but it had been destroyed in the battle at the supergate and Vas hadn't had it fixed yet.

Out of the corner of her eye Vas saw Gosta in a contamination suit run onto the deck and make a frantic leap, not to the hatch, but to his console.

The world slowed as Bhotia forced open the emergency hatch. Vacuum sucked him out along with the air in the command deck. Only for an eighth of a second. Too short to count. One instant Vas felt the air slam out of her lungs, the next it was back and a clear shield held the darkness of space at bay.

Gosta folded over his console, shaking so badly that Vas was afraid he'd been hurt. He'd managed to get the shield up in time.

"Vas?" Terel and Pela came on deck slowly, both also had suits on, but they'd already released their helmets. "Can you move?"

"You're alive." Vas felt a tear come from her eye, then another.

"And doing better than you, I'd say." Pela had gone to Gon and was helping him sit up. The crew was alive.

"Um, I don't want to ruin things, the captain crying, people being alive and everything, but we're currently drifting out of control in a hyper stream?" By the sound of his voice, Gosta had recovered from his race to the command deck.

Vas tried to turn, but the power she'd had before vanished.

"Damn it, I cancelled the code mid-stream. Where's Mac?"

"Dead."

Vas would have been more concerned if it hadn't been Mac's voice she heard. Moments later, Terel and Gosta lifted the pilot up.

"Can you move at all?"

Mac winced as he tried to shake his head. "That would be no."

"Okay, Gosta, take the pilot seat, Mac, talk him through this. I don't care where we come out, as long as it's not what was originally coded in." Everything they'd just been through would be for nothing if they still ended up in the hands of the Asarlaí. Bhotia wasn't the danger, his masters were.

It took a few tense moments of swearing on both sides, but eventually Gosta stabilized the ship and the welcoming sight of a small hypergate appeared. Vas recognized the system it fed into. A nicely populated star system, marginally part of the Commonwealth. Big enough that there hopefully weren't any gray ships there. More importantly, it was not the gate Bhotia had made her enter the command for.

"What do we do now, Captain?"

Vas studied the mess and her recovering crew. The *Warrior Wench* was seriously damaged, her crew looked like they all needed about a month in a recovery lab, and her brains felt as if someone had flung them around the galaxy in a soup strainer. Nevertheless, they survived.

She nodded to where Gon had already begun stacking the dead pirates in a corner. "We fix this ship, we heal, then we get my second-in-command back, we get my *real* ship back, and then we go after the bastards who started all of this. Oh, and we may have to destroy the Commonwealth to do it."

The End

DEAR READER,

Thank you for joining Vaslisha and her crew on their maiden voyage.

I really appreciate each and every one of you so please keep in touch. You can find me at www.marieandreas.com.

And please feel free to email me directly at Marie@marieandreas.com as well, I love to hear from readers!

If you enjoyed this book (or any book for that matter ;)) please spread the word! Positive reviews on Amazon, Goodreads, and blogs are like emotional gold to any writer and mean more than you know.

Thank you again, and we all hope to see you back here for the VICTORIOUS DEAD! Vas will be back, and she wants her ship and her second-in-command.

Marie

ABOUT THE AUTHOR

Marie is a fantasy and science fiction reader with a serious writing addiction. If she wasn't writing about all of the people in her head, she'd be lurking about coffee shops annoying innocent passer-by with her stories. So really, writing is a way of saving the masses. She lives in Southern California and is currently owned by two very faery-minded cats. And yes, sometimes they race.

When not saving the general populace from coffee shop shenanigans, Marie likes to visit the UK and keeps hoping someone will give her a nice summer home in the Forest of Dean.

Proof

Made in the USA
Charleston, SC
20 May 2016